POWERDOWN

POWERDOWN

Peter Tonkin

HEADLINE
FEATURE

First published in 1999
by HEADLINE BOOK PUBLISHING

A HEADLINE FEATURE hardback

10 9 8 7 6 5 4 3 2 1

British Library Cataloguing in Publication Data

Tonkin, Peter, 1950–
Powerdown
1. Suspense fiction
I. Title
823.9'14 [F]

ISBN 0 7472 2316 5

Typeset by CBS, Martlesham Heath, Ipswich, Suffolk

Printed and bound in Great Britain by
Mackays of Chatham plc, Chatham, Kent

HEADLINE BOOK PUBLISHING
A division of the Hodder Headline Group
338 Euston Road
London NW1 3BH

www.headline.co.uk
www.hodderheadline.com

Cham, Guy and Mark

in memory of two good friends:
Douglas Leeds
and
Peter Waugh

and respectfully dedicated to the man who inspired it:

Hammond Innes
1913–1998

The Master

Chapter One

Richard Mariner looked down at the urgent telex then stared narrow-eyed out at the Southern Ocean for perhaps a heartbeat. 'We have to go south,' he said tersely.

As Richard spoke, he handed the flimsy to Colin Ross who towered at his right hand. The Scottish glaciologist gave the matter an instant's more thought before he, too, turned to the captain. 'Aye,' he rumbled. 'South.'

'And I concur,' said young Captain Pitcairn, turning from his guests to the duty helmsman. 'Take her south, please. Not that there's much south left.' It was a feeble enough quip, particularly as they were still north, just, of the Antarctic Circle, but it lightened the tension on *Erebus*'s spartan bridge – tension which had arrived so suddenly with the westerly storm and the unexpected cry for help.

Even as the British Antarctic Survey support vessel began to turn onto her new heading, a ram of wind, threatening, ice-laden and six months out of its allotted time, slammed in from the west. It roared out of the Bellingshausen Sea across the Bismarck Strait and tried to push *Erebus* onto the forbidding coast of Graham Land. Richard strode over to the starboard bridge wing, first recipient of the dangerous new weather, and looked speculatively westward. 'This'll put the visit to Faraday behind schedule,' he said to Colin Ross.

'Aye,' agreed Colin. 'And it'll pull us back towards Rothera. Make a mess of our schedule altogether.' The pair of them were referring to the British Antarctic Survey's (BAS's) two main bases nearby, bases *Erebus* was here to supply as they prepared for the millennium.

'Nothing that can't be put right with a bit of energy and ingenuity,' said Richard quietly. 'And anyway, it isn't every day that a NASA astronaut goes missing at the South Pole.'

Robin Mariner sat silently in their cabin, ten minutes later, and listened while her husband explained. Even their twins subsided into uncharacteristic quietude at the magic acronym NASA. The ship's sudden turn had warned the sea-wise Robin that something was up

1

even before her vividly excited husband had arrived with the first gusts of the unseasonal westerly. Now Richard had to raise his voice to near quarterdeck bellow to make himself heard as the weather thundered against the west-facing portholes of their cabin.

'We've just received a distress call from the NASA experimental base at Armstrong. One of their men went out this morning and the weather closed down on them. They've lost contact with him and they're very concerned. Like everywhere down here they're running on skeleton staff until after the millennium and they need all the help they can get. They have one snow team of their own still on base – but they lost contact with them for a while earlier. Now they'll only send out search and rescue parties if we can offer back-up at the very least. The local scientific stations, even the Argentinian and Chilean ones, are all short-staffed or closed, so they've put out a general alarm which we're answering. It means we're turning back along the track towards Rothera, but not too far. Armstrong experimental base is on the coast at the foot of an empty glacial valley. Not far out of our way. With luck we'll still make Faraday for Christmas.'

'NASA,' breathed daughter Mary, the scientist of the family. 'What are they doing down here?'

'Getting ready to go to Mars,' Richard stated. 'NASA have had teams at Lake Fryxell for years, on the coast opposite Ross Island way down in McMurdo Sound. They used the dry valleys to test their vehicles for the Mars probes. But once they decided to try a manned mission, they moved up here to Armstrong where the conditions were similar and there were more people close by. But something went wrong this morning and now there's an astronaut out there on the mainland, on the edge of one of the most inhospitable deserts in the universe and he's lost in this storm. We have to help look for him.'

As if to emphasise the seriousness of Richard's words, the westerly storm thudded against *Erebus*'s side again. Richard and Robin both felt the ship's head yaw round under the onslaught, then fight doggedly back on line. The whole cabin tilted over a good few degrees to port. Half-packed suitcases slid dangerously near the edges of bunks.

'Wow,' said their son William. 'That was cool.'

'Is Mummy going with you?' demanded Mary. Even at eight, she was sensitive to the slightest hint of a sexist slight, all too well aware even during the few hours she had spent down here so far that the South Pole was something of a Man's Club. Women and children were looked at very much askance.

'Mummy can come if she's asked,' said Richard, glancing up at

Robin over the fierce expression on his daughter's face.

Even under the steely light of an Antarctic midsummer storm, Robin's golden ringlets contrived to glitter. And there was a sympathetic light in her grey eyes too, though whether this was amused understanding for his predicament or the fact that her eyes were identical in colour to the strange light, he would have been hard put to say. Certainly, he had put his last phrase badly. It sounded as old-fashioned and patronising as some of the crusty old characters they had met in the brief interim between leaving the British Antarctic Survey's Dash-7, which had popped them down from Ushuaia to Rothera, and boarding *Erebus*. 'Beards' they were called, these taciturn Antarctic scientists. And it was easy to see why. As Richard had quietly observed to Robin, the natural conservatism of the Polar group – to whom Captain Scott's death seemed an all too recent tragedy – was enhanced by the fact that the only scientists still down here were the men with no reason to be anywhere else for the millennium celebrations. Such Antarctic celebratory plans as had been made seemed largely to involve daring each other to shave, ogling garish pin-ups, dressing up in the kind of clothes the pin-ups were so spectacularly lacking, and wearing an assortment of underwear outside their thermals. *Erebus*, with her more strictly naval regime, seemed to offer the most promising haven from the proposed excesses – but that was far in the future. The immediate plans were for Christmas at the British Antarctic Survey's base Faraday, if the current crisis could be resolved in time. Otherwise, it might well be Christmas at Armstrong, courtesy of the USA's National Aeronautics and Space Administration. Richard himself found the promise of this possibility as exciting as did his children.

Colin Ross suddenly thrust his face into the crowded little cabin. 'You'll need to get your cold-weather gear on quickly,' he said. 'Captain Pitcairn says there's a break in the weather due. They want to send the Westland helicopter on ahead with half a dozen of us in it.'

'On my way,' responded Richard. Colin vanished, no doubt to warn his wife and ice partner Kate. Richard hesitated infinitesimally, glancing across at Robin.

'It's not really my game,' she said, with just the faintest hint of regret in her voice. 'I'll be better here with the twins, though I know we can rely on Leading Seaman Thompson if push comes to shove . . .'

'Never mind,' said Richard. 'You'll only be a couple of hours behind us anyway. *Erebus* should dock at Armstrong before tea time.'

3

'Tony Thompson says we should call it smoko, not tea time,' said William belligerently, his mood threatening to darken. 'Smoko with sausages at eleven hundred and smoko with scones at sixteen hundred. That's the Navy way. Never elevenses or tea – smoko!'

'There you are then,' said Richard as though these facts explained everything. 'Though how you can think of smoko after the lunch you've just packed away is beyond me.' As he spoke, he rose and crossed to the wardrobe built against the wall partitioning the sleeping quarters from the shower room.

Idly, over the head of the quiescent Mary, Robin Mariner's still grey eyes followed her husband as he pulled out a bright all-in-one cold-weather suit, kicked off his shoes and forced his huge frame into it. Only the strength of the suit's construction and the triple stitching of the seams, apparently, stopped it from splitting as he zipped it closed across the barrel of his chest already wrapped in naturally-oiled Shetland wool. But this was illusion, of course. No sooner was he secure within the bright suit with the zips tight up to the huge rollneck of the pullover than he shrugged, settling the all-in-one comfortably, and stooped to catch up a huge pair of fur-lined boots. Of all the things that had almost spoilt their southward-looking plans, finding a pair of boots big enough for him had come the closest – for, with the exception of Colin Ross, it seemed that the men of the South – the beards – were great in spirit rather than in stature. In the end, on Colin's advice, they had simply had them hand-made. Richard stamped his feet into them now and straightened. His eyes met Robin's and he gave a slightly rueful grin. 'Right,' he said.

The door opened again as he spoke and there was Colin Ross, equally garish in his vermilion parka. 'We're off,' said the Scot as though completing Richard's thought, and they were gone, leaving Robin feeling a little becalmed in the backwater of so much energy. Becalmed and faintly regretful. In the past it had been she who shared Richard's every thought so intimately that they finished each others' sentences.

As Richard and Colin stepped out of the port bridgehouse door onto the main deck, they were staggered by the icy force of the squall. The deck beneath their heavily booted feet was awash with water so cold that it was freezing against the metal. The driving snow swirled around the forward face of the bridgehouse, its effect intensified by the overhang of the bridge wing just above their heads. The cold was literally breathtaking and even in their cold-weather outfits they had to stand and acclimatise to the shock.

4

The ship heaved under them and they were thrown towards the suddenly downhill guard rail then forward as the ship's head dipped again. They had hardly taken a step before they were brought up short by the safety lines. The last thing each man had done before exiting the bridgehouse was to shrug on the safety harness and now it was a matter of instants for each heavily gloved and mittened hand to clip the harness to the lines before they staggered off into the roiling murk.

And yet, such were the vagaries of the Antarctic summer weather that they were only halfway towards the aft-mounted helipad when the wind stopped as though someone had switched it off and the blizzard transformed itself from a snow tiger to a kitten. Big, soft flakes tumbled playfully over each other and somewhere high above the suddenly listless snowfall the sun came out. Visibility was not much improved by the light – or rather the glare. To the landside, eastwards, the departing skirts of the squall still concealed everything behind curtains of snow. Seaward, away to the west, loomed a fog bank whose thickness could have hidden islands or icebergs with equal ease.

Although the deck became steady in the sudden calm, neither Colin nor Richard unclipped their harnesses. One after the other they followed the safety lines down to where the Westland helicopter crouched under an igloo of snowdrift. Colin's wife Kate was already there, working with the others to clear the snow, and she, too, had kept her safety harness clipped to the line. The pilot, however, had not been so wise. He had unclipped his safety harness as he climbed onto the undercarriage, reaching up to clear the cockpit of snow. So it was that, when the last heave of the squall came like the flick of a snow leopard's tail, he dived head first onto the decking and tumbled away into the scuppers. As he slid across the icy deck, he left a thin, bright smear of blood which froze solid even before it could be dulled by oxygenation. And behind him came the mass of snow from his helicopter.

'Catch him and brace yourself,' called Richard, suiting the words with the action. Colin heard and obeyed. They were down-slope from the helicopter – it was all sliding down towards them. Even as *Erebus* began to right herself, with much groaning from the Westland, the two men caught the body of its pilot and hung on for dear life. A wall of soft snow, perhaps two metres high, swept over them like a big surf. The weight of it crushed them. The cold of it burned them. But Richard's quick thinking had given them just enough time to prepare themselves and their grips were as tight as death, so that when the

5

wave of snow washed through the guard rail and over the side, there were still three bodies woven together like flotsam at the tide line.

Kate was beside them at once. In thoroughly unwifely style she shoved aside the bulk of her husband's gasping form and pulled the pilot back into the clear and level deck. She hissed as she saw the wound on his forehead. 'Dan,' she called to the crewman with the radio, 'call the doc down here at once. Do you have another chopper pilot aboard?'

'No, ma'am,' the sailor replied. 'Skeleton crew. One chopper man.'

'Then we're screwed,' said Kate roundly.

'No we're not,' said Richard, struggling into a sitting position. 'Robin's chopper licence is up to date. If the conditions stay as clear as this, she'll get us down to Armstrong, no trouble at all.'

Robin handed the not too truculent twins over to Leading Seaman Thompson who promised to spend the next couple of hours showing them how sixteen-hundred smoko was prepared and then allowing them to consume most of it. As she checked her cold-weather gear she thought of her twin children with more than a twinge of guilt. Mary and William had been sent to the boarding school at a very tender age largely because their parents' business commitments kept Richard and Robin rushing all over the world – they had only just extricated themselves from a long-running business entanglement in Hong Kong, for instance, and the last six months had been the first time the family had been in the same continent for any length of time since the Crown Colony's handover to China. It was typical of the Mariners' strange family life that they should be spending the last Christmas of the millennium not safely and quietly at home – but down here at the bottom of the world. Still, it was a once-in-a-lifetime chance and the twins seemed to be having the time of their lives.

Robin left the cabin and walked purposefully along the narrow passage to the companionway. Even now, after the unexpected invitation from Kate and Colin, nearly three months ago, after the excitement and the lengthy preparations, the packing and the never-ending journey via Buenos Aires and Ushuaia to get down here, Robin could scarcely believe that they had made it to Antarctica. But as she shrugged on her safety harness and stepped over the sill of the big door out onto the deck, the lingering snowfall left her in little doubt. It was as unmistakable as the blue icebergs lurking at the heart of the seaward fog bank, as unmistakable as the midnight sun. She had just clipped her harness onto the safety line when an eddy of wind brought

6

a handful of massive flakes into her face. 'Give me a break,' she said to the frozen South – the Big White, as the Americans called it. 'It's only three days after midsummer . . .'

The controls of the Westland were familiar enough to Robin for all that the cabin was bigger than on the little Wasps she was used to. It was designed to take pilot and six passengers. As she went through pre-flight and got to know a couple of new men on *Erebus*'s bridge, Colin, Kate, Richard and a team of bearded scientists from *Erebus* piled in their snow gear and strapped in behind her. So far she and Richard had met only Captain Pitcairn's spruce, clean-shaven Navy crew. The scientists had probably been introduced to them, thought Robin, surveying her passengers in the cabin mirror, but one beard looked much like another to her, and like their companions at the BAS base at Rothera they apparently approved of neither women nor children.

'Fasten your seat belts,' she ordered, quoting from some half-forgotten movie. 'We're in for a bumpy ride.'

In fact to begin with the ride was anything but bumpy. Robin lifted off *Erebus*'s heli-deck in a dead calm and took the Westland straight up above the swirl of snow and loom of fog bank. Up here she could see the tops of the outer islands to the west and the Antarctic mountains to the east. More immediately, she could see the tops of the nearest bergs, though none seemed large enough or close enough to pose any threat to *Erebus* as she fell away behind and below them.

Robin passed all this back as she received heading information, weather and radio frequencies from the NASA base at Armstrong. As she talked, tuned, talked again, she dropped the Westland's pert nose and opened up the throttles. The bright orange helicopter roared south and swung east, whirling with the squall's skirts across the leaden heave of the Bismarck Strait, over the iridescent sprinkle of berg, bergy bits and growler until the black scythe of the coast chopped in beneath them. Then Robin was turning onto her final approach and pulling the chopper's nose up again as the basalt beach became glacier-topped basalt cliff. And, breathtakingly, beyond this first great outcrop of volcanic coast, a sudden bay fell back into a low, broad reach. In calm, clear conditions the view would have been utterly spectacular, but here the southern arm of the squall lingered, pulling a deadly white shroud over black beach and equally black water. Robin was caught in the classic quandary of the pilot in extreme conditions. Should she go up high and try to fight back down onto the landing place – assuming she could make it out – or should she come in low, cutting through the murk, ready to take evasive action should anything unexpected loom?

Confident of her reactions, and all too well aware of the need for speed, Robin chose the latter option. She dropped the Westland's nose again and followed the course laid down by Armstrong's radio man all but blindly.

She had just settled onto the course across the bay when some half-glimpsed glimmer of light or movement had her pulling the controls back into the pit of her stomach as her feet danced on the pedals. Out of the deadly smoke-swirl of the squall, so close that the whip antenna on the highest reach of the radio mast ticked the fat swell of undercarriage, there came and went a ship. Richard, hurled sideways against the Perspex of a window by the helicopter's wild gyration, saw the white bridge of a big icebreaker. He saw the bustle of crewmen on the deck, clustered round a big, red Sikorsky helicopter. He saw her name, painted starkly on her ice-destroyer's bows: *Kalinin*.

The NASA people at Armstrong had put out a series of flares to mark the landing spot. The square of mauve lights gleamed brightly, though the smoke that they gave out streamed away down the wind with the dark swirls of snow. The wind, so much stronger here than north of the ice-capped volcanic headland, was at least steady so Robin was able to factor it in to her landing. The track of the final approach brought them over the bay, past the deep-water anchorage facilities so generously provided by Nature herself at the foot of a southern brother to the black headland, past the less spectacular manmade docking facility on the black beach and over the complex of green Jamesway huts. Out of one of these huts, halfway between pre-fabricated buildings and canvas-sided tents shaped like strange, sectioned tunnels, a little welcoming committee dashed, so that when Richard, Colin, Kate and the beards leaped out into the blizzard they were swept immediately into the next phase of the search without a break.

While Robin moved the helicopter off the landing pad to make way for another chopper that was apparently due to arrive any moment, her passengers were briefed and equipped in the vestibule of the nearest Jamesway hut. Five minutes later Richard was sitting in the back of a bucking John Deere pick-up clutching his borrowed skis and poles, craning to see over Colin's shoulder to the screen of the American scientist Billy Hoyle's laptop. Out of the windscreen he could see that the Westland had vanished and he wondered briefly where Robin could have got to. Then he turned back and gave all his attention to Hoyle and his laptop. On the bright square of the screen there blazed a 3D schematic of the terrain immediately in front of them, broken up into a grid by red lines.

'The lines are the tracks of the laser net we laid down,' the American was bellowing. 'Like I said during initial briefing, we have just enough scientific staff left to keep it running. It shouldn't be possible for him to go out of touch; even if his equipment all goes down, he should still register in one of these quadrants. It's supposed to be foolproof. We were relying on that – especially as there are so few of us left to handle any emergency. I guess nobody told the Big White to lay off us, huh?' Hoyle's thick mitten dangled from a clip at the wrist as his gloved finger danced over the laptop keys. Quadrants on the schematic dulled. 'These are the areas our one little snow-team searched before we went off the screen too and the boss hit the panic button,' he continued. 'Only the distant and difficult sections are left. There must be holes and hollows out here which fooled the hell out of the net. Like the one we went into when we vanished off the instruments back at base. Or maybe the laser beams froze, what do you think?'

'What's that feature there?' Richard leaned forward, pointing at a lateral mark bisecting the topmost sector.

'You got sharp eyes and a good nose, sir. That's a nasty little feature. The whole of this section, everything on the map here, is the floor of a glacier that vanished maybe five million years ago. There's no ice there now, just the huge boulders you can see on the schematic here, some the size of a pick-up, some a little larger than *Titanic*. But on the ground we still got some subglacial features, even though the glacier is gone. And that is one. It's a moraine hill. Crushed rock gathered into a hollow in the original ice-sheet and dumped here. We don't know exactly what it's made of but it acts funny and fucks up our equipment. 'Scuse me, ma'am, sirs. Technical phrase there. And in the middle of this moraine hill there's this deep lateral fissure. If this was ice it'd be a crevasse. It's narrow, mean and nasty.'

'And it's where we'd better start, I guess,' rumbled Richard and Colin together.

'Our chopper flew over it right at the outset, but there was nothing to be seen,' the American said. 'The boss would only authorise chopper searches this far off-base – especially after he lost contact with us.'

'Even so,' said Richard.

Colin nodded in agreement. 'It's not the same as doing it on the ground. What do you think, Kate?'

9

'There's supposed to be no snow on this ground,' said Kate. 'But there are deep drifts everywhere.'

'Likely be gone in the morning,' said Billy Hoyle. 'Not that there is actually a morning, this time of year.'

'You could hide a regiment out here in this and never see them from the air,' Kate observed.

'A tank regiment at that,' agreed Richard feelingly. And after his experiences in Central Africa he knew all too well what he was talking about. Colin and Kate were the ice experts – that was why they were in Antarctica with the British Antarctic Survey, after all – but Richard had spent some time in close association with them delivering a massive iceberg, codenamed Manhattan, from the North Atlantic to the African coast before becoming embroiled in a civil war there. A war which had involved several regiments of tanks. He was, as a consequence, no slouch around ice. Nor around tanks, come to that.

The strange moraine had the eerie appearance of a big black Neolithic burial mound. With the snow streaming off its cleft crest like intense grey smoke, the look of it was deeply disturbing, even from a distance. The sound of it was worse, for the wind caught in the throat of that strange lateral crevasse and it sobbed, cried and howled according to the squall's intensity. This sound began to overpower even the revving of the John Deere's engine. As they drew up beside it, Hoyle spun the 3D graphic with a precise scale. The moraine was the better part of three hundred metres high and three hundred metres wide at its widest point, and perhaps four hundred metres long, tear-shaped as such things tend to be. Its tail pointed up the desolate valley towards the distant, invisible massif which had given the glacier birth, before flicking round into a blunt, south-facing hook.

When they got out and stood beside it, they saw that its sides were nearly sheer and disturbingly smooth, reaching up into the near invisibility of the howling overcast. The squall had cloaked its sides with massive concavities of pallid snow, made all the more stark by the fact that the rock face of the moraine and the floor of the valley itself were obsidian, basalt black. The John Deere had dropped them not far from the central fissure and towards this, up the slope of sugary snow, Colin Ross led them after some lengthy, painstaking ground work worthy of a Native American tracker. The snow, although crystalline and temporary, was firm enough to carry them upwards until they attained the cleft and shuffled forward into it.

For Richard it was as though he had stepped from one circle of the

10

Inferno into another. With ruthless perspective the moraine cliffs on either hand stretched upwards to the tiniest strip of sky above and forwards to the merest, fading glimmer of grey. Everything else was sheer, featureless black, giving the illusion that the towering black walls were closing inexorably in on him, like a vice in Vulcan's smithy. So vivid and disorientatingly overpowering was this claustrophobic impression that Richard was hardly surprised to see Colin Ross suddenly collapse before him, as if borne down by the weight of those terrible, howling rock jaws.

But no. When Richard got to Colin's side, he found his old friend examining a bright piece of equipment.

Hoyle was at their side almost at once. 'That's his back-up radio,' he bellowed.

Richard looked around. 'He came in here to shelter and signal but gave up and went out again?'

'Looks like it. And in a bad way too or he would never have left this. But why would he need shelter?' Hoyle mused aloud. 'The whole point of the suit he's wearing is that it can shrug off conditions like this. Even if there was a fault with the comms he should still have been able to walk out. He could call up the schematic from my laptop on the head-up display inside his visor. Our fifteen minutes in the John Deere is maybe a forty-minute walk home, ten kilometres all in all – and downhill into the bargain – but that was what he was out here to do.'

'Sounds like a power failure to me,' said Richard. 'What sort of power unit was he wearing?'

'That's just it. The whole suit is the power unit. Powerdown is just impossible . . .' Hoyle's vice tailed off. He had clearly said more than he meant to. And Richard, in a moment of revelation, thought of the bulky, five-layered, two-part space suits he was familiar with. Whatever the missing man had been wearing must have been very different to that. Lighter. Less unwieldy. Experimental. And it had obviously failed somehow. What had Hoyle called it? Powerdown.

'Over here,' called Colin, and they followed him silently.

Every now and then Colin would pause and study some sign, but it was not until they got to the far side that he showed his true worth. On the outer, south-facing, slope, the snow seemed to Richard to be as fine and undisturbed as the one they had walked up on the north side. But not to Colin's snow-wise eyes.

'Look,' he bellowed to Kate, gesturing at something invisible to the others.

'I see,' she called, and they plunged forward, side by side, following an uneven track down and back along the hissing slope, away from the wind, inland up the valley.

Richard floundered along in their wake, awed by their ability to read the featureless surface of the snow. As they did so, the wind began to falter and the light to brighten. By the time they reached the teardrop tail of the great moraine, there was bright sunshine in a hard blue sky through which drifted the last few innocent swan's-down flakes. Here the tail of the rock curled right round into a little amphitheatre perhaps three metres high and across. The whole of the hollow was packed with snow, like the curve of a beach-groin packed with sand.

Colin began to dig, with Kate at one side and Richard at the other. Hoyle, protecting his equipment, stood back. As they worked, the day settled into a bright clear afternoon, apparently full of midsummer heat, though in fact it was still about zero degrees Celsius. So still did it become in those few minutes as they worked that the sudden thunder of the Sikorsky burst upon them like a disquieting revelation, and as it did so they found their missing astronaut. As a result, they scarcely spared a look at the hovering chopper. The only recognition they gave it was to be grateful that the outwash of its rotors moved the snow and made their digging easier. It made Hoyle's job harder, however, as he tried to report in to Armstrong over the noise of the Sikorsky.

As though creating a bizarre snowman, they revealed a tall, silver-clad, snow-crusted figure frozen erect there, mirrored visor looking urgently but all too hopelessly westwards to where unattainable safety lay, reaching out with his right arm. How light the suit seemed, thought Richard as the snow fell away. It looked to be little more substantial than tin foil. By the time they had uncovered the body down to the thighs, there was enough of a platform for Hoyle to step in and undo the clasps of the helmet. He lifted it clear to reveal a still, white, wide-eyed face.

Kate pushed her naked fingers onto his throat at once. 'No pulse,' she yelled. 'Frozen solid.'

Richard looked up then, distracted by the fact that she had had to shout at all. Black against the hard blue sky, the Sikorsky still hung immediately above the cleft. As he raised his hand to shade his dazzled eyes, he saw a figure throw itself out of the helicopter's side. Hardly able to credit what he was seeing, Richard watched the falling body curl into a surfer's stance and he realised there was a board strapped to its feet. With a whoop just audible even at this distance – and over

12

the clatter of the motor and the rotor – the figure straightened as the board settled onto the crest of snow which sat along the topmost curve of the black moraine like the fin on a curled eel. Arms spread for balance, gold hair streaming free above the folded parka hood, Ray-Bans gleaming in the hard light, the wild figure hurled down the thin, precipitous line of snow until its momentum dissipated in the jumble their digging had created.

In a fine flurry, the snowboarder came to a stop and kicked his board up into the air. Catching it deftly and swinging it under his arm, he strode forward.

'Hi,' he called. 'The name's Maddrell, Thomas S. I see you found your missing astronaut. Armstrong radioed that you had before we came out on our little pleasure jaunt. Hi there, buddy . . .' He came breezily forward, still on a high from his wild ride, arm outstretched to shake the hand of the frozen corpse.

Chapter Two

The centre of NASA's Armstrong Antarctic base was a collection of Jamesway huts which served for accommodation, storage and laboratories. It was typical that the laboratories were by far the most luxurious. To the west of these lay the bay, with its two black arms like the antlers of a gigantic stag beetle. To the east lay, in succession, an open area with a flagpole, the landing pad for the helicopter, the secure engineering areas and the vehicle dispersal area. Beyond that lay the flat-floored vastness of the glacial valley stretching up to the distant Antarctic mountains.

During the next couple of days Richard, Robin and the twins got to know the camp's facilities pretty well. For Richard and Robin, that acquaintance began in the big central hut which functioned as mess hall, church, assembly hall, recreation room, communal office and, today, coroner's court. The camp's meagre supply of chairs was supplemented by packing cases, plastic boxes, anything of the right height which promised a relatively comfortable seat. The corpus delicti was not present. Together with the radio retrieved by Colin Ross and the helmet removed by Hoyle, it lay in a cold store area – in other words an outer hut which had no heating. No disrespect was intended, but practicalities had to be observed as well as due process.

At one end of the wooden-floored area a table stood athwart the long, narrow room. Behind this sat the man Hoyle called 'the boss', base commander Eugene Jaeger, who carried the rank of full colonel, USAF, but who never seemed to use it. Beside him sat one of Armstrong's two remaining communications experts with a laptop on open two-way video link with NASA headquarters in Washington DC via a powerful dish outside, a couple of satellites and an Internet provider.

Armstrong Base was at 60 degrees west and Washington at 75. The little group in the Jamesway were nearly two hours ahead of their headquarters, therefore, and this seemed fortunate to all of them, for this was the afternoon of Friday, 24 December. As Jaeger began proceedings it was 17.30 local time, and 15.30 in Washington. They had just got through to the Office of Safety and Mission Assurance, and an S&MA team was being called together as fast as possible.

Richard sat trying to assess the likely impact of all of this on their Christmas plans. It looked to him as though Christmas with NASA was a distinct possibility, though with the big camp so lightly manned there would be room for all of them. This part of the process was painstaking, because it would be on the basis of this report that the Associate Administrator of Safety and Mission Assurance would decide whether to despatch his whole S&MA team, one inspector or what. And if either a team or a single inspector came down, that could well slow things further, for this was American soil, and they would want all the witnesses to wait and answer their questions in turn.

Still, thought Richard wryly, that was the way of the world; it was always your good deeds that found you out in the end. And days and deeds didn't come much better than this one. Idly, he looked over the quietly hissing Preway oil heater, past the big card on the wall depicting Santa controlling a helicopter emblazoned 'Season's Greetings from the Ice Pirates' and through the chill-proof clear plastic panel which was the Jamesway's excuse for a window. At the far edge of the dazzling afternoon, where the blue shadows were just beginning to gather into that strange intensity of evening in the land of the midnight sun, he could see *Erebus* and *Kalinin* coming to anchor side by side away out west in the bay, with the tall black arms of the basalt outcrops solid and stark astern of them.

The scientific support vessel and the adapted icebreaker were much the same size, but where one had the slim, if strengthened, bows of a corvette, the other was broad in the beam with a great ram up ahead. He knew which he preferred the look of; but then he knew which he would rather face the ice aboard. They both had big white bridgehouses midships – something that still looked old-fashioned to his tanker-man's eye. They both looked to be state of the art for these waters.

Colin nudged him, and he pulled his mind back to the present and his wandering gaze back to Colonel Jaeger, and the camp doctor, whose name he had missed but whose evidence seemed clear. The dead man, Major Bernard U. Schwartz, had been in the peak of physical health. His vital signs had been monitored that morning before he donned his suit and went out. The doctor had checked the frozen corpse for vital signs and, having determined that there were none, had no hesitation in certifying him dead effective from 16.00 local time today. Of course he would be ready, willing and able to perform a post-mortem examination even though he currently stood without medical assistants, but only after the process of this inquiry made than an accepted option.

The doctor was succeeded by Hoyle, who seemed to have no rank. He seemed to be part scientist, part ice-expert. Hoyle had helped the supremely fit Major Schwartz, universally known as Bernie, don the experimental suit. Hoyle himself was involved with the design team for the suit and usually helped Bernie into and out of it. He had not checked it since Bernie's recovery this afternoon. Bernie had elected to take the suit out today for an unscheduled test because of – not despite – the weather. In theory the suit should have been in secure storage until well into the new year, but the prospect of the squall was too much for Bernie to resist. For the first time this season they were promised conditions which would test the suit to its limits and Bernie wanted to make full use of it. Hoyle's evidence became a little vague after that and Richard realised that once again the scientist was up against the limits of secrets. Were these secrets industrial, military, or political? Richard wondered.

Hoyle's evidence was put on hold while the second – and last – communications expert gave evidence about the manner in which Armstrong base had expected to keep contact with Major Schwartz but had failed to do so. Then Hoyle returned to the stand and gave evidence of the initial search attempts, the brief loss of the snow-team, the call for help and of the later phase when help arrived. Then at last Richard and Colin added their evidence. No one else was called. No one from *Kalinin* – understandably, as they had not helped in the search, though they had expedited the recovery after Thomas S. Maddrell's embarrassing mistake.

The video link was broken at 18.30 local time to allow the great and the good at NASA HQ to deliberate undisturbed. As they waited, the room was rearranged and the little group of witnesses milled around a little aimlessly, not yet permitted to return to their duties or their vessels, not having anything else in particular to do. Richard watched as hard copy of their testimony spooled out of one of the computers. He realised that the same would be happening in Washington in case the decision-makers wanted to refer to any detail there. He crossed to the window again and looked out at the ships in the bay. Colin and Kate were there, also silently looking outward. 'No chance of Faraday now,' said Richard quietly.

Colin shook his head.

The communications laptop buzzed urgently and Colonel Jaeger crossed to it. All eyes remained on him for the few minutes he spent exchanging terse words with his masters. Then he drew himself up.

'Ladies and gentlemen,' he said. 'Washington will be sending one inspector down from the Office of Safety and Mission Assurance. This officer will be here within forty-eight hours, in spite of the season, and will need to speak to us all, including those kind friends who answered our distress call. We therefore extend to you the hospitality of Armstrong base at this festive time and apologise if your charitable actions have resulted in disruption to your plans and schedules.'

As soon as he finished speaking the main door of the Jamesway opened and several people entered. Among these was Robin carrying, of all things, a tray. She came over to Richard at once and thrust her tray under the noses of the little group by the window. Richard looked a little suspiciously at the glasses of steaming yellowish liquid. 'What is it?' he asked.

'Eggnog,' said Robin, grimly cheerful. 'The one nearest you has no alcohol in it. Merry Christmas.'

Chapter Three

The next twenty-four hours went by in a whirl of activity whose momentum gathered pace like an avalanche. The process began with the initial inquiry, then continued with various visits and explorations. By the time the parties got seriously under way, things were already slipping. Perhaps it was the Big White. Certainly on *Erebus* and in Armstrong there was more than a little cabin fever, though everyone contrived to conceal it well enough at first. Then there was the genuine shock of Bernie's death, and a surprisingly large number of them were involved in that, or felt as though they were.

At first, to Richard's wise eyes it seemed that much of it arose from the volatile mix of nationalities, cultures, attitudes and genders all trapped here in these extreme conditions with the threat of the inspector's arrival looming. But then he began to suspect that there was something more complex, and more sinister, at work. That was later, however. Now he stood with his eggnog, watching Billy Hoyle approach. As soon as the American scientist joined them, Richard introduced Robin.

'How do you do,' she said. 'I'm sorry about the circumstances. Is "Merry Christmas" out of order?'

'I guess not,' said Billy. 'Though we'd say Season's Greetings I guess. Bernie was a nice guy but he'd know how much the rest of us need to let off steam right now. He wouldn't mind.'

'You could look on it as a bit of a wake,' said Colin, sipping the thick yellow liquid with some trepidation.

'A wake would be Bernie's style,' agreed Hoyle. 'Though I don't think it's a legitimately Jewish concept. Still, he wasn't too deeply into the faith. He'd have been here for midnight Mass tonight. Drunk or sober he'd have been here.'

Colin surveyed the room. Several people were onto their second drink and the mood was lightening. 'Have you been saving up for this?' he asked quietly. 'I guess even NASA must put liquor very low on their list of supply priorities when they're flying stuff in. Same as our supplies from the British Antarctic Survey. Fuel first. Liquor last. A dram of oil's worth a damn sight more than a dram of single malt down here.'

'Saving up like you wouldn't believe, and we've had a moonshine still going for months – in spite of the obvious difficulties with the heat for distillation. And a lot of the guys who've gone home for New Year's have left their allowances for the rest of us as well. We've been looking forward to this, I can tell you. And nobody more than poor old Bernie.'

'Well,' said Robin so quietly it managed to rob the observation of offence, 'all of you except Bernie seem to have fallen on your feet. You've not only got your own supplies, you have for the time being got two ships to call on too. *Erebus* is as well stocked as you could wish, especially in the booze department. I speak with some authority in the matter because I have seen her Port Stanley lading manifest. And I can't even begin to guess what you'll find aboard the good ship *Kalinin*. But I'll bet my life there'll be lots and lots of it.'

Four sets of eyes looked through the clear plastic window to where the two ships swung at anchor almost side by side, their lines clean and striking in the early evening glimmer, etched against the black wall of the southern basalt cliff. The westerly squall had dropped but the seas were still high and Colin's forehead folded into a frown as he registered the amount of brash ice washing in through the mouth of the bay. 'If it freezes hard again tonight the ships could well be trapped for a while in any case,' he growled.

'Not *Kalinin*,' observed a new voice. 'That old girl could smash her way through a sizeable berg if Captain Ogre ordered it.'

They all swung round to face the breezy new arrival. It was Thomas S. Maddrell, apparently unabashed by his faux pas with Bernie's frozen corpse. As the realisation of his arrival spread through the room, so the animation went out of much of the conversation, in spite of the eggnog. If he noticed he gave no sign, but continued to smile sunnily at his little audience.

'Captain *Ogre*?' asked Robin.

Thomas S. Maddrell removed his Ray-Bans to reveal deep-set brown eyes surrounded by pale-floored laugh lines under thick corn-coloured brows a shade or two darker than the riot of his hair. 'Yeah,' he said, 'I asked too. Her folks come from a little town just south of Riga. What can I say? Lucky they didn't come from Brest. Or Smela.' He turned, languidly, to survey the room, meeting all the gazes aimed at him. 'Or Astrakhan . . .'

'Or Titicaca, come to that,' interjected Robin drily. 'Eggnog, Mr Maddrell?'

20

'Call me T-Shirt. Everyone does. What's in it?'

'Reconstituted egg powder, homemade alcohol, Advocaat – so I'm reliably informed. Why T-Shirt?'

'Sounds irresistible. Partly the initials Thomas S.' He took a yellow glass. Sipped as though it contained Krug. 'But mostly because I always seem to have—'

'Been there, done that, got the T-Shirt,' Richard completed, remembering one of William's favourite sayings a couple of years ago.

Robbed of his punch line, T-Shirt grinned. 'Got it in one, sir,' he said cheerfully.

Richard winced. The way the young American said 'sir' made him feel ready for his Zimmer frame.

'Are there many like you on *Kalinin*?' asked Robin.

'Twenty-five boys, same number of girls. Not one of us even faintly sane. Though I'm the first to snowboard the Big White. Got my reputation to consider. I am sorry about your friend, though,' he said, turning to Billy Hoyle. 'Sad way to go. Sad mistake on my part.'

'Forget it,' said the scientist. 'Bernie was a joker. That was the sort of thing he loved. If he hadn't been dead already he'd likely have died laughing.'

'Nice of you to see it that way. I guess some of the others'll take a little more convincing.'

'They'll come round. They just need someone to blame. Other than Bernie himself, or me, or the boss.'

'Outsiders are pretty useful to closed societies, huh?'

'If it hadn't been you it would probably have been us,' said Robin soothingly. 'They need time to adjust, that's all.'

Richard thought how accurate Robin's observation was. They were all outsiders here at the moment, even though they were here by invitation. 'I think it's time we reported back to *Erebus*,' he said.

'Yeah, I guess the guys on *Kalinin* can't last much longer without me either,' said T-Shirt. 'But I tell you what, if these guys at Armstrong keep on with the cold shoulder, why don't we all get together sometime? I'll put it to Captain Ogre.'

'And I'll ask Captain Pitcairn,' promised Robin.

'I'll add a little extra weight if need be,' promised Kate with an uncharacteristic sparkle. 'Twenty-five more like you I simply have to meet.'

'And Captain Ogre,' added Richard, riding a sudden wave of suppressed hilarity. 'We couldn't miss Captain Ogre.'

'Seems to me,' observed Colin at his most Calvinist, 'that you'll all fit right in.'

Andrew Pitcairn was in anything but a hilarious mood. 'Everyone at the HQ in Cambridge has knocked off,' he said to Richard an hour later. 'I can try and track the director down on his personal phone but since he agreed we should answer the distress call no matter what, he'll order us to stay and co-operate with the inquiry when the S&M investigator gets here.'

'S&MA Investigator,' corrected Richard thoughtlessly. 'S&M is something else entirely.'

'That's as may be,' answered Pitcairn a little huffily. 'We're still stuck here for the foreseeable future, aren't we?'

'We'll have to make the best of it,' said Richard bracingly. 'Are you telling me it won't be more fun here, especially with *Kalinin* in port, than it would have been at Faraday?'

'More fun for *us*, maybe,' said Pitcairn. 'But those poor sods at Faraday were gearing up for something special.'

'Well, perhaps we'll get a chance to make it up to them before New Year. In the meantime . . .'

'Point taken. I'll contact Colonel Jaeger ashore and the captain of *Kalinin*. See what we can arrange. The captain's a woman, I understand. Any idea of her name?'

'Ogre.'

'Really? Are you serious? Ogre? Oh well . . .'

The three commanders and their various advisers met in the central Jamesway at Armstrong after their separate dinners. Richard and Colin accompanied Andrew Pitcairn as well as his first officer Hugo Knowles, leaving the second officer in command while the third assumed the first night watch, it having just turned 20.00. As the chopper pilot was still out cold in the ship's surgery, Robin once again took the Westland's controls while Kate filled the co-pilot seat beside her. The redoubtable Leading Seaman Thompson, relieved of all other duties, was engaged in convincing two defiant rising-nines that it was bedtime in spite of the fact that the sun was still up. And that even down here Santa was bound to call on children tonight. On good children. If they were in bed. Asleep.

'You were right, I think, to keep sea watches going,' Richard was saying, as quietly as the clatter of the engine would allow. 'You may find it difficult to maintain discipline and we don't want any incidents either aboard or ashore while we're held here with nowhere else to go.'

Andrew Pitcairn was young and a little arrogant. The openly offered advice galled him. But he was no fool. He could learn a lot from these four people. The Rosses, both PhDs in various glacial studies, knew more about ice and how to deal with it than all the beards put together. In the young captain's other – more important – world, Richard and Robin Mariner commanded equally awesome heights. As captains they had sailed almost every type of commercial craft across nearly every chartered sea under every conceivable circumstance and situation. From tiny experimental multihulls to massive supertankers; from state-of-the-art toxic waste transporters to clapped-out old tramps, they had commanded the lot. They were legendary on the Gulf oil runs; across the dour Northern Ocean, in the mystic South China Sea. There was nothing they did not know about shipboard life, its problems and their solutions. And although they had gained their reputations in commercial fleets, they were both the offspring of Navy men, and therefore knew something of the Navy way in which *Erebus* was run.

And, Pitcairn admitted to himself, Richard Mariner's finger was precisely on the spot which was worrying him most. His command were volunteers. Shore leave had been offered to those with families. The rest all knew what they had signed up for on this particular cruise. But their plans were coming apart now. The strict discipline which had actually seemed quite lax against the regimes at Faraday and Rothera would look very different compared with the lifestyle on Armstrong, let alone on *Kalinin*. Men whose greatest hope for the season was high jinks off watch and a chance to get legless at Faraday were suddenly presented with a very different set of prospects indeed. The presence of women simply added to the brew. Robin and Kate were bad enough – each already had their fan club aboard. What would happen if and when young, available, willing women appeared, Andrew Pitcairn could scarcely imagine. And yet *Erebus* could not stand aloof from anything planned. At the very least there must be a reception aboard for senior officers and their consorts. And if any cross-command entertainments were mooted, the men would have to join in that too.

It was with a chill feeling of foreboding, therefore, that the captain snapped his seat belt open and rose, Hugo Knowles at his shoulder, to exit the Westland at Armstrong's helipad.

Richard was a little slower to unfold himself from the seat – his long shanks were held to his great thighs largely by steel pins at the knee – and the pause gave him opportunity to catch Colin Ross's eye. 'Young Andrew's worried,' he said quietly.

'He's every reason to be. Let's see what the women think of the situation.'

So the four most experienced experts there followed the two Navy men at an increasing distance. And the two of them were well behind the brightly parka'd, strapping figures which had climbed out of the *Kalinin*'s Sikorsky and followed the animated Hoyle towards the distant Jamesway through the strange, salmon-coloured opalescent brightness of a high overcast crossing a midnight sun.

'He's right to be concerned,' said Kate thoughtfully. 'Things aboard *Erebus* are not quite shipshape. Or Bristol fashion. I've taken to rinsing my own smalls and frilly bits, for example.'

'But you've always done that,' blurted the surprised Colin, his memory filled with washing facilities in numberless basic encampments festooned with such things.

'Only when the going gets tough, my love. Not on shipboard with perfectly good laundry facilities.'

'Then why now?' pursued Colin, who had lost the plot here. 'Why bother aboard *Erebus*?'

'Because bits and pieces don't always come back from the ship's laundry, my darling. There may even, I understand, be a market in items that didn't get there in the first place. The crew is exclusively male, remember. At least it is at the moment.'

'My God.' Colin stopped, thunderstruck. Genuinely outraged. 'Do you mean to say someone's been stealing and selling your underwear? Someone aboard *Erebus*? You tell me who's been doing this and I'll—'

'You see Pitcairn's problem?' said Kate quietly. 'This is a mature, sensible man, well versed in the problems of closed societies under extreme conditions. And the first answer he can come up with involves grievous bodily harm. What chance have the others got? It's all right, darling. I've retrieved everything important and I wash it all myself now, as I've said. I suggest you do the same, Robin. And for Mary too.'

'*What*?' bellowed Richard. 'If I catch one man—'

'Here we go again,' said Kate.

The main area of the Jamesway was now illuminated with a couple of Tilley lamps to augment the columns of thick pink light from the windows. Inside the hut it was warm enough for Jaeger to be in his shirtsleeves and somehow he had managed to get the shirt starched and creased to a thoroughly military neatness, in spite of the fact that it bore no badges or insignia. Richard's party joined Pitcairn and Knowles, as they stripped off the parkas, pullovers and cold-weather suits they had worn for the journey hither. As is often the case, the groups turned their backs on each other as though the removal of coats and boots was something too intimate to be observed by strangers. Thus it was that, turning all at once, they received their first impressions of Captain Ogre and her senior advisers at the same time.

There was no mistaking the captain. She wore full uniform and was tucking her peaked hat under her arm, the gold braid on its front lost against the gold braid hanging from her golden epaulette. In spite of the Antarctic clime she wore tropical whites, every bit as starched as Colonel Jaeger's shirt. The whites might almost have fitted Richard or Colin. If anything, the legs of the trousers might have been too long for them, for the captain's waist was as high as it was lissom, given her overall stature. The flare of her hips was no more concealed by the cut of her jacket than the depth of her bosom was disguised by its double breast. On the considerable slope of a snow-white shirt lay a conservative black tie. Above the perfectly executed Windsor knot rose a pale throat and strong neck which in turn supported a broad, determined chin. The wide mouth turned up, at the corners, matching a faint crinkling at the edge of the eyes, which made the face seem just on the verge of a smile. Though, thought Robin uncharitably, dyspepsia and myopia could easily combine into the same impression. Robin's uncharacteristic lack of feminine solidarity arose out of a combination of the shade of the captain's perfect red-gold hair, the fathomless depths of her limpid blue-green eyes, and the expressions on the faces of her dumbstruck husband and associates.

'I wonder who guards her underwear aboard *Kalinin*,' she breathed into Kate's ear.

Kate gestured with her chin.

On one side of the captain stood a square, thickset man, with a weightlifter's body and a boxer's face. His first officer's whites did not fit him as well as his elegant commander's fitted her. They bulged here and there – at calf, thigh, shoulder, chest and bicep. Behind his collar lay not waves of red-gold perfection but short dark stubble on a roll of neck muscles; stubble which reached featurelessly over his bullet cranium to low on his overhanging forehead. There seemed nothing to his face but jut. The jut of beetling brows, of nose under crushed bridge, of square, spade-grey chin. Eyes and mouth were not

25

immediately obvious. The hand in which he held his hat was slightly larger than the braided headgear.

On Captain Ogre's other side stood a slight, almost girlish figure. No uniform here; rather a simple green dress clinging modestly to a slender, upright figure. Solid, comfortable shoes which nevertheless contrived to be stylish. Long, slim legs. No great flare of hip or bosom, but a long neck rising from square shoulders. An open, well-scrubbed face with clear, girlish skin. Wide, intelligent blue eyes and a shock of auburn hair.

'Ladies and gentlemen, please,' called Colonel Jaeger hospitably. 'Pour yourselves some coffee and let's get down to business. We need to be out of here in an hour to let my folks prepare for midnight Mass. Shall we start with introductions? I am Eugene Jaeger, commander of Armstrong base.'

'I am Irene Ogre, captain of *Kalinin*.' Her voice was soft and deep, the purr of a Siberian tiger. Robin was beginning to hate her on principle. 'This is my first officer Vasily Varnek, and this is my entertainment officer Vivien Agran.'

For reasons which he did not understand immediately, Richard ended up introducing their little group, though to Robin's eyes it was clear that Andrew Pitcairn's reticence was a direct result of Irene Ogre's impact. Then they all sat round the table, each with a steaming mug of Jaeger's fragrant coffee in front of them.

It was Captain Ogre who opened the discussion with a forthrightness verging on the brutal: 'We have a big problem here. For you it is worse than for me but I think we must plan to meet it head on or it will go out of our control too fast.'

Jaeger took a long pull at his coffee, his brown eyes measuring the striking woman. 'I agree, Captain,' he said after a moment. 'I think everyone here has at least thought through the situation during the last few hours. Some of us have already discussed our thoughts. But I think we would all be grateful for your analysis.'

'OK. I will speak plain. No beating about the bush, OK? You are all professional people. Many of your senior staff are military, some of your commands are also and those that are not are scientist volunteers with serious job of work. Yes?'

Heads nodded in agreement.

'Your people have much in common then. They play by the same rules. Even those of different gender are part of the same system. There are no big problems if you all mix together.'

Again, the sage nods of agreement. The captain had clearly not

26

earned her command simply through good looks.

'Then we are, what you say, the cat among your penguins. Yes? We have on board fifty tourists. Extreme tourists. They have paid fortune in passage and insurance to come here for two weeks and play. There is little they will not do or risk for fun and excitement. They take no orders and listen to little advice except from each other. They are not in my control, neither the men nor the women. My job and the job of all my people aboard is to help them have fun, not to advise or control – except where my ship's safety is concerned. You have met Mr Maddrell. There are twenty-five men like him aged between twenty and seventy. They climb, snowboard, bungee jump. They hang-glide, parascend, Base jump. They ride snow scooters, and they ski. All of this, and more besides, they do with fierce competition. Some of them, it sometimes seems, have no desire to see the twenty-first century arrive next week. They are not sane, balanced or reasonable. They are, I say again, not in control. As well as these, and nearly as bad, I have twenty-five women aged between twenty and forty. They are partners, consorts, rivals, friends, enemies. It varies. They are all mad, strong-willed and predatory. And available, if I make myself clear. All here for good time. Yes? And in my command also I have deck officers and engineers who do not like these people already. I have stewards, chefs and galley staff who do not like these people very much. I have entertainment staff, under Mrs Agran here, who are paid to like these people but who are not paid enough. We have no experts on ice, penguins or the breeding of seals. It is not that sort of cruise, you understand. But for the fifty passengers I have sixty crew. Forty men. Twenty women. Many also available on the look-out for romance and adventure. They wish to begin the new millennium with a new relationship. These I can keep aboard if I have to and out of your hair. Mr Maddrell and his friends, I cannot. And I think they will mix in here like nitro mixes with glycerin. Yes?'

This worrying summation of the case caused many a frown of concerned agreement round the table. Every mind there became bent on planning how best to control the simmering mix. Every mind, perhaps, except one. Andrew Pitcairn's mind was simply and solely on Irene Ogre. He had led a monastic existence during the last few years and had sublimated everything into work and his command. He had hardly thought about sex in a year. That was all over now. He sat, coffee untouched, with just enough nous to frown and nod with the rest but in his mind he was undressing Captain Ogre. As she completed

27

her first statement and looked around for some kind of response, he was mentally unfastening the clasp of her considerable brassiere, a fantasy constructed of straining black lace, warm to the touch and fragrant, held tremblingly by a catch between the overflowing cups. By the time Richard voiced his suggestions, the garment was off, Irene stood gloriously revealed to the young man's imagination. And from then on, behind every suggestion he agreed to and every decision that he made lay the underlying drive to get her that way in fact.

Chapter Four

'Silent night,' they sang, 'Holy night . . .'

They all seemed to know the fine old tune. There was some impenetrable Russian equivalent to the words, and anyone uncertain of both Russian and English could settle on the German original, '*Stille nacht, heilige nacht . . .*'

Their deliberations had been curtailed not by any agreed conclusion but by midnight Mass as Christmas Eve became Christmas Day. Then, instead of withdrawing to their various responsibilities, they had all decided to stay to celebrate it with the men and women of Armstrong. As the NASA base had no priest, the service was delivered under battlefield conditions by the commanding officer. No Communion would be offered – though some present stood in dire need of it.

Although all of their voices strove as one to follow the base's eccentric little electronic organ, very few of their minds were on higher things at all. Richard was preoccupied with the command problems that appeared to be of such little interest to the captain of *Erebus*. Robin was praying that the twins were asleep and the presents which Santa had left in her keeping for them remained undiscovered and would prove a welcome surprise later this morning; much later. Colin was wrestling more globally with the problem occupying Richard. Mentally, he was scanning the quadrants of the map on Hoyle's laptop, working up a proposition for Jaeger about allowing *Kalinin*'s mad and bad passengers access to one distant quadrant alone – one sufficiently full of danger and excitement to keep them all occupied. It was a problem because the valley reaching away inland east of the base was largely denuded of snow. Kate, as she always did at this time of year, regretted their inability to have children and yearned to share Robin's problems – thoughts she kept secret from Colin, of course, though sometimes she felt her heart would break with longing. What Irene Ogre and her two companions thought was locked deep within them, for they were secretive people. Andrew Pitcairn fondly hoped his thoughts were pretty deeply hidden too. He had contrived to stand immediately behind the object of his abrupt fixation and was continuing to imagine what the view of her would be without the interference of her clothing. And in this endeavour he was unexpectedly aided by Antarctica, for, as the hour itself stole past, the rays of the midnight sun fell through a thickening overcast before streaming ruddily in through the Jamesway's plastic window, giving to the back of Irene Ogre's skin-tight whites the warm hue of naked flesh.

At the end of the service there was little chance for anything except farewells. Not even the forthright Colin could get Jaeger to listen to his plan, and somehow Pitcairn kept getting between him and the Russian captain. The result of Pitcairn's insistence was revealed in the chopper halfway back to *Erebus* when the excited commander suddenly announced, 'I've arranged a little drinks party on *Erebus* at noon sharp. Captain Ogre, her senior people, Colonel Jaeger and his chaps will be there. You're all invited, of course. Though perhaps the twins might . . .'

'Richard and I can take turn-about with them,' said Robin.

'It seemed a good idea. We didn't come to any conclusion about the situation somehow. Maybe we'll get more done in a slightly more social atmosphere. Formal, of course. We'll play it very Navy, Hugo. Full dress. Pink gins and Christmas nibbles. The works.'

'Certainly, Andrew,' said Hugo Knowles. 'And hold back the men's Christmas dinner till smoko?'

'Good. They won't mind, under the circumstances. We'll need several teams of them preparing, cooking and serving in any case. Better for the galley too; let them fiddle about with their turkeys in the afternoon watch. Oh, and we'd better dispense with sea watches for tomorrow as well.'

He fell silent after that and left the rest of them prey to silent speculation: Hugo Knowles on how he was going to get all this arranged – and the effect on the men of attempting it; Richard and Colin on the possibility of using the gathering to help get some serious plans laid before it was simply too late; Robin and Kate almost guiltily on what on earth among the kit they had packed for adventures in Antarctica they could possibly find to wear to a formal Navy drinks reception.

In spite of the red light streaming through the thinly-curtained porthole like a spotlight for Macbeth, the twins were fast asleep. Their exhausted, preoccupied, extremely unChristmassy parents pulled secret Santa presents from all sorts of hiding places – their strange situation making the oranges and nuts almost as valuable down here as the Little Scientist microscope and the Sony Discman – and pushed them silently into stockings. As they prepared for bed in the adjoining cabin, Richard said, 'What d'you make of all this, darling?'

'It's a mess growing into a disaster. What on earth Andrew Pitcairn thinks he's doing I have no idea. Well, of course I have a very good idea. Are you going to get very involved, dear?'

'Don't want to; may have to. Same as Colin, I think. It's none of our business really, and it stays that way until it starts to look as though it could take us down as well. Then we'll have to get involved.'

'It's a little like being on *Titanic*.'

'That's a bit dramatic, darling. Even so, don't worry. Between us, Colin and I will do a damn sight more than rearrange the deck chairs.' This last was issued from the top bunk as Richard settled as best he could into its restrictive length.

'I know you will,' said Robin sleepily from below. 'Merry Christmas, darling.' But the only answer she received was a quiet snore.

At midday on the dot, as punctual as cadets arriving for their first watch, Richard and Colin entered *Erebus*'s wardroom. They were suitably attired in blazers and flannels. Their wives were still below, swapping bits and pieces by Armani and St Laurent, trying to change a couple of little black New Year's Eve numbers into something more suited to Christmas lunchtime. Almost as an afterthought they were watching the twins. An edge of black silk scarf under her microscope kept Mary happy. William had yet to discover that it was possible to walk with his Discman, indeed to run with it, jump with it and do the things he most liked to do with it, so for the moment he was sitting quietly, simply listening to it.

Andrew Pitcairn, who had placed himself so that he could divide his attention between the door and the aft-facing window, greeted them formally and a little dully. The minute *Kalinin*'s helicopter touched down on the specially-vacated helipad, however, a frenetic fizz seemed to enter him and by the time Captain Ogre and her party entered, he was positively glowing. The Russian Captain was all business and icy formality, however. She handed over the bottle of vodka she had brought as a gift and accepted a Scotch and water. No sooner had this been sorted out than the chopper from Armstrong heaved into view and Andrew was perforce distracted from his pursuit.

Colin stepped in. 'Captain Ogre,' he began. 'I was wondering

31

whether you might find it acceptable to send your tourists exclusively to the furthest quadrants at the back of the valley up behind Armstrong. That is where the moraine is located.'

'Where the dead astronaut was found.'

'Quite so. That is the place where the Armstrong people will be least likely to interfere with them. It is also, unless things have changed overnight, where the best conditions for extreme sport can be found. Your Mr Maddrell has already—'

'He is not *my* Mr Maddrell. But I see your point. This is very clever and may serve well. Vasily . . .' The two of them turned to find Vasily Varnek and Vivien Agran deep in conversation with Richard.

'I didn't realise,' he said affably as they approached. 'Mrs Agran is American, not Russian. She tells me that, although most of the officers and crew are Russian, the galley staff, stewards and entertainers are all American.'

'Indeed,' said Vasily Varnek. '*Kalinin* is Gdansk-built and Russian-crewed, but she is owned by a consortium of Russian and American businessmen who refitted her in St Petersburg in nineteen ninety-seven and staffed her to the highest standard.'

'That will do, Vasily. This is not a promotions evening,' interposed Irene Ogre. 'Dr Ross has come up with a scheme which may be of use to us. I wish to discuss it with you before we take it to Colonel Jaeger. I am not satisfied that our plans for the rest of today will keep everything battened down tight, especially as there will be no darkness again tonight.' Without further ado she bustled Vasily and Vivien Agran into a corner, eschewing brusqueness in favour of simple rudeness.

Richard and Colin looked at each other, but if they hoped for a moment to share disquiet they were out of luck. Colonel Jaeger and his people arrived. Even before the first festive nibbles appeared, Irene Ogre had the men she wanted gathered together discussing Colin's suggestion, gaining Jaeger's wholehearted approval, and setting some plans in motion. This process rather sidelined Andrew Pitcairn but he was a quick-thinking and resourceful man. He joined the group as of right – as the other commander present; then exercised his mind in getting involved. 'I say,' he observed at last, forcing his thought into a pause like a foot into a door, 'won't your people be rather exposed up there, Captain Ogre? I mean this poor chap froze to death in that very spot. What if the weather closes down again? We don't want to give this S&M investigator chap too much to do, surely.'

'S&M investigator?' asked Vivien Agran. For someone so slight

32

and girlish of figure she had a surprisingly husky voice.

'Safety and Mission Assurance,' he explained. 'NASA's sending this chap down.'

'Ah,' she said. 'I understand. But you were saying, Captain Pitcairn?'

'Well, shelter, you see. I know what a premium decent shelter is at down here—'

'We would supply portable latrines and pyramid tents in case of emergencies,' said Captain Ogre. 'Basic survival requires we send such things out with groups expecting to be ashore for more than two hours.'

'I see that,' nodded Pitcairn. 'You can't just go peeing behind any old rock down here. Environment and all that. Besides, your winkle would freeze off.' He waited for a laugh. After a moment of embarrassed silence it began to dawn on him that he had been in exclusively male company for too long. 'If you've got one in the first place, of course . . .'

'Your point is well made, Captain,' purred Vivien Agran, coming to his rescue. 'And you can offer more substantial facilities should Captain Ogre feel the need?'

Andrew shot her a grateful look. 'Yes. Exactly. I can lend a couple of square-frame canvas huts for the time we're here. They've got to go to Faraday eventually, but in the meantime, if Captain Ogre could use them, and perhaps a couple of men to look after them . . .'

The captain's limpid blue-green eyes rested on him for a moment and she favoured him with a sunny smile deeply at odds with the chilly overcast outside. The deal was done and everyone was happy.

A stir of movement began at the door and swept across the room. Still basking in the glow of the smile, Andrew was slow to turn. A waft of Chanel alerted Richard and Colin at once and they both turned. Perhaps it was simple coincidence, but they found themselves, like Pitcairn, right at the back of an admiring little crowd. Richard met Robin's dancing grey eyes over the shoulder of an assiduous Hugo Knowles. 'Your children need you, dear,' she breathed to him.

Down in his cabin, Richard slipped off his blazer and sat where he could divide his attention swiftly and equally between his children. In the event, they both settled into quiet contentment. That was good. It gave him time to think – about the accident to Major Schwartz, the imminent arrival of the inspector and what he was likely to uncover ashore at Armstrong. This should have been the main focus of his

33

concern, but his mind kept drifting to *Kalinin* and the unusual nature of her financing, crewing and fitting.

Typically, Robin had sent him down here as a little teasing game. Knowing how he hated to be away from the centre of things, even to be with his beloved offspring, she had actually arranged for Leading Seaman Thompson to come and keep an eye on them. Thompson turned up within five minutes but it was at once obvious that the young sailor was preoccupied. 'You all right to take over here, Tony?' asked Richard, easing his blazer back on.

'Yes, thanks, Captain. It's a bit of a relief, to be quite honest. All that bitching and backbiting. You'd think it was back to the *Bounty*, a little extra duty and holding the plum duff to smoko.'

'Things a bit tense below decks?'

'Well, first we don't get up to Faraday as planned. That puts one or two noses out of joint. There's a few at either end expecting to do a little bit of seasonal trading and bartering, if you catch my drift. Then there's this inspector bloke. What's he going to inspect? Not the old *Erebus*, I hope. There's a fair bit of this and that aboard here destined for people and places best left undiscussed. I mean, you can see it for yourself, sir, if you think it through. We didn't only get pink gins aboard in Stanley. There's a good few commitments given and markets waiting. And, in consequence, a good few debts outstanding not likely to be repaid in the foreseeable.'

Richard buttoned his blazer deliberately, trying to calculate what might have been smuggled aboard in Port Stanley to go on the black market at Rothera and Faraday. Drugs, alcohol, cigarettes and pornography sprang to mind. Except that he couldn't believe that there was much of a black market in either Rothera or Faraday.

'And then there's the normal traditions of the service out the window. That's raised a few hackles, I can tell you. Where's our extra Yuletide tots? Splicing the main brace and such? Extra duty instead. Where's our Christmas vittles and duff? Shoved off to smoko and the galley hands told to stuff their turkey into the afternoon watch. Captain'd better not want too many favours from the below-deck messes, that's what I say.'

Richard straightened his lapels, visualising the reaction to Pitcairn's order that a couple of Faraday's big huts be unshipped and a squad of men take them up a deserted glacial valley, erect them and guard them. An order likely to be passed down later today, in fact.

'You're right, Tony. Thanks for telling me this. You're better off in here and out of any trouble brewing. You want me to mention what you've told me up on the bridge?'

'God! No, Captain. Thank you, Captain, but no. I mean, if it got about I'd even mentioned it to you – you've no idea . . .'

It was a very thoughtful Richard who re-entered the wardroom a few moments later. He had been away for fifteen minutes. Under Irene Ogre's impatient drive, things had moved forward yet again. The rest of the day was more or less organised for all of them. After this little get-together, all three commands would be put through the same schedule by their different commanders in their varying ways according to their own traditions. Christmas dinner would be served at 16.00 and cleared by 18.00. If there were any high jinks or other expressions of tradition which could not be avoided, they would be over by 19.30 at which time the commands would once again be left commanderless and all would repair to Jaeger's Jamesways. Here, Irene and Vivien would arrange something even more exciting than the current diversion and equally to the taste of refined senior officers and their specially invited guests. While this exclusive gathering was under way, another amusement could be arranged for the lower ranks at Armstrong and aboard *Erebus* while the madcap tourists from *Kalinin* were let loose up by the black moraine, guarded by the men kindly volunteered by Captain Pitcairn, and sheltered as necessary by the huts he had promised to send over and have erected there.

Containing the crew of *Erebus* below decks would be comparatively easy, thought Richard, but keeping T-Shirt Maddrell and his friends safely in one spot ten kilometres up-valley from Armstrong might be rather harder. And yet, like a parent allowing his child to cross the road alone for the first time, he saw that they would just have to hope for the best. Unless they were going to corral and cocoon everybody aboard or ashore until the NASA inspector arrived, then they would simply have to risk it.

And so it was done. Robin and Kate's obvious attempts to uphold the social reputation of *Erebus* in the face of their captain's preoccupation with *Kalinin*'s captain had made them the darlings of the wardroom, so they became guests of honour at the full crew's late Christmas dinner. To Andrew Pitcairn's hastily smothered surprise, it was to them that the choicest cuts were offered first and to them alone that the ship's band played the selection of Christmas and nautical melodies accompanying the repast. Neptune, laden with Santa's sack on one shoulder and a frozen trident on the other, allowed them first rummage and the round of applause when they both opened little

35

packages containing the kind of black and lacy confections that kept getting stolen on the way to the ship's laundry. 'More washing,' said Kate in a faintly despairing voice. The laughter which followed seemed entirely untrammelled by guilt.

If Robin and Kate were closest to these hearts of oak, next in line were the twins. On best behaviour, most unnaturally saintly, they sat through it all, eating what they were given, talking when they were talked to, saying 'please' and 'thank you', often at the right time, and accepting with good grace all the rest of the high jinks. Neptune miraculously arranged matters so that Mary got a hand-carved doll and William a ship in a bottle. Even under this severe provocation they were so cheerfully courteous that Richard became rather worried for their health. He had only ever seen them so unremittingly accommodating when they were sickening for something.

As he led them back to their cabin after the festivities, trying without much success to explain why the loyal toast was taken sitting down by the senior service, he realised that he had seen neither hide nor hair of Tony Thompson since their talk. 'We'll have to take the twins ashore with us if Tony's been assigned to any duties this evening,' he said to Robin.

'I'm afraid we will,' she agreed. 'Let's plan on it and get moving. We're all due over there in half an hour and it looks as though it'll take at least two flights.'

'Thank goodness the pilot's so much better.'

'Too right. Signor Armani did not design this particular outfit with chopper piloting in mind. And I did not arrange this coiffure with headphones in mind either, come to that.'

As things turned out, Richard, Robin and the twins went over first with Colin and Kate. Andrew Pitcairn and Hugo Knowles had to get the promised huts up and over – and the truculent matelots assigned to erect and guard them. The sky between Armstrong and the two ships seemed particularly busy that evening. There was also a chill wind from the west again, pushing more brash into the bay under a sky that looked as though it was largely made of slushy grey ice, and the air between the two was thin and treacherous. The frosty wind kept the lower air clear, however, so the chopper ride in gave everyone spectacular views of the bay with its two hilly arms stretching westwards into the ocean. Behind these, the black pebble beach rose swiftly to the plateau where Armstrong base stood, Jamesways, open areas and vehicle areas all in neat order. Beyond the base the wide, black-bottomed valley reached for icy kilometre after icy kilometre up towards the distant mountains. It was just possible to see ten kilometres up the valley, a pattern of lights and helicopters clustered around the moraine where Major Schwartz had frozen to death yesterday, and where the extreme tourists planned to play in the snow today.

The welcome at the base was warm. As the ladies removed their parkas, repaired hood damage to hair and replaced sensible boots with less sensible shoes, the husbands and the twins were entertained by a character calling himself Old King Pole whose provenance was so obscure – or original – that not even Colin had ever heard of him. This fantastical creature was overpoweringly disguised in a frost beard and an ice crown and was dressed in a cloak of snow. He also dispensed presents and sweets, so the twins at least were very glad to make his acquaintance, and he led them off to a quiet corner to bribe them into acquiescent contentment.

Colonel Jaeger was expansive. Irene Ogre's imminent arrival had put him on his mettle and while not in full uniform he was nevertheless sporting all his honours and badgers of rank. Everyone had obviously dined well, and it was equally clear that everyone, with the exception of chopper pilots, watchkeepers and the ever abstemious Richard, had enjoyed a certain amount of drink too.

'Got your command safely tucked down, Gene?' asked Richard, still worried about the state of morale aboard *Erebus*.

'Sure. We've been saving *Die Hard Four, Hell On Ice* for this very occasion. You couldn't prise most of the men away from the video with a crowbar.'

'That's good. I see *Kalinin*'s chopper is heading up the valley pretty well laden. What are those things slung under it? Snow bikes?'

'I guess. Skiddoos, I think they're called.'

'I hope there's still some snow up there for them to run on,' growled Colin, joining them. 'Looks as though there may be more on the way though.'

'Looks that way to me too,' said Jaeger. 'I hope Andy Pitcairn gets his huts up PDQ. Not just for their safety, either. I don't want that guy T-Shirt or any of his friends trying to gatecrash our party.'

Another chopper whirled past the window, coming in low, and Old King Pole shouted, '*Kalinin* incoming, boss.'

'Thanks, Pat. Now keep a good lookout in case those tourist creeps show up. Good evening, ladies. Excuse me, I have more guests to greet.'

The four of them stood beside the table which had been used for the inquiry into Major Schwartz's death. It was now laden with an assortment of traditional American party food.

'I'm not so sure this was such a good idea,' said Kate quietly.

'We'll just wait and see,' soothed Colin, but his eyes, like Richard's, were soberly clear and busy.

Abruptly, from a hidden sound system, Bing Crosby began to sing 'White Christmas'. The *Kalinin* contingent arrived, without Vivien Agran but with several nervous-looking young officers. All men. Old King Pole had a couple of helpers who began to circulate with trays of light snacks and drinks. Bing started on 'Sleighbells'. Another helicopter thundered past the window.

'There's Andrew,' said Robin. 'I hope he's left everything aboard all right.'

'Well,' said Richard, 'when push comes to shove, what are they going to do? Mutiny? I think not.'

'*Erebus* incoming,' sang out Old King Pole.

Colonel Jaeger went to the door as Irene Ogre approached the group by the table.

'I have here several officers who wish to make your acquaintance,' she began.

Andrew Pitcairn came in through the door with several men whose faces were familiar from the noon reception. But Hugo Knowles was not among them. Richard assumed that the first officer had been despatched up the valley to oversee the erection of the huts. Andrew looked pale and preoccupied, his eyes tired and clouded. Even the sight of Captain Ogre failed to brighten them appreciably. But at least Colonel Jaeger's wide welcome prompted some surface cheer out of courtesy if nothing else. Richard turned his gaze back to *Kalinin*'s captain and the beardless youth she was trying to introduce to him.

By the time Bing Crosby had given way to Nat King Cole, things were going with more of a swing and there was enough good cheer evident to get over 'The Little Boy That Santa Claus Forgot'. One of Irene's young men summoned up enough nerve to ask Jaeger whether there was any music which might promote a little dancing. The colonel was preoccupied, looking out at the glimmering gloom as another chopper thundered down to the landing pad. He nevertheless referred the young man to Old King Pole. A few minutes later Nat King Cole gave way to American Forces Radio and the countdown of the Christmas hit parade according to *Variety* magazine.

As it did so, as though on cue, the door of the Jamesway burst open. Old King Pole the doorman dashed out from behind the tinsel hangings over the radio and CD player far too late to stop the influx of strangers. First among these was T-Shirt Maddrell. Immediately behind him was a slim, dark, intense-looking young man of faintly Mexican appearance with dangerous-looking, street-wise eyes. Everyone's first thought was 'gatecrashers'.

Irene Ogre muttered something impenetrably Russian but probably unladylike. 'Vasily,' she spat. He moved towards the gatecrashers, herding the young officers in front of him. Richard was suddenly struck by how muscular and fit they all looked. As, indeed, did the helpers in service with Old King Pole as they followed Colonel Jaeger towards the mêlée at the door, moving just that little more swiftly than the Russians. The air crackled with dangerous confrontation as the two groups of Americans faced each other, at once so dangerously similar and so destructively different. Even Irene's gang held back in the face of it.

When Richard, following close on Robin's heels, suddenly pushed himself into the no-man's land between them, it was as though he was thrusting himself into the eye of a storm. The gap between the opposing sides was no bigger, it seemed to him, than the overwhelming gap between the jaws of the fissure in the moraine. He had no idea what was actually going on, for no one as yet had spoken. He had no notion of whether anyone proposed to start the fight that crackled in the air. Or whether anyone had come armed in order to do so. If Robin hadn't been there, he sure as hell would not have been either. But she was, so he was, and that was that.

'Hi, T-Shirt,' she said quietly. 'What's the problem?' The one question no one had yet thought to ask.

'Up at the moraine,' he began. 'I think there's a big—'

Two huge strangers pushed through the door, breaking up the tourists' lines. Richard found himself staring into a chopper pilot's visor, concealing eyes very nearly level with his own. The figure was wearing an American Forces' cold-weather uniform with 'Ice Pirates' embroidered on it. Beyond the great square shoulder stood a waif-like figure in a huge open parka. Huge eyes seemingly without colour. Long face with round chin and wide mouth. Long boxer's nose like Varnek's smashed a little out of line by accident or genes. The wide, colourless eyes brushed over Richard to T-Shirt where they lingered, taking in the hair, designer gear, designer stubble, the dark eyes stripped of their Ray-Bans, and a good deal else, before returning to Richard.

'Good evening, sir,' said the slight figure clearly to him. 'Are you Colonel Eugene Jaeger? I am Dr Jolene DaCosta, chief inspector for

39

the Office of Safety and Mission Assurance, NASA. I believe you are expecting me.'

Chapter Five

Jolene DaCosta was used to entering closed societies as the outsider
– the fiercely resented outsider, in most cases. She had built around
her slight, apparently fragile self a hard shell. It never ceased to amaze
her how much she could put up with and get away with simply by
forcing herself to do so. She had little sense of being extraordinary,
but sometimes wondered vaguely why other folk had so much trouble
with indulgences, addictions, diets and the like. She had a strict and
set routine on arriving in any situation, designed to establish authority,
pecking order, responsibility and her own special position, before she
actually began investigating. Like her protective shell and her iron
self-control, it was deeply important to her, though she scarcely
registered it on a conscious level at all.

Jolene had been born and raised in Austin, Texas, and was currently
assigned to the Johnson Space Centre in Houston. She had travelled
widely in the USA, been as far west as Hawaii, but had never travelled
further south than Florida. Or further north, come to that, than Niagara,
and that had been just once. Disastrously. On the honeymoon of her
long-dead marriage. She had received emergency clearances and reams
of instructions from the American Antarctic Survey – all faxed, aptly
enough, from the Xerox Document University in Leesburg, Virginia
– but these hardly constituted in-depth preparation for life on the Big
White. She had received details, though no personnel files or
photographs, about the people at Armstrong, and she knew that a
British Antarctic Survey support vessel and an American/Russian co-
owned cruise liner were somehow involved too. She had been sent
not because she was the best prepared or most expert investigator
with the greatest experience, but simply because she was the one senior
investigator who had not sent in a lengthy leave application for the
next week. And so, accordingly to the personnel files in the big
computer at NASA headquarters, she was still on duty at half past
five on Christmas Eve, and available to come South. The US Navy's
Ice Pirates had brought her the last leg of her exhausting journey in a
big VXE-6 chopper and had supplied her with cold-weather gear suited

to someone twice her size, as well as self-heating field rations and hot coffee, but, again, had done little to brief her about the special conditions here. And once they had delivered her, they saluted Colonel Jaeger – whom they, at least, did recognise – and left her. At least they let her keep the cold-weather gear.

Jolene's first, intuitive impression was that she had walked into a confrontation, perhaps a crisis. Automatically, she took charge and began to investigate what it was all about. 'Are you Colonel Jaeger?' she asked the tall man facing her once again. In her heart of hearts she hoped he was. She would need to rely on Jaeger in ways she couldn't imagine yet and she liked the look of this man's long, square-jawed face a lot.

'Naw,' drawled the kid in the designer gear. 'The colonel's at the back of the room.' Jolene looked at him again. She realised he was a good deal older than she had first supposed. She did not like the look of him. But that might have been in reaction to his disappointing news.

'And you are, sir?'

'Maddrell, Thomas S. Call me T-Shirt.'

Jolene found she was beginning to like him even less. 'Thank you, sir. I think not.'

A solid man whose paunch filled a white shirt decorated with a colonel's rank badges pushed through. 'I am Colonel Jaeger,' he said, defensively.

As she introduced herself again and displayed her ID and authorities, Jolene compared the soft-chinned baggy-eyed balding face of the man she did have to deal with against the long, lean hatchet of a man she would rather have dealt with. That hair. Thick, swept back, so black as to be almost blue. Dazzling, electric-blue eyes. Six foot four and more; impressive, even to a Texan. Colonel Jaeger, on the other hand, was not much for a girl to lean on at all. Ah well, make the best of it.

'And precisely what is going on here presently, Colonel?'

'These young men gatecrashed our reception—'

'Gatecrashed! Hell, mister—'

'T-Shirt was just telling us about a crisis up at the moraine,' cut in the deep voice of the blue-eyed man. 'I think you'd better tell us what the matter is, T-Shirt. If you don't mind, Gene.' Plummy English accent; but his voice came up from his boots, thought Jolene.

T-Shirt took a deep breath. Colonel Jaeger shrugged. 'Hokay, Richard.'

Jolene reckoned maybe she could count on this big guy after all. Then she noticed the tall blonde in the Armani outfit by his side.

42

'Yes, T-Shirt?' the blonde prompted gently, also in an English accent.

'It's the Skiddoos,' he said.

'Excuse me?' said Jolene.

But T-Shirt was explaining earnestly to Richard, paying no attention to the mousy girl buried in the huge parka, inspector or no inspector. 'We unloaded them from the Sikorsky at the moraine, near where the English guys are putting up the big frame huts, and flew back to *Kalinin* for more. But then when we went back, the Skiddoos were all on fire. I kid you not. Blazing like you wouldn't believe.'

'And the *Erebus* men? Were they all right?'

'I don't know. I guess so. The huts were up. But we didn't see them.'

'Didn't land,' supplied T-Shirt's Mexican-looking friend.

'Yeah. Max is right. We just turned and came straight back here.'

Richard swung round looking for Andrew Pitcairn. 'Excuse me, Dr DaCosta,' he rasped. 'We have to check the safety of our men. Andrew, did they have W/T equipment?'

'Yes. Hugo was supposed to check in with *Erebus* every fifteen—'

The door behind Jolene DaCosta, closed by the departing Ice Pirates, burst open to reveal a worried radio operator.

'Captain Pitcairn,' he called. '*Erebus* says they've lost contact with your shore party.'

There was an automatic, concerted, movement towards the door. But three figures held firm. Richard and T-Shirt stemmed the flow, but it was Jolene who called, 'Wait just a moment.' She drew breath. 'First priority has to be safety, not speed. Then security. Who's ready to go now?'

T-Shirt and his people were still in their cold-weather gear, and Richard was already donning his parka and boots. He signalled Andrew Pitcairn to come and do the same.

'Who needs to go?' asked Jolene.

'We do,' said Richard. 'Captain Pitcairn, commander of *Erebus*, and me, Captain Richard Mariner. My first aid is up to A&E level. And Colin. Dr Ross is our ice expert.'

'I'll buy that. Nice to meet you, Captain Mariner. Then the next issue is security. We can't go charging up-country and leave this place wide open. It's severely under-manned and we're in the middle of an investigation here. Who's in charge of camp security?'

Old King Pole thrust himself forward, removing his icy crown and his snowman's head. 'Pat Killigan,' he growled. 'Sergeant, US Marines, seconded.'

'Pleased to meet you, Sergeant. My main priority is the late Major Schwartz, his equipment and effects. What's yours?'

'General camp security, ma'am.'

'Right. Give mine priority. Nice costume, by the way.'

'Yes, ma'am. Thank you, ma'am.'

'Colonel Jaeger, I think you and I had better go as well, don't you? I always tend to assume that anything unexpected that happens on the ground of an investigation during an investigation is relevant to that investigation. And the moraine is in your back yard, isn't it?'

'Ten klicks up-country,' admitted Colonel Jaeger. 'But we've a big yard—'

'Also,' called a forceful, feminine voice, 'we go. Skiddoos my cargo. My responsibility. Like passengers also. Vasily, move.'

As they came out of the door into the open area at the centre of the camp, the sun slid out from under the overcast and threw a clear pink light past the black shape of the departing Ice Pirate VXE-6 onto the waiting shapes of *Erebus*'s Westland and *Kalinin*'s Sikorsky, both powered up and ready to go, unlike Armstrong's own chopper. The Westland was on the helipad and so the Sikorsky had landed almost in the middle of the square vehicle-dispersal area containing mini-tractors, Honda four-by-fours, and John Deeres.

Richard, Andrew, Colin and Gene Jaeger pounded one way. T-Shirt, Max, Vasily Varnek and Irene Ogre went the other. Jolene DaCosta hesitated between them, then, unaccountably, she threw herself towards the more distant Sikorsky and scrambled in ahead of the *Kalinin* contingent. When Irene Ogre, fastest, with the longest legs, scrambled in, the S&MA investigator was sitting, frowning, with her face pressed against the window overlooking the parking area.

Irene broke into her reverie at once. 'You do not need to interview my people. We will leave tomorrow, first thing. Tonight perhaps.'

Jolene looked through the gape of the ill-fastened parka to the gaudy badges of rank on the big woman's breast. 'I don't think so, Captain Ogre. Your ship answered the distress call. Your people came ashore. Your passenger Maddrell was involved in the discovery of the body. There are things I need to ask. You'll have to wait. Apart from anything else, your company's western head office, in St Petersburg, Florida, closed for the holiday after giving us permission to demand your co-operation. And I guess your eastern head office in St Petersburg, Russia, would tell you the same even if they were open now, which I doubt. Face it, Captain, you're stuck here till Monday at the earliest.'

'You've done your homework, Miss DaCosta.'

'That's Mrs DaCosta. Or Dr DaCosta. And somebody else did the homework. But they gave all the answers to me.'

'*All* the answers?' needled T-Shirt.

'All the ones I need in order to get started, Mr Maddrell. I'll find whatever else I need to know in order to wind up in due course.'

'Why don't you interview me now? Get that out of the way, maybe make Captain Ogre's day, you know?'

'No, Mr Maddrell. I'll interview you properly, with due witness and proper record at the right time.'

'Hey!' said T-Shirt, looking round at Max, the captain and Vasily Varnek. 'I think Mrs DaCosta just said she doesn't trust us to tell the truth or bear due witness.'

'You could be right,' said Jolene equably. The sun slid back behind the overcast as she spoke and the sudden, gun-metal light reflected in her strange, almost colourless eyes, made them turn steel-grey for an instant as she looked at T-Shirt. 'And also I haven't decided what I want to ask you. Yet.'

'Look at that,' said Vasily Varnek thickly. 'What is that light ahead?'

'That's quite a blaze said Richard tersely. 'I hope it's only the Skiddoos.'

The Westland dipped and then soared over the black bulk of the riven moraine. As they flew over the great fissure, kicking snow from the long white fin on its slug-like basalt back, the men in the cabin craned forward to see what was going on. At first all they could see was a glow reaching up over the curling tail of rock where the frozen Bernie Schwartz had stood. As they approached, they made out individual spires of flame whose light mingled with the dull evening glimmer under the cloud cover to illuminate a couple of half-erected huts. On the dark side of one of these, the furthest from the fire, stood a group of shadowy figures. 'Seven,' counted Richard. 'How many did you send, Andrew?'

'Nine,' answered the worried captain. 'Two teams of four for the huts and Hugo.'

'OK,' said Richard. Then he called forward to the pilot. 'We want to go close to the huts in case of casualties but not too close to the fire. I don't think Dr DaCosta would thank us for fanning any flames needlessly.'

'You can say that again,' said Colin Ross, choosing his moment to break a long, thoughtful silence.

The Westland started to settle, well away from the moraine in an

45

area clear of the massive square boulders which littered the rest of the flat-bottomed glacial valley. The Sikorsky, immediately behind it, also settled there and in a few moments they were all out together, perhaps a three-minute walk from the huts, less than five away from the fire, though its precise location was surprisingly difficult to pinpoint beyond the big, black, room-sized rocks all around. After a moment or two, one of Andrew's men appeared on the scene, drawn by the sound of the helicopters.

'What's going on here?' demanded Andrew at once. 'Where's Lieutenant Knowles?'

'He's in the hut, Captain, hurt. Have you got a doctor with you?'

'I'm doing first aid,' said Richard. 'Anything beyond me we'll have to chopper back to the doctor at Armstrong. He's standing by just in case.'

'Excuse me, sailor,' said Jolene DaCosta quietly but forcefully, 'can you fill us in on what's going on here please?'

'What?' muttered T-Shirt. 'Without competent witnesses and due process?'

Jolene paid no attention to him. In the night light her face was a serious, pale oval. Her eyes seemed fathomless. 'We need to know what to expect, sailor.'

'Bates, Miss. Leading seaman. I don't know, really. Our team was putting up our tent. Some of the chaps said theirs was slower because the choppers kept blowing it about. The next thing I knew Mr Knowles had taken one of the others over to look at something. There was no chopper there but there was an engine running. Some sort of engine, I'm certain. Then BOOM! It all went up, miss. I didn't see anything or do anything. The blokes doing my hut, we just stopped and looked and some of the others ran over. Apparently there was some of them snow-ski things dropped off by the chopper and one of them caught fire, I don't know . . . But the blokes brought back Mr Knowles. Burned. Scorched, anyway. Unconscious. He's in the hut, like I said.'

Basic first aid training requires that the first aider should be certain of his own safety. As they came past the last boulder and out beside the hut Bates had been building, Richard asked, 'But is the fire contained now? Are the huts here in any immediate danger?'

'No, Captain.'

'I'll go up and check that,' said Jolene.

'I also,' rumbled Irene Ogre. 'Vasily . . .'

'And me,' chimed in T-Shirt at once. 'It's my gear, after all. Come on, Max.'

'Should have brought some wieners,' said Max dolefully. 'And some marshmallows maybe.'

'Colin, I'm going to need warmth and light,' said Richard.

Andrew Pitcairn, stunned to discover that his friend and right hand was hurt, gathered his wits and said, 'No worries there Richard. I sent up Tilley lamps and oil-fired space heaters. You should be well able to see.'

The door of the hut opened and Richard, followed by Colin, pushed past the concerned little crowd into the yellow brightness of the Tilley lamp on the floor. Hugo Knowles lay unconscious in the middle of the square wooden floor. Andrew had sent heat and light with the huts but no blankets. One hardy soul – Richard mentally determined to find and reward him – had taken off his parka and used it as a blanket. Beside this Richard knelt. 'Hugo,' he said. 'Hugo, can you hear me? It's Richard Mariner. I'm here to help you, with Colin Ross and Andrew. Hugo, can you hear me? You've had a bit of an accident . . .' He lifted the parka.

From mid-thigh of the right leg up past the hip, closing round into the waist – front and back, by the look of it, and certainly into the groin – was a scorch mark. Clothing – quilted nylon for the most part – was burned and melted, but it lifted clear of pink, lightly poached skin. Above the waist the effects of blast were added to those of flash. The parka had shredded and the skin looked more seriously scorched. The arm and shoulder were burned. The neck and face were seared, half the hair crisp, its ends seared white. But most of the face was relatively unharmed, apart from a nasty square bruise. And the ear was fine. Close to it, as though frozen into place, lay Hugo's right hand, also seared, as though holding something. The radio, thought Richard. Of course.

He checked for vital signs, thrusting two fingers firmly but gently under the undamaged curve of the left jaw. He felt a strong pulse just as Hugo Knowles took a juddering breath and gave a moan. 'Hello, Hugo, old chap,' said Richard. 'You've had an accident but you're going to be fine. Just lie there a moment while I give you a little something for the pain. Colin,' he continued, hardly varying his tone, 'we need to get Hugo back to Armstrong's doctor at once. Alert the Westland. There's room to lie him across the cabin between the seats. Get some of the men here to carry him over. Now, what about the other missing man?'

No sooner had he asked the question than the door opened and T-Shirt's familiar drawl said, 'Captain Mariner, the fair Jolene wants you up by the bonfire, please.'

'Coming.' Richard began to rise slowly and painfully, flesh, bone, tendons and steel pins all complaining as he straightened his knees. 'Any idea why?' he asked, to cover the slow process.

'Well, sir, I guess she wants you to see the scene and bear witness being as how she doesn't trust us or the Russians and all. And I believe she has formed a positive regard for your own faculties, sir. And I know she knows that you particularly would be able to say what the area in question looked like yesterday when you found the late Major Schwartz there. Certainly with far more authority than the poor fool who didn't even notice that the man was dead before he shook his hand. But most of all, sir, I believe she wishes you to see the new dead man before she calls Captain Pitcairn over to identify him.'

'The new dead man?'

'Yes, sir. Very new. Very dead.'

The new dead man lay in the brightness of the blazing Skiddoos. Flat out on his face, as though he had dived, spread-eagled, from a great height. For an instant Richard thought he was naked, but then he saw that his clothing had been melted and shredded by the blast. It was impossible to tell where blackened vermilion nylon ended and roasted crimson flesh began. Sickened, as much by the thought of the poor fellow's dying agony as by the terrible sight of him, Richard knelt again. But immediately he did so, he saw that the victim would have felt nothing. Wedged neatly into the back of his skull was a piece of metal. At the very least he would have been unconscious when he died. Gingerly, Richard slipped two fingers onto the cool flesh of the dead neck. No pulse.

A shadow moved between the corpse and the dying fire. Richard looked up. Jolene DaCosta was framed in red like a Valkyrie, eyes strangely luminous in her shadowed face.

'No pulse,' he said.

'Thank God for small mercies.'

'This is what killed him.' Richard pointed to the metal in the back of his skull. 'It feels squashy round it.'

'No more touching, if you don't mind. First aiding's done and you are no pathologist.

'True. I'll help to move him, though.'

'In a minute, Captain Mariner. I've called Captain Pitcairn.'

Andrew came up slowly as she spoke. 'There's only one man missing,' he said a little shakily. 'Tony Thompson.'

48

Stunned, Richard took one burned shoulder and turned the corpse's face upward. Leading Seaman Thompson might have been restfully asleep. Jolene DaCosta's hiss broke into his thoughts as he was about to lower Tony Thompson's corpse back to the ground. 'Captain! No! Hold it there.'

Surprised, he did as she asked. She bent to look more closely at the metal fragment which, driven by the blast, had actually killed him. Intrigued, Richard, too, looked over the dead shoulder at the bright metal protruding from the black matted hair. And, just like Jolene DaCosta, he frowned.

He knew nothing at all about Skiddoos and the bits and pieces which went to make them up. But he knew a fair amount about explosives, fuses and timers, and what was wedged in the back of Tony Thompson's head looked like part of a timer to him.

Jolene looked him straight in the eyes and they shared a disturbingly intense, dangerously intimate moment. Then T-Shirt came back and Irene Ogre followed with Vasily Varnek at her side.

'This is very bad,' the captain huffed. 'What we have here is wilful destruction of private property.'

Dr Jolene DaCosta, senior inspector for the Office of Safety and Mission Assurance, looked up, every inch a Federal officer, almost as if she worked for the FBI rather than NASA. 'Oh, no Captain Ogre,' she said quietly, in a voice that carried even over the roaring of the fire. 'What we have here is at least one first degree murder.'

Chapter Six

The two helicopters clattered away across the ten kilometres down to Armstrong base, each bearing one of the victims and a range of other passengers. Andrew remained with the last of his men, finishing Hugo's assignment. Jolene DaCosta remained, her investigation not yet complete. Colonel Jaeger and T-Shirt also remained, because she ordered them to; Jaeger more or less truculently and only for the meantime. And Richard remained because she asked him to.

As the thudding of the Sikorsky faded into far echoes like the drums of a distant army, the four of them began to walk away from the bustle of the huts into the disturbing, twilit silence which separated them from the dying fires and the wrecked Skiddoos. There was no wind. The temperature was well below zero Celsius, but not so cold as to put those in ill-fitting gear at risk. Even Richard, who wore only parka and boots separated by nothing more substantial than grey flannels, somewhat stained at the knee, did not feel his legs were too cold. He was sharply aware that the case would have been very different had the wind been blowing. Had he been dressed like this yesterday in the squall, he would have ended up frozen to death like poor Bernie Schwartz in very short order indeed. Severe cold had to be met with total integrity. Cold would find an entrance through the smallest of flaws and the result could be fatal in a terrifyingly short time.

It was with Major Schwartz very much on his mind that Richard arrived for the first time at the actual site of the explosion. On his right was Jolene and on his left T-Shirt. Beyond Jolene was Colonel Jaeger. As they approached the dying embers, Jolene looked across to T-Shirt. 'You unslung the Skiddoos from the Sikorsky, Mr Maddrell?'

'That's right, Mrs DaCosta. Max and me.'

'Where did you put them?'

'In a line along there, beyond the tail of the moraine. There was some snow left there then. They prefer to sit on snow.'

'Now I don't expect you to be an expert in the behaviour of these machines under extreme circumstances – like during an explosion, for instance – but do you think it's possible that a complete machine could have been hurled right over the tail of the moraine here into this hollow nearest us?'

'Well, our Skiddoos are pretty substantial vehicles. They look flimsy but they're not. And the tail of the moraine's about three metres high where it curls round there. It'd take quite an explosion to throw one that high or that far. Their petrol tanks were full, all ready to go, which would have made the explosions bigger but it would also have made them heavier.'

'So it could have been moved on purpose.'

'I guess so. But why?'

Richard answered that one. 'Because that little area is where we found Major Schwartz. What with one thing and another we never searched the snow he was buried in all that carefully. We just pulled him out and carried him back. But it looks as though someone was worried enough about what might have been left lying around to try and burn out the whole area. And there's another thing. We know where we found Thompson and we should be able to establish where Hugo Knowles was, but just from Thompson's position, the force of the blast must have gone that way, towards the huts. So it couldn't possibly have blown a lone Skiddoo this way.'

'But who would have done such a thing?' asked Colonel Jaeger. 'I mean, look at what you're describing, for God's sake. You're saying there was something suspicious about Major Schwartz's death. That someone knew this and tried to cover evidence. That they used Mr Maddrell's Skiddoos to do that. They were desperate enough to use explosives and to murder at least one person on the side. Is that what you're really saying?' There was a kind of dull hopelessness to the question. Like some medieval householder, thought Richard grimly, asking the guy with the funny face mask, 'so we've all got the Black Death, is that what you're saying?'

A look at their stonily set faces was answer enough for Jaeger. 'All right then, who? I guess some of my guys might be in the frame because Bernie was our man. But there's no proof anyone from Armstrong blew up the Skiddoos. They were Skiddoos from *Kalinin*. There were lots of *Kalinin* people up here, crew and passengers. And there were lots of people from *Erebus*, too, come to that. I mean, they were up here at the critical time. My people were all down at the base. So where does that leave us, huh?'

'Not all your people were down on the base,' said Jolene her voice as cold as the wind in yesterday's squall. 'At least one person was out

52

and about in one of your John Deeres. But I bet you he's back at camp now . . .'

'Where is that bloody man of mine?' demanded Robin explosively.

'Still up at the site of the accident, according to Colin,' answered Kate placatingly. She had never seen her friend so angry, but she could see the reason. It was very late. The party, which had never got started, was totally moribund now. The twins were asleep in a corner beneath a jumble of parkas and Robin wanted to go home. Not just to *Erebus* – home.

But *Erebus* would do in the meantime; *Erebus* and bed.

There seemed to be no chance of either in the immediate future, however. Since the officious little woman from NASA had swept in and out with most of the men, there had been nothing to do but wait and wait. There was no way for them to know how serious the developments up-valley had become so their priorities remained domestic.

But then Colin arrived, with Billy Hoyle in tow. 'Look,' he said tersely. 'There's a bit of a situation up at the moraine. Nasty accident. I don't think you'll be going back to *Erebus* tonight so I've asked Billy here to scare up some accommodation for you two and the twins. The rest of us are in for a busy night by the looks of things but you should be able to get your heads down if you don't mind camping.' His tone as much as his words gave the women pause.

'Kate, if you could bunk in with Robin and the twins. It's not just a case of saving space, though that's important, but you'll be able to make sure she's up to speed with the facilities and so forth. Robin, have you or the twins ever used an ice-station latrine? I thought not. I know you've got no nightwear or anything, but I think we'll be able to get a couple of sets of thermals from central stores. They should keep you snug enough. Now our only immediate problem is if anyone needs to use the major toilet facilities; otherwise I've got pee bottles for you all and they'll have to do until morning. Which isn't that far off in any case as things go.'

Colin and Billy Hoyle carried one twin each, tucked between their parkas and their cold-weather overall bibs. Robin and Kate slipped on their parkas, still warm and redolent of sleeping child, then the four of them hurried through the strange grey gloaming to the little two-bunk pit room that had been cleared for them. The women swiftly changed from party frock to thermals – rolled up at ankle and wrist. They would each take a sleepy child as a kind of restless hot water

53

bottle in their big, fleecy sleeping-bag, but the need for simple insurance, especially here, required that the children be introduced to the pee bottle before tucking down again. William was happy enough – the bottle was well designed for male use – but Mary was much less happy to feel it's cold lip against her warm tummy. After half an hour they tucked down, however, and although each woman was prey to widely different feelings vivid enough to keep them awake for a while, when Colin crept past nearly an hour after his arrival back from the moraine, he was relieved to hear sonorous snoring in two feminine keys. Relieved also to have managed to put them together without having alerted them to his worry about security. He checked the pit-room door. Good. It was securely locked.

The children woke refreshed. The adults did not. Robin ruled that anything but the most basic ablutions should wait until they were back aboard *Erebus*, something that she expected to arrange well before lunchtime. Then, having dressed the children in their warm, weatherproof clothing, was brought up short by the fact that she and Kate had a choice of Armani, St Laurent, parka or River Island all-in-one long johns in which to greet Boxing Day. Kate was inclined to see the funny side of this. Robin most certainly was not. The main function her bloody husband had promised to perform on this family holiday was to ensure that she was waited on hand and foot, and here she was without adequate clothing to face a camp of mostly sex-starved men and a boat full of underwear thieves. Her usually cool grey eyes ablaze beneath a wild riot of normally well-brushed hair, she looked deep into the rather nervous countenances of the twins. 'You find your father,' she said. 'Or you find Uncle Colin. And you get them here now. Do not get lost. Do not get sidetracked. Do not get anyone else or I will personally boil you in oil. Do you understand?'

Two very solemn nods. One nervous 'Yes, Mummy,' in a squeak that could have come from either throat, and they were off.

'Are you sure that's the right way to treat a couple of frightened eight-year-olds, Robin? I'm sure it's not what Dr Spock—'

'Bugger Dr Spock, Kate. I want my husband here. I want some clothes and I want to get back to *Erebus* and I don't care who I have to boil in oil to do it.'

Kate considered being upset by this, but something in Robin's tone made her nod her head sympathetically instead.

The only familiar face the twins could find belonged to Billy Hoyle. Their mother's instructions had been quite clear so they did not

54

approach Billy at first but simply followed him around, hoping that he would lead them to one of their goals. The camp was in a bustle verging on turmoil this Boxing day morning. Normal Sunday routine was well and truly disrupted. Another inquest was more likely than a Sunday service. The doc had finished his examinations of the two Englishmen, one living, one dead, but as with Bernie Schwartz there was to be cold storage rather than post-mortem. More authorities would have to be contacted before any action could be taken in that regard. Suspicious deaths of American service personnel on American soil were difficult enough but the suspicious deaths of serving men from the forces of friendly powers performing humanitarian good deeds on American soil opened a very large diplomatic can of worms.

The doc concentrated on trying to get Lieutenant Commander Knowles into a fit state to be transferred back to *Erebus*. In this worthy endeavour he was aided by *Erebus*'s own surgeon commander, who had been flown ashore in the middle of the night to help. The two men hated each other immediately with the ill-controlled venom which only equally qualified experts in competition can achieve. This relationship looked as though it was going to set the tone for most of the relationships during the next forty-eight hours or so as things continued to slide out of control with gathering pace.

By the time breakfast should have happened, Colonel Eugene Jaeger had had more than enough of that bossy little bitch from head office. He had also had enough of the useless faffing around of that wet blanket of a captain from the Royal Navy. He did not appreciate big Scotsmen with a penchant for giving orders either. And as for Richard Mariner, Jolene DaCosta's bitching blue-eyed boy, he could well get through the rest of his life without ever seeing him again. But far from getting rid of them, he was going to have to go through a re-run of Bernie's inquest with DaCosta in the chair instead of himself and a whole bunch of questions being asked about camp security, like how come folks could slip out and in with John Deeres without leaving trace or record – not even on the fuel manifest. And where was the guard on the explosives store when someone took a couple of kilos of H/E and several timers. And that was just for openers.

His own command, increasingly, was a series of small camps armed against outsiders – especially outsiders with high explosive and lethal intent. And those armed camps were further armed against the English sailors who seemed to have brought this new wave of unpleasantness down on them. And the English, of course, were all too willing to

55

think ill of their colonial cousins, their attitudes, their discipline, their security and such.

Andrew Pitcairn's men had finished putting up the tents in the small hours only to have Colonel Jaeger ask that they be taken down again and sent back to *Erebus*. He had returned briefly to Armstrong at 4 a.m. to find a message from Captain Ogre warning that the instant Dr DaCosta had examined the crew and passengers about the two incidents, *Kalinin* was leaving. Indeed, if Dr DaCosta was not pretty quick with her questions in the morning then she could whistle. In the meantime there would be no more recreational visits ashore by her crew or her passengers. The shelters would therefore not be required. The wreckage of the Skiddoos was the colonel's responsibility and it seemed to her very much as though the cost of replacing them would be his too. In the meantime, *Kalinin*'s contingent – those deemed relevant by Captain Ogre – would be there to answer questions at 09.00. Departure would be at midday, no matter what.

The colonel had passed the message on to Jolene DaCosta who had looked remarkably unsurprised and had returned with Richard Mariner to whatever investigation and measurement they were engaged in. In the meantime, the exhausted Andrew Pitcairn had discovered that he could not get the collapsible huts to fold into the correct size for their crates and had been forced to summon Colin Ross once again.

And so, as the twins began to search for uncle or father, early on Boxing Day morning, Billy Hoyle was rushing hither and thither, preoccupied and distracted. Captain Ogre was expected within the hour to give evidence or depart. Dr DaCosta was expected back then or soon after to start up the formal hearing if she wanted to register *Kalinin*'s evidence. She and Richard Mariner were expected to tweak a few more tails when they arrived, too – starting with the colonel's. At the same time seven exhausted, very irritable English matelots and one grumpy Scot had dumped two big crates in the middle of the compound where John Deeres had a habit of coming and going unaccountably. These eight at least were aiming to make full use of the toilet and dining facilities, blissfully unaware of the storm gathering around them.

Like the need for total integrity to combat cold, the slightest flaw in routine can put everything at risk. On that morning so much was going on that all Armstrong's routines seemed to be coming down like a house of cards. The twins had no knowledge of this. They noticed nothing untoward as they followed Billy Hoyle into the laboratory area and watched him talk to a couple of men in white coats, whom they did not recognise. They followed him into the dispersal area and watched him check the insides of several pick-up trucks. They followed him to the unguarded supply hut where he spent so long ferreting around that they almost went away to search for their father on their own. They followed him past the camp's medical facility to the cold storage hut. Firmly side-tracked in spite of Robin's orders, like the Hardy Twins or two of the Secret Seven, they followed him into the still, silent, shadowed depths of the icy storage hut. They were so close behind the busy young scientist that when a distant voice – belonging in fact to Sergeant Pat Killigan bellowed, 'Hey! Hoyle! That hut's off limits, buster. You get your scientific little ass out of there before I boot it clear over the Pole,' and Hoyle spun round as though he had been shot, there they were, just behind him.

'Hey, kids,' he said easily. 'What're you doing?'

'Looking for my daddy,' said Mary at once. 'Have you seen him?'

''Fraid not, honey. Anything I can do?'

'I don't think so, thank you, sir. Mummy just said we should find him or Uncle Colin as quickly as we could.'

'We-ll,' he drew it out like Ace Ventura, 'I think I can help you there. All-righty then?'

'Yes, please,' said William, who was cold and bored. 'Where shall we look?'

'Let's start out at the helipad, shall we? All-righty.'

Hoyle moved towards the door with the twins trailing a little hesitantly behind him. 'Why is that sleeping man wearing that funny silver suit?' asked William in one of his stage whispers.

'I don't know, William. Shhh,' answered Mary. But both of them hesitated, their interest piqued. There was someone sleeping in a strange suit which seemed to be made of cooking foil. The tables in this place were about the same length as beds. Most of them seemed to be piled with boxes and bundles but at least two of them had been turned into makeshift resting places.

'What is that funny smell, Mary? Has someone been cooking in here?'

'I don't think so, William. This doesn't feel right. Mr Hoyle . . .'

'*Daaaddy.*' William had run out of patience. He had good lungs. The bellow was enough to wake the dead. Almost. Hoyle, by the door, spun to look back at them, his face pale, finger jerking up towards his lips.

'William. That man sleeping over there looks like Tony Thompson,' said Mary loudly.

'Hokay, Hoyle. I heard the sergeant warn you. Now you and the stockade are going to get . . .' Sergeant Killigan's right-hand man Corporal Washington slammed in through the door, immediately behind the horrified Hoyle.

All three of the interlopers swung round and stared at the large, angry Marine.

'Hey, Corporal,' babbled Hoyle. 'I'm sorry. I was just helping these kids look for their daddy. He's the big limey that's in so good with the S&M investigator. Their mommy told them to find him. Isn't that right? William? Mary? Help me out here. Give me a break.'

'Yes, sir. This gentleman is helping us find our father,' Mary confirmed. 'Our mother and Dr Ross have no clothes at present and we need to find our father or Dr Ross to help them.'

'No clothes?' said Corporal Washington, diverted by an entirely inappropriate mental picture. 'Weeeelll.'

Ten minutes later there was a scratch at Robin's pit-room door. Mary's slightly muffled voice whispered, 'Mummy . . .'

Driven to distraction by the length of time she and Kate had been forced to wait, Robin ripped the door wide and froze. Immediately outside stood her daughter and son, laden with cold-weather gear from central stores. Behind them stood Hoyle, Washington and Killigan, united this once by a common dream.

The dream was not fulfilled – not quite. Instead of the nudity that only cabin fever would have made grown men hope for, they were treated to the sight of a woman clad only in an all-in-one so tight and clinging it might as well have been a slightly ribbed, Chanel-fragrant, white coat of paint.

Or that's the way they saw it – until she said in the deepest, most plummy English growl, 'Why gentlemen. Thank you so much for your help . . .' The kids scurried in and, with a breathtaking tensing of long, widely-parted thighs, a deliciously pert twitch of the broad hips, a wonderfully liquid sway of the breasts, the vision in white slammed the door. And the three men returned to the real world.

Chapter Seven

At 09.00 on the dot, *Kalinin*'s Sikorsky lowered itself out of a low grey sky directly onto Armstrong's landing pad. The side swung open. In full uniform, Captain Irene Ogre, Lieutenant Vasily Varnek and a helicopter pilot descended. Behind them, in their own designer-label equivalent, came T-Shirt and Max. As the Sikorsky courteously lifted off and went to squat beside the crated huts in the dispersal area, the five figures from *Kalinin* marched to the central Jamesway. Their arrival was so strongly stated that they got quite a following as they marched across the windswept, snowless central area past the flagpole. Amongst this inquisitive group was Robin, Kate and the children, still unaware of exactly what was going on here.

At the main door into the Jamesway, Colonel Jaeger was waiting. He, too, had with him a group of men expecting to give evidence.

'Well?' demanded Captain Ogre.

Before the colonel could make any reply, the exhausted – but well fed – sailors from *Erebus* arrived, led by Andrew Pitcairn and Colin Ross. Seeing her husband, Kate pushed forward, full of questions. Colin turned aside to talk to her and Andrew Pitcairn found himself confronted with the sparkling eyes of his fantasy woman. They were sparkling with anger and impatience.

'Well?' she repeated.

Andrew reached over and opened the door for her. Even his sudden dislike of this imperious, arrogant woman could not stop a tremble of lust as his face came close to the snowy crests of her bosom. But as the door swung wide she rudely shoved him aside and first she, then her command, then the rest of them trooped into the chilly cavern of the Jamesway.

Helicopters had come and gone all night, most of them up to the moraine and back. Even Colin Ross had lost track of who was where. Such had been the confusion, the lack of routine, this morning that anyone could have been anywhere and no one would have been at all surprised to find the Jamesway empty. But no. There at the table, arranging notes – written, processed and taped – was Jolene DaCosta, as utterly in charge as a school principal in her office.

Jolene was not alone. As the crowd jostled in through the narrow door, pulling off or opening up their outdoor clothing, they saw Richard slouching solidly in a chair at the back of the room, like a minder in a detective film.

He watched Robin pushing through the crowd towards him, twins in tow. She would be really angry with him, he knew. And if he had been in any doubt, one glance at her steely eyes would have settled things. But she didn't know the full story.

'Darling,' he said quietly as he stood and embraced her, 'I've some very sad news, I'm afraid. Hugo Knowles has been pretty badly hurt in an accident up the valley.' He checked that the twins weren't too close. 'And poor Tony Thompson's dead.'

Robin sat down, winded, and he folded himself back down beside her.

'How?' she asked.

'Caught in an explosion. Maybe an accident. Maybe not. That's the problem.'

'That's what this meeting's about?'

'Yup.'

'Then I'd better get the twins out of here.'

'I agree.' Richard raised is voice slightly. 'Andrew.'

Andrew turned from his rather fearsome contemplation of Captain Ogre. 'Yes?'

'I think this is going to take some time. Is it OK if Robin and maybe Kate scoot back to *Erebus* in the Westland?'

'Sure.'

Half an hour ago Robin would have given almost anything to hear this. Now she wasn't quite so sure. 'Wait a moment,' she said. 'Just what is going on here?'

'I expect we'll all be back by lunchtime,' said Richard easily. 'I'll tell you then. But I really don't think we want the twins finding out about . . . you know what . . . like this, do we?'

Robin might have hesitated still, her danger-antennae suddenly twitching. But William asked at once, 'What's you know what? What is Daddy talking about, Mummy?' And that rather settled matters.

As *Erebus*'s helicopter thudded away towards the distant ship, Jolene checked the display on her personal phone and settled it beside her laptop. She eased the laptop's screen slightly to get the clearest picture and typed in a short code. Then she sat back, quite still. As though her stillness had been a signal as powerful as the rapping of a gavel, silence settled across the room. Even the overwhelming Captain Ogre fell quiet.

'Let us begin,' said Jolene clearly. As she spoke she leaned forward and began to type a record directly into the machine in front of her. 'I have very few opening remarks, then I will call for evidence and announce my decision.'

Irene Ogre was on her feet, mouth open. Jolene's busy fingers hesitated. 'In a minute, Captain Ogre. Your people will come and go first, I promise. But there is a form to these things. Due process.'

Irene sat, defeated for the time being. Jolene proceeded. 'It is nine oh five local time on the morning of Sunday, twenty-sixth, nineteen ninety-nine. This is a Safety and Mission Assurance report by Inspector Jolene DaCosta . . .' Jolene spoke briskly and typed at the same speed, glancing down only occasionally, her eyes on her audience for the majority of the time – and, Robin would have noticed had she been here, on Richard most often.

'I was assigned to investigate the apparent accidental death of Major Bernard U. Schwartz under circumstances I am blocking in now . . .' Slight pause as she called up a block of pre-prepared text and pasted it in place.

'Just a minute.' Colonel Jaeger was on his feet. 'You could be adding anything in there.'

'You will get a print-out of the whole testimony at the end of the proceedings, Colonel, as will Captains Ogre and Pitcairn. And anyone else who requires one,' Jolene promised quietly. Then she continued, more loudly and formally, 'Circumstances have dictated, however, that detailed investigation into this incident should wait. Another incident which I believe is linked to it, throwing a very questionable light on it, has since occurred. I will now call in a block description of the facts of that incident. And yes, Colonel, it will also be on your print-out and you may register disagreement with any section you wish. But this section will be supported by testimony. Now, Captain Ogre, I would like to talk to Mr Thomas S. Maddrell, passenger on the ship *Kalinin*, and resident . . . Mr Maddrell, you need not rise or take the oath, just give us your address for the record and tell us about the placing of the Skiddoos . . .'

And so the deposition got under way. T-Shirt had his say, then *Kalinin*'s pilot had his. Finally Irene Ogre confirmed that she had given permission for the whole doomed enterprise, all legal and above board, to satisfy the insurers. Having established that the recreational vehicles were left clear of the moraine, Jolene called for testimony from Andrew Pitcairn's men to establish whether anyone fit to bear witness had noticed the placing of the Skiddoos nearer the time of the explosion. Only Knowles and the unfortunate Thompson had gone close enough to see anything, apparently; and they had clearly seen too much. Evidence was taken from the men who had heard the explosion, found the bodies, moved Knowles in the hope of helping him and left Thompson who was still burning at that stage and clearly dead.

Both doctors gave evidence, in widely differing styles and with directly opposing commentary but with basic agreement as to facts. Major Schwartz had probably died of exposure, and was still frozen in the state in which he had been found. Leading Seaman Thompson had suffered a severe blow to the back of the cranium, probably as a result of an explosion, and had died either of shock caused by his injuries or from these injuries themselves. Thompson, like Schwartz, was awaiting detailed post-mortem attention. Lieutenant Knowles was likely to make a full recovery but he was still sedated and in no fit state to give testimony at this time.

Richard then gave evidence about the placing of the bodies. He was able to place Knowles accurately because his ruined radio had still been on the ground where he had fallen. He also gave evidence about the out-of-place Skiddoo. Jolene then blocked in corroborating evidence of her own and a final deposition about the unaccounted-for movements of at least one John Deere and the missing explosives and detonators.

'My conclusions are as follows,' said Jolene, typing as she talked. 'Sufficient doubt hangs over the death of Major Bernard Schwartz to warrant further investigation. Such severe doubt hangs over the death of Leading Seaman Thompson and the wounding of Lieutenant Knowles as to make charges of possible culpable homicide or perhaps even murder seem likely. My position here allows me to investigate and to report, and advise the camp authorities as to the need for detention in any case until higher military or federal authorities can be summoned. I do not have powers of arrest or detention beyond those of the ordinary citizen – unlike Colonel Jaeger or Sergeant Killigan, for example. However, if I deem the situation serious enough, I can summon higher authority. And this is what I have decided to do. Hearing terminated at ten thirty, date as given. Now, if you will wait for a few moments, you may have your print-outs.'

Richard pulled himself erect and strolled across to the Jamesway's clear plastic window. The sky looked like dark-banded pewter; the nearby beach and distant cliffs were utter black without any reflected brightness and so the lightest part of the scene was the bright, blue-edged brash ice bobbing in the bay between them. Beyond this, *Erebus* and *Kalinin* lay, one dead and dark, with only a glimmer of riding lights, the other bright and bustling, ready to break out of the ice-bound bay, running lights already up and agleam. It was with a feeling of almost profound sadness that Richard realised he would never get the chance to look around the converted cruise ship after all. And if T-Shirt and Max were anything to go by, he would have enjoyed meeting the passengers – if not the crew, perhaps. He turned and looked across to where Irene Ogre and Vasily Varnek were poring over Jolene's print-out. Well, that wasn't quite true. Unlike Andrew Pitcairn, Richard had been more struck by Vivien Agran. He would have enjoyed getting to know the entertainment officer better; she appeared to be an interesting girl. There seemed to be hidden depths to her.

'Right,' announced Irene Ogre. 'This will do for us. You summon who you like, Dr DaCosta. Tell them if they want to talk to us we will be somewhere south of here.'

Jolene gave a half smile from behind her laptop, her fingers still busy. 'I'll tell them that, Captain Ogre. And thank you for your patience and co-operation so far.' She did not rise but dropped her eyes. The captain, her associates, *Kalinin* herself, were all dismissed.

Colonel Jaeger dragged himself away from his detailed contemplation of his own print-out to do the gallant thing at the door. 'Thank you for answering our distress signal so promptly, Captain Ogre,' he said formally, offering to shake her hand. 'I am sorry everything went so wrong so quickly.'

It was a lame speech, made weaker by her failure to take his hand or to answer. He changed the gesture into a salute which she also disregarded. Silently, she looked around the room. Of all the gazes there, only Richard's met hers. Met it and held it. She nodded an acknowledgement and was gone.

The silence in the room after her exit made the sound of the departing Sikorsky seem louder, more final. It was as though the last lifeboat had just pulled clear of *Titanic*.

Apparently casually, Richard crossed to stand beside Jolene again. He looked down into the screen of her laptop, with its symbols and icons.

'This seems about right to me,' said Andrew Pitcairn. 'I'll add it to my logs and the accident report. Then I'll want to transfer all my people, living, dead and wounded, back to *Erebus*. That'll include you of course, Colin, Kate, Richard. Then I'll get onto the BAS people at Cambridge direct, I think . . .' He turned away, trying to summon up some decisiveness.

'Are you going to send this as it is?' demanded Colonel Jaeger at last.

Jolene looked at him, her fingers still on the keyboard of her laptop. Slowly, being very careful to exert no pressure, she stood. 'You have a problem with that, Colonel?'

'Sure I do. It makes it look as though some psychopath has been running around here for at least two days and there's been no security, no records, no leadership—'

'It makes it look as though, in spite of the reasonable precautions normally taken in this kind of place, someone has managed to outwit all of us because we didn't know what he was up to. It makes it look as though now is the time for leadership and security. A lot of both. And if you can't supply them, Colonel Jaeger, then Armstrong base is in trouble.'

That gave Jaeger pause. Jolene gazed at him, her eyes narrow, their pupils gleaming, blue-edged, like the brash ice outside.

'Well, I still don't like it,' he huffed.

'You don't have to like it,' she pointed out coolly. 'Are you saying that it is inaccurate in any regard?'

'Well, not really, but—'

'Yes or no, Colonel?' The voice cracked every bit as authoritatively as Irene Ogre's at her most officious.

'Well, no.'

Jolene's finger fell like the beak of a diving skua. 'In that case, Colonel, I suggest you start looking for the leadership and security you will need for the immediate future. The Feds will be here within twenty-four hours.'

'What? How?'

'My laptop hooks to the Internet via my personal phone. I've just sent that report directly to my office in Washington. I tagged it so that it will transfer automatically to FBI headquarters. The duty office have been waiting for it since I alerted them just after midnight. There will be a team of Special Agents on their way down here before lunchtime. And if you think I travelled fast, you should see those guys move.'

'Hey, now wait just a minute here.' Colonel Jaeger raised his hand as his mind fought to keep up with her words. 'You just called *who*?'

Then the penny dropped. 'You stupid woman, what have you done? You'd better have booked a pretty good return ticket to that tight-assed little office of yours because I want you the hell off my base *now*. Killigan? Killigan!'

'Yes, Colonel?'

'Killigan, if that woman is still on my base in five minutes I want you to sling her bureaucratic little heine in the stockade.'

'Well, Colonel—'

'You hear her, Killigan? She called in the Feds on us. Also she does not have the right of arrest whereas I do and she does not have the right of legal detention which you do. Now if she is here in five minutes I will arrest her and I will order you to lock her up.'

'You only have to obey an order if it's a legal one, Sergeant,' observed Jolene quietly, apparently unfazed by the turn of events.

'This woman's presence here is prejudicial to the good order of my command, Sergeant. If she will not get herself out, I will have to move her to secure accommodation. In the cooler. Until her friends from Washington show up at least. And that is all. In four minutes . . .'

'Andrew,' said Richard quietly. 'Have we got a spare berth aboard *Erebus*?'

Andrew jerked, as though waking from deep preoccupation. 'What? Oh, yes, of course. Happy to oblige.'

'Let's go then.'

'You don't have to keep putting yourself out for me, you know,' said Jolene by way of thanks, halfway to *Erebus*'s Westland.

'Don't mention it.'

'I'm used to this kind of reaction. I can handle it. And myself, come to that.'

'No. No. It's no trouble at all. I assure you.'

'Are all Englishmen like you?'

'What do you mean?'

'So gallant.'

'Mostly. You mean men aren't gallant Stateside?'

'Not so much, I guess.'

'I hate to disagree with a lady, but if *Kalinin* was still here instead of *Erebus*, you'd have been having this conversation with T-Shirt.'

'T-Shirt? Are you kidding? He would not give one good god damn. And even if he did, Captain Ogre would never have allowed him.'

'Is that what you think? Really? I am surprised. Well, I see you have your laptop and personal phone. Where's the rest of your kit?'

'Supplies hut by the vehicle disbursement area.'

'Couldn't be closer or more convenient. We might even make Gene's deadline.'

'Hate to disappoint you, but this girl has an urgent call to make. Ladies cannot get by with pee bottles alone.'

'Are you sure? The facilities aboard *Erebus* are far more suitable. Can't you wait?' He might almost have been talking to Mary.

Jolene might almost have been talking to her father. Almost. 'I don't think so. And look. I spy with my little eye . . .'

Two doctors deep in vitriolic confrontation about the imminent departure of Hugo Knowles. The Westland was not likely to be leaving until they resolved that. Or until Andrew ran out of patience and pulled rank.

'Point taken. I'll take this stuff now and pick up your kit too. See you back here.'

'OK.'

'Oh, and Jolene?'

'Yup?'

'Watch your back, and even more importantly . . .'

'Uh-huh?'

'Use the pee bottle and pour it into the funnel. It's easier. Believe me.'

A certain amount of Jolene's conversation had been bravado. She did in fact feel isolated here. Out of her depth and more than a little at risk. Even the bulky cold-weather gear designed to keep her warm and alive seemed to over-swaddle her, choke her, put too many layers between her and the powerful little lightweight Glock pistol which was her insurance, her court of last resort.

Almost as soon as she left the central square of the disbursement area she felt she was being watched. Watched and followed. She strained to hear any sound which would allow her to focus, but all she could make out were the slow thud of the Westland's idling rotors, the groaning crackle of the restless brash in the bay and the unearthy keening of a wind she had not noticed arriving.

A sudden scream made her jump and look up. A seabird swooped low over her head. A brown skua, though she did not recognise it. That too had arrived, unnoticed, with the wind. Suddenly cold as well as scared, Jolene hurried forward. At last the hut was there before her. She pushed open the door and stopped, her nose crinkling. Twenty-four hours ago she had been warm and safe, winging southwards in the fragrant confines an Air Mexico jet heading for Ushuaia city whence the Ice Pirates would spirit her southward across the terrifying leaden corrugations of the deadly Drake Passage. Then the most offensive smell had been the mouthwatering tapas she was just about to eat. She would frankly rather have been bobbing in a bathtub adrift on the Passage, the stormiest, most dangerous waters on earth, than here now.

'This is a hell of a way to conquer the final frontier,' she muttered to herself, not very boldly going where all too few women had gone before.

In the wall a tube opened out into a tiny urinal, a tiny urinal positioned for a very tall man. Beside it, a good deal lower but not a lot bigger, was something that looked more like a bike saddle than a seat and it sat upon a large tub marked a little threateningly, SOLIDS ONLY. Beside it was a pile of chemical-soluble paper. Jolene saw exactly what Richard had been driving at. She turned, took a deep draught of clean, cold air and secured the door. Holding her breath she adjusted her clothing until it was just possible for her to use the pee bottle. She did this quickly, all too well aware of other urgent needs. Then, with her trousers still half down and her bottom coming close to realising that old saying 'It'll freeze your ass off' she shuffled over towards the drum.

There was the slightest stirring outside, almost drowned by the whisper of the wind. Almost but not quite. As she squatted, winded by the cold, Jolene slid her right hand down the inside of her boot, freeing the new Glock from its neat calf holster. She felt physically threatened. At risk because of her position as S&MA inspector. She assumed she was being followed by whoever had been caught up on the wrong side of the mess she was investigating. She expected to be warned off, frightened away, perhaps attacked. Under the cover of nature taking its course, she eased out the powerful little pistol and flicked on the red dot of the laser sight. She did not take the safety off yet. She did not check the number of shells in the magazine. Professional to her fingertips, she knew how many she had loaded and she could tell from the weight that they were still there.

Another scuffling whisper told her the secret watchers were still there too, but she found herself in a quandary. She was ready to finish up here and leave, but could not use the paper, control her clothing and hold the gun at the same time. The instant she put the gun down and reached for the paper, there was an explosion of sound and action seemingly just behind her. She scrabbled up the heavy little weapon and whirled, cleanliness and dignity very much second to survival in her mind. The wall of the soft-sided hut bulged in and then eased out again. There was a crisp impact, which could only have been a blow, followed by the sound of a falling body. 'Sorry, Jolene,' came Richard's grim voice. '"Watching your ass" is the phrase, I believe.'

Jolene gave herself a quick wipe, adjusted her clothing and tore open the door. There was her guardian angel standing with the half-conscious, black-eyed Billy Hoyle.

'I was watching it figuratively. Billy was literally. Sad. I thought better of him. What do you want me to do with him?'

'I don't know.' Jolene was so completely wrong-footed at finding herself the object of prurient rather than psychopathic interest that she was uncharacteristically indecisive. 'Let the sad scumbag go, I guess. He'll have nothing more to look at when I'm aboard *Erebus*.'

'OK,' said Richard equably. He let Hoyle go and the scientist fell to the ground.

'What's going on here?' came Jaeger's bellow almost at once. He and Killigan came round the corner shoulder to shoulder.

'One of your men peeping into the Ladies,' said Richard, gesturing. 'Should have been christened Tom, not Billy.'

'What is that?' shouted Colonel Jaeger suddenly, unaccountably.

'I beg your pardon?' Richard could not immediately see what the colonel was shouting about.

'That.' He pointed at the still stunned Jolene. 'That *gun*.'

Jolene raised her hand, only now registering that she still held her pistol.

'You can't bring armaments onto my camp without my permission,' snarled Jaeger, clearly glad at last to have got one up over the inspector. 'Sergeant Killigan, impound that weapon.'

'Aw, now, Colonel.'

'Direct order, Killigan.'

'Oh, for heaven's sake Colonel. We're taking it straight out to *Erebus*.'

Jaeger paid no attention to Richard. He had seen the shock and simple hurt in the wide, clear-water eyes in front of him. So he pressed his mean advantage with all the power of a schoolyard bully. 'The gun, Killigan,' he snarled. 'Take it or you're straight on a charge.'

'I'm sorry, miss . . .' said the sergeant softly. He clearly meant it. That, if anything, made her back down and hand it over. She squared her chin and stepped forward.

Richard, fuming, fell in beside her and the two of them walked across to the waiting chopper, leaving the three representatives of the NASA base Armstrong silently watching them go.

Chapter Eight

Richard spent much of the rest of Boxing Day in most unseasonal activities. Between eleven and midday he helped unload Hugo Knowles and get him safely below, then he found himself helping Jolene DaCosta settle into a spare cabin. This was not a hard task: *Erebus* was supplying Farraday and Rothera with equipment – not personnel – and her own scientific contingent was as sparse as Armstrong's. Andrew put her on the scientists' near-deserted B deck corridor, in a room between the Mariners and the Rosses. The first thing she asked to do was to take a shower and Richard could not see any reason why she should not. Then, just after noon, he went along to his own cabin and, finding it empty, went off in search of either his errant family or the captain.

Richard intended to offer himself as watchkeeper in Hugo Knowles's place tonight at the very least, and for some of this afternoon if Andrew would have him. He was well qualified, and probably able to fit into the Navy way – for a harbour watch certainly. The alternative was for the exhausted commanding officer to stand the watch himself, as he was currently doing now until 16.00, according to the youthful third lieutenant Richard met as he left the B deck corridor.

As Richard made his way upwards towards the command bridge at about twelve thirty, he heard his name distantly called from below. He peered over the edge of the companionway and saw Robin looking up. He turned and descended to the less-than-contented captain of his heart. 'Where are the twins?' he asked, planting a kiss upon her cheek.

'First lunch. I popped out as soon as I heard Andrew was up on the bridge; figured you'd be free. At last. What are we going to tell them about poor Tony Thompson?'

'I don't know, darling. They're too young for the truth to mean much. And this was supposed to be a happy holiday. I'm so sorry.'

'Don't be silly, it's not your fault. All you've done so far is to try to pull other people's fat out of the fire.'

'Story of my life. Our life . . .'

'You must be pretty tired or you wouldn't be worrying like this.'

71

'Well, I am tired. And I am worried. We're nowhere near the end of this affair. And we'll not get free of it as easily as Irene Ogre in *Kalinin* either.' Walking slowly down to the ship's dining facilities, he explained to Robin what Jolene DaCosta had done. And, indeed, where Jolene DaCosta was.

Colin, a trencherman when he could get away with it, and Kate were there, sharing the table – and many of the sausages, bacon, chicken, chops and chips – with the twins. When he saw – smelt – what they were up to, Richard suddenly realised that he needed sustenance far more than he needed sleep. 'Three of my favourite Cs,' he said. 'Coffee, chops and chips.'

'Daddy, Daddy,' chorused the twins.

'Two of my favourite Ds,' he said, sitting down and reaching for a cup.

A steward appeared at his elbow with a steaming pot. He did not have to overtax his memory with Richard's brunch order. Or with Robin's either.

Much to Robin's grudging admiration, Richard managed to lighten the atmosphere simply with his presence and his expansive mood. He could darken it as quickly, though, if he was preoccupied or angry.

As they ate, they began to play word games – the 'My favourite Cs and Ds' being the signal. After that they played I Spy until William had defeated them all comprehensively, individually and collectively. But then Jolene DaCosta found her way to their table and over ham, eggs and wholewheat toast, she took on the family nonpareil and gave him a close run for his money, earning his admiration and his sister's ready friendship. Which she was happy to return out of regard for their father, if nothing else.

All too soon, however, Jolene looked at her watch. 'I have to talk to the captain,' she announced.

'So do I,' said Richard. 'Look, darling, I plan to offer to take the first officer's watches for him now and this evening. If I'm not back in twenty minutes, I'll be up on the bridge. Bring the twins up and I'll show them around. Make some plans for this afternoon and this evening. Maybe take out the chopper or the Zodiac, look for some local wildlife. What do you say?'

'Sounds OK. If nothing goes wrong.'

'Oh, come on, darling,' said Richard. 'What on earth could possibly go wrong?'

'I love a man who lives dangerously,' said Jolene as they plodded up the companionway towards the command bridge.

'What do you mean?'

'"What on earth could possibly go wrong?" With those two of yours? With the wind coming up and the sky coming down? Today, the way it's gone so far.'

'We'll keep a weather eye out. And we won't do anything too dangerous. You want to come?'

'I thought going to the john would be pretty uneventful. Shows how much I know about the Big White. Still, can't argue with a confident man . . .'

Erebus's bridge was enclosed, weatherproofed and adapted to the rigours of the Southern Ocean. On the port side of the wide central area, level with the island of the chart table, behind the doors back into the radio room and out onto the enclosed bridge wing, there was an easy chair. It was big, scooped, like an old Parker Knoll swivel. On this slumped Andrew, more than half asleep. There was no one else apparent on the bridge. No need for a helmsman; no immediate need for movements officers or weather watchers. The door to the radio room stood ajar and the sound of gentle snoring came from within so Andrew was not entirely bereft.

As *Erebus* swung gently to anchor, the wide clearview gave a breathtaking view of Armstrong, a collection of tiny huts perched precariously on the edge of a white-skulled monster of black rock, beyond a restless agglomeration stirring brash crust. The sweep of the near arm of the bay reached up, disturbingly close, along the starboard. Jolene walked that way, entranced, as though she could walk onto the bridge wing, reach over, and stroke it as if it was the flank of a beached whale. Richard walked the other way and looked along the long curving line of black water cutting through the brash to where the last trace of *Kalinin* was vanishing round the northern headland. He watched until she was only a smudge of exhaust smoke, brown against the grey overcast. He took a deep breath, almost, but not quite, a sigh. Turned. Swung back, frowning. The underside of the clouds had suddenly taken on a strange white tone. White light moved across them in a disturbingly Biblical way, showing their inverted ridges and valleys as though some plague out of the Book of Exodus was on the way. Richard knew what that meant. He turned decisively and crossed to Andrew. He took him by the shoulder and shook him gently until he stirred.

'Oh. Hi, Richard. Must have dozed off. *Not* the Navy way. What's up?'

'I've come to relieve you if you'll allow it, Andrew,' he said gently. 'You're too important to the command to be wasting your energy like this. Especially without a first officer to support you. But first, have a look at this sky, would you?'

Andrew looked blearily at the dramatic sky. Jolene joined them, also struck by the phenomenon.

'It's ice,' began Andrew.

Colin arrived on the bridge. 'Ice sky,' he announced. 'There's something big out there. Ice sheet or berg and the light's reflecting upwards off its surface. It's a warning. Might mean nothing. But on the other hand—'

The radio buzzed urgently and Sparks, the radio officer, jumped awake with a wet sound. '*Erebus*,' he answered, giving the vessel's call sign as the four from the bridge wing gathered round.

'*Kalinin* here,' came Irene's unmistakable voice out of the loudspeaker. 'Is Captain there please?'

Sparks handed Andrew the old-fashioned hand microphone with its long, coiled snake of flex trailing.

'This is Andrew Pitcairn. What can I do for you, *Kalinin*? Over.'

'I give you early ice warning, *Erebus*. Over.'

'Thank you, *Kalinin*, we were just discussing the ice sky. Over.'

'We also. But we see the cause of this as well. Large tabular berg, bearing – do you have a pencil *Erebus*? Over.'

Andrew signalled to Sparks to write down the bearing as Irene gave it.

'Got that, *Kalinin*. Looks as though it's drifting due east into the mouth of the bay here.'

'That is our calculation also. I am sending up Sikorsky to check the size and rate of drift but it looks big from here. First calculations suggest it will close the harbour within thirty-six hours unless it grounds far enough out to leave a channel clear, but I strongly suggest you do not rely on this. It is pushing much brash ice and bergy bits ahead of it. Over.'

'Thank you for your information and your concern *Kalinin*. May we ask where you are heading, please? Over.'

'We go in search of snowy slopes and sheer cliffs, *Erebus*. Extreme conditions for extreme pleasures, yes? Because of the size of the berg to the south, our course will now be to the north. We will not be far away, I think. *Kalinin* out.'

'Thank you, *Kalinin*. Good luck. Stay in contact. *Erebus* out.'

Andrew signed off and then continued talking, handing the mike back and swinging round. 'We really need to know about that ice.'

'I agree,' said Richard. 'But it's not a crisis. Why don't I take the watch here while you get some rest? In the meantime you can order the Westland up to take a look. Fuel OK?'

'Yup. Even with all that flapping around at Armstrong. And we'll get more at Rothera or Faraday. I left dumps there on purpose.'

'OK. We'll send Colin and Kate in the chopper. They're our best ice experts – unless any of your remaining beards is hiding his light under a bushel.'

'No, I don't think so.'

'Right. So we'll have a briefing at sixteen hundred or so and draw our plans from that.'

'What about alerting Cambridge?'

'Apart from routine contacts I wouldn't make an issue out of this until we know exactly what we're dealing with.'

'Yeah. Fair enough.' The lack of military snap, precision and diction testified to Andrew's tiredness and he was happy enough to go off to bed.

Colin vanished with barely suppressed excitement to scare up the chopper and go look at some ice. Jolene followed Andrew to get her head down. Richard prowled around the bridge, familiarising himself with the layout of the controls. He had had as little sleep as any but he felt full of fizz. Being back on a bridge like this simply excited him and even though he was far from being in command here he felt the old power surging through him like pure adrenaline. Let Andrew get a couple of hours now then a decent night's sleep tonight and he'd be back on his feet. In the meantime, thought Richard, he would attend the briefing when Colin got back, think up some little adventure to enjoy with the twins, fit in a couple of hours' shut-eye after dinner, keep the midnight watch – always a quiet one, especially at anchor – and catch up with a lie-in tomorrow morning. That would all fit in perfectly with their probable movements if Irene's observations were right. *Erebus* would have to pull out of here by the second dogwatch tomorrow afternoon or she would be stuck until November 2001 or so.e

The radio cracked and the Westland began to run through basic pre-flight. Colin and Kate hurried down the deck and climbed aboard.

Richard completed his train of thought piously. I hope to God, he thought, that the FBI team get here before we have to pull out. Otherwise we'll just have to throw Jolene back to the wolves when we go.

75

Robin and the twins arrived then and Richard spent much of the rest of the watch showing the lively and intelligent youngsters everything he thought might interest them. They were familiar with the bridges of ships and much of the equipment they contained, but were of that age when familiarity breeds security and so greeted the Kelvin Hughes equipment, the Differential Shipmaster, the echo-sounder, the Doppler collision alarm radar, the weather predictors and all the rest like old friends.

Mary peered into the gyro compass. 'How accurate is this at these latitudes?' she asked, and Richard began to explain while William took the helm and hurled himself from side to side as though trying to rip the thing loose.

'Don't do that, dear,' said Robin mildly. But William was pretending to be a Formula One racing driver and was lost to reason for the moment.

Later, Richard showed them the big British Admiralty Antarctic Ocean charts and explained to them where they were. Mary traced the long coastline of the Antarctic Peninsula, also known as Graham Land. Even at her young age she was familiar with the conventions of sand-coloured land, aquamarine shallows, paler shelves and white depths with patterns of soundings.

'What's this purple?' demanded William who, past the end of his attention span, had pulled out another chart – that of the whole Antarctic.

'The purple is the permanent ice shelf,' said Richard, and turned back to Mary, who was still entranced.

'The islands have such funny names,' she observed dreamily. 'Lavoisier, Renaud, Anvers, Brabant. So romantic.'

'Named for men, ships, explorers, monarchs, benefactors and dreams.'

'Nightmares, more like,' said William. 'There's one here called Desolation Island.'

'And one here called Deception,' said Mary. 'That sounds bad.'

'Actually, that's good, dear.' Robin took up the explanations as Richard was called into the radio room by news from Colin and Kate. 'It's called Deception because from the sea it looks solid. Big black hills like the arms of the bay just beside us here, reaching right up into the sky – not that you can usually see all that much because of the bad weather. Looks like a massive great place. Home to a range of penguins, all sorts of wildlife. A solid island like all the rest. But appearances are deceptive. Deception Island, see? In fact the whole island is the top of a sunken volcano. Its central area, its caldera, is flooded. There's a tiny entrance—'

'Neptune's Bellows,' interposed Richard, popping out of the radio room in a lull between transmissions.

'Yes, Neptune's Bellows. And if you can get in through Neptune's Bellows then you're in Port Foster, the safest anchorage in the Southern Ocean. Great black cliffs all around you, face on to the wind, no matter what quarter it's blowing from. Nice and calm and peaceful.'

'As long as the volcano doesn't get restless,' added Richard dramatically, like a pantomime villain. 'It's still active, you see . . .'

Colin and Kate came back just after Richard came down off duty having made the acquaintance of Andrew's self-effacing second officer. What with the boyish third Richard had met earlier, it was no wonder Andrew felt as though he had to run the whole show on his own. As soon as the Westland hove into view, Richard sent a nice reviving cup of tea to the commander's cabin and retired to the officers' wardroom which doubled as ops centre for briefings. Here he pinned up a range of charts culled off the bridge, ready for Colin's report, occasional scraps of which had come in over the radio.

By the time the Rosses arrived, the room was already quite full. Andrew and his quiet lieutenants were there. The chief engineer had been called to add his thoughts about power and speed to the more general deliberations. The two remaining beards, known to the crew as Pinky and Perky, were present. Robin and the twins were there too and nobody seemed to mind. The twins' wide-eyed thirst for knowledge was endearing them to officers and crew alike. Jolene DaCosta was the last to arrive and after quick introductions and brief explanations, the main business got under way.

'*Kalinin*'s report looks to be pretty accurate,' said Colin. 'There is a big berg drifting this way. Nothing special about it. Plain, tabular. Not even particularly huge, as these things go. Maybe three kilometres wide and two deep. It's pushing an apron of thick brash liberally peppered by some big bergy bits and smaller bergs in front of it. All in all, then, you're looking at an ice front maybe five kilometres wide. When it arrives it's going to close the bay here. Tight.' Colin strode to the map on the wall.

'What's happened is this. The perpetual west-wind drift has slipped a little south this season. Not by much. It happens. The result, for the time being at least, is that this side of the peninsula is a lee shore to the prevailing wind. God alone knows what's going to be blown in.

77

We'll have to watch out – for the time being at least.'

'And give ourselves some sea room,' mused Richard.

'Can you estimate the speed of drift?' asked Andrew. 'How long have we got before the ice closes the bay here?'

Colin shrugged, glanced at Kate.

'Twenty-four hours,' Kate said, decisively.

The seamen glanced at each other speculatively.

'I'll only need a couple of hours' notice,' said the chief. 'I've had to keep everything fired up below to stop it freezing.'

'Twenty-four hours,' said Andrew, eyes narrow.

'That going to fit with you?' Richard asked Jolene.

'Well—' she began.

'It'll have to, I'm afraid,' said Andrew with unaccustomed rudeness. 'I'm not getting trapped in here for God knows how long. Even when the wind shifts back to a full easterly, the berg is likely to stay wedged across the mouth of the bay. With the mountains up above Armstrong as a wind break, it'll stay grounded until it melts.'

'Hey, look,' said Jolene quietly. 'You've been doing us a favour. Armstrong base, NASA, yours truly. If you can hang on until the Feds pitch up, fine. If not, no sweat. Like I keep saying to tell Richard here, I'm a big girl. I punch my weight, believe you me. I can have the likes of Jaeger for breakfast and still have room for coffee and grits. You can drop me back and high-tail it right now if you'd like.'

Andrew looked at Richard, eyebrows raised; perhaps read in that bland expression the faintest shake of the head. 'No,' he said decisively. 'We'll wait. I've got to talk to Cambridge, warn Faraday and Rothera, and make some arrangements about poor Tony Tho—'

'Kate,' cut in Robin, 'did you see any interesting wildlife out there?'

'Well, yes. Just round the corner of the headland there's a wide shelf and a long beach, invisible from this side but actually quite close by. And there's a penguin colony there. I've never seen so many Adeles in all my life.'

'Oh, how exciting,' said Robin, catching Richard's eye. 'We should see that. What do you say, darling?'

'Can we borrow a Zodiac?' Richard asked Andrew. 'If we're staying here for another twenty-four hours we should have time to take a look.'

'Well, yes, of course,' answered Andrew, somewhat taken aback by the sudden request.

'Come on then, darlings,' said Robin. 'Just think. Penguins. Let's get kitted up at once, shall we?'

With overwhelming energy she swept them out of the wardroom. But even so, the last thing Richard heard as he lingered to apologise and explain was Mary's plaintive question, 'Mummy, what's the matter with Tony Thompson?'

The penguin colony was a great success. This was fortunate for the news about Tony Thompson depressed the twins, even when presented with the softest of kid gloves. They took a Zodiac. Colin and Kate came with them and Jolene tagged along. Although Jolene was the only adult there not expert with a Zodiac, Andrew insisted that a couple of his own men go with them. The Zodiac held them easily – it would have held sixteen. They climbed down the companionway over the side of the ship down to a small landing at sea level, and then took an easy step over into the rubber-sided boat. Down here the water, which looked black from above, seemed utterly clear. 'You should be able to see the bottom at any depth,' said Jolene with simple awe. 'It's clear as glass.'

They sat on the sides with their legs in the central well, looking eagerly forwards as the Zodiac skimmed across clear water between the port side of *Erebus* and the point of the bay's black southern arm. It soon became obvious that the cliff of the bay did not quite reach to the point. A ledge curled back on this side to form a secure little bay. Here the Zodiac was tethered after a brief ride and they all scrambled easily ashore and followed the ledge round the point. The ledge looked narrow and tiny compared with the cliffs above it but in fact, even at its beginning within the bay, it was as wide as a roadway and where it went round the headland itself it broadened as the cliff face leaned backwards. Almost as soon as they had walked round the point they found themselves on an expanse of level shore which degenerated into a rubble of shiny black stones on one side and reached steeply up to the heights on the other. And up those slopes, across the ledge – now as wide as a motorway – and down to the jumble of the water's edge stretched the penguin rookery.

The noise was indescribable. Even out here, still some distance from the outskirts of the throng, it was nearly impossible for the humans to communicate over the cacophony of the birds. Richard and Robin stayed within easy reach of the enchanted children. Jolene, Colin and Kate stayed close to them.

The smell came next, borne on the icy edge of the wind. It was like breathing airborne acid. Richard and Robin looked down at their fastidious offspring but, again, they had underestimated how much discomfort the youngsters would suffer in the pursuit of excitement and adventure. They waded into the throng utterly captivated and overcome.

The penguins, to Richard's eye, seemed to be mainly Adeles and chinstraps, though one or two flashes of colour hinted at gentoos as well. It was not, he knew from his preparatory research, unusual to see the three common types sharing a rookery. They were all of a size, about 75 centimetres tall. The difference between the adults and their offspring seemed to be that the downy chicks looked larger than their sleek parents. They all seemed slumped, round-shouldered and fat; the chicks grossly so. As they carefully picked their way among the nesting sites and the guano droppings, they seemed to go if not unnoticed then at least unregarded. But as soon as the eager children got within a couple of metres of the little creatures, they began to shuffle away warily.

A pattern of action, repeated and re-repeated began to emerge out of the apparent chaos. A little penguin would shoot up out of the impossibly clear ocean as though fired from some submarine gun. Over the rocks she would fly, to land and change on the instant from porpoise to pudding all dumpy and fat. She would waddle forward, flapping her wings for balance and waving her beak, calling to her single chick somewhere in the throng. Four or five would descend on her at once, all making urgent, raucous claims. Her own offspring would likely as not be last among them, certain of his mother's love and sustenance. The interlopers would be screamed at, threatened, clubbed mercilessly with her long beak but would push forward indefatigably, begging for food. At last, apparently giving up, the poor mother would turn and shuffle away. By this time only a couple of chicks would be involved, but still her own would be the last and there would be another round of screeching and beak-batting before the last interloper was seen off and the heir apparent finally got to thrust his beak into his mother's crop and drink the soup of warm krill there.

Here and there among the busy throng sat sad and solitary figures, dressed in rags of down. Leaner, lonelier, more sullen and silent than the others, they seemed to be motherless, bereft, forlorn, soon to be victims. William was so overcome by the sight of one such that Kate had to be called in to shout a terse explanation that these were just moulting and would soon be in the water dressed as adults, fit and well.

But the thought of these jolly little creatures as victims made the adults that much more alert to the grim realities of the place. Eyes probed seaward distances, catching the dark swirls of hunting seals. Colin's eyes, sharpest of all, focused further out. His hand touched Kate's shoulder and he gestured. Richard, looking where he pointed, saw a pattern of tall black fins where a pod of killer whales was closing in to capture the hunting seals. And, away beyond them, just heaving brightly over the horizon, came the blue-white wall of the approaching berg. It was time to take the effervescent children back aboard *Erebus*.

Conversation over dinner was predictably dominated by the children. Never had they seen anything like the penguin rookery and their constant repetition of favourite moments, incidents and characters was interspersed with the names of school chums to be regaled with the adventure. It was exactly what Richard and Robin had hoped for when they brought the twins south and so they let them have their heads. Colin and Kate were happy to join in too, supplying details which only twenty-five years at the pinnacle of their glaciological profession could allow them to know. Jolene sat with them to begin with but children were not her bag, so she soon allowed herself to be seduced away into the company of the junior officers, navigating and engineering.

After dinner the twins tucked down and moderated their usual pre-sleep antics because their father also tucked down next door. They were deeply asleep two and a half hours later when he awoke at ten to midnight. He crept out of the top bunk and padded through to the tiny shower room to dress. Then, fondly assured that he had not disturbed Robin, who gave a couple of very convincing snores as he tiptoed out into the corridor, he ran up into the command bridge as though he was off to enjoy a midnight feast.

'All quiet, sir,' said the third officer signing him onto the log. 'Not too light. The sun's behind those mountains there, though well above the horizon. And the cloud is very thick indeed.'

'It averages seven or eight oktas here every month of the year, according to the pilot,' Richard observed companionably. 'But I'll do my own detailed readings of sky and sea. Give me something to pass the time.'

'Right, sir,' said the third officer and disappeared.

Richard walked forward to the familiar bank of instruments below the wide clearview. Putting his huge hands on their chill surface he leaned forward, utterly at peace, absolutely at one with his environment, completely contented with his lot.

Or at least he was until he saw the first great mushroom of fire explode into brightness amid the distant Jamesways of Armstrong base.

Chapter Nine

'I'm coming with you,' called Jolene DaCosta a little wildly, fighting with the zip on a parka two sizes too big for her. 'For God's sake, they're my people.'

Richard, half in the Westland, his great body shaking to the throbbing of its whirling rotor, glanced back along the deck towards the bright command bridge window where Andrew stood tousle-haired, wrapped in his dressing gown. This was not Richard's call, though he would have taken her had he been in charge.

'What does he say?' he yelled to the pilot.

'If there's room then OK,' the pilot bellowed back, relaying Andrew's decision.

Richard looked around the crowded cabin. Six aboard already, with himself destined for the jump seat. There wasn't room really. But what the hell. 'In the jump seat,' he directed her, hauling her up out of the slipstream. As she slid down and strapped in, he swung himself into the central aisle between the others' legs. 'Go!' he bellowed to the pilot, then hung on for dear life.

The Westland hurled up and forwards, tilting its nose to drop immediately over the land-facing bows. The whole of the chopper's broad windscreen filled with fire. Fire seemed to leap up in bright geysers from tents and the spaces between them. There was fire reflecting off low, light clouds; fire glimmering off mirror-smooth obsidian slopes and cliffs; fire glittering wickedly over carapaces of hard ice; fire striking like lightning off restless brash stirred by the wind of the helicopter's passage.

Andrew had sent his chief, his first engineer and his second officer, the three most competent members of his crew. He had sent Colin and the doc. Kate was assistant to one or the other of them – whichever needed her the most. Richard was there to help anyone who needed it. And Jolene was there.

'Keep our priorities clear,' bellowed Richard, tearing his throat as though battling a hurricane. Which in many ways he was, for he had not closed the Westland's door. 'Find Colonel Jaeger. We can't help effectively till we know what's going on and what he's doing. Even you, Doc. Stay with us until we know the priorities of the men on the ground. Understand?'

'Got you,' they chorused dutifully. Even Colin Ross was happy to take Richard's orders at this stage. Colin was, but Jolene DaCosta had priorities of her own.

'You know what this is about, don't you?' she called back, her words coming and going with the vagaries of wind and slipstream. 'This is part two of the Skiddoo episode. This is where the rest of the missing explosives went, what the other timers were for. This is another fucking cover-up.'

'That it may be,' yelled Richard. 'But our first priority is to help, not to detect. Stay with us, please. At least until we get a body count and a butcher's bill.'

She knew he meant lists of dead and wounded, and in the face of that her investigator's job seemed secondary. But there was a fair number of helpers, and only one inspector.

Richard was well aware of this fact, but he put a different interpretation on it. He considered Jolene to be very much more at risk than any of the rest of them. Particularly if the suspicions they shared about this incident were accurate.

The Westland leaped up over the shoreward storehouses, huts and labs. Up again over the big familiar Jamesway and into the central square. The helipad and vehicle dispersal square were both dotted with flames and people fighting them, so the pilot skipped the chopper over sideways onto a quiet piece of darkness. As he did so, Richard had a clear view of the pattern of the disaster so far. One explosion, by the look of things, had started a spreading circle of destruction in the vehicle assembly and dispersal area where blazing petrol and exploding machines had yet to be got under control. Petrol flooding out of the damaged tanks was running under the bellies of the nearest vehicles and setting them off in turn. Unless the cycle was broken, they would be ablaze soon. And the fire would be hot enough to spread to the closely clustered Jamesways.

No sooner did the helicopter's landing gear settle than they were out and running towards the light and the noise. Richard, first in line and possessed of the Westland's own canister of foam, was sharply aware of a duality of focus he could ill afford. At the forefront of his mind was the need to find Gene Jaeger and get stuck into protecting whatever was recoverable here and despatching helicopters with wounded and for more help. At the back of his mind, a tiny, persistent

84

unscratchable itch, was the knowledge that Jolene would be slipping away about her business at the earliest possible moment – always assuming she hadn't gone already. Well, he'd made the global priorities clear to her. If she turned up on the body count or the butcher's bill, that was something they would have to deal with later. And if necessary he would deal with it. Personally.

Richard arrived in the central square in front of the Jamesway where a wildly dressed handful of beards was milling around. Nothing against beards per se. It was just that the competent beards were probably up at the sharp end helping.

'Colonel Jaeger?' bellowed Richard, towering over the confusion. 'Where's the colonel?'

'Over there,' yelled someone obligingly, pointing to the brightest burning, over by the John Deere section.

Richard pressed forward, his mind shifting gear. A glance over his shoulder showed that Colin was solidly behind him like a prop forward running guard for his fly half on a rugby field.

'Colin!'

The steady Scot came closer.

'How d'you fight fires like this with water at such a premium?'

'The camp security people double as firefighters. They will likely have set up a pump to get a good head of sea water up from the shoreline. Otherwise, buckets.'

'But against petrol they'll have to use foam.' Richard was a tanker man, his response was automatic and immediate. 'Water will just spread burning petrol all over the place. They'll have to use foam,' he repeated, holding up the canister from the Westland.

'If they've got any and if they can get it defrosted in time. Still, most of the four-by-fours and all of the John Deeres have foam canisters, and from the feel if things they'll be defrosted soon enough.'

'Other than that, isolation? Pull everything back and hope it burns out before it sets anything else alight.'

'That's about it. At least it looks as if transport rather than shelter has been hit.'

'So far.'

They burst through into the vehicle dispersal area and there was Colonel Jaeger at the head of a motley crew of firefighters, parka gaping, shirt open. It was hot enough for June. A swift glance around showed that Billy Hoyle was there, pulling himself up in Richard's estimation by wielding a canister from one of the John Deeres. Sergeant

Killigan had swapped his role as security guard for that of fire chief. As the foam choked off the pools of blazing petrol, carefully targeted jets of brine fell hissing onto the red-hot skeletons of the burned-out vehicles, quenching tyres, seats, interiors. But half a dozen vehicles were still wildly burning, and as the group from *Erebus* arrived, another went up as though it had just been hit by a mortar round.

'Get in the John Deeres and the four-by-fours,' Jaeger was bellowing. 'Move them out of harm's way. Killigan, we need more foam. Come on, the rest of you, move these vehicles.'

But even the most intrepid of his little command were hesitating to do anything so obviously suicidal. Colin and Richard both knew that it could be done in relative safety, with a little intrepidity and self-control. 'Leave that to us,' they bellowed as one and the team broke up. Kate and the doc went off to look for wounded; the drivers followed Richard and Colin.

'Is this wise?' gasped Colin.

'It's a distraction,' answered Richard with more certainty than he felt. 'One charge, exploded now. Maximum disruption. It's working so far.'

'Distraction from what?'

Richard opened his mouth to answer when behind them the first of the tractors went up amidst a babel of shouting and screams.

Jolene DaCosta walked quietly but purposefully through the huts at the far side of camp. Her fists were thrust deep in her parka pockets, gathering the loose bulk of the garment round her slight frame. None of the fire's heat penetrated this far, but shafts of yellow brightness cut through the midnight glimmer and she wished the warm garment was not so brightly coloured. She also wished she still had her gun. She had no doubt that she was putting herself into very great danger here but her first priority had to be to her investigation. That meant that while everyone else was trying to protect the living, she had to look out for the dead. She knew the Englishman held at least part of a clue wedged in his shattered skull. The FBI would have to help her with that and so she had to be sure he was there for them to examine when they arrived, if she could. She was certain that Major Schwartz, too, held some further hints about the facts in his own death, the identity of those responsible for it, and their motives. Her duty here was clear. She just wished it was not also so blindingly obvious.

Jolene opened the door of the hut and froze. Subconsciously she had adjusted to twenty-four hours a day daylight very well. It came as a genuine shock to find the interior of the hut absolutely dark. Unlike the well-fitted labs and the social Jamesway, there was no need for windows in mere storage huts. The light of the midnight sun was cloud-obscured, far too dull to penetrate. The doorway was well shadowed from the blaze in the parking area. Wishing now she had a torch as well as a gun, she stepped in.

Automatically, she felt around on the inner doorframe for a light switch, and found one. A cord dangled. She closed the door carefully, making sure it was tight. Then she pulled the dangling cord and the hut was filled with dull white light from a low-wattage bulb in the roof. A sudden wind thumped against the outside of the hut, making the canvas walls flap thunderously. She jumped, but even this strong hint from Mother Nature failed to alert her to how flimsy the glorified tent really was. Enough light escaped through the weatherproofed walls to make the whole thing glow like a danger signal to anybody watching in the murky daylight outside.

Jolene had not yet had the opportunity to examine the late Major Schwartz and it seemed to her a good opportunity to combine the duties of guard and inspector. She had gained her first degree, in criminology, at the University of Texas, but her doctorate in forensic science had been earned on the West Coast. She could perform a pretty fair autopsy on Major Schwartz herself, if the need arose. Certainly his stiff, icy corpse held no terrors for her. She unzipped the plastic bag it was in and went deftly but carefully to work.

Which is what she was still doing a minute or two later when the light went out.

On the instant the darkness came, Jolene dropped to the floor so that the first bullet went over her head, through the space she had occupied an instant ago. She knew the quiet spit of the gun as well as she knew her own heartbeat and rolled onto her back looking for the red dot of the laser sight. She lay still, face up like a corpse herself, mouth wide and nostrils flared, swallowing air without the slightest susurration of breath. So quiet that the only giveaway was the echoing beat of her heart. She counted seven – a lucky number with her. Nothing. Not even the red glimmer of the Glock's sight. Tension screwed at her like an emotional rack. 'He's waiting for me to move: do not move,' she thought. 'He knows exactly where I am. If I don't move he will creep up and kill me anyway.' She moved her head infinitesimally. She heard the slither of the hood beneath her cranium and stopped, eyes as wide as her gasping mouth, striving to soak up enough dull light to discriminate shadows and silhouettes. Instead she saw the faintest of red lines cut through the rising column of her frosted breath.

Panic. Did he see it? God, what a giveaway. How could he miss it?

Faintest of footfalls. Whisper of nylon. He was on the move. Was there a rhythm? Could she move at the same time using his movement to cover her own?

Whisper of nylon against nylon. She rolled. *Bang!* The shot smashed into one of the bodies above her.

'That was a little big edgy,' some calculating part of her psyche said coldly, 'shooting a dead man.'

Whisper of nylon on wood . . . She rolled again, tensing herself for the shot. There was none. She lay face down now under Major Schwartz's table. Arms folded and tensed, ready to push as she leaped upward. Had he come against her at that moment, she might have done just that, hurling her stiff, frozen evidence into her would-be murderer's face, no matter what the cost. But he did not come. And her reason whispered, 'You cannot harm the evidence. You are the inspector . . .'

And so, even without another whisper, she rolled sideways away from temptation. She saw the floor where her face had been the instant before she rolled; rough wooden boards illuminated by a bright red spot. She understood that but for her movement that deadly mark would have rested unsuspected on the back of her head. She kept moving by a sheer exercise of will, tearing her muscles through the incapacitating shivers of revulsion. The red-marked floor exploded upwards and she closed her eyes, rolling again, calculating with the most intimate of knowledge how swiftly the next round would pump up into the chamber. Rolled again, remembering with photographic precision that the table behind Schwartz was piled with boxes two metres high and more. Hurled herself erect, the shoulder of her parka whispering past the table edge.

A black wall of boxes stood between her and her would-be killer. Let him not think to shoot under the tables, she thought. Her legs flinched, slowing her as she danced away. A tunnel between the piled boxes gleamed red. The laser sight shone on the inner surfaces. Something spat through, making the table lurch; spat through to whine past her ear and thump out through the wall behind. Three shots gone, she counted. She had to calculate on a full load. She was still in terrible trouble, from an attacker she had neither seen nor heard. And her own gun! She had time to curse that pompous, inefficient bastard Colonel Jaeger. Then she gave the loudest and most blood-curdling scream she could manage and threw herself sideways. She landed on her right shoulder, rolled, and powered up onto her feet again. The layout of the hut was like a map in the laptop of her visual memory. She was exactly at the junction of the space between the tables. If she stopped going sideways now and started rolling forwards she had a good chance of reaching the door.

With no further hesitation she threw herself forward. Precisely into the cold grip of Tony Thompson. Together, like Romeo and Juliet awakening, in a kind of sickening slow motion, slightly louder than the arrival of an Amtrak locomotive, they rolled onto the floor. Still Jolene did not stop fighting. She took the corpse by his shoulders and lifted. Her feet skidded on floorboards slickened by some nameless dead-person slime. She pushed him away. A red brightness defined his shoulder. His right; her left. He slammed ardently down on top of her, dead flesh as bullet-proof as Teflon-coated Kevlar. 'Fuck you!' she screamed. He knew where she was. There was nothing to lose by making a noise until he lost sight of her again. 'I know who you are,' she shrieked, hoping for nothing more than to give him pause. 'I'll see you fry, you bastard . . .'

And the distant door opened.

'That's not very ladylike,' said Richard Mariner, peering into the darkness.

'*Gun*!' she bellowed, tearing her throat.

Tony Thompson's heavy corpse slammed to her left, the weight of the next bullet pressing it down again. She threw it left and rolled to the right. Her hair caught in the splintered floorboards and she all but scalped herself coming up but still she did not hesitate. 'Get help,' she bellowed at the gaping door.

Outside, there was a flash of movement. Richard's shoulder, she guessed. Inside, there was a blur diving sideways across the dull square of doorway. She saw nothing more than a figure in cold-weather gear, apparently flying. Her foot hit more of the slippery liquid from whichever of the corpses and she went down hard. By the time she picked herself up, everything was quiet and Richard was running back in through the gaping portal.

'Did you see anything?' she asked, her voice ragged.

'Nothing. No one.'

'He went this way.' She led Richard to the last place she had seen the figure. In the canvas wall of the storeroom there was a long, clean cut.

'So,' said Richard thoughtfully, 'he had a knife as well as a gun.'

89

'Yes,' said Jolene. 'But what else did he have?'

'What do you mean?'

'I mean did he have a bomb?'

He hesitated. 'That's why he was here I'd say. What do you want to save from in here?'

'Can't we—'

'Search for it, find it, disarm it in time? I think not. We're already living dangerously.'

'Then it's the bodies. Schwartz first, with everything of his we can carry.'

They worked in a frenzy. Everything around the spaced-suited corpse was piled willy-nilly on his firm flat belly. Then they simply caught up the square corners of the table he was resting on and ran him out through the door. Richard was first, running backwards, slipping and almost falling down the steps onto the icy ground. 'Keep going,' he yelled at her.

Two huts away, on the edge of the flame-bright central area, they left him and turned to go back for Tony Thompson.

'What are you doing?' came Colin's distant bellow. 'Can we help? We're all done here.'

'Stay back,' bellowed Richard in the loudest voice Jolene had ever heard. Then he was gone past her, heading back in for Tony Thompson. Still game, though deeply convinced now that she must be mad, she turned to follow her intrepid helper.

Then suddenly his great black form was silhouetted against white. She saw him spread against the ballooning detonation like a chiaroscuro in an animation. The exploding atoms of force tore past him and then she was flying and possessed the deep knowledge that she had seen him take wing as well.

Richard flew backwards into the wall of the next Jamesway whereas Jolene, further back behind him, missed it and flew out into the parade ground, sliding almost to Colonel Jaeger's feet before she stopped. The soft wall of the rigid-frame tent broke Richard's fall, and he was not too much the worse for wear. Unlike the Jamesway. The weight of his body wrecked the wall on which he landed, and the searing heat set the frame and wooden floor alight. He rolled sideways over the fire-retardant material of his safety net and contrived to be well away before the whole lot went up in flames. Still running – and a good deal more shocked than he realised – he hurled into Colin Ross who was returning with the other firefighters from their successful efforts in the vehicle dispersal area. 'Here we go again, Colin,' he said, very loudly, half deafened by the explosion.

Colin could see that. So could the others, particularly as the wounded, with two doctors and Kate Ross, were pouring out of the burning building that had broken Richard's fall: the base's medical facility. Running forward, well practised now, the firefighters set up their teams again. This time they did not need to worry so much about foam. The fire-retardant walls of the huts contained the flames until they reached ignition point. Then the huts exploded, spreading flame like a virulent contagion. The fire teams soaked the walls with sea water as best they could, but after the medical facility, two of the laboratory huts went up too, the chemicals within them making the explosions larger and more deadly. It was these explosions, the last before the flames began to come under some kind of control, that claimed Killigan and his right-hand man Corporal Washington. Singed, seared, almost as badly wounded as Hugo Knowles, they were dragged aside and replaced, until the sullen flames began to die back at last.

After that it was just a case of quenching wooden floors, contents and packing cases. Half an hour's work which, unfortunately, robbed Armstrong of almost all its medical supplies.

'Where is he?' asked Jolene the moment she came round.

'Richard?' said Kate Ross, dabbing her last anaesthetic disinfectant wipe on a combination of blast sear and gravel graze on Jolene's forehead. 'He's back fighting the fire.'

'Not Richard. Major Schwartz.'

'Over there, taking his ease where you left him. I warn you, though, that since the infirmary went up he's beginning to drip a little.'

'I've got to get him somewhere secure.'

'That's up to you, dear. But dead people are low on my list. I've got wounded and dying to take care of. And not much left to do it with.'

This statement was a little over-dramatic in fact. Kate had no one that near death's door, but she did have several who were pretty badly burned and blast-damaged, Killigan and Washington among them. A couple of scientists, Fagan and Mendel, were a cause for concern; Mendel particularly, the last to leave an exploding hut, had been badly seared by the blast.

As the last fires came back under control and the exhausted men and women of Armstrong base began to look around themselves it became time to take stock. The gathering light of a new day at the beginning of the last working week of the millennium revealed that they had lost one store hut, two labs and the medical facility, as well as half their transport pool. On the plus side, they had shelter and supplies to continue their work. They even had enough medical equipment to tend all but the worst cases, for the labs all had well-equipped first aid boxes, just as the vehicles had all had foam-filled firefighting canisters.

Looking around his battered command like Colonel Travis at the Alamo, Jaeger said hoarsely, 'We are due for relief at the end of the next month. We can certainly expect a full re-fit before we close down for the winter in March. We still have a lot of work to do and everything we need in order to get on with it.' He took a deep breath. 'I don't want to hold any of you here against your will, particularly in the face of the FBI's imminent arrival. But anyone who wants to stand with me and get on with the work we were sent here to do is welcome.'

'Not me,' came Jolene's clear voice. Heads swivelled to look at her standing thin and straight beside the silvered corpse of Bernie Schwartz. 'I'm asking Andrew Pitcairn to take me and my evidence out of here until I can guarantee security. I'm not sure what is going on here but I am certain that almost all the violence over the last few days has been aimed at a dead man – this dead man. And everyone else who has been hurt or killed has simply gotten in the way. We're outta here, so maybe you folks can sleep a little easier. If the Feds don't like it, you just tell them to come talk it over with me.'

'Nice speech,' said Richard sotto voce beside her. 'Think Andrew'll take you and your Trojan horse?'

'He will if you ask him,' she said.

'Dr DaCosta's right,' said Kate Ross suddenly. 'I vote she goes and we take half a dozen of the most severely hurt with us, if you agree, Colonel Jaeger. Sergeant Killigan and Corporal Washington both sustained bad burns when the second lab went up. Billy Hoyle's got pretty severe blast damage and a scalp wound from flying debris, though no one's quite sure how or when that happened. Two of your scientists . . .'

Colonel Jaeger agreed with Kate's proposal. He talked to Andrew Pitcairn and the deal was done. The Westland lifted them all back aboard *Erebus*, including Major Schwartz, zipped securely in his strong plastic body bag, and swiftly-gathered possessions and dunnage for each of them that needed it.

By the turn of the midday watch everything was settled, signed and sealed. Then, with Andrew on the bridge still, his parka over his green plaid dressing gown, *Erebus* cast off and pushed her way slowly through the thin ice along *Kalinin*'s track, out of the bay, past the thickening skirts of the incoming iceberg and away into the Bismarck Strait.

Chapter Ten

As *Erebus* pulled out between the tall jaws of the bay, Richard was standing below the after end of the rear-mounted helipad, leaning back against the stern rail, his shoulder against the little flag staff there, the ensign snapping in the air above him, the lanyard rapping and tapping in the wind. All around him the wind sighed, whispered and chuckled in the lines securing the Westland into place.

The twins had been with him until the penguin rookery passed out of sight, then they drifted away. But as he watched the slim ship's wake he rather wished he had been able to hold their interest for a little longer. As *Erebus* swung onto a northerly heading, scant metres away to port, the brash ice began to pile into something like the permanent pack, and what appeared to be only a couple of hillocky kilometres beyond that stood a cliff of blue ice stretching from edge to edge of the southern horizon. It was illusion, he knew; a trick of light, scale and thick cold air, but the effect was magnificent. The monstrous berg did not come unattended. Beneath the piled brash seals were hunting the fish which fed on the krill in the cold currents created by the berg and the plankton growing on and around its submarine surfaces. Above, a range of penguins came and went with much the same feeding habits as the seals; they had young to feed and raise before winter closed her icy grip again in March. Briefly he remembered the pod of killer whales Colin had pointed out from the penguin rookery. They would be down there too; toothed whales, baleen whales, predators of all sorts. Sharks too, in all probability, from the harmless to the fearsome.

Richard stretched, unconsciously making a throwing motion with his arm. A skua screamed in low over his head, hitting the water where any titbit would have landed. Richard smiled and shook his head. Even these wild and fearsome hunters of the air had learned to feed from the hand of man.

Even down here.

He turned, and there was Colin halfway down the outer aft companionway, waving a white flimsy like a flag. He'd better be careful a skua doesn't have that off him, thought Richard, raising a hand in acknowledgement and starting back.

In fact Colin was holding not one flimsy but two: a print-out and a fax. Both showed more or less the same thing. Colin began to explain it to Richard as they went up the companionway but it was not until they were back on the command bridge with the white papers spread beside the big chart that the whole picture became clear. Now that she was under way and out of the harbour, *Erebus*'s weather-watch equipment was up and running again, and, just as she received her first ice map from a low-orbiting weather satellite above them, so *Kalinin* faxed over a copy of the one she had just received. Put against the long sand-coloured tongue of Graham Land, the two maps made the situation unequivocal. Under the influence of the westerly drift, the Bismarck Strait, Grandidier Channel and Crystal Sound below it were all silting up with ice. This was particularly significant because, although Faraday had been *Erebus*'s next scheduled port of call, Rothera, on Adelaide Island to the south, was closer, an important consideration with wounded aboard.

'But now,' said Richard, tracing the course on the chart with a broad finger while Colin and Andrew watched, 'to reach Rothera we would have to go right out round the Biscoe Islands, nearly doubling the length of the journey. Faraday is now the closest BAS station.'

Andrew leaned forward, pointing to the chart and dropping his voice to a slightly more conspiratorial level. 'Frankly, that fits well with my overall game plan. The American base at Palmer, here on the edge of Arthur Harbour on the coast of Anvers Island, is well manned and right on the way there. I have every intention of stopping off at Palmer to drop off our unwelcome guests, living or dead, before running on over to Faraday for the New Year. What do you say?'

'Sounds like the best idea to me,' agreed Colin. 'And in the meantime every country with any pretensions to international standing has some kind of summer base up and running between us and them. From the USA to Uruguay. From Chile to China. Any more problems, we pop into the nearest. Simple.'

Richard nodded once. Somehow he could not bring himself to believe it was going to be that simple.

Robin's first aid qualifications were almost as advanced as Richard's and every bit as up to date. Her gender and demeanour, moreover, made her as welcome a nurse as Kate. Andrew Pitcairn had been persuaded to release another crewman to replace Tony Thompson as

96

child minder to the twins because Kate had asked Robin specially to help in the ship's infirmary to settle the American wounded in and to protect them from the shock of meeting the doc. Surgeon Commander Cedric Chapple was generally known among the crew as Dr Crippen. He was a short-tempered, cantankerous, dyspeptic man, thin of stature, bald and deeply lined. A fastidious, punctilious man, he behaved as though the worst, most arrogant excesses of hospital consultants were normal medical practice. His one saving grace – and he was a man who needed a saving grace – was that he was excellent at his job.

'Well,' he said, after his first round of the after-luncheon session. 'I have a good number of genuine cases and a couple of malingerers. If they were British sailors I'd soon have them up and about their duty, I can tell you. But they do things differently in the colonies I dare say. Breed less hardy stock.'

'Should we direct the medical orderlies to any particular cases?' asked Kate.

Chapple used Kate as a kind of matron or staff nurse. This added to his feeling of self-importance and kept the common jack tars out from under his feet. His pallid blue eyes rested on her.

'Keep a close eye on Sergeant Killigan. The scalp wound is worrying. Please keep checking for concussion as the patent begins to stir. Keep an eye on Washington, and on Mendel, the more serious of the blast victims. It will be a while before anyone can call him "a beard", what with all his hair singed off, eh? Eh?'

'Yes, sir,' said Kate tranquilly. 'Anyone else?'

'Experience suggests that the next most troublesome after the severely unwell will be the malingerers. Hoyle in particular will bear close watching. Nowhere near as ill as he pretends to be and he'll be up to all sorts of games the minute your backs are turned. If you were my nurses,' he concluded, 'I'd advise you to wear spare knickers and keep your pretty bottoms well padded around Mr Hoyle, eh? Eh?'

'All of your nurses,' spat Robin, 'are men.'

'His nurses are only men at the moment,' Kate soothed her steaming friend when the doc had gone, 'because all the Wrens on the crew list have gone home for the New Year. Not many women mad enough to be down here at this particular time.'

'Well, you can see why. God! Why did I allow that bloody man to talk me into this?'

'Same reason as I let my bloody man talk me into it. And in any case, it was neither of our bloody men who did this. I did it to you, and I really thought you'd love it. I still think you'll love it, when we

97

get out from under all this doom and gloom. You enjoyed the visit to the penguin rookery yesterday, didn't you?'

'Yes. So did the twins. Even this lunchtime it was all they could talk about.'

'There you are then. We'll get sorted out here and see if we can arrange more adventures like that one.'

'OK. One more round, then one of us goes up on the bridge to see what's really going on. Deal?'

'Deal.'

Some of the below-deck crew, the hard men, thought sickbay watch was an easy option, for lazy oiks and nancy girls. Not so Ernie Marshall. Ernie was content to put in his sickbay time and put up with that prat Doc Crippen because it gave him the two things a man in his line needed most of all – freedom and privacy. It also gave him a place to store his stash, which no one ever checked, though a man of his experience and talents would have been able to find a secure corner anywhere. The innocent might assume that his position would also give him access to various substances for which there would be a ready market among his weaker shipmates but, like his namesake, the doc was careful about his poisons and kept a very accurate drug log, updated on a carefully irregular basis usually every week. Still and all, where there was a market, Ernie could usually arrange a supply.

Ernie was physically fit but by no means large. He was fast and tough. He could hold his own against bigger men but rarely had to. He preferred to out-think his opponents rather than out-fight them. To go with his scheming mind and devious character, Nature had given him an open, boyish countenance and wide blue eyes which Ernie schooled himself always to reflect a direct honesty. He was popular with the officers, with the doc who trusted him more than most, and with the two women who were helping in the infirmary.

At the end of their shift, Robin and Kate handed over to Ernie for the first dogwatch and went off about their business while he got ready to do a little of his own. He watched them walking down the corridor side by side. They were in Shetland pullovers and jeans – hardly designed to arouse much libido under normal circumstances. But aboard *Erebus*, with all the Wrens flown, Whistler's mother would have made it as a pin-up – had Ernie not been there with a range of alternatives, of course.

Ernie's innocent blue gaze focused on the seats of the women's jeans, lazily comparing the way they were filled. Not bad for old

98

broads, he decided. He let his mind dip beneath the blue cotton, and he could do so with more authority than most, considering the little stock of underwear he had in his stash, not to mention the range of videos, books and magazines he had also accumulated. No fetish unfettered, no taste uncatered. With his personal slogan in mind, he decided to do a quick tour of the sickbay then down to check his stuff.

Everyone seemed well-sedated and fast asleep. He went back through the ward like a ghost and returned to the quiet little anteroom where the doc usually did his briefings. Here he kept his stash behind a grille in a big duct. Within moments the old kitbag was out on the table and Ernie was sorting through the contents with one eye on the long corridor along which anyone would have to approach the room, giving him plenty of time to get everything hidden again. Anyone, that was, coming down from the bridge. Someone coming up from the ward would be able to surprise Ernie very much more effectively, which was why he had checked so carefully earlier. Carefully, but not carefully enough.

Ernie was just sorting through some magazines he had managed to acquire during a visit to the Scandinavian camps in Queen Maud's Land last summer when a shadow fell across his garish wares. 'Hey,' drawled a quiet voice. 'Now this stuff makes *Playboy* look like the *Church Times*. You must be a guy it's good to know.'

Ernie looked up into eyes every bit as cheerful and open as his own. 'Hi,' said the stranger, sticking his hand out socially. 'My name's Billy Hoyle. It's a pure pleasure to meet you.'

No sooner had Robin relieved a lucky crewman of twin-watch and fed them their smoko than Richard appeared. 'Come on out again,' he said, full of bounce and enthusiasm. 'There's a really clear view of the berg just behind us, all sorts of wildlife stirring. Bring the camera.' And, as if to emphasise his words, a split in the clouds let the sun through. Robin allowed herself to be swept up by Richard's enthusiasm and within ten minutes or so they were all bundled up, ready to face the deck again.

Richard led them up the companionway that Colin had descended with the flimsies earlier. This steep set of stairs led upwards to the highest open deck of all, at the foot of the communications mast, right above the command bridge. Here they were able to look back past the funnel, over the top of the Westland and away into the heart of the sun-struck berg. It towered even more majestically from this angle, and the sunlight sparked a range of fires from it, all of which were blue. They were close enough to see slopes behind the great vertical cliffs, like thick, twisted, bubble-filled glass in ancient blue bottles. For every snowy surface there was a crystal depth. For every craggy headland – undercut for the most part and fiercely beaded with icicles the size of stalactites – there was a glittering grotto fathomlessly deep where shades of sapphire darkened into inky richness and mysterious darkness. But no sooner had the unutterable beauty of this scene imprinted itself on their minds than a sound like the rolling salvo of heavy guns opened up. Both children had been to the Imperial War Museum and knew well enough the sound of the great barrages of the First World War. Now they looked across the berg as though expecting it to transform itself into the Somme. As they did so, a line of smoke rose up along the highest ridge of the cliff, exactly as though the barrage had found its target.

'Daddy!' screamed the twins. Robin stepped forward and took Richard's arm. The whole cliff nearest to them began to fall. It was an indication of the real distance they were from the berg that it all seemed to happen so slowly. Boulders of ice – as large as houses, many of them – sprang free and began to fly in individual parabolas. Then the slopes behind and below them began to slide, gathering momentum, throwing up clouds of blue ice-smoke as they did so. And the first great blocks, destined to become bergs and bergy bits, became subsumed in the whole massive slide to destruction. Green spray, wet and heavy, exploded out of the ocean and rained down where the ice-smoke was snatched away by the wind. And it seemed that the ice-smoke and the thunderous sound of the main avalanche reached them simultaneously, for as they strove to catch their breath in the face of air which reverberated like a drum roll in their chests, so the burning prickle of ice crystals, like sand grains made of fire, fell onto their faces. As they looked on, too shocked and entranced to move, the brash ice apron all around the berg heaved up into great solid waves.

Like everything else about the spectacular scene, the waves moved in loud slow motion, the liquid heave of the water overmastered by the inertia of the sluggish cowl of ice. Like waves of oil or gelatine, without spray or foam, the great rollers came. The ice did not even seem to split, apparently heaving like thick, slow cream to the dictates of the fearsome forces beneath it. Only as the little family, still rooted, saw the waves begin to near did the creamy surface seem to fracture into lines like a shattered windscreen. Lines of black at first, then green-hued valleys, then green-floored, blue-throated abysses.

'You'll be surprised,' bellowed Richard reassuringly, 'how small and sedate the swells will be when they reach us.'

Out of nowhere, as though summoned by his reassuring words, a great flock of arctic terns screamed by, seemingly just above their heads. This was very nearly too much for the children and William cried out, ducking down under his father's protective arm. As the birds whirled past, the first wave emerged from beneath the ice, in truth a good mile and more astern. It was not all that big, as Richard had said, so much of the energy which gave birth to it soaked up by the force required to move the ice at all. And, from its leading surface, a gentle slope of bottle-green, there soared half a dozen dolphins. The dolphins, coloured precisely and distinctly black and white, leaped out of the rushing heave, flew ahead of it like birds and slipped back into the water without a ripple or a splash, heading directly for *Erebus*'s fleeing stern.

The best view now would be from the helipad and it was all Richard could do to stop William and Mary pulling him headlong down the steep companionway. They arrived at the stern-most section of the ship a little before the first wave did, and so they were able to see, from a much lower and more intimate perspective, the arrival of the hissing green wall. From down here it looked higher, faster and more threatening. The twins' trepidity would have returned, but the dolphins exploded outward again, gambolling so playfully that first Mary, the naturalist, entranced, and then William forgot to be frightened by the prospect of the wave's arrival.

Richard looked up toward the bridge wing, hoping that whoever was on duty up there was well awake. *Erebus* might sit better during the next few minutes if she was moving a little more determinedly north.

A flash of movement. Half a dozen heartbeats later the revs – which they could not hear but which both Richard and Robin could feel quite – rose appreciably. Deep in the heaving green below their feet, the long shaft spun *Erebus*'s single, three-finned, variable-pitch propeller up towards her maximum revolutions. The ship gathered way, seeming to surf forward on the crest of the first wave, joyfully joined at this interface of the liquid and the gaseous elements by the frolicking, flying dolphins.

But even as *Erebus* gave that first surge forward, as though taking flight with the sleek mammals dancing in her wake, a great shuddering *bang* echoed through the whole ship. It was as though she had run aground but there was no catastrophic lurch in her forward progress. Instead a deep thrumming seemed to come from underneath them and the sleek ship lost way, sliding off line so that the next wave took her on the port quarter, making her roll as well as pitch. The engines stopped.

'The propeller,' bellowed Richard. 'She's struck something.'

Side by side, each with a twin in one hand, Richard and Robin leaned out over the aft rail behind the helideck. And there, bobbing up into the sluggish wake, came the culprit. A piece of ice the size of a big John Deere. Deep blue. Yielding nothing to the green of the ocean or the suddenly returning overcast of the steel-grey evening. Iceberg heart-ice, ten thousand years old at least. Older than mankind, maybe, oozing down off Antarctica over centuries without number, compacted, hardened, everything of liquid squeezed out of it with the lighter shades of the spectrum until only the steely blue registered. Half as old as coal and every bit as hard as iron, it had smashed into the whirring blade just at the most critical moment; and God alone knew how much damage it had done.

Chapter Eleven

It was the chief engineer's quick thinking that saved the shaft. Now it was the chief's right-hand man who was going to be lowered over the stern to check on the extent of the damage. First he had to be made proof against hostile Antarctic environment, the pressure ten metres and more down and the possibility of attack. As Richard helped get the diving suit ready for the young engineer and his colleagues secured a winch in place to lower and raise him, Richard was suddenly and forcibly struck by just how light and apparently fragile Major Schwartz's suit had been. He was as knowledgeable as most people about space hardware and he knew about the great, multi-layered, pressurised, space-strengthened monstrosities most astronauts wore. The major's suit, which had been designed to withstand the hostile environment of Mars, must have been a thoroughly extraordinary piece of kit, he thought to himself. He wondered how much Jolene actually knew about it, and just how important that knowledge might be. Certainly, when the engineer was ready, it was easy to see why the winch was necessary, with the heating lines, the power lines, the life-signs monitor line, the two-way radio line, the videocam monitor line and, of course, the air line. And this man was going ten metres out of his element at most, thought Richard. Ten metres, for half an hour or so.

By the time the young engineer was winched back aboard, most of those who had remained on the deck were well aware of the gloomy predictions and the tutting and headshaking with which the chief had greeted the video pictures of the damage. While the pair of them went off with the video and the engineer's observations, Richard and the rest cleared up and stowed away. During the hour or so that they had been drifting since the accident, the great berg, given new impetus by the act of calving, had swung onto an even tighter course for the bay where Armstrong was, and had picked up speed so that retreat was forbidden them now. They could not get back into the bay even if they wanted to. With everything packed away, Richard stood looking back across the sudden mountain range which had risen with volcanic swiftness between the ship and the shore. They could walk back to

Armstrong, if they wanted to, he thought.

The accident to *Erebus* was not an uncommon one. It had happened to one of Robin's ships in the North Atlantic. Typically ingenious, she had contrived to pull the stern of her command high enough out of the water to put a new propeller in place. Not a luxury likely to be afforded Andrew Pitcairn, thought Richard. Then, more prosaically, his stomach growled. He looked at the quartz face of his old steel Rolex, amused as always that the quartz was over the display, not in the movement. Coming up for seven. Dinner time.

Immediately after dinner, while all the senior people were still in the dining salon, Andrew and the chief came in.

'It's not quite as bad as we thought at first,' said Andrew. 'As I believe you all know, the chief's quick thinking saved the shaft from any damage. The only immediate problem is the propeller itself. Chief?'

The chief was a plain, blunt Newcastle Tynesider. He took no bull and gave no quarter. 'Aye. Well, shaft and engines are fine. The propeller's another matter. The propeller's got three variable-pitch blades. One of these is severely twisted and locked. It is absolutely firm, however, and poses no danger to the hull or the other blades. It's twisted out of its normal line and cannot by my estimation be returned to it. Even if we cut it off – if we could, out here – we could not re-attach it firmly enough in a more acceptable position. We do not have spare parts to allow any alternative make-do and mend. However, if we set the other two blades very carefully and make no attempt to sail at any great speed, then we should at least be able to proceed under our own power.'

'That speed should be about five knots or so,' supplied Andrew. 'We should be able to make the American base on Anvers within forty-eight hours and, with luck, they may help us without too excessive a salvage fee. Alternatively, we could make for Faraday and have some spares flown out.'

'Aye,' said the chief. 'In a safe anchorage, with the correct parts and a little leisure, I believe we could get her A1 again.'

'So there you have it,' said Andrew. 'We'll come up to speed at the chief's convenience, enjoy tomorrow night at sea – that's Tuesday. Then with any luck by Wednesday the twenty-ninth we'll be at Palmer base dropping off our American friends. Then over to Faraday by Friday evening at the latest for the celebrations.'

Jolene listened to the captain's words, but only the early part of his address really interested her. Of all the Americans aboard she was the only one well enough to be in the dining salon. She knew nothing about the American base at Palmer on Anvers Island but she was quite heartened to be going there. At the very least, by the sound of it, a couple of Federal Special Agents would be only a couple of hours' flight time away, courtesy of the Ice Pirates. But that knowledge abruptly focused her mind. There was still a lot of investigating to be done. And now was a good time to do a little more.

She went downstairs to talk to Sergeant Killigan if he was awake, or Billy Hoyle if he was not. But when she got to the sickbay, she found Killigan and Washington were still sedated and Billy Hoyle was nowhere to be seen. Thinking nothing much of it, she went to the little anteroom where the sailor on nursing duty was sitting reading a book. 'Excuse me.'

'Yes, miss?' he supplied, looking up.

'You seem to be missing one patient here.'

'Oh no, miss. He went off with my oppo, my opposite number, Ernie Marshall, at the end of the first dogwatch when I came on. Just for a look around, like, all legal and above board. Though don't tell the doc or Mrs Ross or Mrs Mariner, if you wouldn't mind, miss. We have a saying in Britain, "Least said, soonest mended", if you follow my drift, miss.'

'I do. May I sit with Sergeant Killigan, please?'

'Of course, miss, and I'd be pleased if you would. He's been restless and I expect he'll wake up soon. Nice to see a friendly face, I dare say.'

So Jolene went to sit by Pat Killigan and soon, as the orderly had predicted, the sergeant woke. At first he did not remember where he was or seem to understand why his face and bits of his body felt pain and sticking plaster. Most especially he did not seem to recognise the woman with eyes as clear as water sitting smiling by his bedside. It was the perfect situation for a little close questioning.

'Hi, Sergeant,' said Jolene brightly as she saw Killigan begin to stir. 'How are you feeling?'

'Not good. Where am I?'

'In the infirmary. You'll be fine. Do you remember anything?'

'Anything about what? How did I get here?'

'We brought you. The doc says you'll be fine. Do you remember anything about the fire?'

'What fire? Jesus, I hurt like a son of a bitch. What happened to me?'

'You're a bit burned. Don't you remember anything about the fire? How it started?'

'The first John Deere went up right on . . .' Killigan lifted his blankets to steal a quick glance beneath them. 'Hey, I got no underwear on. Who took my stuff?'

'One of the nurses, I'm sure,' said Jolene, aware that the sergeant was playing for time in the face of her questions. 'The John Deere went up right on what?'

'What nurses? There are no nurses at Armstrong.'

'Right on time?' she probed, using the last of his disorientation.

'No women at Armstrong at all'

'There are nurses here. You'll be all right. But the John Deere. It went up right on what? Right on schedule? Right on plan?'

Silence.

Killigan looked up, suddenly clear-eyed and frowning. 'Right on that fucking chopper's landing gear. You're the S&MA inspector. Jolene DaCosta. I got you now.'

'I'm glad you're feeling stronger. Can I get you anything? Food? Drink? Reading matter?'

'So where am I? This isn't Armstrong. Hey, I hear engines. This is a boat.'

'That's right. The British ship *Erebus*. It's evacuating some of the wounded from the fire. You weren't caught in the first explosion, though. You were caught when the store shed and the labs went up.'

'No kiddin'?' said Killigan, his eyes narrow, giving nothing away now. He began to pull himself up a little. He winced.

'You'll get good treatment aboard here,' Jolene told him. 'These facilities are better and warmer than anything left at Armstrong, and you'll be dropped at Palmer in a day or two. We will, rather. I'll be coming ashore there too. What's there? At Palmer, I mean? Do you remember?'

Killigan frowned, clearly giving it all he'd got. 'Permanent base. Bigger than Armstrong. Good helipad. Raised. Metal. All-weather, near as dammit. Proper landing strip. Four hundred metres, if memory serves. You'll be able to fly in FBI by the shitload there. Fly out whatever you want too. aIf there's anything left for you to fly anywhere.'

'I still have Major Schwartz.'

'You do? You are a persistent person, Dr DaCosta.'

'Thank you. May I get you anything? Food? Drink?'

'A babe with a Martini would be a good start.'

'Any particular babe? Vodka or gin? Shaken or stirred?'

'What've we got?'

'American girls? Only me. Captain Mariner and Dr Ross if you want British women. Among your men, Billy Hoyle up and about. Otherwise, anything you fancy.'

Killigan's narrow eyes slid away. 'Billy Hoyle,' he said to himself. Then, more firmly, 'Vodka. On the rocks. Bring a pitcher.' He held up his hands. They were singed. Shaking.

'And a straw.'

'Oh, l think not,' said Dr Chapple, pulling aside the curtain briskly. 'The only container you're going to need for the next few hours, Sergeant, is a bedpan. And they don't come with straws.'

On the way back up the sickbay, Jolene noticed that Billy Hoyle was back on his bed, hands linked behind his bandaged head. 'Hi, Billy,' she said equably. 'Where did you vanish off to?'

His eyes flicked over to the distant doctor, but Jolene had spoken softly; the termagant had not heard. 'Just making a few acquaintances aboard. Settling in,' he said.

'Don't get too settled in. We'll be at Palmer in a couple of days.'

'Palmer?' His gaze was suddenly calculating. A door opened behind those bland, shallow eyes, showed her a racing intelligence reckoning odds like a card sharp. Then it slammed closed. 'Good old Palmer. Well, what do you know? When do we get there?'

'Forty-eight hours,' she said. 'On the dot if it all goes to plan.'

'Two days,' said Billy. 'Two days and a night.'

'Two nights,' she said, frowning. 'Tonight and tomorrow night.'

'But I'm a sick man. Tonight I gotta sleep,' said Billy Hoyle and closed his eyes.

They all slept well that night, or seemed to do so. The full sea watches reported nothing untoward above or below decks. Kate and Robin's dedication to first aid stretched as far as a late check and the promise of another first thing, but only the medical orderlies prowled the sickbay in the middle and morning watches, with orders to disturb the doc in dire emergency only. The twins, overcome by the mixture of terror and elation which had characterised so much of the day, slept very nearly as soundly as Major Schwartz in his icy drawer. Their parents, only a little less exhausted, went out like lights and stayed that way. Even Andrew Pitcairn slept, though the restfulness of his slumber was more than a little undermined by visions of Captain Ogre wearing nothing but her epaulettes and the golden badges of rank which matched so exactly the luscious over-abundance of her hair.

Jolene DaCosta woke. She was burning. She sat up in her bunk, gasping the thick, almost liquid air. She could feel the perspiration trickling between the tense hillocks of her breasts and running down her belly like raindrops on a windowpane. She pulled back the blanket and the starched perfection of the Navy regulation sheet. Somehow the tissue-fine cotton of her travelling nightdress had got all bunched up around her waist. She swung her long legs out of the bunk and stood, waiting an instant as the nightdress slithered languidly into place, falling with that familiar little kick into place just below her buttocks' flare; just below the deepest curve of her tummy. Lingeringly she smoothed it into place, feeling how hot she was beneath its gauzy surface.

The gentlest rapping whispered at her door. She crossed the cabin, heart aflutter, feeling each tuft of carpet with super-sensitive toes. She turned the lock and the door swung silently inwards.

He was tall, but not as tall as she remembered. Little more than a collection of light-limned curves, emphasised by bottomless deeps of shadow. Hair like silver in the perpetual light of midnight here. Hands like white doves upon her. As though she was weightless he picked her up and carried her to her bunk. His palms and fingertips were like warm down drifting beneath the nightdress that was little more in substance than a fragrant breath. But his knee between her thighs was rougher, denim-clad. She rubbed against it gently, not wishing to hurry things too much. Her own fingers were busy, sliding under the paler, softer, warmer woven cotton of his T-shirt.

'Oh my God,' said Jolene.

Her lover raised his head. His eyes twinkled knowingly.

'Richard was right,' said T-Shirt. But his voice was her own voice.

Jolene woke. She was cold.

Because her dream was still so vivid in her mind she pulled herself out of the bunk and checked the door. It was open. And that was very bad because she had locked it before she went to sleep.

Chapter Twelve

Jolene slept no more that night. She dressed, feeling at risk and invaded. She checked the simple door lock. It was capable of being unlocked from either side and looked easy enough to pick. She went through her stuff, most of which was laid out on the top bunk of the little double room. Nothing had been taken. Nothing seemed to have been touched. Then, investigator that she was, she went through the room again, looking for clues. In the face of another blank she fell to reasoning. Who? Why? Or rather, why and then who. If the motive was sexual, it could be pretty much anyone on the sex-starved crew. If the motive was almost anything else, then the suspects could probably be narrowed to those who knew who she was and thought they knew what she was up to.

Having got that far in her logic, typically Jolene took action. With no further hesitation, not even pausing to check the time, she went out, locked her door, pasted a couple of hairs across the jamb with spit and went for a prowl. The hairs on the door ploy was a bit James Bond and they would fall off when the spit dried but there was a certain security in knowing that little bit more than any potential burglars. Thus empowered, Jolene crept down towards the sickbay, right palm itching for the reassuring weight of her Glock.

It was probably just as well that she didn't have the gun because when Robin called, 'Morning, Jolene. You're up early,' from just behind her, she got such a fright that she'd probably have shot her if she had been armed. Then how could she have asked Richard for his advice and help?

'I need,' said Jolene a little while later, 'a knight in shining armour.'

'Oh?' said Richard. He did not sound particularly convinced. 'What's the problem?'

Jolene explained about the break-in.

'I'd have thought changing the lock would be no problem,' said Richard, being practical. 'Ships are self-regulating, self-repairing entities. No matter what you want doing in that line, there'll be someone aboard to do it. If you want a new lock the first officer will

109

know if there's one aboard, and if there is, a chippie will fix it.'

'I think my lock was picked. Anything stronger? I was thinking maybe bolts.'

'Bolts if you insist. But they tend to be frowned on. Prime directive on any ship is safety. In an emergency the head of your station or assembly point should be able to open your door with a master key – in case you were knocked out, gassed, fainted, hurt. If you're bolted in, they're screwed and you're dead.'

'I'd say the chances of that are pretty slight. Slighter than robbery or ravishment in any case.'

'So you think the motive might be intercourse rather than information?'

Jolene's eyebrows rose. 'You mean you don't think so?'

'You fishing for compliments? I'd say that most of the men aboard would queue up to get at you, if that's what you wanted.'

'But if whoever it was broke in for information, why didn't they take any?'

'You woke up. Disturbed them. Frightened them off. What was in your mind when you woke?'

T-Shirt Maddrell, you clever bastard, but she did not say it. 'Well . . .'

'No impression of movement, someone leaving?'

'No. Nothing like that. Maybe it was just someone trying to put the frighteners on me.'

'Scare you? Did they succeed?'

'Well, no.'

'Right then. Tell you what, I'll ask around about locks and bolts, all right?' Richard stood without waiting for an answer, turned away from the preoccupied woman and left.

Her clear eyes followed him, taking a little cloudiness from the day. She continued speaking to his departing back, at a level calculated to be inaudible to him, 'Well, yes, actually. If they were trying to scare me they did a pretty good job. They got me jumping at shadows and asking strangers for help. The guys at Safety and Mission Assurance simply would not believe it if they could see what a mess I am becoming here.'

Having delivered the last of this monologue to the door which closed behind Richard's departing back, Jolene pulled herself to her feet and crossed the room. She had work to do. The investigation could not proceed without more detailed facts. She really needed to reconstruct the circumstances surrounding Major Schwartz's final mission a little more precisely. And she had the ability to do that if she just bestirred herself. She could examine his failed space suit. She had some briefing notes about it and would be able to see if anything was obviously wrong with it. She could call on the expertise of at least one of the wounded beards, both of whom had been involved in aspects of the design. She could talk to Killigan again, but about security this time – of the vehicle compound, the explosive store, the off-limits area where the priceless, revolutionary, experimental, clearly flawed space suit was kept. She could talk at greater depth to Billy Hoyle who had been involved with the practical applications team as well as with communications and back-up and who had helped the major dress. She could also talk to him about how the search was organised in its early stages and so forth.

Filled with a bit more energy and assurance, she made her next decision. Billy Hoyle knew most. Start with him. Pity he seemed such a scumbag.

As she passed a decorative mirror, she caught a glancing reflection of herself all bundled up in pullover and jeans, not so much dressed as fortified. The way to Billy Hoyle's brain, she reckoned, if not to his heart, probably lay through his gonads. She had a tight, executive little office number in her case, all cleavage and the promise of a glimpse of panties. That would distract him while she dug a little deeper.

She ran up the companionways to the corridor where her cabin was with a good deal of bounce, but as she turned into the corridor, some of her excitement dimmed. The doors were all closed. The corridor itself was shadowy, lit only by a glimmer of light from the porthole in the big door at the far end. Apart from the all-invasive background rumble of a ship at sea, it was silent, deserted. She walked slowly, stealthily, rising onto tiptoe. She began to linger outside the cabin doors, listening for sound, movement. She would have given much to have had even Richard's terrible twins in tow.

She reached her own door. It was closed. Exactly as she had left it. And yet . . . She checked the jamb, scanned all round its edge. No hairs. She put the slightest of pressures against it as she checked. It moved. Not only was it unlocked, it was open. She jumped back, as though from some venomous creature; sucked in a silent breath, hoping it would still the thumping of her heart.

A scuffle of movement. There was someone in there. Another nearly silent slither of sound.

Jolene stood back. She regretted the absence of the Glock even

111

more keenly. But she was not absolutely defenceless. Since she took up this job she had changed her preferred form of keep fit, giving up dance aerobics in favour of martial arts. She knew the falls, rolls, kicks and strikes. She had sworn a timeless oriental oath that she would only use these skills for exercise and never against any person. Screw oriental oaths for a start, she thought. They never stopped Bruce Lee or Jackie Chan. Or the Teenage Mutant Ninja Turtles, come to that. So she kicked the door wide and hurled herself inward, using the momentum to set up her first attacking blow.

And nearly killed the sailor changing her bed sheets, through a heart attack if nothing else.

The day proceeded. *Erebus* picked her way slowly and carefully through the still-gathering brash out of the Grandidier Channel and into the Bismarck Strait. Her course was carefully laid to swing her out around the western reaches of Anvers Island, a preferable if slightly longer route than the cramped inner waterways between Graham Land and the chain of islands just off it. As Andrew put it to Richard, looking at the next ice-warning sheet, 'With this lot packing in on the west wind, I'd rather have sea room than speed. Not that speed's all that much of an option.'

'I'd have to agree,' said Richard, looking at the satellite picture and the chart. 'The ship is well found and in no danger. Ice-strengthened hull, the works. All you need to be worried about is further damage to the propeller. And that's more likely to happen in choked-up channels than with nothing up wind of you.' He stopped, frowned, the chart of the Antarctic Ocean in his mind. 'Nothing up-wind of you at all.'

'What d'you mean?' asked Andrew vaguely, his mind else-where.

'It's nothing important. Just a fancy. But it's literally true, I think. There is nothing up-wind of you round the whole of the world.' He turned to the starboard bridge wing. Its far end looked almost due east at that moment, onto the distant mountain spine of Graham Land. 'That,' said Richard, 'is the next land, the only land, to the west of you.'

Andrew looked at him as though he had taken leave of his senses. 'To the east,' he said.

'Yes, to the east. But to the west as well. At these latitudes, that thin little mountain chain, and a couple of islands beside it, is all the land there is.'

112

Jolene did not stand naked in front of a mirror and say, 'Right Billy Hoyle, which bits of me will distract you most if I give you glimpses of them while I ask you questions?' But she might as well have done so. Perhaps she was getting a touch of cabin fever too. Perhaps it was reaction to being a victim, a sex object, having been already the subject of Hoyle's voyeurism, but she decided coldly to use her body as a weapon against him. And once she had made that decision, she followed it through to the hilt. Perhaps it was fortunate that the mirror in which she checked her armoury was fairly small, for she did not in truth look much like Sharon Stone.

Jolene had one see-through bra. She slipped it on. One pair of lacy panties – thankfully white. Thankfully clean. Miraculously still here. She stepped into them. Her tights were all heavy and sensible, chosen for the environment, not the fantasies of the men trapped in it. It was a bit obvious, but she would have to leave them off. Thinking that the term 'obvious' was being given new meaning here in any case, she reached up for her one light blouse. It had a sensible button-front, which became less sensible as fewer buttons were fastened. She possessed a tailored skirt. She pulled it high, sucked in her tummy and rolled the waistline discretely. He wouldn't notice the waistband if she got the hem line right. There was a matching jacket, fashionably baggy; plunging lapels emphasised how much sense was now lacking in the buttoning of her blouse. Seeing the way her cleavage looked, she fastened two more buttons.

Then unfastened one. She sprayed a little Tommy Hilfiger, not too much – there were limits to what she wanted to waste on Billy Hoyle. She put on her black slingbacks with the thickish soles and the half heels and went out hunting.

Richard arrived when Jolene was little more than a fragrant memory. He had the chippie in tow, the junior engineering officer who doubled as ship's carpenter. Chippie was possessed of a new two-cylinder door lock with a pair of keys, though as he pointed out, he had to ensure the door could also be unlocked from the outside in an emergency. 'Unlocked' was a fine term. At Richard's request he also had a small bolt. 'Nothing fancy,' Richard had insisted. 'And nothing large. It has to be strong enough to calm the lady's fears and at the same time, when push comes to shove, it has to be weak enough to yield to a good firm shoulder in an emergency.'

'Right, Captain,' said Chippie, diplomatically. 'I understand.'

113

Richard watched as he took off the handles, extracted the shaft, unscrewed the plate and eased out the lock; slid in the new one and reassembled the door. Fortunately, the doorframe itself was quite thick so his second task, securing the bolt, was easy enough. 'That'll come loose with a good hard shove?' asked Richard.

'It's not something I can demonstrate, really Captain,' said Chippie. 'But you just take my word for it. Will it be you doing the shoving, Captain?'

'Certainly,' said Richard. 'I'll make a point of it.'

'I'm looking for Billy Hoyle,' Jolene told him. Ernie Marshall was sitting with his feet on a chair cushioned with an old and rather dusty kitbag. 'Have you seen him?'

'Just stepped into the head, miss. He won't be a moment, I'm sure.' Wide blue eyes crinkled trustworthily. Open, boyish countenance grinned, full of innocence. Jolene didn't notice.

'I need to talk to him alone,' she said. 'Where can we go to be private?'

'Well, you can talk in here if you'd like, miss. I'll be popping down into the sickbay in a tick myself. Duty calls.'

Jolene looked around the little area. It was not quite a room – one door and one archway down into the ward; but it was not quite a vestibule either – the door closed and the archway had a curtain for privacy. It boasted a central table, with four plastic chairs. There were three easy chairs put side by side like a sofa along one wall. It would do very well. 'Can we get a cup of coffee in here?'

'If you don't mind instant, miss, I'll fetch it along myself.'

Billy Hoyle returned to find Jolene waiting for him, loaded for bear. She was sitting on the mock sofa of three easy chairs. She had beside her a cup of coffee and there was more awaiting his attention on the table. 'Take a seat,' she said. 'Take a cup.'

He took both and looked down at her. 'She's setting me up,' he thought. But he put the cup to his lip and sipped, sneaking a long look over the rim at the way her blouse had sagged to reveal the inner curves of two surprisingly well-filled lacy cups. 'What can I do for you, Inspector?' he asked.

'There are some details I have to get straight,' she said.

'Anything I can do . . .'

'You mind if I tape this?'

'Not at all'

As she turned to the little recorder beside her, her blouse gaped

114

wider, allowing him a far more intimate glimpse than anything she had planned for. His eyes lingered appreciatively. His memory flashed up some shots from Ernie's Scandinavian selection. His libido stirred. It occurred to him that maybe she had been aroused by his attempt to spy on her in the john. That this was a genuine come-on. Had he been the man she thought him, his fantasies would have switched off his intelligence there and then. But there was a little more to him than that.

Jolene sat back, uneasily caught between her twin roles as interrogator and vamp. She adjusted her blouse. Fastened two buttons without thinking. Long fingers played with the third.

'The day Major Schwartz died,' she said, 'no excursion had been planned?'

'That's right.'

'So how much notice did you have that he was going out?'

'Minimum allowable. He got the colonel's OK then came to me. Told me to get him geared up.'

'Were you surprised? Taken by surprise?'

'Yes and no. We'd been working on the suit. Mendel had been checking it the night before for something – it'll be in his log.'

'I have that.'

'Normally we'd have had enough notice to do another set of checks. Six hours was the usual. But not this time. It was up and out, more or less. But we did the basics. Got it all set up by the book. "According to Hoyle", like they say. It's in my—'

'Log. Yes, I know. I've scanned the top-copy digest. I have all the detailed logs downloaded from the network on Armstrong.'

'Well, you'll see what w7e did then.'

'I see what you logged.'

'It's the same thing. Mendel and Fagan checked the suit according to the rules. The major came in in a hurry; weather was closing and he wanted out in it. I helped him, checked the life support, comms, other stuff, by the book—'

'According to Hoyle, yes. I know a good deal about the suit. Not as much as Mendel and Fagan, though.'

'You can check that out whenever. They're both in the sickbay.'

'I know. Though Professor Mendel may be out of communication for some time.'

'At least until his beard grows back. I understand.'

'So you checked the major's suit and all was well?'

'Couldn't have been better.'

'Then what went wrong?'

'Damned if I know. I mean, it was one of those things, you know? You could almost feel fate closing in. Like it was going to go wrong right from the outset. I guess that's why we were so fast off the mark – when his line went dead and I realised we'd lost him.'

Jolene uncrossed her legs. Paused. Re-crossed them. '*Fate*, Billy? You felt fate closing in?'

'Well, ah . . .' he drew his hand over his mouth, like a silent movie actor trying to portray lust. 'Well, you know, it was an extra test. The suit was up and packed away. Mendel and Fagan had checked it and bagged it for the duration. It wasn't due out again until next millennium, you know? And the major, he just comes in out of nowhere demanding one last run out into the worst weather of the season. "Make or break". That's what some of the guys called him, you know. Make or break Bernie. Well, he didn't fucking make it, did he?'

Jolene uncrossed her legs, placing her feet flat on the carpet half a metre apart. Without thinking, she leaned forward, elbows to knees, eyes fixed on his like a couple of steel rivets. He had not seen so much warm lace since his last visit to a girlie bar.

'So the suit was packed away. It wasn't due out again for weeks.' She leaned even further forward. 'He came unexpectedly because he wanted to test the thing one last time in the unforeseen squall. The beards had closed it down and packed it away for a fortnight. Logged it off. Procedure requires at least a twenty-four-hour start-up schedule if a suit is logged off, so you doctored your logs and gave it a quick once-over. The major took it out. And all of a sudden it didn't work. Why?'

Billy Hoyle was so shaken by her summation he stopped trying to see through the shadowy lace of her panties. 'Total powerdown,' he said.

He may have been hoping that the jargon would faze her. No such luck. 'Powerdown would kill his life-support and communication,' she said. 'But it wouldn't kill him and it wouldn't kill his back-up communications or his locator beacon fix on your laser grid.'

Billy looked at her, stunned by how much she knew. 'Of course it would,' he said. 'Total powerdown would do all of those things if the stupid, arrogant little fuck went way out in weather better suited to midwinter than midsummer. You got the weather records for the day? In the heart of that squall it was thirty below. Thirty Celsius with the wind-chill. So he had powerdown in the back of beyond with no chance of calling in or registering on the monitor. He tried to call us up and he tried to walk back and the sorry fucker froze to death. End of story.'

'Not quite. Not from where I'm sitting, Billy. Because you know and I know that even with total powerdown the major could only have frozen in that suit if some part of it had been left wide open. Wide open or missing altogether. I don't see any record of that in your logs. Or did you tidy them up again?'

'I don't know what you're getting at. I never—'

'Yes you did, Billy. You, Mendel, Fagan; you three at least. You tidied up the whole shut-down procedure so you could get it out again for the major with a minimum of fuss. What else did you erase from those logs before you saved them down for the record?'

Billy Hoyle looked at her, open-mouthed. Her eyes were blazing. She stood up. The hem of her skirt was exactly level with his chin. 'It's fortunate for me,' she spat, 'that the network automatically saves each old file as a back-up each time a new one is saved on top of it. The system has been programmed to do that not just once but four times. So I have your top-copy official log, Billy; yours, Mendel's, Fagan's and the rest. The top copies and the four separate back-up copies, one on top of the other.'

'Who's the lucky man?' asked Richard a little later, gesturing at Jolene's outfit.

'What? Oh, Billy Hoyle,' she answered distractedly.

'I beg your pardon?'

She looked down again. Buttoned up her blouse. 'It's an interrogation device.'

'Really? In my day they used thumbscrews.'

'Well. It worked. Maybe too well. But that's not your problem. What can I do for you?'

'In that outfit? You've already done it, my dear.'

'Very funny. And I expect that's why you're following me to my cabin. What is it really?'

'Here we are. Now I can show you. New lock, see? New key, and new bolt. Good and solid. No more casual break-ins. Better?'

'You are a life-saver, sir.' Spontaneously she went up on tiptoe and pressed her lips to his cheek.

Far below, Billy Hoyle was sitting glumly, looking across the little alcove at Ernie Marshall. 'I think she suckered me,' he said. The English sailor, an obvious soul mate, had become friend and confidant almost instantly. Confidant for much that Billy wanted to unburden himself of, but by no means all. 'It was that get-up she was wearing. Screwed with my head just when I needed to think straight.'

'Tarts,' sympathised Ernie. 'What can you do, eh? Still, if you're into her, so to speak, I can let you have the nightie she was wearing last night. And I've got a magazine somewhere that shows a Scandinavian bit that looks just like her doing some really interesting things with a bowl of fruit. Well, not the bowl so much . . .'

'Aw, come on, Ernie. Get real. This is serious. The bitch can really hurt me.'

'I thought she was going to hurt me this morning,' admitted Ernie feelingly. 'When she came through the door of her cabin like that I thought she was going to kick my head in where I stood. I kid you not.' He paused. 'God, I wish she'd been wearing that little miniskirt then, I tell you.'

Jolene did not go down to luncheon and spent the afternoon watches going through the back-up records stored with the downloaded central network on six 3½-inch floppy disks which she could slip in and out of the port in the side of her laptop. The two systems were not quite compatible and she found her investigations slowed by pages of impenetrable computer babble. As she worked as swiftly as babble and due care dictated through the mass of information and records, her mind became freed of the icy shackles of the Big White and her position here on the edge of it. She became again what she was most supremely: a lively mind on the shores of the third millennium; a child of the next century. And she began to wonder how much of this mass of information on Armstrong's network was confined to the network.

Colonel Jaeger had put his report straight through to NASA HQ using the base's satellite phone. She had done something similar herself, though her system was state of the art and far in advance of anything she had seen down here. But how secure was the network? There were stringent locks and bars in place to prevent hackers breaking in from the outside, but what was to stop someone on the inside simply sending information out on the Internet? There were places – France, Japan and Russia sprang to mind – where just the specifications of Major Schwartz's suit would be worth a fortune. Though Russian fortunes weren't what they once were, these days. Not the legal fortunes, at any rate, if such things still existed in the mafia-haunted economic Armageddon of the Republic. Nor were

Japanese ones, come to that. She should have a look at the records of satellite phone time over the last few days – assuming they could be trusted any more than Hoyle and his cronies' logs, the vehicle movement and fuel consumption records, and the explosive materials book. 'Going round in circles here, Jolene,' she decided eventually. She stretched until her shoulders popped, looked at the time and realised she was so hungry because it was dinner time. She had missed not only lunch but smoko and the quaint, old-Navy 'pour-out' at eighteen hundred hours. She didn't mind that; she was an abstemious person. Somewhere in the back of her mind, however, she remembered that in spite of the fact that it was a Tuesday, the day's menu on the wardroom display board promised roast beef And that was something that the British seemed to do even better than gallantry. Knight-errantry, she thought, unfastening the bolt, exiting and locking the door with her big new key.

Robin gave her a welcoming grin and gestured her over to the Mariner table as soon as she entered the dining salon. Jolene was pleased enough to go, aware of all too many eyes upon her, in spite of the fact that she was back behind the battlements of pullover and jeans.

The meal was superb. Replete and relaxed, bed beckoned. The twins had been so saintly that they had been allowed to stay up late. It was Richard and Jolene who took the pair up together, for Robin and Kate were down doing their last quick tour of the sickbay.

Jolene was still feeling gently and indulgently motherly when she went to bed. Before she removed any clothing she turned her new key in her new lock and slid her new bolt home tight. Her sense of security was only briefly undermined when she could not find her fine cotton nightdress. Still, it had been a bit too flimsy in any case. Jolene drew out a clean, lengthy, very much more substantial garment. Wrapped up like the oldest of old maids, she tucked down, virtuously determined not to dream of T-Shirt Maddrell – or any man at all if she could help it.

Jolene woke up. She was hot. Very hot. The whole of the end of her bed seemed to be burning against her feet. She sat up and her face filled with smoke. Her cabin was on fire. An alarm bellowed out of the tannoy. Feet scurried in the corridor outside. The whole ship must be alight. Refusing to panic, though choking for breath, Jolene swung her legs out of bed. The floor was blessedly cool against the scorched soles of her feet. She reached over to switch on the light but could not find the switch. Disorientated, fighting for control, she sat in the resounding darkness, fearful of breathing in the smoke and aware that she had no more time to look for the stubbornly elusive switch. Still thinking quickly and coolly, she knelt. Her life jacket was under her bunk. She should take it and go to her assembly point. On the floor there was less smoke. She gulped down a draught of clearer air. Her head began to clear too. What else should she take? The laptop with the records. Had she any chance of getting Schwartz's body out of cold storage? Almost certainly not. Smoke billowed down upon her. She pulled the life jacket free, sucked clear air from the floor and pulled herself to her feet – and found herself in a blinding, choking, disorientating world where clear thought, clear sight and clear lungs were impossible. Her right hand held the life jacket, grim as death. Her left hand once again sought the light switch – in vain. Gave up, sought the strap of the laptop's travelling case instead. Thank God she had packed it all away last night, neat and tidy as always.

She swung it off the bunk and onto her shoulder. Heart thumping painfully, self-control wearing thin, chest as vividly aflame as her cabin seemed to be, she walked blindly to the door. It wasn't there. Panic rising, she felt along the wall, searching for the reassuring handle. She transferred her life jacket into her left hand and searched with her right, willing herself not to breathe, call out, cry. At last, unlike the light switch, there it was. She turned it. Nothing.

Turned it again. The door would not open. Panic welled dangerously close to the surface, incapacitating, deadly.

You stupid woman. You locked and bolted it. The voice came into her head clearly, as though someone was standing behind her talking.

Life jacket swinging into and out of the way, she managed to find the key. Turned it. Wrenched the door. Stopped. Controlled herself with an epic exercise of will. While her right hand squirmed round the warm doorknob, she raised her left hand, life jacket and all, and found the neat little handle of the bolt. She had just enough strength to pull it back if she was quick. Just enough strength before the smoke choked her or the fire broke through. Her fingers fastened on it, guided and controlled by her unshakeable will. But it would not move. It was stuck fast. As though wedged there. As though soldered into place, the bolt simply would not yield to her.

Her self control failed her then. The volcano of panic erupted in her breast and the icy control in her head was swept away. For the last few instants of her life she sobbed and screamed and railed against the bitter helplessness.

And the door burst back into her face, charged open by a big square shoulder dressed in a blue and green plaid dressing gown. With the shoulder came in fresh, clean air so that her lungs, gasping after her sobbing screams, sucked in life-giving oxygen.

'OK?' said Richard's voice from somewhere beyond the orbit of Pluto. 'Lifeboat drill, I'm afraid. Still, we need to be ready for the real thing . . .' He stopped talking as he realised her cabin was full of smoke.

And, in spite of her best intentions, she fainted into his arms.

Chapter Thirteen

Erebus's routine lifeboat drill became a genuine emergency. While the passengers and crew shivered at their assembly points, a team of firefighters went to Jolene's cabin. Half an hour's work revealed that the emergency was not too serious. A few old rags, oily and combustible, had become wedged in the ducting and had begun to smoulder; they had not even really caught fire. The heat she had felt came from the ducting which passed by the end of her bunk. There would have been no real emergency at all, they concluded a little huffily, had she not insisted on having the bolt fixed to her door. Even those who found her attractive were less than sympathetic. It was generally agreed amongst the crew that she had brought the whole thing on herself. And so it was left to the slightly more understanding civilians to arrange the tea and sympathy she really rather needed.

The whole emergency was over by 2 a.m. on the morning of Wednesday, the 29th. Under the circumstances, Andrew declared himself satisfied and did not call for the lifeboats to be swung out, whereupon Jolene rose in everyone's estimation again, for the weather was closing in once more and swinging out the boats would have been a cold, unpleasant business.

The dazed Jolene returned to her smoke-smelling cabin, which had been declared safe if not wholesome. She closed the door, locked it and reached automatically for the bolt. It was hanging off of course, separated from the doorframe by the thrust of Richard's shoulder. She was in the act of pushing the screws back into the torn wood, wondering whether her nail file would prove a strong enough substitute screwdriver to re-secure them, when she noticed something which turned the accident into something very much more sinister.

As she moved the little brass bolt, trying to settle it against the frame, its shaft caught the dull light from the cabin bulb, making a glassy carapace glitter for an instant. Jolene looked closer. All around the shaft, where it crossed from door to jamb and slid into the second section, there was some sort of hard coating. Numbly, Jolene opened the door and looked at the frame. A section of it had broken off and was attached to the door. Jolene tried to prise it free, but it would not move, secured there by some powerful glue. Superglue by the look of it.

During the night as she had slept, someone had crept silently past her door and squeezed Superglue into the crack so that it dripped over the bolt and glued it locked. The logical conclusion to be drawn from this was that whoever had glued her door shut had also filled her air duct with smouldering rags and waited for her to choke to death. The murder plot would have worked perfectly but for the lifeboat drill.

Jolene crept to her bunk and pushed her shaking shoulders into the corner between the bedhead and the cold, vibrating wall, drew up her knees and spent the rest of the night watching the door.

What would have been the dawn came grudgingly and dully. The slow swoop up of the sun was distantly obscured by lowering battlements of cloud, piling in out of the west, driven by the same great weather machine which was piling icebergs so unseasonably along the west-facing coast of Graham Land. There was a sense of dull foreboding to it, of distant threat inevitably drawing closer.

'I don't much like the look of that,' said Richard as he came onto the bridge after breakfast.

Andrew looked up. 'We'll be all tucked up safe and sound in Palmer before anything hits,' he said. 'But I don't think it'll be all that bad really.'

'Hmm,' said Richard. He strolled across to the weather prediction equipment. Like the ice-watching equipment, much of its information was satellite-generated. Low necklaces of weather sats were hung around the more turbulent weather bands. There was one above them now; a chain in series watching the roaring forties, the stormy fifties, and the huge unstoppable weather systems which whirled around them, unmoderated by any intervention of land. The conversation Richard had already had with Andrew about there being no land at their latitude except the spindle of Graham Land reaching up towards the dagger-point of South America stirred again in his mind.

'Have you got a picture of the weather system out there?' he asked the watch officer.

'Yes, sir. That's the latest one there.' Beside the ice picture on the chart lay a satellite picture of a classic southern weather system, a perfect reversal of a northern hemisphere depression. Lines of latitude and longitude gave a clear location for the centre of the cloudy whirlpool 65 South and 70 West, just where it could make most trouble with the pack ice around Alexander Island, then sweep it all up towards them as it followed its generally eastward track.

'Does this thing get you weather-sat pictures from anywhere you want?' asked Richard. He was fairly confident with the new hardware but certain areas of the twenty-first century stuff left him floundering.

'It certainly does, Captain. Just key in the figures and it'll take the snapshot. If the nearest one can't, it'll pass the order round the chain. The further away you ask to look at, the longer it takes to come up with the goods, that's all.'

'Fair enough. How about our latitude but right round the other side of the world?'

'Sixty-five South, then; and, what, one hundred East?'

'Let's say a hundred and ten East.'

'OK, Captain. That shouldn't take long. What with the earth's curvature, it's not actually all that far away. And nobody much will be asking to look at some lump of ocean not quite south of Australia anyway.' As the lieutenant talked, he typed in the co-ordinates.

The machine began to print almost at once and a darkly swirling picture emerged, tighter, deeper, blacker by far than the picture from their own side of the world.

'Holy Moses,' said the young lieutenant, awed. 'What in heaven's name is that?'

'That,' said Richard thoughtfully, looking away to the west, 'is the squall that killed Major Schwartz. In the last five days it has crossed Graham Land and gone out over the Larsen Ice Shelf into the Weddell Sea. It has fallen off the ice shelf into the storm factory between the permanent pack and the Antarctic Convergence about level with Bouvet Island. It has run south of Tristan, over Prince Edward and Kreugen Island and it has been given a new lease of life by the conditions there which on the average day generate about the same amount of energy as ten big nuclear power stations. Have you seen the original *Star Trek* movie?'

'Well, no, sir.'

'It's about this little spacecraft, the *Voyager*, which goes out from Earth, gets captured and adopted by an alien race which makes it the heart of a massive machine the size of a planet and then sends it back again. The people on the Starship *Enterprise* have to stop it before it destroys Earth.'

'I see. Very interesting. If you like old sci-fi movies. However—'

'That's what's happening to the squall that killed Major Schwartz,' said Andrew as he crossed the bridge. He took the picture of the storm

125

from the confused lieutenant and looked at Richard, frowning with concern. 'It's spent the last four days growing out of all proportion. And now it's on its way back.'

'With no land to moderate its force. Nothing but sea and ice and winds to make it worse. And it'll be here in four days tops.'

'Four days,' said Andrew, looking up at the calendar automatically. 'Happy New Year.'

'Happy New Year indeed,' said Richard.

'Richard, I think someone's trying to kill me,' said Jolene, meeting him as he came down from the navigation bridge, frowning.

A lesser man might have raised an eyebrow, laughed aloud. Not Richard. It was not in his nature to mock. But he was worried about Jolene. The possibility of cabin fever did not seem too wild. He had seen it happen. Like most travellers and seafarers, he had read widely so he knew well enough that just being down here could affect the unwary as potently as an unsuspected drug.

'What's more important?' he asked. 'Who or how?'

'I don't know who yet but I'll obviously have to get to them before they get another chance at me. As to how, I'll show you.'

There was nowhere aboard *Erebus* large enough to accommodate all of her complement, scientists, guests and wounded comfortably. But, with several on watch above and below as the weather worsened from the west, some still bedridden and at least one dead in his gently vibrating drawer, there was just room for everyone to stand in the dining salon. This they were summoned to do the instant luncheon was cleared away.

'It has come to my attention,' Andrew Pitcairn said loudly, 'that there has been some dangerous horseplay going on. Some utterly unacceptable bullying.' Bullying was the worst he could bring himself to believe of his own men. And even his American guests seemed variously incapable of anything much worse. 'The object of this unwanted attention has been Dr DaCosta. Her cabin has been searched; her clothing disarrayed and misappropriated. Last night smouldering rags were placed in her cabin ducting on purpose and the bolt on her door tampered with. All of this childish horseplay will stop forthwith. I will not single out Dr DaCosta further by placing her under guard, but she and her quarters will be watched carefully until we can offload her and her associates at Palmer in six hours' time. Do I make myself clear?'

The officers and crew of Andrew's command made supportively

awed positive noises. The Americans in particular looked askance at this sledgehammer approach, especially when the threats – and their objects – were so vague.

But still, as the captain said, six hours to Palmer base. What could possibly go wrong in so short a space of time?

'What do you think of that?' Billy Hoyle asked Ernie Marshall on their way back down to the sickbay.

'Put up the price of that nightie,' said Ernie calculatingly. 'Might have made me a packet. Why?'

'Six hours,' said Billy. 'That's just time to give her one more good fright. I really want her wetting herself by the time we get to Palmer. I need a little space.'

'Wetting herself,' said Ernie, rather savouring the prospect. 'We should be able to arrange that, I guess. What had you in mind?'

'She's got all the records from Armstrong's network downloaded onto disks.'

'Yeah?'

'Well, disks are only of any use if she can read them, so I was thinking maybe . . .'

'Steal her laptop? A bit dicey.'

'No. More subtle than that. She'll likely as not be using it this afternoon, getting everything ready for when the Feds arrive in Palmer. But laptops are pretty fragile, you know? You got to be careful about things like current and feedback. So I was thinking, could we arrange a power surge? Up to her cabin? We'd be well away. Out of trouble. She would be there, with any luck a little bit braised, if you know what I mean, with her hard drive in ashes and her laptop melting all over the place.'

'Jesus, Billy, I don't know. I'd have to bribe some engineers pretty good. That'd be expensive. Difficult. Lot of – what do you call it – collateral damage. I think we can do it but it won't come cheap.'

'Well, it just so happens that I came aboard well-equipped to pay for expensive favours, Ernie.' Billy slipped off his big, thick-soled boot. Lifted the lining. Took out a box that filled the heel. 'Here we have just what your market has been crying out for. Happy pills.'

Engineering Cadet Baines was a young man whose sanity had been eroded more than somewhat by the whiteness of his environment. He worked in white-painted engineering sections overseeing banks of alternators supplying power to the bridgehouse and the compressors

127

in the diesel motors which drove the ship. He found with increasing disgust that he hated and loathed the white environment above as well. The snow. The ice. The clouds. The fog. The horizon. The whole fucking lot. He made no secret of it among his mates, though he kept it from the officers, of course. And this time of year it was worse than ever. There wasn't even any darkness to give him a break from the white. So when Ernie Marshall discovered a magazine containing nothing but pictures of black girls, he knew exactly who would appreciate it most.

At three that afternoon, in the last hour of his watch, Baines paused to consider the ebony perfection of an outrageously alluring centrefold. She seemed almost alive to him. He had taken a happy pill as well and his grip on reality was consequently very weak indeed. His breathing quickened; the girl of his dreams was about to detach herself from the page in all her gleaming cocoa-liquid perfection. At least that's how it seemed to him when he threw the switches and sent the biggest surge of power he could manage through *Erebus*'s elderly system. For an instant everything burned as whitely as the snows Baines hated; then it all went as dark as the girl he wanted.

Jolene had not been present at Andrew's briefing. Having agreed with Richard's suggestion to call in the highest authority aboard, she had felt it best to stay out of the limelight herself. In any case, having confronted Billy and clarified her suspicions, it was now time to go through the records again, looking for evidence to hand over to the FBI investigation team. She had never been involved in anything like this before, although she had dealt with fatal accident investigations. Now she was calling in outsiders and like any senior executive jealous of the reputation of her company, she wished to hand things over in the best form she could.

Battery power to personal laptops was expensive, quickly consumed and impossible to replace out here, so Jolene prepared for a long session by connecting to the ship's electrical system. Power in the bridgehouse of *Erebus* was supplied via electrical cables which ran, like the air and heating ducts, down the outside of the walls. The most convenient point for Jolene to use was situated below the light switch whose location was now cemented into the forefront of her mind just beside the right side of the door. Below this was a shallow table which would serve as a desk. Having checked the wattage of the power supply, Jolene set her universal adapter correctly and plugged in the laptop. After that, time ceased to have any meaning for her.

When Baines's power surge came, its effect on the laptop was every bit as effective as Billy Hoyle and Ernie Marshall could have wished. It was fortunate, therefore, that it came when Jolene was away from the machine with one disk in her hand as she searched through the other five. A crackling hiss was accompanied unaccountably by a dazzling flash of light. As the light from the bulb above her died, she whirled to find her laptop on fire, the upright square of the screen black, sagging, beginning to melt and run. Sparks danced across the keys. Jolene's hands reached out in automatic sympathy towards the old friends in their dying agony. Luckily the machine – and everything else in the bridgehouse – died before she could touch it, though the shock she thus avoided would have been painful rather than fatal.

Dull, overcast afternoon light streamed like dirty water through the porthole onto the cabin floor. Jolene did not touch the light switch, saving herself from a nasty burn. She pulled open the door instead and walked out into the corridor. Everything was so silent. She could hear the wind. *Erebus* gave a strange lurch.

The door next to Jolene's opened. Richard came out, his shadowed face further darkened by a frown.

'What is it?' she asked.

'It's what happened to your Major Schwartz,' he answered grimly. 'Total powerdown. And let's hope we can fix it more quickly and efficiently than he could, or we'll all be just as dead as he is.'

Numbly, Jolene followed Richard up onto the bridge. It was the silence of the ship that was so unnerving. Jolene had got used to the constant vibration of alternator, the insistent throb of engine. To be without them now was to be without heartbeat, dying all too quickly. And the silence allowed in other, more threatening sounds: the keening of the wind, rising without reason or expectation into howls and battering thumps against the bridgehouse; the rumble of the sea against the suddenly pitching hull; the grumbling roar of the closest ice. Ice they no longer had the power to avoid.

As Richard hurried onto the bridge, the lights came back on. Lights but little else. No heating. No throb of alternators. No engine.

Andrew was in the radio room.

'Right,' said the radio officer, obviously partway through a conversation, 'I'll try and re-establish contact now.'

'Battery back-up,' said Richard to Jolene. 'Lighting, some navigation aids. Radio. That's all. And it won't last very long.'

He walked across and stood beside the helmsman. The pair of them looked out towards the west where the first squall front of the approaching storm was closed down tight on the black seas. Abruptly the engine room telegraph sounded.

Richard picked it up without a second thought. 'Bridge'

'Captain?'

'No, Chief, this is Richard Mariner. Andrew's with Sparks. What can I pass along to him?'

'Bit of a mess down here. One of my men seems to have gone crazy. We've got him under restraint but it won't be so easy to undo the damage he's done. No power for a while, I'm afraid. No engines till we get the power back. No light after the batteries go down so I suggest we conserve it for radios and emergencies, navigational and otherwise. No heating or hot water. Lucky she's a sound old lady or we'd be pumping by hand as well.'

'Thanks, Chief. I'll pass it on. But he'll want some kind of time frame.'

'Tell him to ask after the dogwatch.'

'The first dogwatch?'

'Second.'

The chief rang off and Richard glanced up at the chronometer above the clearview. As he did so, the first shower of rain splattered across the glass; splattered and ran, obscuring his view because, like everything else, the clearview was no longer working. Andrew came out of the radio shack, rubbing the back of his neck in worried exasperation.

'I've just been talking to the chief. I've got his report,' said Richard.

'Tell me the worst.'

Richard told him.

'Bloody hell, Richard. That really puts us up the creek. We were talking to Palmer when the lights went out. They were just saying how lucky it was we would be there within the next few hours because the depression is pushing enough ice up ahead of it to close the coast as tight as Armstrong. We get in and out during the next watch or we're screwed.'

'We're screwed then,' said Richard. 'The chief says at least five hours for power. Then he'll have to see about starting up the motor. Then we'll have to see about making up lost way because this lot out here'll be pushing us eastwards at a couple of knots, I'd say.'

'No way for six hours,' said Andrew, stunned.

'If then. And from the sound of things, nowhere to go when you get her under way.' Richard walked back towards the chart table, his mind already busy with plans.

130

'It's not as bad as that, there's always Faraday,' said Andrew, rallying.

'If you're lucky you'll drift over there before the second storm hits,' said Richard.

'Oh, we'll all be tucked up safe and sound by then,' said Andrew, doggedly cheerful.

'Can't argue with a confident man,' said Richard with a laugh. 'But in the meantime, what about the rest of us?'

'Yes. That's a worry, isn't it?' said Andrew. 'We can't have sick and wounded people with no power or heating, no fresh water, no hot water. No light.'

'Not just sick people,' said Jolene. 'There are quite a few perfectly fit people who'd find that hard to take after a while, believe you me.'

Andrew looked at her, his face a mask as his mind sought to come to terms with what was happening. 'You're right,' he said. 'Jesus, this is a mess.'

Sparks stuck his head through the radio room door. 'I have Captain Ogre for you, Captain. *Kalinin*'s just been talking to Palmer and is apprised of our position. She can be alongside us here in four hours from now if that would be any help.'

Chapter Fourteen

No one wasted the next four hours. On the command bridge, Andrew, with Richard and Colin adding such advice as they could offer, set up literal watches – ice and weather watches to replace the dead machines. He made a series of decisions and gave a range of orders designed to ensure the comfort of the sick and wounded.

Erebus had stores aboard bound for Faraday; these were raided for Tilley lamps, cooking stoves, extra blankets, Karrimats, stretchers, and the like. The walking wounded, like Killigan, Washington and Billy Hoyle, joined in this work, for it was warm, dry and relatively light. The largest and most unwieldy item they had to move up out of the storage hold was a coffin, bound for Faraday's emergency stores but now detailed for more immediate use. It was the only safe vehicle anyone could come up with for the unfortunate Major Schwartz.

The sickbay staff were relieved from their other duties to ensure that warmth, warm food and warm drink got to their charges on a regular basis. Ernie Marshall, more than a little shaken by the overwhelming success of Baines's action, joined in this enthusiastically and was soon busy brewing hot chocolate. But his eagerness for this cushy number waned when he discovered he was also expected to supply the watches up on the bridge wings and out on the freezing forecastle head with a regular supply of hot drinks. So he contrived to join Hoyle and the others in packing boxes and baggage with possessions they had brought aboard and which they hoped to take off with them again. This was a wise move. The rest of the deck officers and seamen were preparing the ship for her meeting with *Kalinin*. Lines were readied – vicious work, out on the deck. But worse than that was the rigging of the buffers. Great old tyres, heavy rope-filled hammocks, any other form of protector aboard was slung over the side. The weight, unwieldiness, the simple cross-grained cussedness of these great barriers made this an unpopular duty at the best of times. To carry them across the pitching deck awash with water so cold it froze on contact with whatever it touched, to rig them in the running bilges and sling them over the streaming, heaving, icicle-

133

fanged sides was a chore come directly from hell. And yet it had to be done. When the two ships came together in this pitching tumble of ocean, their sides would have to be protected. And come together they must. The weather was closing down slowly but relentlessly. The wind was increasing, gusting at unexpected strengths from undreamed-of quarters. The Westland was well tethered but even so was twitching uneasily like a dog dreaming. To unloose her would mean disaster; to try and fly her, suicide. The sea was a metallic grey, like the surface of a giant rasp file, filled with deadly little traps of ice, death even for the trusty Zodiacs.

After having talked to Cambridge, the Admiralty and *Kalinin*, Sparks wearily went down the list of all the local stations from Arctowski and Esperanza to Arturo Prat. Then he scanned the airwaves, military, commercial, ordinary and emergency, for contact with anyone who could offer any help. Apart from *Kalinin*, only Faraday could. And Faraday was where they were going anyway. Eventually. With luck.

The only spot of brightness in the whole of that dreary afternoon on the bridge was the return to duty of Hugo Knowles; battered, bruised, bandaged, still a little bloody but chipper, on form and raring to go, he said. No sooner did he appear, however, than Jolene also appeared, keen to drag him to one side and question him about his memory of the explosion.

'I remember putting up the cabin with the second team,' he told her. 'I remember Thompson calling me out – it was a bad time, I think, though I can't remember why. Maybe because it was coming up to report time, I don't know. I can't remember why he called me out either, come to that. That's about it, I'm afraid. I'm sorry.'

'It's early days yet,' said Jolene understandingly, hiding her disappointment.

He shrugged in silent apology, and, swept away by a sisterly sympathy, she gave him a hug and a kiss on the cheek, an act which brightened him up enormously and earned her a good deal of goodwill generally – and his friendship particularly.

Below decks things were just as busy. With the exception of Engineering Cadet Baines who was locked in his cabin rather queasily awaiting the moment his captain could spare the time to see him, everyone was working flat out to rectify the damage he had done. There were electrical lines to be checked and where necessary repaired or replaced. There were circuits to be tested, repaired or replaced. As the stock of spares diminished, decisions had to be made about high and low priority areas. Almost every light bulb aboard needed renewing. The cook went to the captain at the end of the morning watch. Some of his ranges worked by gas, he said. The gas bottles were full. Could he cook the men some hot food even though the lack of electrically powered extractors would make this absolutely against regulations? The captain hesitated – until he saw the state of his deck crews. Then regulations went out of the window.

Scientists and passengers fitted in as well as they could, depending on experience and ability. Richard and Colin went onto the bridge and offered advice on seacraft and icecraft. Andrew would hardly be holding this command if he needed much of either but he welcomed the company, particularly Richard's because of the bond they shared as captains. Robin and Kate would have been able to offer advice and company every bit as well, but Richard and Colin would have made lousy nurses. So the women worked below, their professional expertise severely under-used for the moment, as was that of a couple of the beards, PhDs in the cryobiology of phytoplankton, whose only relevant qualifications allowed them to change light bulbs.

Jolene, too, found that it was her gender rather than her qualifications which fitted her to work with Robin and Kate. For the time being she allowed her professional drive to take a back seat as she worked with the team in the sickbay. As time went by, however, the professional expertise of both Robin and Kate became more important. Having made the few remaining bedridden patients warm and comfortable under the most trying and basic of conditions, their next task was to prepare them for transfer onto *Kalinin* through conditions which were very far from being warm and comfortable. Here, Robin's experiences as a ship's captain – and particularly one who had been icebound – were invaluable. And, with the possible exception of Colin, Kate knew more about Antarctic conditions and how to survive them than anyone alive. While Jolene and the attendants, led by Ernie Marshall, kept an eye on the bedridden, Kate and Robin went off to search for a supply of water- wind- and ice-proof equipment to make the transfer more comfortable for most and less fatal for the rest.

'No matter how ill he still is really,' said Robin quietly to Kate as they left, 'Hugo is certainly safer up on the bridge.'

'It'll mean he stays aboard for the duration,' said Kate uneasily.

'The doc's staying. He'll look after him.'

'That's a bit eccentric, even for the doc, isn't it? To send all the patients away and yet to stay aboard himself?'

135

'He's sending away the current patients,' said Robin, 'and saving himself for the next batch.'

The wind thumped against the side of *Erebus* like a Roman quinquereme at ramming speed.

'He's probably wise,' said Kate, watching distantly as Killigan and Washington carried the sinister shape of the coffin through the ward towards the cold-storage facility.

When the holds had been emptied of useful items now no longer bound for Faraday, Ernie Marshall had agreed to help prepare the wounded for transfer. Time would be short in all probability, but the nursing staff on *Erebus* felt that each patient transferred would be happier, and therefore more disposed to recover well, if they had a package of personal possessions with them. This was supported by the doc, and so while Robin and Kate were finding weatherproof supplies for the transfer, Ernie and the others found a kitbag for each patient and inquired what they would most like to see packed within it. Fagan, oddly, wanted shaving equipment and some old *National Geographics*. Mendel was still comatose. Billy Hoyle packed his own kitbag, in negotiation with Ernie, fizzingly full of excitement at the prospect of the new market *Kalinin*'s passengers promised to supply, independent of her entertainment staff, stewards and crew. While Billy plotted and Ernie planned, the other, more serious, patients and nurses worked. Killigan and Washington, having brought the coffin to the cold store, lifted the major gently into it They put the lid on the box but did not secure it; Jolene was due to come below later and check on it.

'She's going to take the major in that box,' Billy Hoyle said to Ernie, quietly.

'I'm not too much surprised, mate. She's a persistent little tart.'

'I don't know. This isn't working as we planned it.'

'As you planned it, Billy. I bet she wet herself, though.'

'You'd better hope so, my man. They've got Baines. Is he going to stand firm?'

'Good point, mate. I'll check when I get the chance.'

Ernie Marshall wished to the bottom of his heart that he could bring himself to trust Billy Hoyle. He knew pretty well how little merchandise the Yank would be taking aboard *Kalinin*, and while he had no doubt of Billy's ability to parlay it into a sweet profit, the potential was nothing compared with what might have been possible with his own stash to boot. But Ernie simply could not bring himself to yield up his hard-won investments to his new friend in the dimly distant hope of a return sometime, somewhere.

These thoughts carried Ernie down to the locked door of Baines's cabin. Under normal circumstances, given the heinous insanity of Baines's crime, there would have been a guard on the door. Now there was not.

'Baines,' whispered Ernie. 'It's me.'

'Piss off, Marshall.'

'Is that any way to talk to a shipmate as made your dreams come true?'

'Up yours, Marshall. If you think I'm going down for this on me tod, you'd better think again. If it gets me one second less in the brig then you're coming with me.'

'You sorry little shit, Baines. You knew the score. No names, no pack drill.'

'Well, you'd better pack your pack, Marshall you bastard. 'Cause you'll have hard drill every watch for the rest of your service, mate.'

While Ernie was having this conversation with Baines, and Robin and Kate had turned their attention to the twins and their own dunnage, and Jolene had gone to prepare her own possessions and the precious disks for safe, dry transfer, Billy Hoyle thought about what he had said to Ernie earlier: 'She's going to take the major in that box.' He decided to go back down below again.

He wasn't the only one.

Later, when Jolene went down to check on her charge, the coffin lid was screwed down tight and there was no time to loosen it – nor, apparently, any reason to do so.

Kalinin came nosing brightly out of the sleety, freezing murk halfway through the second dogwatch, dead on time. She did not come unannounced. In fact she had been checking in half-hourly through the first three hours and latterly every fifteen minutes. Everything and everyone was ready for her. And that was as well, for the wind was continuing to gather and it was bringing with it rather too much ice for comfort. Hardly a pitching heave passed by *Erebus* without the ringing impact of ice on metal. All the forced cheeriness and Dunkirk spirit was used up now. Those waiting to go and those doomed to stay alike sat silent and exhausted. Apart from the engineers, they had all completed their duties and reached the end of their tether. At the change of the dogwatch at pour-out, which never came, the chief switched on the lights. Those with new bulbs blazed for three minutes then died. The chief contacted the bridge. Estimated completion time was now the end of the first night watch. Immediately afterwards, Palmer came on. The bay was blocked; the way in and out was closed. Each transmission received from *Kalinin*, however, spread a little brightness through the gloom. The earlier ones did, at any rate. The later ones, falling on fatigued ears, only served to drive home the twin facts that those leaving were going out into a fair amount of danger and discomfort on the way, and those who were staying, were staying.

Richard and Colin privately agreed between themselves that they would do as much deck work as they possibly could themselves and keep the number of *Erebus*'s men required outside to a minimum. They, at least, had heat, brightness and dry clothes to look forward to. The men remaining aboard had none of these things. Moved by exactly the same impulse, Robin and Kate planned to oversee the movement of each patient personally across the deck and onto the rescue ship before they themselves went aboard. Jolene agreed that she would be first over, to check the incoming casualties and assure their disposition. Even on a pitching deck, stormbound on the rim of the Antarctic Circle, this was little more complicated than simple secretarial work and easily within her ability, though having never been in anything fiercer than a ten-minute squall on the way out from Rockport to Matagorda Island, she was glad to have discovered she was not prone to seasickness.

For reasons best known to himself, Ernie Marshall went all the way up from the sickbay to the command bridge to assure himself – on the doc's behalf, he said – of the exact arrival time of *Kalinin*. On being brusquely informed that she was at this moment closing to come alongside – something he could have seen clearly for himself had he looked through the portholes on the starboard side – he turned to run back below. He had reached the top of the final companionway when the two hulls crashed together. The impact sent him crashing into the side of the corridor opening at the stairhead. He spun as though shot in the shoulder and pitched headlong down the stairs. Robin had finished preparing the twins down in the sickbay and was about to go on deck with Kate when she saw the tumbling body pitch out of the well at the far end of the corridor. Bouncing off the walls as the hulls ground together again, she ran to him, crouched down and carefully turned him over. A quick examination showed that he was battered but not too badly broken. Kate arrived. 'Add him to the sick list,' gasped Robin. 'Bundle him up and bring him along with the children and all the rest.'

* * *

138

As that first bellowing impact went shuddering through *Erebus*'s hull, Richard ran out of the A-deck door, clipping his safety onto the lines as the great icy hand of the wind tried to slap him into the sea. The converted icebreaker's hull stood a good two metres taller than *Erebus*'s. The effect was claustrophobic, as though a tall white wall was trying to close over on him and crush him. The first team on the forecastle head had caught the foreline and were securing it to the winch there. At the stern, in the relative shelter beneath the reach of the helideck, the second team would be doing the same. Each team leader was wearing a hands-free radio tuned to a waveband agreed between Andrew and Irene Ogre.

No sooner had Richard arrived midships with Colin solidly beside him than the black avalanche of the scaling net crashed down at his feet. Old-fashioned, unhandy and downright dangerous as it might be, the net was still the easiest and quickest way to transfer walking wounded, Karrimats and stretchers, not to mention kids and corpses in coffins. Richard's huge hands closed on the black strands of the net and pulled it back to the nearest securing points. Half a dozen safety lines whipped down and he clipped these in place too so that anyone slipping off the net would be held safely, hopefully well clear of the grinding jaws of the ships' sides. When the safety lines were rigged, Richard yelled into his battery-powered radio, 'Ready! Warn the sickbay.'

Another bundle of cordage slammed down onto the deck and he looked up to see a solid davit reaching out over *Kalinin*'s side like a small white crane. 'For the coffin, Karrimats and dunnage,' he cried to Colin. 'Catch hold of it, would you?' As the massive Scot hurried off to do his bidding, his radio buzzed.

'On their way up from the sickbay,' came Andrew's faint voice. 'And they've got one customer more than planned.'

'OK. *Kalinin*, you hear that?'

'We hear,' came Vasily Varnek's voice in his ear. 'We will prepare.'

Jolene arrived, wrapped up like a kid in her parent's parka. 'Bernie's coming next,' she yelled. Richard nodded to show he understood and took her across to the net, clipping her harness from one safety line to the next and checking it carefully for her. Gamely, she waved, turned and scrambled up the heaving, streaming web of the net.

'Hope none of those guys up there work for the KGB or whatever they call it these days,' growled Colin, his voice carrying even against the brute bellow of the wind.

'I think she's more worried about her own side,' said Richard without thinking. 'Industry. That's where the money is. International inter-corporate stuff. Political espionage is dead and buried.'

'I suppose so,' said Colin.

'I beg your pardon?' asked Andrew distantly. Richard swore silently. He had forgotten his radio was still on.

Bernie Schwartz arrived in his coffin carried by two of Richard's team, Killigan and Washington. Richard sprang into action, helping to run the coffin across to where Colin stood. While the crewmen secured it to the pulley rope, Killigan and Washington staggered across to the netting and secured themselves to the safety lines. Then, as two of the less badly hurt, they waited to help the others up.

Jolene's head and shoulders flashed into view with Varnek just behind her. And, behind them, another figure, framed against *Kalinin*'s lights. There was something unutterably sinister in the scene for an instant.

'Bring him up,' screamed Jolene, her voice only audible via Varnek's VHF.

The coffin began to stir, swinging upwards as though part of some magic trick. Then the first of the walking wounded stumbled out of the A-deck door, preceded by the twins. Richard and Colin both ran back to take the children in hand, and as they did so, the wind took the coffin, making it spin and swing, out of control.

Unaware of this, for it was going on behind his back, Richard made sure the twins were well secured to the safety lines. Then he held them back, looking around for Robin and Kate to accompany them to the net. Robin left the wounded and ran over to him. When the little group reached the foot of the net, Richard clipped the children to their lines and clipped Robin securely between them. Only then did he return to his team.

They really had their work cut out as the stretcher cases came. Colin and Richard had to rush back from the net and prepare to carry the Karrimats over to the foot of the winch. Only when the first lay safely there did Richard turn, just in time to see disaster strike.

The twins were halfway up the net. Robin was between them, with Kate and some of the wounded just behind. Providentially, Killigan and Washington were there too, having followed the women, children and wounded upwards, so that when the two ships suddenly wrenched apart, slamming the net into terrible tautness and throwing everyone upon it up into the air, there were strong hands ready to help.

Richard always felt he loved Mary more than her twin. She was quiet, academic, affectionate. She gave as good as she got but never

140

gave it first. William, on the other hand, was moody, self-absorbed and capable of a spiteful meanness when one of his dark moods was on him. But when his son cartwheeled off the taut net and flew towards the gaping, foaming gulf below, Richard received a salutary re-education. He could not have felt more terrified agony if all three had fallen. Robin instinctively clutched at the flying Mary. Killigan and Washington threw themselves sideways, Washington reaching out to catch William's safety line and pull him feverishly upwards. As he did so, the hulls, having jerked apart, swung down towards each other again, making the net sag dangerously between two closing walls of steel. And the coffin swung over into the narrowing gap as though Major Schwartz hoped he could hold the hulls apart. Instead, the foot of the coffin slammed into the two soldiers, smashing them backwards into the slack netting. Washington, who took the first impact, let go of William's line.

Richard was off. Leant wings by sheer terror, he raced to the net. He did not pause to clip himself on but threw himself over the rail, onto the swinging netting. Up he swarmed, over streaming, ice-slippery strands, over the bodies hanging grimly onto them. Up past Robin he went, past the inverted, bleeding bulk of Killigan. Even Washington was trodden underfoot as Richard caught at William's safety line and heaved with a power that tore his back and shoulder blades. As he strained to pull his son upwards, he looked up, perhaps even heavenwards. And there, heading straight for him like a medieval siege engine, came the major's coffin. In the moment he saw it and realised that it was going to smash him down like Killigan before he could pull William up, he saw something else. A figure leaped easily outward off *Kalinin*'s deck, caught the line like Tarzan himself, and came sliding down the whipping rope to slam onto the coffin with an impact like a bomb. The coffin's movement moderated under the sudden added weight of the man and instead of battering Richard, it swung harmlessly to one side of him as his hands closed around William's vital little body.

'Abseiling.' Shouted T-Shirt exultantly from the top of the major's coffin. 'Wow, what a rush.'

Half an hour later it was all but done. Everyone was safely aboard, though Washington and Killigan were back in the sickbay, both unconscious, and the twins were unusually quiet. Richard and Robin, Colin and Kate stood on *Erebus*'s foredeck, stiff and sore from reaching and stretching, pushing the dead weight of helpless men on heavy

141

stretchers up a steep pitching hill to a swooping plateau from a heaving, rolling base, all the while being strafed by a barrage of chunks of ice under an unceasing Niagara of rain and spray. At last, Andrew's voice came faintly over the W/T: 'That's the lot, Richard. Over you go. Report in from *Kalinin*'s deck and we'll cast off. Farewells from *Kalinin*'s command bridge. OK?'

Richard and Colin pulled themselves back onto the net after Robin and Kate, hooked themselves on and scrambled up for the last time. As Richard heaved himself over the safety rail onto *Kalinin*'s main deck, he was for an instant dazzled by the brightness all around him. He turned and looked down to *Erebus* where his team was already unhitching the scrambling nets. He looked around at the blaze of deck lights, impressed both by the smart lines of the ship and by the smart movement of her deck crew retrieving their nets and safety lines. He clipped himself to *Kalinin*'s lines, though it hardly seemed necessary to do so, the big ship was so solid and steady it seemed that the very storm itself had moderated, awed by her size, the height of her gleaming bridgehouse, the power of the huge, ice-crusher's motor throbbing beneath his feet.

'All aboard, Andrew,' he called. 'And safe and sound. At last.'

Andrew's reply was so faint that the clap of Varnek's hand on his strained and burning shoulder and the hiss of his gesture towards the bridgehouse drowned it out.

Richard strode over to the side and looked down into the dark, departing pit of *Erebus*'s well. He tore off the radio, gathered its leads and batteries together, heaved it over and down to his team. A glimmer of movement as the falling kit was caught. Distant wave of thanks and farewell. Then *Erebus* rapidly fell away upwind as *Kalinin* turned.

Varnek's hand patted his shoulder again and Richard followed him to the blaze of the bridge. He stepped, dazed and dripping, into warmth and quiet. Halfway between a hospital and a hotel, the bridgehouse closed around him. One of Varnek's men took his wet gear and Varnek himself led him without delay into the lift and up.

Up and up the smart lift sighed until it hissed to a stop and the doors whispered open. Richard stepped out into the pristine perfection of the prettiest and best-fitted command bridge he had ever seen. It was quite simply palatial, as though the passengers were expected to disport themselves expensively up here as well. Irene Ogre turned, a commander in perfect accord with her command.

'Welcome, Captain Mariner,' she said. 'You wish to report to Captain Pitcairn, I think. Then you will look to the disposition of your people, no? Varnek here will help you.'

'Thank you,' said Richard simply. He crossed to the radio room following Varnek's gesture, and took the handset the radio officer offered him. It was like a walkabout phone. There was no line, just an aerial connecting it to the main radio. 'Andrew?' he said, walking automatically to the bridge wing.

'Hello, Richard. Glad you made it all right. We're off to Faraday as planned. Should be there in thirty-six hours. I'll be back in contact the instant we have power. Keep it short in the meantime to preserve the battery. *Erebus* out.'

'I hear and obey. Good luck. Mariner out.' He gave up searching the streaming murk for any sign of her. There was none. It was as though in the moments it had taken to walk to the lift and ride up here, the BAS ship had simply vanished off the face of the earth, sucked to who knew what sub-Antarctic doom. But he knew she was out there, working her way intrepidly up to full power and safe haven.

Irene Ogre caught his eye and smiled. She believed in Andrew and his crew as well, Richard realised.

Chapter Fifteen

'Two thousand pounds a week,' Robin said. 'Two thousand pounds a week *each*. Half for each twin. Damn near a grand a day for all of us. That's what this lot ought to be costing. Drinks, excursions, equipment, room service, other facilities all extra.' She dropped the brochures, booklets and room-service menus on the table.

'At first glance,' answered Richard, 'I'd say it was worth it.'

They were in a stateroom, by no means *Kalinin*'s most expensive. A double bed snuggled comfortably beneath a white satin-covered swan's-down duvet, at its foot, a good few white-carpeted metres distant, there was a wardrobe, drawer and vanity table unit, all, like the other fittings here, pristine white. Such was the width of the room that inboard, on Richard's left as he looked, there was room for a sofa to fold out into a second double bed, also reclining warmly beneath a swan's-down duvet. On the opposite side of the room a desk sat comfortably beneath a brass-rimmed porthole, and the sleet-shafted dirty gloom this revealed was the only thing about the room not gleamingly perfect.

'I don't think the twins should even be allowed to walk on this carpet,' said Robin half jokingly.

'They certainly should not be allowed anywhere near this lot.' Beside the desk stood a bar fridge topped by a little table holding equipment for making coffee and tea.

'And look.' Robin opened a door on the inner side of the bedhead to reveal a neat, bright, gleamingly white shower room and toilet.

Richard sat on the bed, a little overwhelmed. It was not that he wasn't used to such luxury, even aboard ship, but after the restrictions of Armstrong and the privations of *Erebus*, the contrast was a little disorientating.

'The smooth young steward who showed me around said there would be a hot meal in the main dining salon on Bellingshausen-Peary Deck at twenty-two hundred hours. Or we can order up from room service whatever we like, at no charge, for tonight alone.'

'Bellingshausen-Peary Deck?'

'The three passenger decks other than Main Deck are named after famous Antarctic explorers.'

'So we're on what, Hempleman-Adams Deck? Ranulph Fiennes Deck? Scott-Shackleton Deck?'

'No, dear. This is Palmer-Hall Deck. Byrd-Ellsworth is below us, then Bellingshausen-Peary, then Main.'

'Give me strength. I suppose Main is also known as Wilkes Deck. That more or less covers it for major American explorers. But wait a moment. Why Bellingshausen? This is an American ship.'

'Co-owned by Russians.'

'As if we could ever overlook that with Irene Ogre aboard.' Richard let the quiet wash over him like a warm bath. 'Where are the twins?'

'Gone off with the steward to explore.'

'Was that wise?'

'Not wise. Unstoppable. You want to make something of it?'

'No. I'm too tired. We'll fight later. What d'you want to do in the meantime?'

'Eat and sleep. Not necessarily in that order.'

'What about our charges? I'm in command of this lot, by the way; Irene says.'

'Kate and I, good as gold, went down to tuck them in. But Dr Glazov did not require any help and saw us off in no uncertain terms. Terrifying. Makes Irene Ogre look like Winnie the Pooh.'

'Really? He must be quite something.'

'*She* certainly is. Kate heard somewhere that the passengers call her Dr Fuckov. I've seen her bedside manner. I am not surprised.'

'So, as is not unusual among captains at sea, we have all the responsibility but nothing whatever to do.'

'That would seem to be about the size of it.'

He pulled himself to his feet. Made light-headed and a little silly by the narrow escape they had all had, he put on his best Charles Boyer accent. 'Komm vis me to ze . . . not the kasbah. . . What was it? Ze Bellingshausen-Peary Deck.'

'OK,' she said indulgently. 'I've always been a sucker for a sailor with a silly accent.'

The passengers' dining salon looked to Richard only slightly less sumptuous than *Titanic*'s had been. In spite of the fact that dinner had already been served to the paying passengers, who were currently, apparently, dividing their attention between the latest Bruce Willis blockbuster – the American print not due out in England until next

146

spring – and a lecture on base jumping, the galley staff and stewards had prepared food and ambience to five-star standard as though for the first time this evening. Richard was not alone in having his breath taken away. Typically down-to-earth, however, Colin leaned across as his friend sat down beside him. 'Keep all your credit cards and cash locked up tight,' he growled in the chilly accents of a Morningside accountant. 'Especially after tonight when the freebies stop.'

'Is there going to be a personal account for each of us?' asked Kate, a little concerned. 'Or will there be one big bill at the end?'

'That's a worry for me,' said Jolene quietly from the far side of the table. 'I'm on a very limited expenses budget here. I'll have to account for every penny and they can be tough at head office. One of our guys liaising with the European space people in the depths of French Guiana got a hell of a rocket for drinking Perrier water when the local supply went bad. He should have just got dysentery cheaply and quietly, they thought.'

'I'll find out in the morning before anyone has a chance to get in too deep,' promised Richard. 'In the meantime, let's sit back and enjoy this evening while it's free.'

A slim young man appeared at their table, rose excitedly on his gleaming toes and said gently in the French accent of a Brooklyn-born trainee restaurateur, 'Good evening, mesdames and messieurs, I am Francis, your waiter. May I say what a pleasure it is to welcome you aboard. In a moment the sommelier will bring your bottle of champagne, with the captain's compliments. In the meantime, are you ready to order? Tonight, Chef has prepared the following starters: pâté de fois flavoured with Amaretto served on a bed of rocket, a hot green salad of young quails, and lightly poached Pacific prawns with dill mayonnaise . . .'

Francis's mellifluous flow was interrupted by the arrival of the twins dragging an exhausted but grimly courteous steward. A close brush with death had gone apparently unnoticed by the pair of them, except that they were even more full of life and mischief than ever. But the waiter quickly established that the charming English children wished to sit between their doting parents and wanted hamburgers and French fries. Then he returned to the serious adult business, quite unruffled, while his lesser colleague staggered off to rest and recuperate.

In spite of the sumptuousness of the meal, what they ate was light and well balanced, and soon fatigue began to overtake them. Even the twins made little more than token complaint when Richard and Robin took them off to the stateroom on Palmer-Hall Deck. The little kit they had brought with them had been unpacked in their absence and stowed away. There was nothing for them to do but to get undressed and tumble into bed. Richard and Robin quietly prepared for sleep as well, but when they tucked down in the perfectly sprung supportive firmness of their bed, Richard for one found sleep elusive. Their all too intimate brush with death, Colin's warnings and Jolene's worries kept jumbling around in his head, so that, after half an hour or so, he climbed out of bed, pulled jeans and sweater over his pyjamas and pushed his feet into an old pair of trainers big enough to serve as lifeboats. He looked back from the doorway but none of the rest of his little family stirred. He slipped out like a shadow, closed the door soundlessly and went for a prowl through the silent ship. The instant the door closed, Robin sat up and looked around the dimly-lit room. At least the children were innocently and absolutely asleep.

Jolene was standing in her white panties regretting the disappearance of her fine cotton nightie. It was the only one really suited to the comfort of her single cabin on Bellingshausen-Peary Deck. The heavy, almost full-length alternative was too dowdy and far too warm. She had just decided to tuck down as she was when the lightest of scratches came at her door. She pressed herself against it, finger on the lock. 'Yes?'

'It's T-Shirt, Mrs DaCosta. Can we talk?'

Had he come to her last night, the answer would have been no. But what he had done this afternoon, though cloaked in a laid-back, self-mocking assumption of cool, had impressed her. T-Shirt Maddrell was not simply a foolish and self-indulgent pleasure-seeker. He was capable of cool thought, calculated action and a great deal of bravery. He really rather deserved his place in her hotter dreams. 'Yes . . .'

'No, I mean face to face. Can I come in?'

'No!'

He misunderstood the reason for her sharp rebuff. 'Hokay. We can meet on neutral territory. I just want to talk about tomorrow.'

'No, it's all right, you can come in. Just give me a minute, would you?'

'OK.'

Jolene stepped back into her jeans. They were still warm. She buttoned, then zipped them, and reached into a half-open drawer for a clean white T-shirt. It was not warm and as she slipped the cool cotton over her torso she felt her nipples tense. But that might not only have been because the cotton was so cool. She reached across, flicked the lock and stepped back.

T-Shirt stood there, all blond curls, sparkling eyes and mauve bandanna, with Max behind him. Both were dressed almost exactly the same as she was herself. She stepped back and T-Shirt entered with a broad grin.

'See you, Max,' he said.

'See you, bro,' said the ever cheerful Max and vanished.

The cabin was not large but was well furnished and comfortable. An upper and lower berth filled one wall. At the bedhead end, a vanity table and drawers crossed to a narrow wardrobe. The top of the vanity table turned over into a washbasin. At the foot of the bed was a little table, chair, tiny bar fridge, door into the shower room and toilet. T-Shirt swung the chair out and sat. Jolene took the lower bunk.

'Nice,' said T-Shirt looking around. 'Like the one Max and I are sharing up on Byrd-Ellsworth.'

Jolene looked at him, wondering what to say. It had been a long time since she had done anything like this. And her lack of current social practice was complicated by the fact that she still hadn't finished with him professionally. After shaking his frozen hand, T-Shirt had helped pull Major Schwartz free of the snow. With Richard and Colin, he was the last one to see that area in any detail before the man with the Skiddoo set fire to it.

Suddenly aware of the silence, Jolene snapped back to full attention. T-Shirt was sitting quite contentedly looking at her breasts, displayed to some advantage by her slightly round-shouldered posture under the upper bunk, clad only in fine cotton tight enough to flatter.

'You must be well used to seeing white slopes by now,' she said tartly.

He gave a bark of laughter. Raised his eyes and met her gaze. 'I'll never see enough of white slopes,' he said.

'So you just popped in to sneak a look at the view?' she enquired, a little too blandly.

'No. No, actually I came to ask if you'd ever done any jumping. Base or bungee.'

'What?'

'Word is the weather'll moderate overnight. Some of the guys're going off the top of this cliff tomorrow. Black rock pinnacle higher than Angel Falls. It's what they came for. Base jumpers jump with a parachute and try to ride down without becoming strawberry jam. You know what bungee jumpers do. There's this old Welsh guy, looks

149

like Sean Connery, sixty something, he's a Base jumper, up for it with half a dozen others. Max. Me. Thought you might want to see, that's all.'

'Base jumping,' she said. 'Tell me more about it.'

'Base is an acronym,' he said. 'It stands for building, aerial, span, earth. The four things a Base jumper is supposed to jump off. With a parachute, of course. Most of us have done the usual jumps. But there's the chance of something pretty special down here. And I wondered if you wanted to be a part of it? It's a once in a lifetime—'

'See,' she said firmly. 'Not do.'

'Well, you couldn't Base jump. That's heavy. You need to be right up to speed for that or you'll just be a little red streak on the big black rock. Most of us have spent months getting in practice and the last few days getting prepared for this particular jump. And the last few nights undoing the good work, I guess. But we could scare up a bungee for you if you're keen. I'm up for that myself after the Base jump if there's a good solid anchor. Bit of an anticlimax, though; but I'd do it to keep you company.'

'Big of you. Thanks,' snapped Jolene. Then she said 'Thanks' again, very much more warmly. There was a companionable little silence then she continued, 'Is that all you're down here to do? Try to kill yourselves?'

'That's about the size of it. Adrenaline junkies, the lot of us. We should each have a warning from the surgeon general tattooed across our foreheads.'

'You all came down here together?'

'All fifty of us? I think not. No, most of the guys are like me, made it on our own from all over. Literally. All over the globe. From Carmarthon to Chatanooga, near as dammit. Carmarthon's in Wales, next to England. That's where the old guy's from. Expert Base jumper. Dai. What a name for a guy in his business, I tell you! Dai Gwyllim. We christened him Dai the Death. I think it amuses him. He doesn't care what we say all that much. He knows none of us'll live to be anywhere near his age. He's the only one with a partner – his wife Jilly. Thirty years younger than him, from Adelaide, Australia. They met on the Internet. What can you do with them, eh, the older generation? But most of the rest of us, guys and girls, are single, carefree, out for a good time. Use it up before it just wears out, sort of thing. But ordinary working folk. Saved up, worked extra, night shifts whatever, here to do or die.'

'What about you, T-Shirt? What do you do?'

150

'Bum about. Labouring. Stevedore. Shelf filling. Pump attendant. Security guard. You wouldn't believe the collection of union cards I got. Spent the last couple of years, off and on, re-programming company computers to make them year two thousand resistant. But apart from what I need to live I wire everything into this big bank account I got at the First National Bank in Lordsburg, New Mexico.'

'Lordsburg. You from around there?'

'Nope. Never been there. Just liked the sound of it so I keep my money there. Kept. There won't be any much left after this little experience.'

Jolene, sensible, conservative, inward-looking, careful, shook her head in stunned disbelief. 'Well then, tell me,' she said, striving to come to terms with his bohemian lifestyle, 'what brought you down here to the Big White?'

'*National Geographic Magazine*,' he said without hesitation. 'Volume one ninety-three, number two, February nineteen ninety-eight. Saw it in a doctor's surgery in downtown New York. Got it in my cabin now if you want to see it. I was working for an accountancy firm, getting their computers ready for the twenty-first century. I'd saved up to go whitewater rafting in the Klondyke and I needed to get some shots for the insurance but I saw this article about these guys Lowe and Anker climbing these fantastic rocks in Queen Maude Land. Cancelled Klondyke at once. Been saving up ever since. I'd hoped to do a Base off this face these two guys were climbing – pinnacle spire more than twice the height of the World Trade Centre. But this was the closest I could get. But Dai the Death says this spire we go off tomorrow is pretty epic.'

'You look fairly normal,' said Jolene, 'but you're totally certifiable, you know that?'

T-Shirt grinned. 'Come on, Mrs DaCosta,' he challenged. 'Live a little.'

'I've got a job to do. Responsibilities to meet,' she declared severely, drawing herself up haughtily. She promptly hit the back of her head on the bunk above and slumped forward, seeing bright lights. He laughed and refocused on her bosom with frank appreciation.

'Think it over,' he said. 'There'll be time enough to tell me in the morning. I'll give you a knock, first thing.' He pulled himself to his feet still grinning widely.

She rose and opened the door and he was gone, leaving her frowning slightly. She locked up, stripped off, washed and tucked down, her last waking thought being, 'he's too good to be true . . .'

151

'Hi there, T-Shirt,' said Richard as they bumped into each other on the companionway at Byrd-Ellsworth level five minutes later. 'Mind if I thank you again for saving my family and me, then pump you for some information?'

'Sure. I mean you can ask what you want. That's cool. As to what I did this afternoon, don't give it another thought.'

'Where's the best place to talk?'

T-Shirt shrugged amenably. 'Library and video lounge back here.'

'Lead on.'

T-Shirt switched on the light as the pair of them entered. It was a comfortable room, well furnished with tables and chairs. Bookcases stood along two walls. A big wide-screen digital TV sat on a specially designed trolley at one end with the tables pulled back and the chairs facing it. Its wide screen was full of no-signal snow. It emitted a quiet hiss. Immediately below it, on the lower shelf, sat a state-of-the-art video player. Opposite this, on the fourth wall behind the door, stood a computer, its screen lazily questing through the universe, its screen-saver configured like the bridge of the Starship *Enterprise*. As the two men entered, the tape in the TV system ran out and began to rewind automatically. The picture switched to television on the open video channel, abruptly and graphically showing an attractive, well-oiled couple making love. Unfazed, T-Shirt crossed to the machine and switched it off. 'Kids after a good time,' he said indulgently. 'What'cha gonna do with them?'

'Who?' asked Richard.

'My fellow travellers. Most of them. You want to know about them, ask Jolene DaCosta. I filled her in earlier.' T-Shirt looked up, eyes crinkling with intelligent insight. 'But you don't want to know about them, do you? Not yet, at any rate.'

'You're right. I want to know about the ship and her complement first. I may have to start some serious discussions with Captain Ogre tomorrow. We'll need to go through the full detail of our position aboard here and the Captain's plans for us – and I may want an edge.'

'An ace in the hole. Yes, I can see that.'

'Any background would do. This ship is a little beyond even my experience.'

'You can look round the ship itself any time. Ask for the guided tour. It's free. But I think maybe you want some gloves-off, no-holds-barred actionable slander about the Captain and her jolly seadogs, right?'

'If that's what you've got on offer, I'm in the market, yes.'

'You read *Treasure Island*? Of course you have. Well, it's not like that. Not quite. No one-legged Seafaring men called Silver, Pew or Hands. But then again I don't think the people on the bridge are as much in control as they seem to be either. Captain Ogre gives the orders, but the men jump to it quicker when Varnek's about. Though to be fair, where she is, he is also, for the most part, as you've no doubt noticed. If this was an old-fashioned Russian cruise ship I'd think he was the political officer, the KGB man, you know?'

'I've read about it in books.'

'Really? Me too. But the old ways are dead now and the KGB's been wound up. So who does Varnek work for?'

'Anyone aboard?'

'I think not. There are others aboard of equivalent power, perhaps, but it's difficult to put your finger on. Wheels within wheels.'

'I'm not sure I follow you.'

'I mumble a little. Let me see if I can be clearer. I had this job one time in this New York law firm. No big deal. Getting their computer system ready for the millennium. But I got a feel for the place. It was the subject of a couple of hostile takeover bids, you know? Bigger sharks looking to snap it up. It meant there were three structures in the place. The old guy who set it up and the people working for him. The people who were already sold out in their minds to shark A and were effectively working for him. And the people who had more or less done the same to shark B. It was all really quiet and intense and the old guy never knew. Never seemed to know, at any rate. But all of a sudden shark A made him move. Old guy and his people out. Shark B people out.'

'And you?'

'Shark A had in-house programmers.'

'So. Captain Ogre is trying to run the ship all legal and above board and most of the crew work on her orders straight down the line. But you think behind her back Vasily Varnek is maybe working for someone else. A bigger organisation. Shark A. The Russian owners maybe?'

'If it's just the owners, why isn't the captain answerable? Why do they need to spy on her?'

'It's been known. Who's your other double agent? Who's really working for shark B?'

'I can't be absolutely certain, but I'd say our entertainments officer.'

'Mrs Agran?'

'Mrs Agran,' agreed T-Shirt. 'To whom there is more than meets the eye.'

'What do you mean?'

'For a start, her nickname is more than just wordplay on her name. So I have been told.'

'Her nickname? What is it?'

'Viagra. It is said that there is nothing she can't get up, if you follow my drift. And if she can't do it personally, then she's bound to know a boy or girl who can.'

'Vice? You think she runs a vice ring aboard?'

'Maybe putting it a bit strong. Maybe she just takes her entertainments duties a bit too seriously. This ship is full of young passionate pleasure-seekers with more than their fair share of death wishes, after all. But then again . . .'

'Viagra. Well, I'll be damned.'

'I'll be damned too. We'll make it a race, shall we? But you got to allow me time to catch up.'

'That's your way of saying "end of conference and no more embarrassing thank yous", is it? But you've given me enough to start with.'

The two men left the library, each bound for a different level of the bridgehouse. A few moments later, a little doorway hidden by the bookcases opened to reveal a well-stocked audio and video library. Out of this sneaked Ernie Marshall and Billy Hoyle. The battered would-be vice merchants stood looking down the empty corridor.

'You understand any of that crap about sharks?' asked Ernie, scratching his gauze-bound cranium.

'Not one word,' said Billy. 'It was worth creeping out and risking the wrath of Dr Fuckov, though, just to get the lowdown on that other stuff. We have a contact, and maybe a market for our wares, my man. It's time we pooled our resources for the greater good. Fair do's all round. Let's run along back to bed tonight and tomorrow we'll see what this lady called Viagra can get up for us.'

Chapter Sixteen

When the sun began its upward swoop from well above the fogbound western horizon to signal the beginning of Thursday, 30 December, it soon lifted clear of the low-lying white and soared into a sky of unbroken blue. The wind had fallen with the departure of the last tails of the Southern Ocean depression during the morning watch and those on *Kalinin* astir for early breakfast at 08.00, the start of the forenoon watch, found the good ship cruising through an apparently tropical day. As the sun pulled itself up into the royal blue reaches of the morning sky, it threw long golden spears magically defined by the topmost wisps of the distant, settling fog, to glitter and glance off the mountainous section of coastline up which they were sailing. As though the vessel had been transported to the fjords of Norway overnight, sheer rock battlements soared on either side, only the white lines of their ice-crested tops distinguishing their blue-black basalt faces from the indigo zenith of the heavens.

A low moon hung in the north, dead ahead, tangled in the last late glimmers of the Southern Cross. Below it, as though playing lazily in its pearly track, a pod of right whales broke the surface of the placid ocean and added their breath to the drifting haze.

Right from the start there was a magic in the air, which, real or imagined, swept them all into its spell as the hours ticked by. It was a special day; a calm between the storms in almost every possible way.

Richard woke first, coming up out of a deep, refreshing sleep to sit up, glance around and step instantly out of bed. He moved so silently beneath the steady throbbing of *Kalinin*'s motor that Robin and the twins did not stir. He crossed to the porthole, lifted a corner of heavy curtain, looked out and whistled quietly to himself. In an instant he had pulled the curtains back and let the full power of the glorious morning in. 'Come on, sleepyheads,' he called to the twins. 'It looks like a terrific morning out there.' No reaction whatsoever.

Robin stirred. 'Too bright,' she mumbled, and he laughed. Leaving the curtain wide to awaken his sleepy family in their own good time, he slipped into the bathroom, showered and shaved. As he pulled his

155

razor over the square jut of his chin, he planned the first part of his day. He had to talk to Captain Ogre. For a start, where was she proposing to take them? *Kalinin* had accepted them aboard in an emergency. Did Captain Ogre intend to depart from her schedule and drop them somewhere whence they could be sent to their various homes? Or would they have to wait, fitting in with the ship's routine, until a moment convenient to her passengers and crew? From what Robin had said, the fifty or so passengers had collectively paid the better part of half a million dollars to be here. How much would they have to pay? And when? The insurers would have a field day with this.

Then there were the sick and wounded. They needed checking, in spite of the fearsome Dr Fuckov. They needed talking to, checking with. Their families might need contacting. Their superiors, at Armstrong, aboard *Erebus*, needed checking with. Andrew Pitcairn ought to be contacted in any case to see if he had his power back. Jolene needed to find her place in this. It was just possible, he supposed, that the FBI team had got through the weather yesterday to set up their investigation at Armstrong but it was far more likely they had been delayed and would be arriving there today. Even if they thought very quickly indeed and tried to extend the scope of their inquiry to fit in with Jolene's, there was little chance of them getting aboard here before the weather closed down again. And that meant that Jolene would be pushing her inquiry forward alone as the people she needed to talk to recovered. But her legal position aboard was so questionable, unless Irene Ogre was willing to back her. And, from his conversation with T-Shirt last night, even if Irene was willing to back her, God alone knew what cans of worms she might open if she went ferreting around aboard *Kalinin*.

Then there was the time. Not just the time of the year, though that was bad enough in terms of getting decisions made and things done, but the time of the decade, the century, the millennium. If they didn't get sorted out today, then they were stuck aboard for the foreseeable future. Nobody much would be working tomorrow, New Year's Eve, and Saturday and Sunday were write-offs for all but the most important of emergency services.

The weather was another worry, he thought as he rinsed off the shaving foam. He was not fooled by the smiling tiger outside. He had seen the weather system which killed Major Schwartz, how it had grown, where it was headed. He suspected that half the people aboard *Kalinin* tomorrow would be preparing for the party of the year. The rest would be preparing for the storm of the century.

He was reaching for a fluffy white towel on the convenient, warmed towel rail when Robin slopped round the door, barefoot in a massive old T-shirt with Nelson on the front, which she was using as a nightie. 'You look thoughtful,' she yawned. 'Worried about something?'

Richard gave her his widest grin. 'Now what could there possibly be to worry about on a beautiful day like this?'

Irene Ogre sat behind her desk wearing a frown which Richard recognised from his own shaving mirror. Without her uniform jacket and gold braid, her hair seemed to gleam more brightly, though that might have been the sunlight falling across it. She wore a plain white short-sleeved shirt, open at the collar, perfectly starched and laundered. No jewellery, rings or badges of rank. Her watch was simple, its digital face clear and functional. She looked at it as she held the phone to her ear. Richard could read it also as he listened to the faint ringing tone. It was 09.00 here, 11.00 in St Petersburg, Russia, 07.00 in St Petersburg, USA. Irene told him she was calling her Russian head office, though she warned him that final rulings would have to wait a couple of hours until someone senior arrived at the office in Florida.

The ringing stopped, a deep voice answered. Irene launched into a flood of Russian. Richard crossed to the porthole and looked out. The captain's office overlooked the foredeck and here there was a gathering bustle of activity as the passengers gathered in preparation for today's expedition. Some would be going ashore in Zodiacs, walking, climbing, exploring. Others would be going ashore in the helicopter tethered on the helipad aft. Richard hadn't talked to Jolene and T-Shirt yet today, hadn't talked to anyone except Robin. Hadn't even had breakfast yet, so he knew nothing of the Base and bungee jumping plans. He saw T-Shirt's blond shock and Max's black head beside him at the heart of the excited crowd. They seemed to be talking to a tall older man with a moustache and long grey hair pulled tight back into a pony tail.

Richard turned round again and his position by the porthole gave him a clear sight of the captain's work desk and, upon it, a computer screen. From the back the computer had looked little more than a word-processor. But it was obviously very much more than that. The screen was divided into ten sections in graphic overlay. There were four square sections, one in each corner, and a fifth section in the centre; the four corner sections were split in two by lines running out from the corners of the central area to the corners of the screen itself.

157

The central square was also divided in two, but from top to bottom. The effect was oddly like the British Union Jack flag. Within each section there were ranks of icons. The configuration did not look unduly complex or cluttered – quite the reverse, in fact – but the writing was Cyrillic and therefore impenetrable to him. One of the icons on the central screen was lit up and flashing, and when the connection with St Petersburg was broken, its brightness and activity also died.

'Well?' he asked as she hung up.

'No decision. Their first thought is to make no charge as long as you take no part in expensive activities or indulgences and as long as we do not have to deviate from our course. The next port of call is Ushuaia, the southernmost port on South America. We're due there next Monday the third.'

Richard smiled. 'That's more or less back on our itinerary. We're due to fly from there to Buenos Aires on the fourth.'

'Lucky for you,' she said slowly.

'Less so for the others, I should imagine. And you've still got the problem of Dr DaCosta and her investigation. That won't wait.'

'I knew all about that when I invited you aboard. We're in it also, remember.'

'But she called in the FBI. There will be no FBI here, will there?'

'No.'

'Unless something happens to her, of course. Under the circumstances, if anything happened to Dr DaCosta, you and your head offices would be up to your armpits in FBI.'

'True, unless any accident was explained and proven and anything else which happened was solved so that the investigation was fully completed on her behalf.'

'Not very likely, I'd have thought. She is probably the only person able to close her own investigation to the satisfaction of the authorities. Her or her colleagues from the FBI.'

'I take your point,' said Captain Ogre. A little silence followed.

The icon next to the one which had been flashing during the phone call started to blink. Irene did something Richard could not see and her phone buzzed. 'Incoming radio transmission,' she said. 'I'll have it put through here.'

The silence lengthened as a distant buzzing passed from the handset into the captain's ear. 'Right,' she said after a few moments, switched into Russian, gave a series of orders and hung up. 'That was *Erebus*,' she said. 'Good news. They have restored partial power and are

158

heading for Faraday. They should make it by the time the good weather breaks tonight or tomorrow.'

'Partial power?'

'Not much in the way of lighting by the sound of things. Enough for emergency heating and propulsion. With their damaged propeller, they are making five knots and have steerageway. We do not need to worry any more, I think. I have asked that the others in your group be informed at once.'

'In the meantime,' said Richard, 'we have to wait for Florida to wake up before we can get any further.' And, he added mentally, we don't have to start worrying about Varnek and Agran till then.

'That is so. But there is no need for us to waste that time.'

'I don't intend to. I want to check on my people in the sickbay.'

'I think not, if you don't mind. Dr Glazov has a strict morning routine. No one is allowed into her domain before eleven. No. I would like, if I may, to show you my command.'

'I know Robin and the twins—'

'Captain, Mrs Mariner and your charming children will be offered the package tour. As will the Rosses. I wish to show you round myself. Alone.'

'I see,' he said amenably, although he didn't really. Was this some sort of professional gesture? Some sort of personal gesture? Desire to show off? Cry for help? After his conversation with T-Shirt, he reckoned it could be just about anything.

'I saw you looking at the monitor while I was on the phone,' she said quietly. 'It is a good place to start. Here, let me show you.' She pressed a button on the keyboard and an invisible line seemed to move down the screen, magically transforming everything from impenetrable Cyrillic to plain English. As the transformation happened, Irene continued speaking quietly. 'Every system aboard is computer-controlled and every control system computer-monitored. All the information from these monitors feeds back centrally and is displayed here, and at several other monitors in areas useful to myself, the senior navigating officer, the chief and the entertainment officer.'

'Why her?'

'She is also personnel officer, and in overall charge of several important sections. There, the screen is clear. Now you can see.'

Richard leaned forward. Irene's fingers were long but businesslike. Her nails square-cut, unvarnished and strong-looking. The index finger of her right hand began at the midday position and traced the eight outer sections of the screen, clockwise. 'This section is the propulsion

159

monitor. Each icon is to do with the engines, alternators, ancillary equipment. Next we have lading. This includes stores, fuel, the helicopter and so forth. Next we have accommodation. Accommodation of the passengers of course, but also of the crew, the entertainment staff and so forth. Next, we have the galley records. These include the records of food orders at every level from what you want for dinner tonight to what Chef will want in the way of foie gras next time we are supplied. Next, the entertainment monitor. What we have planned, minute by minute, every day and night of the trip. Which passenger is down for what, which member of the crew or staff is involved with them. Who has responsibility. The next section is records. Surprisingly important. Everything we need to know about every member of the crew, the staff and the passengers, including detailed medical records. Confidential, of course. There are more security cut-outs in this section than in any other. Next, environment. Again, this is important. As you no doubt discovered when power went down on *Erebus*, environmental monitoring is hugely important here, even at this time of year. The ambient temperatures of every area of the ship are monitored and adjusted according to requirement, from the coldest freezer to the hottest sauna. All the crew sections, all the passenger sections, every public area, each private cabin. From the largest space-heaters right down to the individual radiators in each cabin. Finally, on the outer ring, weather. Present, predicted. State of sky and sea, including detailed ice-watch westward and adventure-watch eastward.'

'Adventure-watch?'

'Like the little excursion they are setting up for now. This needs planning. Planning takes time and requires accurate weather predictions. We knew before we picked you up that the weather would moderate to a clear calm today. Marry that up with position and navigation info and there you have it. Jumping.'

'Jumping?'

Irene explained. Richard tried to keep his eyebrows below his hairline.

'Are they mad?' he asked.

'Utterly,' Irene answered. 'And the madness is contagious, I believe. Dr DaCosta may be joining them.'

'Well, I'll be damned.'

'For me these two central areas are the most important. That is why I have my screen configured like this. They are communications and navigation. Navigation speaks for itself. Course, heading, speed

– engine revolutions, propeller pitch, hazards, neighbours – what do you say, animal, vegetable, mineral. Anything, living, dead, mechanical. Anything that might do us damage or that we in turn might damage. And then communications. We have many levels, as you might expect. We communicate with satellites for a range of purposes. Navigation, GPS, weather, ice-watch. It all comes in here. Satellite TV stations, logged and monitored. They have it tuned to South Atlantic Adult at the moment. They are like children with their dirty movies. We have satellite dish for telephone links such as the one I have just used. You saw the icon flashing. We have Internet access. Again, monitored. We have a services supplier contract and try to keep to that, though some individual systems are so powerful now they can give personal access even down here. And of course we have state-of-the-art radio equipment And this monitors band, wavelength, contact ID.'

'Everything aboard,' said Richard, shaking his head. 'That's pretty amazing, Irene.'

'There is more. Look.' She rolled her fingers over a little ball set on the right of the keyboard, touched an icon with the cursor that scuttled across the screen at her command. A name and location jumped into clarity. 'Mrs Agran is in charge of that section, accommodation,' she said. 'This tells me where she is. If I click again I will contact her. Every section has a crew member directly responsible for it. They are in overall charge of the individual computer systems that monitor their sections in more detail and are generally responsible for the relevant programming, maintenance and oversight. But this is all just a static display. To show you the systems in action and interaction we must go up onto the bridge. Follow me, please.'

'So,' said Irene ten minutes later, 'we are here and we wish to go there.'

'Here' was a point on her big Antarctic chart spread beneath the Perspex sheet on her chart table, a bright point on the satellite read-out Global Positioning System video screen and a gesture out past the bright bridge wing to the actual sea. 'There' was another point on the chart, a point already fed into the Differential Shipmaster automatic guidance system, and a distant loom of towering black cliff gleaming on the horizon on the starboard quadrant of the glittering clearview.

'To achieve this, what do I do? Do I get my lookouts to observe the state of sea and sky? Do I ask my man on the forepeak to assess the draft with shot and line? Do I double-check our position with my trusty sextant? Of course not.'

161

'Do you possess a sextant?'

'Yes. And I can use it. But I do none of these things. I do not even ask my officers to check in the collision alarm radar. I do not ring down and discuss with the chief the state of weather, water, power of currents, revolutions or propeller pitch. All I do is this.' Irene pressed a button below the Differential Shipmaster.

'Now my computer is using my navigation slave systems to make all the checks for me. It is communicating with the chief's computer, which is using all the engine room slave systems to deliver optimum performance, and it is delivering us to the desired point safely and swiftly. As it does so it makes constant checks and minor adjustments so as to be able to react to any emergency.

'But of course that is only part of the story. Our objective in getting to "there" is to deliver a set of people onto the shore ready, willing and able to have fun. So, as navigation and engineering talk to each other in the mainframe, so our other systems are checking who wishes to do what, and ensuring someone on Mrs Agran's staff has talked to them. The galley computer is asking the navigating computer for an ETA. Then it will inform Chef about who wants what sort of lunch. It will already have checked with the records computer, so it can remind Chef's staff about dietary requirements. Now it will check ahead for weather and navigation in order to start preparing lists for tonight's meal when they all come back. To get the weather accurate, it will not only check with our weather computer but automatically use the communications computer's digital memory to update itself with reports from local weather stations.'

'It is amazing, Irene. To have everything linked to such a degree, with so much intercommunication is incredible.'

'Ha!' she said. 'You think this is incredible, you wait.'

Chapter Seventeen

By 11.00 Richard's exclusive tour of *Kalinin* had come full circle back to Irene's workroom. In the corridor outside, Vivien Agran was waiting to speak to him, so while Irene was on the phone to her American head office he answered quite a searching set of questions about personal and medical background, status of visas and vaccinations, dietary preferences.

Richard's responses were tapped straight into a hand-held notebook computer, and a little red flashing light in its top right-hand corner allowed him to guess, from his tour with Irene, that the information was being transferred automatically into the mainframe. Idly, he glanced up to try and work out what the red dot was communicating with and saw a little box like a motion detector for a burglar alarm, also with red dot flashing; noticed, with a little prickle at the back of his neck, a small glass panel at the lower end of the box. A camera? As Mrs Agran courteously declared herself satisfied with his information, he looked beyond her down the corridor, mentally counting the pattern of little boxes he had unaccountably failed to notice before. Each with its flashing red light, each with its sinister little square of glass. No wonder Irene could speak with such quiet confidence about knowing where everybody aboard was.

No sooner had Vivien Agran turned away than Irene's door opened again. Richard went in and sat down. Irene was clearly in two minds about the information she had received.

'They take everything out of my hands,' she said, characteristically coming directly to the point. 'I dare say they mean to help but they treat me like a helpless infant now. They will contact all authorities and insurers. I am not to worry my pretty little head. I have more than enough to do getting my little boat here along Graham Land and across Drake Passage to Ushuaia on time through projected bad weather and the unknown effects of the millennium and without bumping into any icebergs or losing any passengers. They wrap me in diapers and treat me with boxing gloves, those men.'

Richard manfully put aside the mental picture aroused by her lapse

163

in idiomatic English and focused on the anger that had generated it. 'I've often wished head office would take all responsibility for some unexpected problem off my shoulders like that when I'm at sea,' he said.

'Then you are a foolish man. You own your own head office. You tell them what for.'

He laughed, and her eyes flashed up to see if he was mocking her. Then her own eyes crinkled into a rueful grin. 'I was very rude,' she said. 'I apologise. But now that is all settled for us, yes? We worry about nothing and play our games like good little girls and boys. The big daddies at head office will look after all the grown-up business for us.'

It was, perhaps, as well that Irene had given Richard the guided tour before the phone call to the States, for her temper now turned moody and introspective and he was glad to be able to get away. He was at once swept up into the preparations for this afternoon's epic jumps. The frenetic activity dominated everything that the passengers aboard were doing, for even those not involved or spectating were being offered exciting adventures of their own ashore. Needless to say, the twins had been attracted by all the bustle and excitement and had dragged their mother along with their irresistible, imperious energy. Richard found them at the outer edge of the crowd around the Sikorsky, listening as the tall, Welsh, Base-jumping expert took the jumpers through the various situations they might expect to encounter free-falling and then parachuting down a mountainside without meeting the black rock face to face.

Richard was fascinated by the erudite authority of the lilting Celtic tones and would have liked to stay, but he had other obligations. He called the nearest seaman and had a steward summoned. By good fortune – he thought at first – the steward who came was the steward who looked after their suite and who had taken the twins in tow last night. Brutally unfeeling, Richard handed them over again, then he and Robin went below into the sickbay. Except, of course, that on *Kalinin* it was not a sickbay at all. It was a hospital.

With a charming but gimlet-eyed nurse following in their wake, Richard and Robin did their own rounds. Apart from Major Schwartz in the cold room next door, Sergeant Pat Killigan was the most severely injured. Corporal Washington was also pretty bad and Richard was keen to keep an eye on their progress. He reckoned he owed them quite a vote of thanks; perhaps even William's life. The two scientists, Mendel and Fagan, were awake – Mendel only just – but they were

164

both apparently content to sit and read while their bodies recovered and their beards grew back. There was a fundamentally contented feeling in the little ward. Even Billy and Ernie seemed much happier to be here than at Armstrong or aboard *Erebus*. Looking at the facilities, Richard could easily understand that.

Richard's next duty was to update Andrew Pitcairn and Armstrong base as to the status of their people. As he and Robin left the ward, Vivien Agran's people came in, clutching their notebook computers, ready to record all but the most intimate details about the patients. The most intimate details, thought Richard acutely, would already be in Dr Glazov's records and the relevant section of the mainframe.

While Robin went to find Kate, Richard made his way to the bridge. 'PASSENGERS ARE ALWAYS WELCOME ON THE BRIDGE' said a notice Richard had failed to notice earlier at the bottom of the companionway up to the bridge deck. Of course he hadn't, he thought with a shake of his head; Irene and he had ridden up in the lift. Automatically, he glanced beyond the welcoming notice and saw a little box blinking at him from the top of the wall. Passengers are welcome but never unannounced, he thought. And indeed, as he walked into the airy spaciousness, there was Lieutenant Varnek, waiting, his smile of welcome ready, A few moments later *Kalinin*'s radio officer adjusted the frequency and checked the volume for Richard as he put through the first of his calls to *Erebus*, informing Andrew that Ernie Marshall would be dropped at Ushuaia on Monday next. Everyone else would be too, of course, but only Ernie was from Andrew's crew.

'Fine,' said Andrew. 'Regular supply planes come down to us from there as well as Stanley. As you know. You came down on one. Over!'

'Right. We'll be back on itinerary. Colin and Kate will probably return with Marshall, though. Over.'

'Keep me posted. Before I sign off, Hugo wants to talk to Dr DaCosta. Is she there? Over.'

'Not immediately. I'll see if I can scare her up and get back to you. Over.'

'I don't think it's urgent. He's remembered something about the explosion, I think. Something's coming back. But it'll wait. *Erebus* out.'

'OK, Andrew, I'll tell her. *Kalinin* out!'

Where was Jolene? Richard wondered as the radio officer made the necessary adjustments to contact Armstrong. Perhaps he should get Varnek to check his computer; that almost certainly contained the information. His silent speculation was interrupted by the clatter of the Sikorsky lifting off and heading inland, the Base jumpers all packed aboard.

'. . . Armstrong Base. Colonel Jaeger speaking, over.'

'Gene. It's Richard Mariner here, to let you know about your people on *Kalinin*, over.'

'Hi, Richard. Good to hear you. That will be welcome information.'

Richard went through the patients, updating the colonel on his sick and wounded. And their likely destination on Monday.

'Ushuaia's a big place,' said Jaeger. 'Anyone still bad can go straight into the hospital there. The others'll hitch lifts back with the Ice Pirates. That'll work fine. Is Dr DaCosta there? Over.'

'Negative, Gene. You want me to get her for you? Over.'

'No big deal. I just wanted to tell her the Feds have arrived. A Special Agent named Jones. Going through the place with a fine-toothed comb even as we speak. Over.'

'I'll tell her as soon as I see her. In the meantime, *Kalinin* out.'

'Thanks, Richard. Armstrong out.'

'Is that all, sir?' asked the radio officer as Richard put down the handset.

'I think so, thank you,'

But it was not all. As Richard strolled out onto the airy vastness of the bridge, the buzz denoting an incoming signal followed him. The radio officer answered at once. Richard, struck by the majesty of the white-capped sheer black cliffs so close at hand, lingered, paying no attention, until Radio Officer Kyril popped his head out of the radio room. 'Captain Mariner, do you know where Dr DaCosta is? I have a Special Agent Jones calling urgently from Armstrong.'

'No, sorry,' said Richard.

'I know where she is,' said Varnek. 'She's over there,' and he pointed to the distant red spot which was all that could be seen of the Sikorsky labouring up the far black skyscraper of cliff.

'You're not jumping?' Dai Gwyllim's Celtic lisp made the 'j' of jumping sound almost like 'ch' to Jolene's entranced ear. She shook her head in preference to testing her voice against the thrumming bellow of the Sikorsky's motor. She looked down at the coil of bungee rope on the floor – what she could see of it under the pile of carefully-stowed parachutes. She looked up. T-Shirt was watching her. He grinned. Winked. She smiled a little weakly. She had never in all her life been so scared. Or so excited, come to that. This was even more poignant than her wedding night at Niagara with the late, unlamented,

166

Mr DaCosta. And, she suspected, it would be a good deal more memorable.

'So how're you going to get down?'

Jolene's eyes switched back to Dai. His eyes were deep-lined, calm blue, like far skies.

'I'll hitch another lift,' she said, hugging the seat's solid armrest. 'Meet you at the bottom.'

'That's wise,' called Jilly, Dai's dazzling young wife. She was leading the bungee team and Jolene hoped she had a good strong bra on for the jump or she would likely batter herself to death when her breasts swung up alongside her head. 'Don't you do anything you aren't comfortable with. We'll all be taking the chopper down too, after we've been hauled back up. It's only the death or glory boys here who'll make it down under their own steam.'

Apart from Jolene herself, there were fifteen aboard. Ten bungee jumpers, mostly women, and five Base jumpers, all men. The other thirty extreme tourists were either with the set-up team waiting to watch the fun or down in the bay below, powering ashore in one of the two Zodiacs, a walk through a penguin rookery and a look at a seal colony in prospect, together with the promise of some of the most spectacular scenery they would ever see in their lives.

A fluke in the wind, an errant zephyr in the near dead calm, swung the Sikorsky round so that Jolene could see the second Zodiac leaving *Kalinin*'s side, its black, rubberised flat-iron shape packed with scarlet parkas. Then over the silent perfection of the picture swung the long, wide-winged shape of a wandering albatross. She caught her breath, entranced.

In the very far distance, just beyond the edge of her immediate understanding, the radio buzzed and the Sikorsky's tannoy whispered, 'Dr DaCosta, call from FBI Special Agent Jones for you.'

It was only when Dai leaned over, shook her shoulder and said, 'Call for you,' that she realised she had heard her name. Struggling up the body of the Sikorsky to the pilot's cabin, she felt a sense of almost personal invasion that the FBI should intrude itself into the jewel-bright preciousness of the adventure. But as things turned out, reception in the cockpit was so bad that she could make out nothing of the Special Agent's message and she was happy enough to cut him off. Their destination was in sight.

They called it the Razor. On the inland side it rose nearly three hundred metres above the mountain-ringed plateau to a triangular pinnacle which looked tiny from the air. On the seaward side, the point of the triangle stood out from the plateau cliffs above a plain of black rock sliding into a wilderness of white shore ice just a little under a thousand metres sheer. The apparent smallness of the triangular top was simply a refusal by the mind to accept the massive size of the Razor. There was plenty of room for the Sikorsky to land and for the excited team to bundle out without even in the least cramping the collection of crew members and spectators waiting there.

Jolene, wracked by her professional conscience, slid into the jump seat beside the pilot and got through to Armstrong base. But Special Agent Jones had gone off again and was nowhere to be found. 'This is a bad place to be calling from,' she yelled into the handset, projecting her voice under the thrumming of the rotors. 'Tell him I'll be back in contact when I get aboard *Kalinin* later. DaCosta out.' And that was that, for the time being. Her mind filled with speculation as to what the Special Agent wanted to tell her, she ran crouching to the open doorway and dropped onto the ice-crusted rock. Still crouching, she ran forward through a whirling storm of downdraught as the Sikorsky lifted off. Then she straightened, suddenly, apparently, alone; all thoughts of the FBI and her investigation pushed aside by the view which greeted her dazzled gaze.

The broad base of the triangle, over which the chopper had just hopped and soared away, overlooked a frozen sea of milk maybe a hundred miles across, or so it seemed. Away at the far side, containing the milk like the rim of a childhood beaker held up for a bedtime sip, rose a ragged black ridge of mountain peaks. Between the Razor and those distant mountain peaks lay only that sleeping sea of snow, three hundred metres down. The sky was vast, electric blue, seeming to attain the indigo of evening, up at its zenith somewhere just below the stars. The gentlest buffet of wind nudged her and she felt as though she would be swept away over the edge, as light as an albatross's feather. Then she turned. The sun reflected up off the carapace of snow, bringing out of the blue clarity of the air an extra range of hues, most of them shades of red. Surprisingly distant, for all they sounded close by, the group of people from *Kalinin* had gathered at the Razor's edge.

There were two distinct groups of them and as she drew nearer she could see why this was so. The Base jumpers had first choice of jump-off point. The wind was light but appreciable. They would need to take much more notice of it than the bungee jumpers. By the time Jolene joined them, Dai had made the choice and the preparations were under way. The bungee base was being anchored to a series of cracks in the rock edge and, before he strapped his parachutes on, Dai came and crouched down to inspect this work as well. Seeing Jolene's frown, he grinned, strong teeth flashing. 'No sense in giving myself a safe landing if the wife has a hard fall,' he rumbled. 'But that's as solid as can be. Right, boyohs, we know the plan, eh?'

T-Shirt and Max nodded, as did the two others Jolene did not know.

'Good luck,' she called to all of them, but it was T-Shirt who grinned at her and winked again, sparking with impatience and excitement.

'Jilly?' called Dai.

She answered, 'Ready, bach,' in her strong Australian accent.

Jolene saw that they were planning to jump together, he with his chutes and her with her bungee, each at a slightly different angle off the sharp point of the arrowhead of rock.

As they tensed themselves to run for the void, Jolene looked past them, out over the Antarctic Ocean. The water was like indigo ink, spotted with clouds and streamers of ice. Far, far away *Kalinin* sat, no bigger than a toy, tiny and peaceful. Beyond her, on the very rim of the horizon where the edge of the sky and the lip of the sea met in a milky distance, loomed islands dark as thunderheads and icebergs like sapphire cities afloat. Jolene found that her arms were up level with her shoulders as though she, too, was about to take flight.

And when Dai shouted, '*Go,*' she tensed to run with the rest of them.

But something held her, setting her thighs like marble, and she walked forward sensibly, with caution and control.

From here at the very top it was possible to see that the Razor's edge had been weathered by westerly winds into great hollows so the top where they stood overhung the middle sections five hundred metres down. On either side, shrinking figures flew downwards and outwards. Beneath them, Jolene had a flashing impression of black rock and white ice. Nothing more, no real sense of scale or distance. Then Jilly's bungee lines snapped taut as the elastic soaked up body weight and gravity force. In lingering slow motion, Jilly's jerking body swung inward towards the cliff. Out on the upper air on the opposite side, Max and T-Shirt were planing, arms and legs spread, falling in formation, their little throw-away chutes in their right hands ready to jerk their wing-shaped canopies free. The last two Base jumpers were sprinting for the edge.

Jilly's body swung gently against the rock face, her bungee beginning to pull her up again and, just as this happened, Dai let go of his throw-away, releasing his chute, and a flock of big brown skuas that had been nesting on the sheer black slope exploded outwards, disturbed by Jilly's arrival. Not a flock. Skuas do not flock. Six pairs nesting in unusual proximity on the cliff wall. They swung outwards, away to the right, before turning, as was their nature, into the attack. But the interloper that they set upon with all the vicious power they could muster was Dai. As his canopy came out, the big birds like black-backed gulls turned into hawks, tore into it and into the man below it.

The balletic grace of Dai's descent faltered as he was forced to fight back. The line of his drop wavered, fell away, slipping with dangerous speed downward and outward, over the black rock, towards the sea-stirred jumble of white.

Frozen with horror, rooted to the spot, Jolene saw T-Shirt and Max vary the angle of their own flight, following their stricken friend outwards, away from the cliff, the black rock beach and the shore. In perfect unison, the pair of them let go of the tiny mushrooms of their releases and their canopies blossomed, side by side, the space between them filled by the more distant image of Dai's 'chute, torn and flapping.

The sound of a little two-stroke engine coughing into life jolted Jolene from her horrified stillness. The *Kalinin* people had looped Jilly's bungee round a small winch and were pulling her back. Without thinking, Jolene ran towards them calling, 'Get the chopper back. Quickly.'

One of them caught her eye and nodded. He was already talking into a little radio.

Jolene turned back to look for T-Shirt and the others and gasped. How far they had fallen and how distant they had become. She fought to keep an eye on the three of them as they skidded away seawards, leaving behind them a trail of birds returning, victorious, to their nests.

Jilly arrived a little before the chopper. Wordless with shock and rage, she watched the distant parachutes settle onto the coastal ice.

'Well, they're down all together,' called Jolene over the abrupt rattle of the chopper's rotors. 'Coming?'

'Too bloody right I am,' spat Jilly.

Ice was really amazing stuff, mused Richard. From *Kalinin*, this belt of coastal white looked as solid as a chalk rock shelf. But as the Zodiac's bulbous bow neared it, the apparent uniformity proved to be entirely illusory. What they were approaching – entering – was a maze of floating brash. The ice seemed mostly ancient; weathered into fantastic shapes, varying from glassy clearness to milky

170

impenetrability, stippled, bubbled, veined and striated, undercut, icicle bearded, it all bobbed sluggishly around them, sometimes as high as shoulder height. The great blue-hued maze of it slid sluggishly back as the coxswain controlling the outboard wove them effortlessly through, in an almost direct line to the black-pebbled beach.

Richard would have loved to have discussed the beauty of their surroundings with Robin or the twins who were beside him, but the cacophony around them made conversation out of the question. It was not just the grinding, rumbling ice, on the larger sections – nowhere near large enough to be called floes – adelie and chinstrap penguins added their screeches to the racket. The thin, icy blade of the breeze, mostly headwind, was full of wild odours, ranging from the timeless scent of the sea through the familiar almost cucumber smell of icebergs to the occasional sickening richness of weed and fish-based guano. Amid all the palaver, a Weddell seal sunned itself fatly on a piece of brash just big enough to support it then rolled with lazy grace and slid soundlessly into the water. A few seconds later it bobbed up inquisitively just beside the Zodiac, wide eyes liquid black, its nose twitching and its whiskers glittering with drops of water, its panting breath a fog of fish smells. Even over all the other sounds, the twins' squeals of delight were clearly audible.

As was a sudden thumping crash. Richard looked up just in time to see Dai Gwyllim's parachute fold into the floes perhaps fifty metres ahead. He turned to the coxswain shouting and gesturing, but the sailor had seen. Abruptly the seal fell far behind and the rubber sides of the Zodiac bounced off the taller floes, pushing them roughly aside. Richard, alerted to the sky now, looked up again to see a pair of 'chutes like gulls' wings settle into the lower blue, the figures beneath them tugging hard at control ropes, obviously using all the skill at their command to bring them down beside the first man.

Along the floor of the solid little craft lay oars and a gaff. Richard picked up the lengthy wooden pole and with an ability he had forgotten he possessed began to fend the ice away as the Zodiac came to full speed. The pair of parachutists eased themselves into the gentlest landing the uneven, unsteady ice would allow, both abandoning their canopies the instant they landed. Controlled or not, their landing took them through the treacherous skin of brash and into the freezing water.

As they landed, the Zodiac broke through into a little kind of bay on whose far shore the two, now identifiable as T-Shirt and Max, were hanging unsteadily onto the slopes of a bobbing ice floe, half awash, desperately pulling at the lines of a parachute, trying to drag

171

the unconscious Dai Gwyllim to the surface of the thick, sub-zero water. Dai would be dead within two minutes unless they got him up and out. And the bits of themselves that were immersed in the water were going to start freezing irreparably within two or three minutes after that. Richard bellowed at the top of his lungs but the two rescuers did not seem to hear him, each one totally focused on keeping his left hand wedged in bobbing ice and his right hand tugging the sluggish ice-bound parachute lines.

As the Zodiac arrived on the scene, so did the chopper, pouncing down out of the hard blue sky just above them. Even the well-wrapped, absolutely dry people in the Zodiac were rendered breathless by the freezing downdraught. What it must be doing to the soaking skydivers half on the ice went far beyond anything Richard could imagine. But he and Robin saw what had to be done and turned to the coxswain together. 'Is there a knife?' bellowed Richard and Robin must have called something similar for when the man gestured to a big box by his feet she came up with two good, long, sharp ones. At once, the Zodiac was beside the three parachutists and Richard and Robin pulled Dai up through the thin crust of surface ice and half into the boat, chopping away the lines of his parachute as they did so. The instant he was free of the tangle, they pulled him right in onto the wooden floor. T-Shirt and then Max hurled their upper bodies off the floe and over the inflated rubber side. With Robin holding one pair of stone-cold hands and the twins' minder the other uneasily beside her, the Zodiac was off, pulling the young Base jumpers through the water. Richard knelt astride the rubberised bow, repeating his performance with the gaff. And he needed to do so. Some of the ice was as sharp as knife blades, some of it rough as tarmac; and over all of it T-Shirt and Max's cold-numbed legs were being dragged.

The shore was a long, fairly level pebble beach. One end of it was a penguin rookery but the other, for some reason, was clear and the Zodiac headed there with the shadow of the helicopter following it.

The Sikorsky had settled onto the sloping shore before the Zodiac beached, and the two women were out of it to greet the little crowd which carried Dai up the beach. They took him and laid him in the Sikorsky, wrapping him in anything warm they could find while Richard, Robin and the Zodiac crew supported the shuddering rescuers up to the chopper as well. Then Richard and Robin staggered back to the Zodiac and the twins as the chopper lifted off and headed for *Kalinin*.

* * *

172

While Dr Glazov examined the three half-frozen men, Jolene was fully occupied in comforting Jilly while worrying about T-Shirt and how well he had survived yet another heroic act. So it was that the evening was quite well advanced before she found herself free. On the doctor's eventual assurance that Jilly could see Dai – asleep – and that no lasting harm seemed to have come to his two young rescuers, Jolene rushed up to the radio shack before seeing T-Shirt, getting something to eat or even checking Major Schwartz's coffin, so quickly packed away on their arrival last night.

Jolene's mission was to contact Special Agent Jones at Armstrong, but before she could get Radio Officer Kyril to tune his radio to Armstrong's wavelength, she received an incoming signal from *Erebus*.

'Jolene DaCosta here. Who is this? Do I say "Over"? Over.'

'Dr DaCosta, it's Hugo Knowles here. I don't know whether or not it's important, but I've been trying to remember more about the explosion of the Skiddoos and I'm much clearer about what happened now.'

'I'm sure it is important, Lieutenant Knowles. I'm just not sure I'm the right person to be telling it to any more. Still, never mind. You go ahead. I'll pass it on if need be. Hello? Lieutenant . . . Oh. Over.'

'Thompson and I were attracted away from the hut we were building by a noise. I don't know what exactly. Thompson heard it and called me. I remember I was a bit stressed at having to go out so near check-in time—'

'Check-in time? What is that? Over.'

'I was checking in every so often with *Erebus* on the radio. It was time to check in and I wanted to make my report, not go wandering around in the snow. But Thompson said he heard something so could I come and look. And sure enough, there was some kind of motor. And Thompson said there had been another engine earlier too, like one of the Skiddoos being moved. The one I heard was deeper. Like a truck pulling away in the distance behind the big moraine. There was a line of Skiddoos. We could see where they had been left, but one of them had been moved. It was strange. Thompson thought it was strange too. He went over for a closer look and I didn't stop him. I suppose it was because I was thinking of checking with *Erebus* anyway, but I thought I'd check with *Kalinin* before kicking up a fuss or anything . . .'

'Yes. I can understand that. So?'

Radio protocol was well out of the window now. Jolene was using

173

the contact like a telephone. But it didn't seem to worry Hugo Knowles.

'So while I was keying in the correct frequency for *Kalinin*, Thompson took a closer look and came running back, calling "I say, there's something odd over here . . ." Or something like that.'

'I see. And then?'

'And he'd just taken three or four steps when I made contact with *Kalinin*. That's when the whole lot went up.'

Jolene remembered the square bruise on Hugo Knowles's face, the shape of the radio, imprinted by the blast. 'So let me get this straight,' she said. 'You think Thompson must have seen something – the bomb. And he was coming to tell you about it when it went off. Could he have disturbed it? Set it off himself? Over.'

'Could have, yes. Over.'

'Was he calling loudly enough to set it off? Over.'

'Possibly. Yes. I hadn't thought of that. Over.'

'Anything else? Over!'

'You'll know as soon as I think of anything. Out.'

With this conversation still whirling like snowflakes in her head, Jolene made contact with Special Agent Jones. His voice was unexpectedly deep, resonant, redolent of Mississippi. She didn't know whether to imagine him as a character out of *Men in Black* or *Huckleberry Finn*.

Like Jolene herself, Special Agent Jones made scant use of the traditional proprieties of radio traffic.

'Inspector DaCosta?'

'Special Agent Jones?'

'Happy to talk to you, Inspector. At last.'

'What can I do for you, Agent Jones?'

'We have several things we need to get straight, Inspector, not the least of which is what you propose to do with the body whose demise we are here to investigate and which is now once again under Federal jurisdiction, I understand.'

'Major Schwartz is safely here with me, yes. And this ship is technically American soil for the purposes of the investigation, I assume. You might need to take that up with the owners, though. If this turns out to be Russian soil we're all screwed, I should think.'

'We have made certain, Inspector. I understand that the American owners hold fifty-one per cent of the stock in her, so she is legally American soil, and therefore within your remit as well as mine. So I hope, Inspector, that you are pursuing all lines of inquiry and preparing to hand over facts, testimony and evidence to us in due course.'

'There's a grey area there, Agent Jones.'

'I see that, Inspector. We prefer things black and white at the Bureau. But in a case like this that is not always feasible. We can bend with the breeze if we have to.'

'Meaning?'

'We give and take. Co-operate. Sort out the niceties Stateside whenever we can.'

'Suits me, Agent Jones. Feel free to ask for information or to suggest lines of inquiry and I will do my best to oblige.'

'It all seems to turn on the space suit. You have the suit because Major Schwartz is still wearing it. It is the only suit because the others went up in the explosion here at Armstrong the night you left. First question. Have you examined the suit?'

'A cursory once-over. Why?'

'So this is the spirit of give and take?'

'It is, Agent Jones. All cards on the table. Face up.'

'On an open line, Dr DaCosta?'

'You think we're being tapped? Bugged?'

'I'm saying it's possible, Inspector, and should therefore be factored in. Consider the ease with which you have communicated with head office in the past yourself. Every word we are saying could be going anywhere in the world. In the universe, actually. And beyond. That might be important, given who you work for . . .'

In Jolene's mind, Agent Jones moved a step or two from *Tom Sawyer* towards *The X Files*. She began to rather like him.

'I take your point, Agent Jones. Even so, we need to get to the nitty-gritty here. I have enough information to check on the current status of the major's suit with regard to obvious damage, completeness, condition and so forth. I do not have a lab capable of discriminating between programmable carbon multilayer and Bacofoil. I do not have the facilities to check whether the superconductor elements are working worth a damn, particularly given that it's all supposed to be powered by the heat differential between the astronaut's body and the ambient air temperature. There currently *is* no difference between the astronaut's body temperature and the ambient—'

'Understood, Inspector DaCosta, and I particularly appreciate the manner in which you have concealed the sensitive elements of the situation from inquisitive ears. It is the integrity of the suit that concerns us at the moment.'

'*Integrity*. Why, Agent Jones, I'm sure it could even run for President—'

'Inspector, we think we may have found traces of a section of it here where it has no business to be.'

Jolene stopped playing with Jones. 'Can you tell me what you have found and where?'

'Certainly, Inspector. We were doing a routine examination of one of the John Deeres and we found traces of programmeable carbon and superconductor on the driver's seat.'

'But that could only come from a Power Strip. Could you have a piece of one of the back-up suits, blown up in the explosion?'

'Unlikely, given its condition and location. Especially as no one was ever allowed to drive when suited-up. Presidential candidate or not, please check whether that suit is all there and zipped up tight.'

Chapter Eighteen

Richard looked down at his battered old steel-cased Rolex. Midnight. Midnight here at sixty degrees west, at any rate. Away round the world, the hour varied every fifteen degrees of longitude. And that consideration would be important on this brand new day, for it was 31 December 1999, the last day of the old millennium.

Even the most die-hard of the passengers were asleep. For them the carefully planned party would begin soon after breakfast when midnight and the new millennium came westwards across the international dateline and swung into New Zealand in eight hours' time. For the crew also, a good night's sleep was a basic necessity. The cooks, waiters, stewards and entertainers under Vivien Agran's aegis would have the busiest day of their lives today. The deck officers, engineers and seamen under the control of Irene and Varnek would also have a busy day, for the storm Richard had seen coming half a world away was due to arrive at sixty west longitude, sixty south latitude with the new millennium – and with even more devastating effect.

The squeak of the mortuary drawer pulled Richard's attention back to the matter in hand.

Jolene would have preferred to have had T-Shirt Maddrell helping her inspect Major Schwartz, but Dr Glasov had given all three Base jumpers a heavy sedative so T-Shirt was *hors de combat* at the moment. After T-Shirt, Richard was the next best option for a range of reasons. He was strong enough to lift and turn the body, an important consideration, for she herself was not. Also he and T-Shirt had been there during the major's removal from the site of his death and so could give an authoritative view as to whether there had been any tampering since. And then there was the hour and the nature of the task – and the fact that they had just walked in here without a by-your-leave and someone would probably have to face up to the captain, the first officer or the dreaded doctor any minute now. Jolene was not superstitious, scared of corpses or easily brow-beaten, but everyone could use a friend in need.

177

'This looks untouched to me,' she said, her voice quietly conversational, just powerful enough to rise above the steady pulse of the engines. 'But I don't know who closed the box on *Erebus* and opened it again here.'

Richard looked down over her shoulder into the coffin. Jolene's hands were resting on the body bag he had seen zipped round the frozen corpse a week ago. The clear, slightly clouded, heavy-duty plastic showed the body in its silver suit clearly.

'Is the helmet still in the box?' he asked.

'In back, at his feet.'

They hesitated. Neither of them saw any real need to check further for signs of whether anything might have been put in with the corpse in transit. Their focus was firmly on the body and the suit in which it had died. But then neither of them knew the uses to which Hoyle, among others, had already put the major's coffin.

'Right. What's next?'

Richard's question was answered by a long whispering susurration as Jolene unzipped the body bag. The sound brought a flash of memory to Richard's mind, for it echoed uncannily the sound of a snowboard sliding down the back of a moraine. The reaching arm, which T-Shirt had mistaken for a gesture of welcome, had been gently forced down by the men at Armstrong, its rigid length lowered inch by inch to the major's side, until it fitted into the bag. Richard looked over. Yes, the arm seemed exactly as they had left it. A combination of rigor mortis and freezing temperatures had preserved the body like a marble statue. There seemed to be no sign of decomposition. Except that the eyelids had shrunk back a little, opening the brown eyes wide again, staring, hypnotic. And the major needed a shave.

'May I ask what you are doing here?' purred Varnek's voice, surprisingly close at hand. Richard certainly had not heard him enter.

'Examining the body. Special Agent Jones asked me to check on one or two things as a matter of urgency.' Jolene had her answer pat and calm.

'At this hour? A little macabre eccentricity?'

'I had people to see. Questions to ask. I did the questioning first so they could get to bed. It's going to be a busy day for everyone aboard when they wake up. Except the major here.'

Richard suspected Varnek knew about the questioning well enough. Even through the usual evening rush of getting the twins fed, amused, washed and tucked down, he himself had been aware of Jolene quietly pulling aside Colin and Kate, Billy Hoyle, the newly-awakened Killigan and the others, one after another, for a few more questions. Robin had escaped, the only one to do so apart from T-Shirt in his drugged slumber and Washington in his. 'Would you come down and check him out with me?' had been the last question she had levelled at him. Clearly, her talk with Agent Jones had fired and focused her investigation once again – the talk, he suspected acutely, plus a certain amount of guilt that she had been out with T-Shirt at the Razor instead of hard at work this afternoon.

Richard met Varnek's suspicious gaze equably. 'I'm just the hired help,' he said. 'Consider me as Dr Watson.'

The Russian's eyes narrowed. His mind was obviously racing. Perhaps he had never heard of Sherlock Holmes.

Jolene had dismissed the first officer from her mind already. 'Nothing obviously wrong at the front,' she said. 'Richard, can you lift him up for me and lie him on his side? I want to see the back of the suit.'

'Of course.' Richard turned away from Varnek. Jolene handed him a pair of surgical gloves which he had a bit of trouble pulling on. Varnek vanished. No doubt to alert the captain, thought Richard. Or Dr Fuckov.

But if he did, nothing came of it. With the gloves at last in place, Richard took the corpse's shoulder and rolled the stiff body onto its side, holding it there while Jolene examined the back of the suit. The cold of the frozen flesh struck into his fingers. A slightly bitter, faintly acrid smell wafted past sensitive nostrils. Other bodily functions, apart from hair and nail growth, had continued after death. Things would get pretty messy once the suit came off, thought Richard grimly. But there was another vaguely familiar odour there as well; something not bodily at all . . .

'Richard?' said Jolene, her voice inflecting into mild surprise.

'Yes?' He pushed consideration of the strange smell to the back of his mind.

'Are you sure the body didn't look disturbed at all?'

'The zipper may have been pulled down to expose the face a couple of times, but other than that he looks untouched to me. He's set like rock. Anyone could roll him around and you wouldn't notice afterwards, but no one could have taken the body out of the bag and moved it much I'd have said. We're the first people to have moved him like this since we zipped him in the bag, I'd guess.'

'Sounds logical.'

179

'It's the best I can do. Why is it so important?'

'Because there's a section missing back here. The suit looks fine at first glance but it's not. The most important section of all has gone. If he went out without it, then that's what killed him.'

'That's it, then. Case solved. He should have taken this bit with him but he forgot. He tried to tell them what was going on when he realised but he couldn't get through. Accidental death.'

'No. You don't understand. He *couldn't* have gone out without it. It's just not possible. Unless someone set him up. Sent him out on purpose. We're talking about the Power Strip, the most important part of a top secret, experimental space suit. It's worth the annual budget of a small country. If it's not where it should be then where the hell is it?'

'OK,' said Richard. 'Case not solved after all. Case complicated. Two motives in prospect: either someone murdered the major, cold-bloodedly and with malice aforethought, and removing this special bit is how they did it—'

'Or someone stole the Power Strip earlier and the major was unlucky enough to go out in the wrong suit at the wrong time and got caught up as collateral damage.'

'Yes, except you said it couldn't be quite as simple as that,' said Richard, rolling the stiff corpse back into place. 'By your own account nobody could have been so incompetent as to fail to notice the thing was missing, unless they skipped or fudged their tests for some reason. The more likely explanation is that they were involved with the theft of this Power Strip and let him go out without it knowingly!'

'Billy Hoyle,' she said. 'Billy helped dress him. I know they skipped routines and fudged procedures then made up their case notes afterwards. And I've got all the records backed onto the six floppies in my cabin. I was going through them when the power surge on *Erebus* burned out my laptop.'

'Really? I didn't realise.'

'And Billy knew I was. I'd already said . . . Richard, could he have been behind the power surge himself? Bribed or blackmailed that poor man to pull all those switches? The one everyone thought had cabin fever?'

'I wouldn't have thought Billy would have known who to bribe or blackmail, not being part of *Erebus*'s crew. But I wouldn't put it past his bosom buddy Ernie Marshall.'

'Is there any way we can check?'

'We can ask Hugo Knowles. He'll be on watch aboard *Erebus*.

They're keeping watches up even though they've made it to Faraday now.'

'If Varnek will let us make the call.'

'Why shouldn't he?' said Richard decisively, pulling off his surgical gloves. 'We can only ask.'

Varnek was happy to oblige. He would have woken the radio officer for them, but since *Erebus*'s call sign and wavelength were in the radio's digital memory, Richard could handle things himself. He raised not Hugo but Andrew Pitcairn.

'Oh, hello, Richard. Yes, doing the midnight stint myself. Letting old Hugo catch up on some sleep. He's still a bit below par, you know. What can I do for you?'

Richard explained.

'Well, oddly enough,' answered Andrew at once, 'I was going to call Irene about Marshall in the morning. Yes. Baines, our fevered engineer, has coughed, as they say. He did it all for love of a dark lady in a magazine at the prompting of Marshall and the request of one of the Americans. Chap called Hoyle, I understand. Both need a close eye, I think.'

'I think we can arrange that,' said Richard grimly. 'A very close eye indeed.'

But for once he was wrong. As he spoke, it was just turning 1 a.m. Billy Hoyle was in hiding, terrified, and Ernie Marshall had been dead for more than ninety minutes.

The evening had begun so promisingly. Dr Glazov had completed her last ward round at half past nine and the two would-be wiseguys had crept out of bed unobserved and made their way to Mrs Agran's cabin, laden with their trade goods and evil intentions. Less observant than Richard, though with much more reason to keep a careful lookout, they had no idea that their approach was closely monitored.

Vivien Agran's cabin was the most lavish of all aboard except for the largest staterooms. She had fitted it out according to her own taste in a restful over-abundance of chairs and chintz, frills and prints. It was a room whose every velvet hanging, every silken whisper, every lingering scent of incense promised much. Even the office-cum-reception area boasted a statue in glazed terracotta of naked youths and maidens disporting themselves with a great bull in the Minoan style. The desk was massive, with ornate brass feet cast in the shape of dragons' claws clutching big brass balls in their knotty grasp. A charcoal print hung above and behind the desk, in which Adam and

Eve were involved in a lingeringly intricate discussion on the nature of good and evil with a suspiciously Freudian serpent. On the wall between the print and the bedroom doorway stood an unusually large porthole, clamped shut, and above it in watercolour a long Diana soaked herself languidly in a classical Greek river under the voyeuristic gaze of a hidden Actaeon. At the bedroom doorway itself, heavy draperies in red velvet were held invitingly open by a naked ebony youth on the right and a naked ebony maiden on the left. Behind the draperies the door stood open but the light remained off, velvety darkness concealing who knew what further pleasures.

None of this had much impact on Billy or Ernie because on either side of Mrs Agran sat two Bunny Girls, real, live, actual, with the trademark velvet throat bands, the ears, the tight, well-filled, black satin costumes. The little white cotton tails too, in all probability, but they were sitting demurely upon those.

'Welcome to my quarters, gentlemen,' said Mrs Agran, rising as her visitors entered. 'Please just sit over there for a moment while I complete a little business.' She sat again, fingers busy and sure upon her keyboard as she spoke. 'Right, Gretchen, Anoushka. That was a good rehearsal. Well done. You will be on at about ten tomorrow night. You know which cakes to come out of later and what to do after that. Good enough.'

The two men watched, fixated, as the two white cottontails wavered out into the corridor.

'Now, gentlemen, what can I do for you?' asked Mrs Agran smoothly, looking up over the top of the only obviously modern thing there – her computer. Her fingers were still busy on the keyboard.

Ernie did the talking, at his most open and ingratiating. The effect was only marginally undermined by the fact that he kept looking directly at her perfectly presented cleavage. 'We got a range of stuff which might be of interest to the, ah, well, the captive market you got on board here, Mrs A., and we hear that you're the gel to ask.'

'Stuff?'

'Magazines, videos, adult CDs, pills. All good gear, as you can see. We brought a selection up with us.' Actually they had brought everything, still in Ernie's duffel bag, exactly as they had snatched it out of the major's coffin where Hoyle had managed to conceal it. 'The magazines obviously cater for all tastes. The straight stuff is probably of less interest to the passengers. They can get the real thing obviously. But the other stuff should go well. And there's always the crew. The videos and CDs are pretty much the same. Wide range of—'

'What sort of pills?'

'Happy pills. A variety of types. Nothing too heavy. Recreational rather than mainline.'

'Let me see.'

Ernie pulled a selection of merchandise out of his kitbag and dumped it on the desk. Mrs Agran leafed through the magazines, sorted the videos, ran a finger through the little pile of bright pills, her face set, expression closed. Then she popped a CD into her computer and called up the contents.

Unable to remain seated, Ernie was up and standing at her shoulder. From this favoured position he was able to divide his attention between the screen and the fragrant depths of her *décolletage*. 'Ah, you chose a good one,' he purred. '*Nude Raider*. Based on the kids' game. But with a difference. In you go . . . There. Now you see the delightful Tara Loft has even less clothing than her counterpart, though equally large assets. Not quite so well animated, perhaps, but then . . . Of course the main objective of the original game is for the central character to keep out of trouble and kick ass. Here it's rather the opposite. There. You see. If you just fail to miss those creepers . . . Well! Whoever would have thought a plant could do that, eh? And things get a good deal hairier further in. Poor Tara. She really has a very rough ride, especially at the higher levels. There are lots of other CDs, of course; live action ones. Much less sophisticated. More basic and immediate, if you follow my drift.'

'I believe I do, Mr Marshall. Now, what exactly had you in mind for all these goods?'

'Well, either to sell it to you direct if you want to add it to your own stock, or to sell it to your market ourselves, giving you a cut, of course. All fair and above board.'

'I see. Add it to my stock.' Vivien Agran rose, crossed to the wall beneath the charcoal sketch of Adam and Eve. There was a wide cupboard here which neither visitor had noticed. Vivien opened one side of it. 'Take a look at my stock,' she invited.

As soon as she moved, Billy Hoyle, sensing danger, tried to catch Ernie's eye, but Ernie was focused on the manner in which Mrs Agran's bottom, out of the chair now, filled the seat of her black satin skirt. And before Billy could take his arm or break his rapt concentration, Ernie was doing his hostess's bidding. In the cupboard in the wall stood rank after rank of videos. The tapes left littered around the TV two decks below were mostly adult and explicit. The channel to which the TV itself was tuned routinely showed endless variations on the basic adult theme. These tapes, however, were designed to cater for those with more specialised, more expensive, tastes. They went far beyond anything Ernie had ever seen or imagined. Even the unfortunate Tara, currently doing some very unusual gardening indeed, paled into comic insignificance in the face of what Mrs Agran had to offer. The other cupboard door opened. Books, magazines, CDs. Again, merchandise at a level undreamed of by the two visitors.

Ernie had never met a woman he couldn't charm, bamboozle or, if push came to shove, bully, so he pressed on gaily, laying on the Cockney charm with a trowel. 'Now this is what I call gear. The biz. You got management? Protection for this lot? I bet I could do you a lot of good, dahlin', if we could get to a mutually satisfactory compromise. What d'you say, gel?'

'I say you're well out of your league, Mr Marshall. You really do not know what you are dealing with. I would pack up my tent and move along if I were you.'

Ernie crowded up towards her, caught between lechery and threat. His arm pressed into one of her pneumatic breasts, unbalancing the perfection of her cleavage. Then their eyes met and he stepped back. On the second step he turned ugly. 'Now you listen here, Viagra, or whatever they call you. You might be big stuff aboard this little tub surrounded by powder puffs, nancy boys and bunny girls, but I trained as a marine and I—'

'Look,' she said placatingly. 'You haven't seen everything yet. What about these? They are really something special. Virtual reality pornography.' From the back of the cupboard she pulled two headsets which looked like thick pairs of wrap-around glasses and offered them to the men. 'Sit down and take a look at what we've really got to offer,' she tempted.

The pair of them sat and looked up at her, as gullible as Adam and Eve. They sat in the chairs beside her desk. They fitted the headsets over their eyes and, as they did so, she switched them on. Choking gasps came from tiny speakers in the arms of each one, sounds which could have been masculine or feminine; denoting pleasure or pain. Both men leaned forward, reaching out as though blind, their minds engaged instantly and disorientatingly in the drama that was being played out for their enjoyment.

As soon as she knew they were wholly absorbed, Vivien Agran rose and crossed silently to the door. She swung it open and there stood Vasily Varnek, summoned by the message from her computer to his. She glanced across the room to her unwelcome guests and raised her eyebrows. They were not the first who had tried to grab a piece of her action. They wouldn't be the last. She and Varnek had an understanding and made a good team. He gestured silently with the blunt spade of his chin and she left. He entered silently, swinging the door shut soundlessly behind him. As he crossed the room, he pulled out of his pocket an old-fashioned cosh – a large egg of lead sitting on a heavy steel spring twenty centimetres long, wrapped in strongly stitched black leather. Without even pausing in his stride he brought the cosh down on the top of Ernie Marshall's head, and swung round to do the same for Billy Hoyle. The stroke was meant to incapacitate, not kill. Varnek wanted the men dazed, helpless, open to reason – he planned to have a little talk with them. But it didn't quite work like that. Ernie exploded upwards, his skull unexpectedly strong. The headset went spinning and he hurled himself straight at his assailant. Varnek turned, his blow smashing down onto Billy Hoyle's shoulder, cracking his collarbone. Then Varnek rammed his elbow back, into Ernie's face. The Englishman reared up and Varnek back-handed him across the forehead with the cosh.

Ernie flipped backwards as though poleaxed and landed on the back of his head with the full weight of his body. His head caught one of the dragon's claw desk feet and there was a sharp report, like a gunshot, as Ernie's skull shattered. Varnek had little leisure to worry about him just at that moment, for Hoyle had torn off his headset and was fleeing to the door. He tore it open and collided with Mrs Agran in the corridor. He tore past her and sprinted away into hiding. Varnek went after him, but he stopped at the doorway when Mrs Agran saw Ernie and screamed. Reluctantly the Russian turned and together they re-entered the room.

Five minutes later, Mrs Agran, white and shaking, only just in control of herself, was twisting the latches on her unusually large porthole. 'He goes out here,' she said. 'If you're absolutely sure.'

'He's dead,' said Varnek bitterly. 'We'd better get our alibis straight and prepare for a "man overboard" when Glazov does her rounds in the morning.'

'He'll be a popsicle by then,' she giggled, on the edge of hysteria as the body slid past her and out into the bitter night.

The wave of hysteria threatening to overwhelm Vivien Agran frightened her. She hated to lose control. She sometimes saw her intelligence as something independent of her body and its occasionally overpowering demands. Her intelligence very clearly needed to rely on her body now. Her body needed to be quiet and calm so that she could maintain that icy control. Experience had taught Mrs Agran the quickest way to render her body submissive to her will, but it was not something she could do alone.

'Vasily,' she said to Varnek's back just as he reached for the door.

Varnek glanced at his watch and then turned slowly. Vivien was standing, shaking, framed against the velvety blackness of her bedroom door like a candle flame. She briskly pulled her blouse out of her skirt's waistline. Even before Varnek had taken a step towards her she had unzipped the skirt. She let it fall and flung the blouse to one side. She turned, sliding her fingers into the waist of a half-slip. He followed.

By the time Varnek's square bulk filled the bedroom doorway, Vivien had switched on the bedside light and placed her foot on the bedcover, rolling her stocking down swiftly. Her bedroom was the opposite of her office, functional, impersonal. There were no pictures or statues to alleviate the white walls, the teak shelving. The only spot of colour came from the cover of a paperback, open and face down under the light. It was Tom Wolfe's *The Bonfire of the Vanities*, Varnek noted distantly. She glanced across at him, seeing his great square hands rise to loosen his tie. The big, raw-knuckled hands were capable of surprising gentleness, she knew. Vasily himself was capable of unexpected tenderness and sensitivity. He was a very competent, complete lover. But sensitivity was the last thing Vivien needed now. She met his hot stare. 'Do not,' she said, and stopped. Her voice was shaking as badly as the rest of her. She took a deep breath. 'Do not be gentle with me,' she ordered, more loudly than she meant.

She had no sooner removed her second stocking than he threw her down upon the bed and tore her brassiere and then her panties off. King Lear's line came into her mind as his sinewy power bore down on her. 'Like flies to wanton boys are we to the Gods. They kill us for their sport . . .' She closed her eyes and surrendered to the thrust of his body and the brute grasp of his hands.

As soon as they were finished they both rolled off the tumbled bed. Her legs were firm again and her breathing steady. She stooped and caught up the rags of lace, mopping herself briskly as she checked in her mirror that he had left no bruises anywhere they might be seen. As he pulled himself to his feet, she opened the small porthole and hurled her underwear out after Ernie Marshall. He could have made a fortune out of those, in certain circles, given the state they were in. But Ernie no longer occupied even the smallest corner of her mind. 'I will go to bed now,' she said, her voice steady and low. 'I will check the videos of the corridors first and wipe any showing either Hoyle or Marshall near here.'

'I'm on watch any moment,' he rumbled. 'But I think I'll take a look around before I go up. I'll certainly pay the hospital a visit.'

'Hoyle won't be there. He's not stupid.'

'You're right,' he said, zipping up his trousers, 'but I'll check anyway.'

The man overboard alarm was raised long before Dr Glasov did her first round in the morning, and Ernie was by no means a popsicle before the Zodiacs were in the water searching for him.

It was Richard and Jolene who raised the alarm. After their brief conversation with Andrew Pitcairn, the pair of them went straight down to the ward and found the two beds still empty. A report to Varnek resulted in a detailed search of the ship. The ship's library of surveillance videos was consulted, but no clues lay there, possibly due to an unexplained failure in sections of the system between ten and midnight.

All common areas from keel to truck were given a thorough search, then the more obscure ones. But it did not occur to any of the searchers, for neither Varnek nor Vivien told them, that they might be searching for a terrified, injured, comatose man whose one ambition was to stay hidden. So they called out and passed on. Only when every other avenue had been explored did the reluctant captain call emergency stations and rouse everyone aboard, passengers and crew alike, from their beds, berths and bunks for a head count. Only the patients in the hospital escaped. By this time it was two thirty and Ernie had been bobbing in their wake for more than two hours, held up in the thick ice-oily water by lungs still filled with air, but beginning to frost over under the blustery overcast, floating and freezing; and lucky he was dead.

Irene was reluctant to allow Richard to go in the Sikorsky, but he managed to cajole her into letting him. The thing that struck him most forcefully as he ran across the benighted but still light deck was that the wind had shifted. Shifted in sinister fashion. The instant he felt it on his cheek he paused, looking at the sky. Obligingly, the midnight sun showed a blood-red gathering of mackerel skies overlaid with low purple wisps of mare's tails. This traditional cloudy warning of severe frontal weather was given added impact by the effect of the blood-orange sun. There was no doubt in Richard's mind as he hurried down the deck after his apparently oblivious companions that this

187

was a red sky in the morning – and any sensible sailor would take a very clear warning.

Of course they knew their search held only the dimmest of faint hopes. They were looking for little more than a couple of heads, possibly frosted white by now, bobbing somewhere in the wake of the ship as much as six hours' sailing time back. Moreover, the restless ocean was already littered with pieces of brash. They looked like blood clots floating in a sanguine sea. The light was so thick and garnet-tinged that only the magnesium power of the Sikorsky's searchlight offered any hope.

The Sikorsky ducked and dived through gusting air. The temperature seemed to be falling off a cliff. And that probably meant that the barometric pressure was doing the same. During the hour of the search flight, the overcast gathered and darkened, making the strange night-time scene look like an almost infinite abattoir full of slowly congealing gore.

They never found Ernie Marshall. The thickening brash under the strengthening wind finally caught him, crushing the air-filled balloon of his upper thorax between the jaws of a couple of clashing lumps of ice. He sank in a shroud of bubbles to abysses far deeper than Shakespeare's five mere fathoms, where his eyes may very well have set like pearls, though his bones never made coral. The smear he left on the ice that crushed him was indistinguishable in the blood-red light, and was erased soon enough in any case when the storm rains came.

Chapter Nineteen

The dining salon was sparsely filled at 07.00 breakfast. After the disturbances of the man overboard alert, most of the people aboard were investing a little more sleep against the planned exertions of today and tonight. Not so Richard, whose internal clock had switched over to ship-handling time and who found a few hours' sleep had left him full of energy and intellectual power. And Jolene DaCosta, spurred by the frustration of never quite being able to get to grips with her investigation, was filled with a burning need to be up and doing. T-Shirt Maddrell, who was almost unique aboard in having slept through the alert, now felt there was much to catch up on and rose from his bed in the sickbay to do just that, apparently none the worse for his swim in the Antarctic Ocean. He left Dai and Max still deep in the arms of Morpheus.

Richard, Jolene and T-Shirt sat in a corner of the salon beneath a square window on one wall and a porthole on the other where Richard could keep an eye on the worsening weather, and where they could talk without being overheard by Vivien Agran's minions who were completing final preparations for the round-the-world, all day party. The dining salon was to be one of the entertainment centres, with great big television monitors receiving pictures of celebrations all over the world, one or two already showing the wind-up programmes under way in Australia and the Far East. Between them, hanging high where everyone would be able to see it clearly, a big digital clock was already set to count-down.

In fifty-four minutes the millennium would cross the International Date Line where east meets west in the Pacific at 180 degrees of longitude; it would be midnight in New Zealand and the celebrations would start. In twenty-three hours and fifty-four minutes the witching hour would arrive in Tonga, Samoa, Midway and Wrangel Islands, and the wild party would be over, bar the shouting. It was going to be a long day.

'Lets go over it again,' said Richard.

Even with her back to the window, Jolene's wide eyes seemed to have picked up something of the troubled turmoil of the clouds outside. 'What's missing is the Power Strip,' she said. 'Just telling you about it can't be giving away too many secrets or breaking any laws, I guess. And it'll help me focus.

'The whole of the major's suit is a computer. The fabric it's made of looks like silver foil but it's actually made out of the new programmable carbon. They've taken the programmable molecules, put them into fibres, woven the fibres into cloth and layered it up with integral circuitry and a combination of the new photo-chips and micromachine parts. The whole thing is a computer programmed to perform a number of functions, and give a range of information to the person wearing it and to the people monitoring him. It also has other properties – strength, lightness, durability, ability to withstand pressures varying from seven or eight atmospheres to absolute vacuum.'

'But it's the computer section that's important,' prompted Richard.

'From our point of view, I guess. Except that one of the properties is its ability to protect the wearer from extremes of heat and cold – if it's all there and on properly.'

'Which in this case it was not?' hazarded T-Shirt, catching up and catching on pretty quickly.

'That's right,' said Jolene. 'The Power Strip is designed to run from the nape of the neck to the base of the spine. It's a little over two centimetres wide and nearly a metre long. In many ways it's the most revolutionary element of the suit. Two layers of programmable carbon tissue, plus a range of other stuff, separated by a layer of material impervious to heat coated in the latest generation superconductor. It's designed to turn the heat differential between the inside of the suit and the outside of the suit into enough power to make the whole thing work.'

'But Major Schwartz went out into very severe weather wearing a suit which had no Power Strip on it,' said Richard grimly.

'Looks that way,' nodded Jolene, her eyes slate-grey and stormy.

'What would have happened to him then?' asked T-Shirt.

'He probably wouldn't have noticed at first. He'd have tested the major functions with back-up power because it takes the Strip a little while to come up to speed. The heat differential needs to be established and locked in. He'd have ridden to location in a John Deere, still none the wiser. In the back, which has been specially adapted. Never in the front. He'd have been dropped off. Standard practice says the drop-off vehicle should stay at the drop-off point until the man in the suit is happy and gives the word; but they were pretty lax about that. I guess the major saw that all the suit's functions were running OK – he had a head-up display projected onto the inside of his visor faceplate – and off he went. Then after a while he would have switched across to power from the Power Strip. And everything would have gone dead on him.'

'Just like that?' asked T-Shirt.

'Pretty much. Total powerdown. He had back-up radio and there should have been a locator beacon—'

'But there wasn't,' interjected Richard. 'His first thought would have been to radio in. But with his suit functions down and a very nasty squall blowing, he was disorientated. So he looked for some shelter and found the cleft in the moraine close by. He went in out of the wind and tried to call for help but he didn't realise that the rock itself was blocking his signal. I suppose he must have thought the radio was packing up as well, because he put it down or dropped it and began to follow the cleft to the far side of the moraine looking for shelter. I don't know when he would have begun to feel the cold . . .'

'He may never really have done so,' supplied Jolene, taking up the tale again.

'Remember, because of what had been removed from his suit, the whole of his spinal column was exposed directly to very cold temperatures indeed.'

'I don't know if it's important,' said Richard, 'but when we went into the cleft, the wind was coming very strongly through it, following the line he must have taken. So it was blowing directly onto his back too.'

'That may have made all the difference,' said Jolene. 'Walking away from the wind he might have felt things were improving when in fact they were getting worse very quickly indeed. When he came out of the southern side of the cleft, he must have been nearly dead, but he may not have realised it. It's a wonder he could still walk. If he had fallen, his spine would have shattered like glass. But somehow he kept going, lost, disorientated, probably thinking he was walking the right way to get back to camp, keeping the wind at his back, I'd guess.'

'Until he found himself trapped in the little amphitheatre of rock at the far end of the moraine. He must have realised then,' said Richard sadly.

'He must have,' agreed Jolene. 'He just had the strength to turn round, reach out . . .'

'And turn to ice,' said T-Shirt quietly. 'It's like something out of the Bible.'

'The whole place is,' said Jolene, gesturing vaguely east and south at the Big White. 'It's like the wrath of God.'

They sat for a moment in silence as the first squall of the impending storm thumped broadside into *Kalinin's* west-facing port quarter.

'OK,' said Richard, riding the uneasy heave of the deck unconsciously. 'That's a convincing scenario but it doesn't end there, does it?'

'Nope,' agreed T-Shirt. 'Because we were all involved pretty soon after that too.'

'By accident or by design?' asked Richard. 'I mean, could there be a sinister side to the sudden disappearance and reappearance of the search and rescue team?'

'Come on,' said T-Shirt. 'Who'd want a British Naval Antarctic Survey vessel and a cruise ship full of tourists cluttering up their neat little plan?'

'Someone who wanted to get away from Armstrong no matter what?' hazarded Richard.

'OK,' conceded T-Shirt. 'Also I guess someone who had contacts or a market waiting aboard one of them.'

'That's pushing it too far, I think,' said Richard.

'Maybe. But then it's a bit of a village down here. And I guess it's easy enough to get gossip from Ushuaia. Or from the Net. Folks can live in each other's pockets pretty well down here. A guy from Armstrong wouldn't find it too difficult to discover the identities of passing ships at any particular time. Especially if they were owned and run by a competitive foreign power in the market for the same hardware. Like, say, the Russians.' T-Shirt looked around the dining room.

'Who in Russia has enough money to buy something like that these days?' asked Richard.

Then he and T-Shirt answered the question together. 'The Russian mafia.'

'But all that supposes that the men who pilfered the Power Strip from the suit want to sell it.'

'Sell it, barter it, trade it for power, honour, sex, drugs, rock and roll,' said T-Shirt. 'Why else take it?'

'That's not what I mean. What if they don't want to sell the thing itself? What if they just want to pull it apart, understand the whole design, then sell the information? They could do that over the phone.'

'Is that possible?' said Richard. 'Surely there'd be a lot of, I don't know, graphics, say.'

'Easy,' said T-Shirt. 'Use the Internet. Get your design, your specs, your graphics – down to the molecular level for the programmable carbon, chips and micromachines – shove it all into a computer with a modem, and a satellite dish down here, and sling it onto the Internet. Very tight security. Complex company code. Limited access destination website. Couple of minutes to send. Couple of hours to download maybe, but once it's in the e-mail tray or whatever, who gives a damn?'

'So,' said Jolene, 'we seem to be looking for a team rather than an individual. There's got to be a fixer, a scientist and a computer freak in it at least. Not to mention a murderer.'

'At first,' said Richard, 'I was tempted to think of him as a saboteur. The major's death could have been almost accidental; the explosion of the Skiddoos could definitely have been a piece of contrived sabotage which killed poor Thompson by accident. Even the fact that no one was actually killed when the transport and storage all went up at Armstrong could point to that.'

'But the bastard came after me on purpose to kill me,' said Jolene. 'Came after me with my own gun, Richard. Don't forget that.'

'No. I'm not forgetting that,' said Richard quietly. 'And it's something we have to bear in mind if we're right and these people are on board here now. You could well still be a target. Especially if they found a way to smuggle guns from one place to another, as well as everything else.'

'Any way we can prove any of this?' asked T-Shirt. 'Test it, even? Without putting Jolene at any more risk?'

'Well,' drawled Jolene, 'the guy who was put in charge of the Glock was Killigan. He was head of security so he should be able to tell me about the suit and how it was being held when it was tampered with.' She looked round the table. 'I need to talk to him. I'll put that on my list of things to do next. Meanwhile, can our little group break down the Power Strip and put it on the Net at Armstrong?'

'Only if Gene Jaeger is involved, or if they've got independent access like the system you brought with you,' said Richard. 'The colonel's procedures may be a little slack, but he's got a tight personal hold on communications. Did Agent Jones mention anything about independent access to the Net?'

'No,' said Jolene.

'OK. Say Gene is not involved. They can't get to the Net from

Armstrong unless they go through him.'

'Or over him,' said T-Shirt.

'Or find some way of fooling him. They'd need open access, private time, nobody paying much attention.'

'They'd get that today, I guess,' said T-Shirt. 'Please, Colonel, can I say Happy New Millennium to the folks back in Old Moscow; couple of minutes on the Net?'

'OK,' said Jolene. 'But there's a problem. The Power Strip isn't at Armstrong. At least it's nowhere the FBI can find it. They found traces of the suit but that was all. The Strip itself isn't there. Which means it's nowhere useful. And since the second explosion and the fire, most of the labs are out and the computer system's none too hot.'

'Then it came out somewhere along the line. Or the information about its design did. Or both,' said T-Shirt.

'Onto *Erebus*,' said Richard. 'But it's not much use there. Limited access to labs. Very limited access to computers. No access to the Net at all.'

'Then it's here,' said T-Shirt. 'The Strip itself or its design specs. And the guys who stole it and want to send the information out are here.'

'I'll buy that,' said Jolene. 'So, could they have sent their information over the Net already?'

'Under the noses of Irene Ogre, Vivien Agran and Vasily Varnek?' said Richard. 'I think not.'

Jolene opened her mouth to respond but her voice was drowned out by a massive shout of, *'Five!'*

The three of them looked up, and realised that while they had been talking the room had filled.

'Four!' yelled the voices.

Richard looked across to the doorway and there were Robin and the twins running in, the twins adding their voices to *'Three!'*

Distracted, he glanced out, still far removed from what was going on immediately around him, struck by how much darker and more threatening the weather had become. He felt the deck heave and wondered whether Irene had put out the ship's stabilisers yet.

'Two!'

Then Robin and the twins were beside him. Colin and Kate, their faces aglow, were just behind them. Richard rose and turned as everyone chorused, *'One!'*

He looked in the same direction as everyone else was and saw the great screens filled with a picture of a clock tower framed with darkness and television lighting. Showing the time ticking down, second by second, to midnight, as everyone, himself included, bellowed, *'Zero!'*

The big clock by the screen showed 08:00 local time, but they were all cheering and clapping with the people of Auckland and Wellington. Both here and there, the champagne corks were popping and the parties getting seriously under way. For in New Zealand, and all points north to Kamchatka, the Siberian Sea and the deserted, benighted North Pole, and all points south to the Ross Ice Shelf, and to Amundsen-Scott South Polar base itself if they chose to recognise it, the new millennium had begun.

As the cheering was echoing round the room, interspersed with the tolling of the first midnight bells, the screens flickered and died. An uneasy silence fell and as it did so, the wind made its presence known by throwing itself against the ship, massive, grey and intractable as an angry rhinoceros. As though shocked back to life by the power of the gust, the signal flickered back onto the screen, catching an effusive commentator in mid-platitude. The cheers began again, though a little muted this time. Richard hugged his excited offspring, swapped a grin with Robin, and began to move away from the table.

'Where are you off to?' she yelled.

'Business. This lot's going to last all day. It's sixteen hours to midnight at this longitude.'

'I know, but even so. Let the twins get settled in, at least.'

Richard felt a flare of irritation, instantly smothered. The family were here at his behest. In twelve hours' time, at supper time this evening, it would be London's turn to count down to midnight and the twins, William in particular, would be upset by the parties and excitement at home he was missing. One sight of the Millennium Dome in London would probably set him off. The only positive way through was to make sure they were having so much fun that they didn't mind. But the atmosphere here was resolutely adult, the fun on offer entirely unsuited to two rising nine-year-olds. Only he and Robin could work the magic needed.

And yet, here he was, caught up in Jolene's investigation, with heaven knew what dangers threatening.

'Ten minutes,' he said. 'Give me ten minutes. I'll be back, I promise . . .' And he was gone, shouldering his way through the cheering crowd, turning down champagne and kisses alike.

Jolene and T-Shirt caught up with him in the corridor outside.

'I'm going to talk to Killigan,' said Jolene.

'If we're going to get sense out of anybody we'd better be quick,' warned T-Shirt, and Richard nodded his agreement. He suspected he was the only tee totaller aboard. And alcohol was the least of the stimulants – or depressants – on offer.

'I'll go up on the bridge. We're always welcome there,' he added with a glance towards the nearest flashing box. 'I expect Varnek and Irene will be there, though I don't know the duty officer, the third. In any case, someone will be able to tell me if anyone's booked to use the Internet at any time in the next twenty-four hours – or, indeed, if anyone sneaked onto it in the last twenty-four without anybody noticing.'

'Right,' said Jolene. 'Then where will you be?'

'I'm a twenty-first-century man, near as dammit,' said Richard. 'I'll be looking after the kids, of course.'

Irene Ogre was in the big chair by the radio room looking worriedly out at the morning. Soiling the otherwise virginal white of her lap was a print-out of the storm currently tearing the heart out of the Bellingshausen Sea, all too near to the west of them. A great black-based wall of cloud was sweeping towards them with the self-assured majesty of an unstoppable army. There was little light left in the young day and it had the pathetic demeanour of a sickly child. The last of this light glimmered westwards and the Stygian depths of the approaching clouds were shafted by cold blue brightness as though some devil had thrown open the gates of a frozen hell.

'There's a lot of ice out there still,' said Richard automatically.

Irene stirred, separating the two flimsies in her lap to show that beneath the storm so unflinchingly delineated by the satellites safe above, there was a wall of ice equally unmistakably defined.

'You're running hard north?' he asked.

'We are due at Ushuaia on Monday on the morning tide,' she said.

'The wind will hit hard from the west then swing to the south.'

'During the next twelve hours, maybe sixteen,' said Varnek, crossing towards the two captains. 'Then we might get a couple of hours' quiet before it hits again hard from the north.'

'It's a very tight system,' said Richard, looking closely at the portrait of the storm. 'What does it seem to be doing?'

'Tightening,' answered Irene a little dully.

'Typical,' said Richard. 'Barometric readings?'

'Going through the floor,' said Varnek.

'Through the lower basement floor,' added Irene.

'Wind speeds?'

'Gusting past force twelve and strengthening. But that's only an estimate. There aren't any ships out in the Bellingshausen Sea today,' said Varnek. 'There was an automatic weather ship of some kind but it's stopped transmitting. Registered a gust of one hundred and thirty-five knots and closed down.'

'Safe havens?'

'None. All west-facing; all of them choked with ice from the last few days' activity, like Armstrong and Palmer.'

'And Faraday,' added the radio officer, entering into the conversation suspiciously cheerfully.

'Kyril?' said Varnek with a frown though his tone was accommodating, 'have you been at the vodka? It's nowhere near time.'

Kyril beamed at them. 'Not so far off time,' he said. 'It will be midnight in Magadan in,' he looked at his watch, 'thirty minutes. Chef is from Magadan and has given a few favoured friends some vodka in case we cannot be together to drink the toast with him at nine this morning.'

'We'll have to ride it out then,' said Richard thoughtfully, paying scant attention to the happy radio officer. 'The islands should give you some shelter and maybe keep the ice off you too. In any case you have an ice-strengthened hull and some of the most up-to-date equipment I've ever seen. Put the stabilisers out and hope for the best.'

'The stabilisers,' said Irene glumly, 'have been out since the morning watch.'

Richard looked at his Rolex. Half an hour. He had promised to be back in ten minutes twenty minutes ago. 'I know this may sound fatuous,' he began, wondering suddenly whether Russians would understand the concept of fatuousness, 'but has anyone booked to send messages over the Internet recently?'

'Many,' answered Varnek at once. 'We have men and women aboard from almost every state in Russia. Many have asked to send messages. Not to their families directly, of course – who can afford a modem in Russia these days? – but to businesses, local contacts . . .'

'Any of our people?'

'Of course. Most of the passengers, I believe. But they will not wish to send their messages until midnight our time or later, to arrive at midnight in their own time zones.'

'Anyone else?'

'Only one,' said Varnek. 'Billy Hoyle, one of the men we brought aboard from Armstrong base. But he will not be able to use his booking, I fear.'

Billy Hoyle sprang awake, the whole of his right side on fire. He was curled on a floor behind piles of stuff whose outlines he could only see in vague security lighting. Then he remembered where he was. And why he was there. He tried to move his right arm and groaned in pain. Trained in basic first aid, he lifted his arm, then lowered it across his chest and tried to hold it there. The best he could do was to shove his numb right hand through his shirt front like Napoleon. He probably looked stupid, but he felt better. Then he tried to sit up again. This time he made it with his back against the pile of softness which had seduced him into slumber – how long ago? He checked his watch. Jesus, more than ten hours ago.

He began to panic. Fought to control the fear. It was so late! What in God's name was he going to do now? That stone killer bitch! Had she any idea what she and her pet thug had done to him? He opened his mouth and began to pant like a dog, hyperventilating, hoping to force some positive energy into his battered, scrawny body. Grimly, he began to enumerate to himself the range of chemical stimulants and depressants which would stiffen his spine and deaden his pain, all of them in the possession of the ice bitch Agran now; just when he really needed them.

Billy gasped, and groaned aloud as the pain lanced through his chest from the point of his right shoulder to the lowest of his left ribs. He wondered briefly if he was having a heart attack. 'Come on there, Billy boy,' he said to himself. 'Move.' And he pulled himself up onto his knees.

He was in a storeroom in the engineering sections, a deck or two below the weather deck, and lucky still to be undiscovered. But he needed to communicate with the world now, no matter what the risk. It was, literally, more than his life was worth to hesitate. At least he remembered to reach up with his left hand when he finally made it to the door.

The door opened inwards and Billy swung back on it, dazed by pain and light-headed. So that it seemed quite logical that a couple of cherubs should approach him suddenly; a boy and a girl cherub, wide-eyed and curly-haired; vaguely familiar.

'Hello, Mr Billy,' said the girl. 'You look as if you're in trouble. What can William and I do to help you?'

Chapter Twenty

Robin had never been so angry in her life. First Richard had dashed off on one of his wild-goose chases, leaving her in charge of a couple of bored, intransigent children in the middle of a party, and then, the instant her back was turned, the pair of them had vanished. *Kalinin* was a big ship. They could be anywhere, up to anything. Robin simply did not know where to begin looking for them.

But she knew a woman who would.

Mrs Agran had her finger on the pulse of the social side of the ship. She was in charge of a crew of entertainers, stewards and cooks, and according to Richard she controlled a security system comprising a network of cameras capable of scanning at least the common parts of the ship.

Robin knocked on Mrs Agran's door, keeping her fingers crossed that the entertainments officer was overseeing her army of helpers from her command post rather than in person.

'Come in,' called a cheery voice, and Robin opened the door.

She took in the décor of the room with one sweep of her cool grey eyes. Whatever impression the velvet hangings, terracotta nudes and interesting prints made on her, no sign of it was evident in her expression. She explained her worries quickly. Mrs Agran courteously invited her to sit down and while she did a quick sweep of the common areas via her computer, Robin accepted a cup of tea from a tall blonde assistant called Gretchen.

The tea nearly slopped into the saucer as *Kalinin* gave a sudden sideways heave. Sidetracked, Robin put the cup and saucer down on Mrs Agran's desk and rose. She crossed to the big oval porthole and looked out at the day with a frown. She was on the starboard side of the bridgehouse, looking over a sheer drop down the ship's side and out to the black-fanged volcanic coast of Graham Land as *Kalinin* plunged north. Away ahead and to the port quarter she saw the chill blue light brushing the black bases of the approaching storm clouds. Then, suddenly, as though a curtain had been closed across the day, the first torrent of rain whirled up against the thick glass – and froze into opacity on contact.

'No sign, I'm afraid,' said Mrs Agran. 'Would you like to take a look around yourself before we institute a full search? They must be in the bridgehouse – unless they've slipped down into the engineering areas. They can't get out onto the deck unless they are very strong indeed. Some of my big boys and girls can't even open those heavy bulkhead doors.'

'Yes,' said Robin. 'That's a good idea. I'll have a look around first.'

'Gretchen here will lend a hand. I have another assistant as well if you like, Anoushka.'

'No, the two of us should be more than enough. And if you can contact my husband, perhaps he could help.'

'Of course. Do you know where Captain Mariner is at present?'

'I have no idea, I'm afraid.'

She thanked Mrs Agran for her help and left the office with Gretchen dutifully in tow.

Robin headed first for the command bridge where they came across Richard and as soon as he heard what their mission was, he joined them, his face creased in a worried frown. As he searched for his missing children, however, part of his mind remained preoccupied with the other problems he was trying to deal with. Billy Hoyle had booked a slot for access to the Internet at 17:00 this evening. Kyril the radio officer had been quite certain about this because it was a very inconvenient time. One or two people had booked calls via satellite phone, radio link or Internet to the cities scattered between Magadan and Novosibirsk in Siberia as the midnight line moved relentlessly westward through the day, but the lines did not really get busy until 2 p.m. when midnight reached the big centres of Tashkent and Ykaterinberg. Thereafter things were destined to get very busy indeed as call after call was booked to families in the populous western Russian conurbation's on this side of the Urals. And busiest of all would be the hour of 5 p.m. when midnight arrived everywhere from Riga to St Petersburg.

The American had given no destination for his proposed message through the Internet, but if it was a seasonal message it could only be going to this area, unless he was calling someone in East Africa, of course. In Hoyle's homeland of America, it would not be midnight until well after it was midnight on *Kalinin*. The lines would be pretty busy then, too, as the American entertainment staff all tried to get on the line at once. Why wasn't Billy Hoyle's booking in with this rush rather than the Russian one?

'Come on, Sergeant,' chided Jolene gently, keeping her voice low so as not to disturb the sleeping Dai Gwyllim, 'surely you can come up with a better answer than that.'

'It's all there is, Dr DaCosta,' grated Killigan. 'I can't remember anything. It's all very well to tell me about security systems I can't detail and thefts you say must have happened, but I simply can't remember. You can tell me that the fires were started deliberately and that there were bombs set. And that there was some lunatic with a Glock running around trying to blow you away. But all I remember is trying to bring a fire in a big John Deere under some sort of control when the whole lot went up in my face. Then I remember the Limey boat and that's all. Maybe the major's coffin gave me amnesia as well as concussion when it thumped me in the head, huh?'

T-Shirt was sitting close by on the end of Max's bed listening to his friend's snoring. In the next bed along from Killigan, young Corporal Washington lay, more severely injured than the big sergeant, swathed in bandages and apparently asleep. While Jolene's attention was focused on the man she was questioning, T-Shirt's eyes drifted towards the corporal and he saw the flicker of a frown flit like a shadow across the young man's face as Killigan spoke.

T-Shirt's eyes narrowed thoughtfully and he pulled himself up off Max's bed. While Jolene continued to go over, step by step, the events at Armstrong on the night of the fire, trying without success to drag some more information out of the big sergeant, T-Shirt wandered away down the ward, checking the deeply sleeping Dai and then more generally, getting a feel for the place and the people in it. Mendel and Fagan, the scientists, were engrossed in a game of chess, both of them well enough to sit up now, strength returning with thickening beards. Billy Hoyle's and Ernie Marshall's beds stood side by side, empty. At the end, between a pair of empty beds and the doorway to the ante-room, another doorway led out into the toilets.

In Billy Hoyle's bedside locker lay a thriller. Apparently bored by Jolene's unsuccessful attempts to extract more information from the sergeant, T-Shirt perched on the edge of Billy's bed and became engrossed in the novel.

After about ten minutes, Corporal Washington shuffled by, heading towards the toilets. T-Shirt didn't appear to notice, licking his finger thoughtfully and turning one page, then the next, before putting the

201

paperback down and rising. He went into the toilets just as Washington was turning away from the wash basin.

'You're next, I guess,' said T-Shirt easily, crossing to a urinal and unzipping. 'So you'd better get your story straight, eh?'

'What do you mean?' asked Washington, watching him suspiciously in the mirror. The ship heaved and rolled slightly. T-Shirt did not answer, focusing on keeping his aim true and his boots dry.

The motion eased. 'If you're going to back Killigan up.'

Silence. But at least Washington was still there.

'I mean,' said T-Shirt, zipping up, 'I can see that you'd want to stand by your boss. And he's head of security, after all. Responsible man. Wouldn't need very much. Probably just a little white lie, huh? What's he after? Some sort of award? Looks a good age for a military man. Trying for something extra to retire on? Commendation? Purple Heart? Extra pension?' His eyes met Washington's for the first time, in the mirror. Then he looked down again, turning on the taps.

'If he is, you can't blame him,' said Washington, stung. 'He's a brave man. Good noncom. Given a lifetime of service. He's a good soldier.'

'Course he is,' nodded T-Shirt, washing his hands slowly and carefully. 'Can't take that away from the man. But he wasn't by the John Deere, was he? When it went up? He was away somewhere else, up to something else. Certainly, that's where he was found, no matter what he says he can remember now. He's lying to the inspector, isn't he? Looking for a bit of glory?'

'Well . . .'

The temporisation was enough for T-Shirt. He was no inspector. He didn't have to make it stand up in court. He reached for the towel. 'Nuff said, then,' he purred. Enough said for the time being, is what he thought. The implications of Killigan's lie needed some careful consideration. Then it would be time for discussion with Jolene.

'I can't budge Killigan,' Jolene said ten minutes later as they walked back along the corridor. 'And Washington backs him up. Perhaps they were both there fighting the fire at the John Deere then out in back of the huts after all. I'll have to double-check with Colin Ross and Richard.'

'Think Richard's found out anything on the bridge?'

'I expect so. He has a habit of finding things out. Sorting things out. He's quite a guy.'

202

T-Shirt was about to answer, when the subject of their conversation came down the companionway.

'We've lost the twins,' he said. 'Either of you seen them?'

'No,' said Jolene at once. 'They're definitely not in the sickbay. Want us to help you look for them?'

'It's all right, thanks,' said Richard with a rueful grin. 'We've got a good few people searching already. You've got work to do. People to see. Files to consult.'

'Parties to go to?' suggested T-Shirt hopefully.

'I think not yet,' said Richard. 'The only person who's booked time on the Net today, Jolene, is Billy Hoyle. He's on at five this evening.'

'If he comes back from wherever he's gone,' said Jolene, thoughtfully.

'Back from the dead?' suggested T-Shirt grimly. The other two looked askance at him and he shrugged. 'Well you all searched the whole ship for him and his friend last night,' he said. 'Where else could they be?'

Billy was in one of the storerooms two decks further down. He was still in pain but was beginning to feel a little better. The children were like miracle workers. Working as a team, they had joined in his camping game and set him up in a neat little bivouac well out of sight at the back of the room. Sneaking out on secret missions unobserved, they had slipped into the cabins of the crew who were up in the passenger areas keeping the party going or up in the ship-handling areas keeping *Kalinin* going. From the cabins they had purloined towels, clean clothing, bedding and a range of stuff at Billy's request. Now it was time for them to venture further afield. The need for bandages and painkillers had been pushed aside for the time being by torn bedsheets and a bottle of vodka from one of the engineers' cabins. What Billy needed now was food. He had not eaten since his ill-fated visit to the witch's lair.

'Lissen, kids,' he said. 'I got to eat. Was there nothing in those guys' cabins? Pretzels? Bagel chips?'

'Sorry, Mr Billy,' said Mary sadly. 'We couldn't find a thing.'

'If we go onto the upper decks there should be plenty,' William observed. 'They have a party going on in the dining salon on Bellingshausen-Peary deck. There's bound to be crisps and peanuts.'

'Naw,' said Billy swiftly. 'Someone would see you and that would spoil our game.'

'The galley's not far from here,' said practical Mary. 'Chef will probably be pretty busy making more party food. We should be able to get something in for you from the galley, Mr Billy.'

'Hey, that's not a bad idea. You two'd fit right alongside with the Hardy Boys you know?'

'More like the Famous Five,' said William as they sneaked out of the door again. 'This is fun!'

'It is,' agreed Mary, but there was a little frown extending the straight line of her nose up between her level eyebrows.

The galley was easy to sneak into and rob. It was all bustle and stir, with stewards coming and going, increasingly laden with party fare. And Chef had arranged the galley tables in a row by the door so that his minions could load them with the canapés he was producing, though as it was not quite 9 a.m. yet, he was holding back in anticipation of a swell in demand three hours hence. And another nine hours hence, running through until after midnight.

Because Chef had moved the galley tables, they were out of their usual clamps on the deck and so they slid a little with the rolling of the hull and juddered with the labouring of the engines, adding a stuttering rumble to the normal noise of a busy kitchen. The ship's movement also jangled cutlery and cookware, crockery tinkled and glassware chimed. Nobody marked the surreptitious entrance of two small figures through the side door into the crew's quarters. They chose their supplies with care – a plate of sandwiches and a small cold roast chicken, a pile of late-breakfast waffles and syrup, and a litre bottle of Coke.

Had it not been for the waffles, Chef would probably never have noticed. But they were a special order and the steward expecting to collect them asked about them as soon as he arrived and saw they were not on the tables. Even then, he was nearly shrugged aside, for the hour was approaching nine. Although Chef had no relatives to call in his native Magadan, he was determined that nothing would stop him, and those he had chosen to share his vodka, from drinking the health of every other native of Magadan when the millennium arrived there, at 9 a.m. local time.

'The waffles,' called the impetuous steward again. 'A twelve stack, maple syrup and a litre of Coke.'

'They are on the table there, ready to take,' called Chef impatiently, his eye on the computer clock, which was permanently set to Magadan time so that no matter where in the world he happened to be, his equipment was attuned to his home.

'You've been at the vodka, Chef,' called the importunate young man, living dangerously. He was a Cossack from Rostov, young and arrogant.

'Now you listen,' retorted Chef, his professional temper aroused. 'My computer has not been at the vodka. See, here, on this screen. Order 12/31/99/P27. Filled. On the table.'

'Well, don't look at your computer, Chef. Look at the table. Order 12/31/99/P27 is not fucking there!'

So Chef missed out on drinking to his city at the very stroke of midnight there, because he was looking at the table – at the lack of order 12/31/99/P27. Amazed he looked back at his computer again. But the screen was blank, as if the whole thing had been switched off.

'Waffles! You guys are the biz! Chicken. And what is this? Knockwurst on rye. How'd you know I'm from New York?'

'We just took what we could get, Mr Billy. And here's some Coke.'

'William. Mary. What can I say, guys? But I'm getting worried about your folks. Won't they be wondering where you are by now?'

'Doubt it,' said William promptly. 'Daddy will be on the bridge or somewhere, doing something important.'

'Mummy will be worried, though,' said Mary gently. 'You're right, Mr Billy. We should get back before we're missed. Have you got everything you need, do you think? For the time being at least?'

'I guess,' said Billy cheerfully. 'But I'm relying on you guys.' He put on a cod drawl. 'You come along back now, y'hear?'

'Yes, Mr Billy,' they said.

Gretchen found the children, down at the end of the crew's accommodation, on the outer edges of the pool of consternation which was the galley.

'Where have you two been?' demanded Robin, coming up next.

'What do you mean, Mummy?' asked Mary.

'We haven't been anywhere,' added William.

'Where could we go?' asked Mary, as innocently puzzled as her brother was manfully confused. 'What's the matter with Chef?'

'Who knows?' answered their mother long-sufferingly. 'Come on, you two. Let's go back up to the dining salon. Don't drift off again.'

'No, Mummy.'

'Course not.'

'Here you are,' said Richard, coming down the campanionway. 'Where on earth have you been?'

205

'Nowhere.'

'Here.'

'I see,' he said sceptically. 'Sounds like moonshine to me. What have you two been up to?'

'Nothing, we—'

'Honestly, Daddy. What could we possibly get up to?'

'You two? No end of trouble! Where are you taking them now, darling?'

'The dining salon.'

'Back to the party, eh? Is that where you'd really like to go?'

'No, Daddy,' said William at once.

'Fair enough. Where *would* you like to go?'

'The bridge,' they chorused.

The bridge did not seem as airy and spacious as usual; nor, indeed, as welcoming. The gathering storm had obscured the furthest views so that the seaward aspect was indistinguishable from the rugged reaches of the black shore on whose dangerous weather side they lay. The light was gone. There were no more hellish blue gleams on the fat black bellies of the clouds sweeping down upon them. Cold rain spat bitterly across all the windows and froze on all except the clearview so that everything was weird and twisted by thin films of ice except the view northward which was frost-framed but clear. *Kalinin* seemed to be running through a larger version of the cleft in the moraine where so much of this had started. Sheer blackness gathered on either hand, pressing in like the jaws of a vice.

'Is there any ice ahead?' asked Irene Ogre as Richard, Robin and the twins came onto the bridge.

'The radar sees none,' answered Varnek, looking up from the screen immediately in front of him.

'Weather sat?' asked the captain, quietly, tensely.

'Clear,' called the second officer, whose name Richard did not yet know. 'Nothing ahead from the latest transmission.'

'Come to full ahead,' decided Irene. 'At the very least it will stabilise her.'

Richard found himself nodding in agreement. He looked across and saw Robin, frowning, automatically doing the same.

'But keep a weather eye out for ice,' added Irene. 'It's coming in hard from the west and I don't want it taking me by surprise.'

'Isn't that what *Titanic*'s captain said?' asked Varnek, straightening.

'No, sir,' chimed in William. 'First Officer William Murdoch was

in command of the bridge when *Titanic* struck. And he never asked
for any more speed.'

Chapter Twenty-One

Jolene was little more in charity with the library's computer equipment than she was with Sergeant Killigan. She had secured herself a corner of the otherwise deserted library, equipped with a computer. Like the other computers aboard, this one in the library was linked to the ship's network, but it had individual CD-Rom facility and twin ports for 3.5 inch floppies. She had also, remarkably, found a CD of Glenn Gould playing Bach's *Goldberg Variations* in the library. She slipped it into the system, then called up onto the screen the computer network's word-processing system. In she went through Windows 98, reacting to its first question by electing to communicate in English rather than Russian, German, Spanish or French. Then she began fiddling around with icons as the intellectual intricacies of the Bach's piano variations, humanised by the gentle droning of the performer humming along with the tune, soothed her subconscious.

After a few moments' exploration, Jolene chose the word processing program she liked best and called it up. She asked the computer to look at the files on the six floppies she had brought with her. The network at Armstrong was not directly compatible with the system on her late laptop but she had nevertheless been able to get into some of the files before the thing was burned out by the power surge. She should be able to get in more easily, quickly and deeply on a machine as large and modern as this one, she thought. She called up READ ALL FILES, and the names of the most recently saved network files came up into the box on the screen.

She focused on a file called HOYLE.NWK and called that up. The first five pages of the file were computer garbage: squares, ampersands, carets, asterisks, exclamations, dots, dollar signs, line after line of 'e' acute and 'a' circumflex and, most infuriatingly, nearly one whole page of question marks.

'Jesus,' she said to the screen, lightly striking it low on the face, like a mafioso insulting an opponent. 'And this is the clear top copy. What are the back-ups going to look like? I'm never going to get at them at this rate.'

'You sure you're going in the right way here, Jolene?' asked a lazy voice right behind her.

She jumped so badly she bruised her thighs on the table. 'God T-Shirt! What are you trying to do? Give me a heart attack here?'

'Sorry,' he said quietly if not very contritely. 'Whatcha doin'?' He pulled up a chair and sat down beside her.

She explained.

Under T-Shirt's sure direction, the machine searched for and tagged all the files she was interested in. By the time they had finished, there were four files stored in the C drive.

'Now, we want to rank them in order of writing and saving, don't we?' he asked.

Jolene just nodded. Her eyes remained on the screen as he keyed in the request, and beside each of the apparently identical file titles there appeared a date and time of saving down to one-hundredth of a second, logged by the central clock in Armstrong's network. Between the top, official, file and the first back-up file, there were fifteen minutes. Between the first back-up and the second, fifteen minutes more. But between the second back-up file and the third back-up, whose existence Billy Hoyle had not been aware of, there was a gap of nearly four hours. And it didn't take much calculation for Jolene to work out that it was in those four hours that Major Schwartz had got lost and frozen to death.

'That one,' she said. 'Call up that one first.'

T-Shirt obliged. Computer garbage filled the screen again. 'Wait a minute,' he said. His fingers danced across the keys and the screen darkened, lightened, cleared from white on black to black on white again. The computer garbage shrank to black boxes and dots, and the words were large and clear on the screen. 'Now, do you want to read this on the screen as it is; do you want me to call up the next one back and run them in parallel, split screen, or would you like me to print this out and call up the next one to print into hard copy too?'

'Print them out,' said Jolene without hesitation. 'I'd rather read a sheet than a screen any day. In fact, if you can, print out all four. Comparing them will be easier and quicker on paper. And I may want to make notes.'

'Consider it done.'

And within fifteen minutes, it was. Jolene held in her hands the details of Bernie Schwartz's ill-fated journey. Or Billy Hoyle's versions of those events. One written before and the rest written after he knew the major was dead. One giving facts, the others giving cover-ups. And those cover-ups, by definition, pointed the finger of guilt.

While Jolene and T-Shirt were at work, Richard and Robin brought the twins back down again. The bridge had been quite a success, but both parents felt that a family heart-to-heart and some strict guidelines were called for. But finding the time or the place seemed difficult just at the moment. Really, they wanted a corner where William and Mary would feel happy and cared for. The party in the dining salon, under-supplied with food for some reason no one would go into, was raucous and no place for children. The television pictures were now showing the preparations for the arrival of midnight in Eastern Australia and Tasmania, Hobart, Sydney, Brisbane, up through Port Moresby in Papua New Guinea to various places in Russia that even the crew had never heard of. Except for the third officer, apparently, whose family came from Okhotsk.

It was twenty to ten in the morning aboard *Kalinin* and far too early to ask excited, buoyant twins to settle down to anything quiet. What they really needed to do was to go for a run around the deck, but as their visit to the bridge had established all too clearly, that was out of the question. None of the ship's facilities would really serve either.

But one thing, oddly, seemed to beckon, and that was the sick bay. Mary had seen her mother and Kate go down there and although she harboured veterinary ambitions herself, she was interested in any kind of healing. Since his view of the Base jumping yesterday, William had been dying to make the closer acquaintance of Dai Gwyllim. And Richard and Robin were well aware that 'thank yous' were owed by both children to Killigan and, especially, Washington for their help on the net yesterday evening. So Richard and Robin agreed to allow a little exploration down towards Dr Glasov's domain, on condition that if either patients or doctor seemed uneasy, all four of them would come away again, post haste.

Dr Glasov had allowed a television to sully the medical calm, but its sound was turned so low that one had to strain to hear it, so a gentle buzz of conversation filled the little ward instead. Dai was up, though not yet about, his elderly frame battered but tough, and Jilly was brightly by his side. Together with Max, they had overcome the shyness of Corporal Washington and the reserve of Mendel and Fagan apparently. But they had been unable to breach Killigan's gruff defences; something, Jilly vouchsafed to Robin immediately on their

211

arrival, that probably could not be done without a generous amount of alcohol and several strippers.

'So he'll be much more cheerful later on, then,' said Robin breezily.

'Well,' said Jilly, 'the alcohol, yes. But the strippers? Not on board Mrs Agran's ship, surely.'

Dai grunted. His sign for amused disagreement.

'Please, sir,' said William to the Welshman, very much on his best behaviour, moving before his parents could drag him across to the overpowering sergeant or the shy corporal, 'could you explain to me about Base jumping?'

Richard, too got caught up in the ensuing conversation, and as the time ticked round towards ten o'clock, a cosy atmosphere built up in the ward, with Jilly and Robin discussing Mrs Agran and her minions, Washington reading a body-building magazine left by Max when he went upstairs to find T-Shirt and join the party, and Mendel and Fagan playing a chess game close enough to the television to hear the commentary and occasionally discuss a point of interest with Killigan who was the only one actually watching it.

Such was the level of cosy relaxation, in fact, that Mary found it perfectly easy to sneak out without being noticed and vanish unremarked down the corridor towards the storage areas.

Lieutenant Borisov, third officer, should have held the forenoon watch but the captain was on the bridge, and with her was Second Officer Yazov, the navigating officer, and First Officer Varnek who was keeping an eye on the weather – a close eye. Borisov was not exactly at leisure, however. He had been assigned duties as lading officer by Varnek and so it was his duty to be up-to-date with everything aboard which could be used or consumed. Chef bought in and sold on his food under Borisov's aegis. Which was one reason they were friends. The second was that they were both military buffs, specialising particularly in post-revolutionary Russian strategy and tactics through to the end of the Great Patriotic War. The third was that they came from towns relatively close to one another, Okhotsk being only a few hundred kilometres west of Magadan, though just inside the next time-zone.

So it was that as 10 a.m. local time drew near, Third Officer Borisov was strolling through the storage areas on his way down to the galley with a bottle of vodka in his pocket because midnight was approaching Okhotsk, and with it the millennium. A passenger appeared out of nowhere, a young girl who saw him, hesitated, turned as though to flee, turned back and walked past him. Borisov was too preoccupied to pay her or her strange behaviour more than passing attention. He noticed her. He noticed what she did. He noticed she was carrying a bottle of Coke. 'Cheers,' he said in Russian and laughed gently as they passed. And that was all really.

Certainly, the child vanished from his mind immediately he arrived in the galley, for there was his friend the chef fuming and shouting in a highly unusual manner. The normal order of the place – the military precision, the commissariat control – were gone. Little squads ran hither and yon as though under fire. The culinary campaign this Voroshilov among chefs-general had degenerated into a messy blitzkrieg, as though he was no more than the merest Goering.

'My dear fellow, what is the matter?' cried Borisov, striding through the wreckage of stewards, brandishing his bottle of vodka.

'The bloody computer is down again,' said Chef, the gloom on his countenance lightening at the sight of friend and festive cup alike. 'The last time we were in dock I had it checked. Those bastards in Petersburg swore it wouldn't happen again. They think it is a joke, of course, to use a computer to run a kitchen. Let them try to do their jobs without computers nowadays. Bastards.'

'Well, never mind,' said Borisov. 'I have brought the twin of the bottle I toasted you with an hour ago. Let us toast each other now, for it will be ten o'clock in thirty seconds' time. Does any man here,' Borisov turned and spoke to the assembled mess of stewards, 'come from east of Lake Baikal? What, none of you? You poor western weaklings.'

'The chief steward comes from Yakutsk,' said one of his minions. 'But he is not here. He is updating the accommodations programme.'

'Then we will drink to him in his absence,' said Borisov. 'As for the rest of you, you are decadent and western and weaklings and I spit on you all.'

He probably would have done so literally, but the red second hand kissed the black minute hand on the tip of ten o'clock just then and so he drank instead, passing the bottle to Chef who took a hefty gulp in his turn. Then they both drank solemnly to the chief steward. The chief steward, of course, had the best vodka; better than the captain's, it was said – even better than Varnek's, it was whispered. There was no doubt that Babushka Agran would have had the best if she had wanted it but she was American in so many of her tastes, though married to a man – probably happily deceased – from Irkutsk, and she preferred bourbon whiskey in preference to good vodka like the chief

213

steward. So the pair of them would be off on the lookout for him at eleven when midnight rolled over Yakutsk.

'It wouldn't be so bad,' said Chef after his third swig, 'but I'm pretty sure the computer crash is just a cover for some major pilfering. You should check your computer also, Borisov. You've got a lot more worth stealing in your charge than I have in mine.'

'That's easily done,' said Borisov, more suggestible now that the fiery spirit was beginning to sing in his Russian veins. 'I have a terminal through here in the storeroom we share next door. Come.'

Borisov and Chef went through into the storeroom where their responsibilities overlapped, one in charge of supplying the plates kept in here and the other in charge of filling them. There was a little terminal on the wall. Its screen was black and blank. Borisov crossed to it and threw the switch. The two stood, swaying slightly, feeling the roll of the ship. The computer screen remained blank. Borisov reached down and snapped the power on and off a couple more times.

'Same as mine,' said Chef. 'Bloody thing's dead as a Tsar. You'd better check your other stores, Borisov.'

Borisov came out into the corridor almost at a run. Varnek would blame him for this and his life would get very unpleasant very soon unless he could shuffle off responsibility and blame. And if someone was using all this confusion to pilfer stuff, then he wanted to stop him in any case.

A picture came into his vodka-brightened memory. A small girl with a large bottle of Coke, coming out of the galley, guiltily.

The first storeroom he checked was quiet. Dark. 'Liddle kirl?' he cried in his best English. 'jou in this place, liddle kirl?'

Silence, except for the engines and the distant raving of celebration or storm. He went on to the next. And the next. He found her in the fourth one. And a great deal more than he expected to find as well.

Billy Hoyle sat, white as a sheet.

'You may question him if it is crucial,' said Dr Glasov, Billy's guardian angel, 'but he has been beaten, probably by this brute Borisov, and he seems to have a broken collarbone. I will not allow much time or any further brutality.'

'Why were you hiding, Hoyle?' demanded Captain Ogre.

'I was scared,' slurred Billy. 'I owed these guys money. I thought they was going to kill me.'

'These men. Who are they?'

214

'Dunno. Guys on the crew. Big guys like this officer Borisov here. Ernie Marshall owed them too. You seen Ernie lately?' He read the answer in Irene's eyes. 'Thought not,' he said with a kind of sickly triumph. He was well aware that this was a very shaky story. Easy to check on; easy to disprove. But it was all he could come up with, and it would serve his primary purpose, which was to keep him at the centre of the captain's attention. He was terrified of being alone where Agran or her lethal thug Varnek could get at him. Even if they lined up the crew and made him do an ID parade on the whole fucking lot of them, it wouldn't matter. The objective was to stay alive until he could find some way of getting to Agran. Getting to her and negotiating with her.

But the fact was the weather was closing down almost as fast as the hours of millennium day were ticking past and everyone aboard had far too much to do to line up and smile for Billy Hoyle, let alone check his story.

Irene Ogre made her decision. 'Very well. Dr Glasov, this man is in your charge until you are satisfied he is well enough to go into secure accommodation. You are responsible for him. He does not leave here. He does not go out of your sight or that of your staff until he is locked up or this matter is cleared up. For all we know it is he who has made Mr Marshall vanish. We could well have a murderer aboard.'

'Right,' said Robin. 'You two have a lot of explaining to do.' Her voice rang around the stateroom, overcoming the rolling grumble of the storm wind outside.

Mary knew better than to protest and even William bit back on a self-excusing whine.

'Look,' said Richard more quietly. 'You've done something Mummy and I think is a bit silly.'

'Very silly,' snapped Robin.

'But clearly you don't think you were being silly at all. Now why is that?'

'Because they have no idea what a perverted little—'

'We helped Mr Billy because he helped us,' said Mary, her huge eyes fastening earnestly on her father's. 'It was Mr Billy who carried me to bed the night Mummy and Aunt Kate slept in that funny little room at Armstrong. And when we came out in the morning to look for you or Uncle Colin because Mummy and Aunt Kate had no clothes, Mr Billy helped us again.'

'How did he help?' demanded Robin, remembering suddenly three

215

burning pairs of eyes trying to see through all too thin a covering of cotton thermal underwear.

'We couldn't find Daddy like you told us,' chimed in William. 'So we looked for someone we recognised.'

'And we found Mr Billy. He was talking to the scientists – the two in the sick bay – and he was talking to lots of other people . . .'

'But he told us where you might be and we followed him into this hut.'

'But don't forget William,' said Mary, 'before we went in, Sergeant Killi—'

'Oh that's right, Sergeant Killigan told Mr Billy not to go in there but we still went in. It was very cold in there. And we looked around but we couldn't see you there. Then Corporal Washington came and took us out and brought us to Mummy. Someone had been cooking in there, I think. And Tony Thompson was sleeping there.'

'And the Tin Man,' said Mary uneasily.

'The Tin Man?' asked Richard, intrigued. 'The one from *The Wizard of Oz*?'

'No, silly,' said Mary. 'This one was in a plastic sleeping bag. Wearing a suit made out of kitchen foil.'

Vivien Agran went slowly back to her office and sat for a while, thinking. Then she leaned forward and snapped on her computer. The ten-section screen lit up. She guided the cursor round the screen to the records section. She double-clicked and the section expanded to fill the whole screen, and a series of icons lit up. During the next half-hour she browsed through these, examining what she had on the visitors first, beginning with Hoyle. After the visitors, she checked some of Dr Glasov's team. Then she went through a series of records plucked apparently at random out of the crew list. Finally she checked three of the files under her own list of stewards and entertainers. She sat back, deep in thought.

Then she reached for her internal phone and dialled the chief steward's office.

'Steward.' He always called himself that to avoid confusion with the other chief, the chief engineer, who did call himself 'Chief.'

'Agran,' she said, though he would have seen her extension number on his phone display. 'Call up the accommodation records.'

The sound of keys clicking came over the phone to her. The whisper of a mouse over its mat. Distant thunder. She looked out through her wide porthole. The sky was dark enough for thunder, she thought.

She tapped on her own keyboard with a long red finger nail. 'Steward?' she said.

'It's up,' he said. 'But please wait a moment, there's someone at the door.'

'No,' she said, too late. The handset thumped gently down, picking up voices. Borisov: 'Hey, Steward! Come on, it's almost time. Where's the good stuff?'

Steward: 'Borisov! And Chef. What are you doing here?'

'We've come to wish you Happy New Year. It will be midnight in lrkutsk in a couple of minutes. Come on, where's the—'

'Sit down, the pair of you. I'm on the phone. A moment or two will make no difference on a day such as today.' The chief steward's voice grew louder as he came back to the handset on his desk. 'Mrs Agran wishes me to do something.' There was a leathery sigh as he eased his solid bulk into his chair. 'Now, Mrs Agran,' he said. 'What is it you want me to do?'

'Look up the secure accommodation,' she ordered. 'I have records of all the suites and cabins but your computers are the only ones with details of what is secure and what is not.'

'Starting now, Mrs Agran.'

Distantly, a cheer wafted down the line to her. Then, very much closer a hiss of surprise. 'Mrs Agran! I'm sorry. There is something not right here . . . I was just . . . And it died. The whole thing went down before my very—'

Communication was abruptly cut.

Frowning, Vivien Agran called up her overview section of the chief steward's accommodation records. The screen filled with the accommodation program but there was something awry with the icons. When she put the cursor on one and clicked, the screen simply filled with a storm of strange snow, a mixture of white computer gunk on a black screen sweeping downwards. A cold chill went through her. Her fingers flashed down to her keyboard, pressing CONTROL; ALT; DELETE all at once. The snow died and the familiar blue-backed, ten-sectioned screen jumped up. She clicked on records and her program came up. She breathed a sigh of relief and thought no more of it. If the accommodation program was down, that was just too bad – for the chief steward. It did not occur to her to check the other sections.

And the three men sharing a bottle of truly legendary vodka in the steward's office also failed to wonder why it was that their computers had gone down while no one else's had. As yet.

* * *

Billy Hoyle came out of the doctor's examination room into the sickbay just after eleven. He was all strapped up and back in pyjamas. He looked bad and felt worse. And not just medically. He glanced around. Time was limited and the stakes were high. As high as his neck. The doctor was only washing up, she'd be out in a second and then he'd be screwed. Washington was off somewhere. More than likely in the john. The Australian bit was out of sight, and her ancient husband was fast asleep. Mendel and Fagan were wrapped up in a chess game as usual. Killigan was lying in bed.

Billy snuck across the ward as fast as he could sneak. 'Killigan!' he hissed. 'Killigan, you got to help me. I'm in deep shit here. That bitch Agran's a stone killer. She had Ernie Marshall offed like she was swatting a fly. Offed him, broke my arm and took his bag. It's got the Power Strip in it. I know you've got the specs on disk now and don't need the Strip any more but you shouldn't let her keep it, you know? You got to deal with her, Killigan. Come on, you owe me. Deal with her and keep my ass out of the sling. What do you say? Killigan? Killigan?'

Killigan made no sign of having heard. And nor did anyone else.

Certainly not Dai Gwyllim, who was awake and had overheard every word.

Chapter Twenty-Two

It didn't make any sense. Jolene had expected Billy's first set of notes to reveal obvious errors of procedure, which she assumed would be papered over in subsequent re-writes. But it wasn't as cut and dried as that at all. The sequence of events established in the earliest set of notes seemed quite clear and unremarkable.

Billy, together with the scientist Mendel, had packed the suit away on Thursday, 23 December at 18.00 hours, as ordered by Major Schwartz and Colonel Jaeger. Camp security was not all that lax, it seemed, for the suit was then placed in secure storage overseen by Sergeant Killigan at 21.00. On the morning of the 24th, the weather closed in and Billy Hoyle's original notes told of the major suddenly demanding the suit be taken out again so it could be tested in extreme conditions. Billy argued against the idea. Killigan point-blank refused until Colonel Jaeger overruled him at 10.00 hours. Only then did Billy and Killigan return the suit to the area they called the 'launch pad' and start kitting the major up. Such was Killigan's concern over the failure of agreed procedure that when Mendel came in to help with the final testing, the sergeant sent Billy to get written authorisation from the colonel a little after 11.00. Only with this in his hand was Billy allowed to proceed. He and Mendel completed the testing and a John Deere was requisitioned to take the major out at 11.30.

In the second, third and top version of events, however, the record stated that Billy himself had taken the suit to the secure storage and locked it away. And it was Billy who had taken it out again when asked to do so on the 24th. He had tested it with Mendel and Fagan before taking the major out in the John Deere and leaving him at the agreed point to walk in under his own steam between 12.00 and 13.00 hours; a simple test which should have taken little more than an hour, even under those circumstances. There was less detail, the time was more vague and had shifted back, and Killigan's insistence on written authorisation was omitted, but otherwise the main difference seemed to be that the latest copies included an account of the search for the major, well under way by 14.00 when the first general calls for help

219

had gone out. The search details were pretty accurate, according to the corroborating evidence she had already.

Had she missed something? She doggedly began to re-read the twenty-four A4 single-spaced sheets.

'I'm not trying to shift responsibility for them,' said Robin. 'If need be we can sit down here and read *The Famous Five* cover to cover, followed by the collected works of Roald Dahl—'

'We could if we'd brought them.'

'But the fact is there has to be something aboard for them to do, to keep them safely out of the way and out of trouble. They're eight, for heaven's sake. They can't be expected to amuse themselves all the time. And they've shown they don't have enough good sense to be left to their own devices.'

'They thought they were doing the right thing.'

'Of course they did. Both times. But they're out of their depth here. A little frightened, I think. And not without reason.'

A fist of wind seemed to close around the ship, deadening all sound as it lifted and tilted the vessel. The pencils on the table where the twins were drawing with silent concentration began to roll. A glass of water, tinted aquamarine with watercoloured paint, slid grumbling across the teak veneer until William stopped it.

Richard and Robin had had a good twenty minutes of very forth-right discussion with the twins. But they could not keep their offspring cooped up in here today of all days. They needed entertain-ment.

'The only person who could possibly help is Mrs Agran,' said Robin. 'I must say I'm by no means one hundred per cent confident in her but she's worth a try. Why don't you wait here with these two and I'll go and ask her.'

'You sure? You don't want me to go?'

Robin thought with wry amusement of the impact the paintings and assorted statuary in Mrs Agran's office might have on her straight-laced husband. 'No, it's all right,' she said. 'I've been down to see her before. I'll be happy to pop down again. With a bit of luck we can call on that Gretchen girl who found them the first time. She at least seemed to know what she was doing.'

'Just as you like. Give her a ring first. Make sure she's there and knows why you're coming. She might even be able to check her records there and then.'

'Good idea, darling.'

Richard and Robin were not the only pair discussing Mrs Agran after half past eleven that morning. In the sickbay, Dai Gwyllim had limped off, supported by the solicitous Jilly. Washington, shy but by no means unpopular, had been seduced aloft to join in the party. Even Fagan and Mendel had gone off to check out the action up on Bellingshausen-Peary Deck. Billy Hoyle and Killigan were alone.

'This woman had this guy Marshall killed? Just like that? You really expect me to believe this?'

'Not herself. She called that thug Varnek and he laid him out with some kind of club. Honest. Looked like a blackjack. Used the same thing to smash my shoulder but I think he was aiming for my head. As for Ernie, I dunno if they killed him or not. They may have him stashed somewhere. All I'm saying is, I ain't seen him since. And I do believe she'll come after me. She's a strange broad, Killigan, you got to believe me. You should have seen the stuff she has in that room of hers. It's like something out of *The Godfather*, you know?'

'You telling me she's connected? She's a wiseguy? A goodfella? I ain't never heard of no broad running stuff for the Firm, Billy. You got to be dreaming. Or popping your own happy pills. Hey! You been using your own stock, Billy boy?'

'Naw, Killigan. I swear to you, she's got stuff down there like you wouldn't believe. Books, mags, videos, gear, the lot. Even these, what do you call them? Virtual headsets. Programmed like you've never seen. And she's got Ernie's duffel bag, with all his stuff in it and all my stuff in it. So she's got the Power Strip.'

'The Power Strip should have gone back to the major after Mendel had finished with it. Mendel or the major should have it. That was the deal.'

'Mendel gave it to me to put back. I was about to do it when you gave me all that grief about the hut being off limits.'

'Because you had a couple of snot-nosed limey kids all over your ass, you dumb son of a bitch.'

'Well, I risked it anyway. Kept them busy looking for their dad. I just about had it all cool when Washington came in all gung-ho. I swear to God, the next chance I had was that night when everything went up. I was trying for it again when everything went kaplooie. And the next thing I heard, you and Mendel were injured. And Fagan like to die and that NASA inspector insisting the major's body should come out of Armstrong altogether. Jesus, Killigan, I did my best. I even hurt myself bad, to cover—'

'But still you never put it back, or gave it back to Mendel or got rid of it.'

'Get rid of something worth all that money? I know Mendel put the design details on disk but even so, I wasn't going to just flush it down the john. I was waiting for you to come round. I couldn't believe you'd gone and got yourself blown up, you of all people. But there you go. I did my bit. I did good! You've got your line out on the Internet, booked in my name with no destination. I knew you'd need a line out, Killigan. That's at two local time. It's real busy but I booked a slot as soon as I could. Other than that, and guarding the Strip and watching your ass while you were out of things, I didn't know what to do for the best. I was planning to ask you what to do, the instant you came round. It was all I could think of to do. But then . . .'

'But then, Billy?' snarled Killigan.

'By the time you did come round, it was too late. Ernie was out of it and I was hiding and the Agran broad had all our stuff. And the Strip.'

There was silence for a moment. Then Killigan shrugged and said, 'You're right. Maybe I'd better go see the lady, huh?'

'Don't you underestimate her, Killigan. She really did have Ernie seen to. And I know she'll do for me if she gets the chance. And she'll be looking for the chance.' He looked nervously around the sickbay as though there might be assassins in the bedpans. 'You better go in tooled up and loaded for bear.'

'Well, it's a funny thing, Billy boy, but I got the space inspector's little red-dot Glock. Slipped it in the major's coffin and got it out again when you thought I was well out of it, you sorry little amateur. But even a lightweight Glock should just about outgun a blackjack. Whaddya say?'

Dai Gwyllim didn't much care for chairs so he wedged his body into the right angle between the wall and the floor of T-Shirt's cabin. Max lay on the lower bunk, T-Shirt occupied the little table, and Jilly was on the chair. They, too, were discussing Mrs Agran, or rather what Dai had overheard Billy say about her. Their reactions mirrored Sergeant Killigan's; they found it difficult to believe she could have murdered the missing man as Billy had alleged. Their conversation wandered over various possibilities, most of them centring on Billy's sanity, before T-Shirt suddenly sat up.

'What is it?' asked Jilly.

'It's Killigan. Why Killigan?'

222

'What do you mean?'

'Of all the people he could have gone to aboard, why choose Killigan?'

They began to give reasons. The sergeant was head of security, a familiar face among strangers, a colleague, perhaps a friend . . .

But what was a man like Killigan doing with someone like Billy Hoyle as a friend?

'Well, there was something else, something I didn't understand,' said Dai.

'What?'

'Something about a Power Strip. Something like that. And Hoyle said its specifications were on a floppy disk so maybe Killigan didn't need it any more, but he should get it back anyway.'

T-Shirt hopped off the table. 'I have to tell Jolene about that right now,' he said. 'And she might be interested to hear about Billy and Killigan being such good friends as well.'

'Yeah,' said Max. 'But let's get this sorted quickly, huh, T-Shirt? There's a hell of a party building out there and we don't want to miss it.'

Dai used a long, heaving roll of the ship to slide erect up the wall at his back, which was no longer quite so vertical. 'Ha,' he grunted. 'That's not the only thing building out there, boy.'

Killigan was the first of the supplicants to arrive at Vivien Agran's door. She called 'Enter' at his knock and met him standing, with a slightly puzzled expression.

'You are very welcome, Sergeant,' she said coolly, 'and it is good to see you recovering. But forgive me, I was expecting someone else. Mrs Mariner, in fact. She just called down.'

'This won't take long, lady.' Killigan sat.

'Very well. She said she'd be down in five minutes. I can give you till twelve. What can I do for you?'

'I got Billy Hoyle telling me you had Varnek kill his little friend.'

'I see. Do you believe him?'

'I could be convinced.'

'Then what are you doing here, Sergeant?'

'What do you mean?'

'Why are you not telling the captain? Asking her to arrest me? Asking her to send for the Special Agents from Armstrong or whatever?'

'Lady, if you think I'm going to call in the Feds on Billy Hoyle's say-so, you don't know me at all.'

'Well, Sergeant, perhaps I should get to know you better.'

'I'm an easy guy to know,' he said.

'I'm sure you are. And I'm an expert in getting to know people. That's my job, after all. Getting to know people. Their dreams. Their desires.'

'Yeah. I bet. Their secrets, their faults, their weaknesses.'

'Their deepest wishes. And I can fulfil them.'

'For a price.'

'Oh yes,' she said. 'For a price. And what is your price, Sergeant?'

'Hey, that was pretty quick, lady,' said Killigan with guarded respect. 'I came here to proposition you.'

Vivien Agran leaned forward suddenly, her eyes narrow. 'Really, Sergeant? What proposition did you have for me?'

'Well,' said Killigan, 'it seems to me that you're living on borrowed time here. Even an outfit like this can't just *lose* a British sailor. As soon as the weather clears and the millennium thing calms down, there'll be an inquiry. And if Billy's still singing his song then, you and Varnek could find yourselves in a pretty tight frame.'

Mrs Agran said nothing. Her eyes watched Killigan's face with unnerving concentration. Killigan opened his mouth to speak, but a brisk knock at the door forestalled him.

It was obvious to Robin at once that Mrs Agran was preoccupied, but she was courteous and businesslike when Robin inquired about the possibility of help with the twins, to keep them out of mischief. 'Of course,' said the entertainment officer. 'I should have thought of it at once. Just let me consult my records and I'm sure we will come up with someone well qualified to help mind your children during the next couple of days before we drop you at Ushuaia. You may be here by accident but I see no reason why you should not enjoy yourselves as well.'

As she spoke, Mrs Agran leaned across towards her computer. Keen to distract the wise grey eyes of her guest from looking too deeply into the shadowed recess of her bedroom where Killigan was waiting, she swung the face of the computer round so that Robin got a clear view of what she was doing. The records section of the ten-part screen was in the lower left quadrant. Mrs Agran's strong fingers moved the mouse to guide the cursor onto it. Just as she clicked, her phone rang. 'Excuse me,' she said and picked up the handset as the screen began to fill with the records program.

Robin heard a distant sound of merriment and calls of congratulation over the instrument. 'Is it?' said Mrs Agran. 'Really? Happy New Year, then. But I am busy here. I will call back.'

As Mrs Agran spoke, Robin's eye glanced up at the clock. Midday. In some part of Russia it was midnight. Somewhere associated with Mrs Agran, by the sound of it.

Robin's eye came back to the screen. ERROR, it said. CANNOT READ PROGRAM. Two little boxes stood grey against the blue. One said RETRY, the other said QUIT.

Vivien had not noticed the message yet. 'My first husband was from Irkutsk, originally,' she said as she put the receiver down. 'Some of my friends think I should call him there and . . .' She stopped talking when she saw the screen. 'Oh dear,' she said. 'Computers! They really are . . .' She moved the cursor to RETRY and clicked on it. The screen cleared and they were into the records program. But the coincidence lingered in Robin's mind. That they should switch it on exactly at midnight and that it should fail at once.

But of course it was midday here. It was midnight far away in Irkutsk.

A few moments later, Vivien phoned her assistant, Gretchen. She would be happy to help out. She had apparently been a First Grade teacher in her home town of Ames, Iowa, before the wanderlust bug had bitten her. It was as though Mrs Agran had read Robin's mind. Or overheard the conversation she and Richard had had just before she came to the office.

The momentary failure of her computer was the furthest thing from Vivien Agran's mind as she bid farewell to Robin. All through the interview it had been Killigan who was at the forefront of her thoughts. It seemed so neat that one nuisance should be offering to rid her of another. As long as the big sergeant did not want anything too demanding, they would reach a deal – for the time being, at least.

Vivien lived in a strange world where some contracts were forged in steel with a wink or a nod and others were made of jello although reams of lawyer-generated paper had been signed. She had started out as an accountant with a Chicago firm which she later discovered was rather less law-abiding than it seemed at first. She had been one of an acquisitions team sent into the financial wreckage of Russia in the mid-nineties and she had been swept off her feet by her contact there.

The contact, Sergei, from Irkutsk, had turned out to be a member of the Russian mafia. In Russia, she had soon found out, you belonged to the barter economy of the countryside or you did a little dealing for the mafia, the only people with big access to roubles, let alone American dollars. They became an excellent team. He had murky contacts and she had shiny currency. They began to make some remarkable profits. And they weren't at all choosy about how they diversified.

A combination of Vivien's feeling for Sergei and some flaw in her psyche had made her fall in love with his work as well. The very illegality of it, the lack of conventional rules, the constant exhilarating threat of violence had been a seductive cocktail for her. But the lifestyle, like the man himself, could not last. He had revealed one or two weaknesses in his character and she discovered one or two drawbacks to her own. The relationship cooled but didn't really sour. She still called him her first husband, though they had never been through any ceremony. She still used him and his contacts when she needed to.

Even in the fiercest heat of their relationship, Vivien had remained cool-headed and refused to give up her precious American citizenship, so, when the time had come, she had been able to go home. But like a double agent in a spy thriller, she had been turned around. She was well-connected in her own right now, and of use to other organisations, especially American organisations keen to work with their Russian counterparts. Her second husband Mr Agran came and then went, hardly more than a useful contact. But a rich, well-connected contact sitting on the cusp between the mafia and the shipping business – at the boardroom end rather than the longshoreman end. And, after Mr Agran departed, *Kalinin* came. A fortune afloat, and in the right hands, capable of generating an even greater fortune. Owned and fitted by the men Sergei had introduced her to; financed and controlled by Mr Agran's associates. It was a joke, really, that they should both have their headquarters in a town called St Petersburg. And here she was sitting pretty in the middle. Or she had been until she lost control with those two arrogant, patronising little no-hopers eyeing her up and trying to muscle in on her turf. She had made a mistake and she would sort it out. Was sorting it out. Irene Ogre might hold the title of captain, but they both knew who was mistress here. Vivien smiled to herself. She was a mafia *capo* on board a mafia-owned ship, crewed by men like Varnek, hired through men with Russian mafia contacts in St Petersburg, away at the far end of the world and effectively untouchable. She could stay ahead of the game easily. Sending her right-hand girl to keep a close eye on the English couple, the Mariners, was part of that. She did not trust the woman's intelligent, inquiring eyes at all. But the Mariners' main focus was on Jolene DaCosta's business, not her own. Which left her with only two things to worry about.

'Come back, Sergeant,' Vivien called to one of them, 'We still have a lot of talking to do.'

In spite of her invitation to talk, Sgt Killigan and Mrs Agran soon sat face to face like a pair of card-sharps in the old West, each trying to work out what was in the other's hand while revealing nothing of what was in their own. She did not reveal, for instance, that Vasily Varnek was already prepared to destroy this pair of importunate Americans on her say-so. He did not reveal that he had every intention of killing her himself with the Glock in his baggy right pocket unless this negotiation went very smoothly indeed.

The Power Strip now lay on the desk between them but neither of them looked at it for fear that a downward glance might miss something important in the poker-face opposite. 'It's useless to you on its own,' grated Killigan calculating the repercussions of reclaiming it at gun point. 'Unless you've got access to scientists – experts – and a whole bunch of other stuff. Even if I let you keep it there's nothing you can do with it.'

'Except to sell it. I don't have any scientists or equipment here – any more than you do – but I know people who do. Rich people. If you let me keep it and deal on your behalf.'

A brief silence fell, broken only by the throbbing of the engines and the battering of the wind. Each player weighed up the implications of what the other had said. Killigan began to wonder to what extent he might explore Mrs Agran's actual ability to 'deal' on his behalf. He himself had managed to reawaken an old market on the ruins of the Russian economy, half KGB, half Russian mafia. But he was unable to offer them the Power Strip itself. They were expecting the design specifications Mendel had transferred to a priceless disk during the last few days at Armstrong. On receipt of an agreed section of the information Killigan's contacts would wire five million dollars to an agreed destination and he would send the rest on confirmation of the funds' arrival, then oversee its distribution amongst his associates. But here was Mrs Agran offering to sell the Strip as well.

Mrs Agran was more subtly reading between the lines of what the Sergeant had said. If the Power Strip was useless commercially to both of them at the moment, then he had to be in possession of something that was saleable. And that could only be the design specification of the Strip. Mrs Agran's ready intelligence leaped through the reasoning swiftly. She leaned forward, unconsciously for once, well beyond such simple tricks as distracting him with her cleavage. 'And I can deal on your behalf when it comes to the disks as well.'

For a moment Killigan's mind span out of control behind his granite poker face. Had Billy double-crossed him after all? More likely the pathetic bastard had let something slip. His right palm itched for the handle of the Glock. That would solve a lot of things here and now. And he would take care of Varnek and the rest in due course if he had to. As long as the disk was safe.

But then the detail of her words registered. She said 'disks'. She didn't know that the whole thing was safely stored on one. There had been no slip-up, no betrayal; simply a lucky guess. Killigan's palm stopped itching and he continued to reassess this woman and what she could do for him. Hoyle was right. She was a wiseguy all right connected to the Mafia back home. If so, then he could, perhaps, deal with her – for anything up to the disk. But not for the disk itself. Not for anything. He and Hoyle would be popping that little mother onto the Internet as arranged. Nothing could be allowed to get in the way of that. His deal cut both ways. If the information on that precious little piece of plastic didn't get to its destination as promised tonight not only would Killigan be down the promised five million, but the remainder of his life would be a short, painful and probably bloody affair indeed.

Even so, Killigan leaned back in the chair with an assumption of confident ease. 'OK, lady,' he said. 'Let's treat this like a first date – see how far we can get before somebody gets their face slapped.'

Half an hour later Mrs Agran was the little consortium's American agent, in for a little slice of the Russian fortune, offering the actual Strip to her contacts Stateside for whatever else could be garnered; seeing what the information on the disk might fetch, even second-hand. She decided to warn Varnek to keep away from them for the time being. And Killigan had decided that she would remain undamaged as long as she remained of service to them – and as long as he kept his hands on their ace in the hole – the disk.

Gretchen arrived at the Mariners' stateroom just before one. The tall, blonde girl was an instant hit with both the children. Self-possessed and cheerful, she told them about her six little brothers and sisters away at home in the States, recounted tales of the classroom, and

228

swept them up into her cosy little world. She quickly sorted out everything she could find which might be counted on to amuse the twins. And so she settled in, freeing Richard and Robin of parental responsibility so suddenly that they felt a little disorientated.

'Right,' said Richard, testing his new freedom. 'Let's find Jolene, tell her what the twins told us, and then maybe look for Colin and Kate and see what's planned for the rest of the day partywise.'

Robin grinned. 'I know you better than that. After you've found your little inspector and checked out how her investigation's going, you'll want to get up to the bridge and check on the storm. You're just about the least convincing party animal on the face of this earth.'

'Hmm,' conceded Richard. 'That's as maybe. But let's look in on the dining salon at least. To begin with. Take it from there.'

So out they went, leaving Gretchen and the twins playing 'hunt the thimble'. As she closed the door, Robin thought what an excellent game that would be for anyone wanting a good look round their quarters. But then she remembered that the stewards had unpacked and put away everything they possessed aboard, and they would certainly have reported to Mrs Agran.

The party on Bellingshausen-Peary was beginning to spill out of the dining salon. Because lunch was being served, those who wished to drink and watch the television were out in the main bar area.

Richard saw Jolene in a quiet little corner near the library, deep in thought. He joined her and told her what the twins had said about Billy Hoyle and his activities in the base. 'That fits,' she said grimly. 'But did they mention anything about the Power Strip, a long piece of silver, like tin foil?'

'No,' said Richard.

'Tell you what, then, why don't you go off and relax a bit while I find T-Shirt and get him to help me do some more digging. We'll catch up later, maybe chew the fat a little more.'

'Chew the fat,' said a passing passenger, a tall, deep chested Caribbean girl with an athletic body and a wide smile. 'Good phrase. Have you been in to lunch yet?'

'No,' said Richard. 'Why?'

'You'll see,' chuckled Jolene, and she joined the boisterous crowd in search of T-Shirt.

Richard and Robin found Colin and Kate enjoying a light lunch. 'Very unusual,' said Colin. 'You order what you want then you eat what you get.'

'Which is not the same thing at all,' chimed in Kate cheerfully. 'It

229

seems to go like this. The system relies on waiters keying in orders on notepad computers which beam everything directly to the galley computers. These apparently process the orders, prioritise what needs preparing in what order, signal where everything can be found and print out the odd recipe or two, I shouldn't wonder. I guess real people pick up and cook the ingredients somewhere along the line, then tell the computer to signal that the meals are ready to serve. No longer. Now we have a bunch of men and women laboriously taking orders on paper in writing it is difficult to read and passing them on by hand to a kitchen whose computer is no help at all in finding, sorting or prioritising anything. The cooks therefore are doing the best they can but taking so long about it that your waiter will probably end up bringing you the order he took last sitting or the one before. We ordered egg salad and pickled herring and ended up with vegetable soup.'

'OK,' said Richard, summoning a harassed-looking waiter. 'I'll try for the cold chicken. Darling? The salmon for you?'

They sat and waited, the women sipping champagne, Colin sipping a very light whisky and Richard working his way down a blue bottle of Ramaloosa, watching midnight roll across the whole of regimented China at a stroke and then arrive in Java, Sumatra, Mongolia; continuing to swing across the Russian Steppes, arriving in Novosibirsk. Then, after a few more minutes, Richard enjoyed a salad of duck's liver pâté with oranges and some French bread, while Robin essayed the Chef's special seafood salad with tiger prawns.

'That's not fair,' teased Kate. 'You two at least got to eat the right species. We couldn't even manage that.'

As they ate, they discussed the festivities planned for the rest of the day. 'The grand banquet from eight till midnight will be a bit flat if Chef doesn't sort himself out,' observed Kate, looking a little jealously at Robin's salad.

'The alternative is the Karaoke Bar,' warned Colin darkly. 'That runs from ten.'

'We might be tempted,' said Robin. 'That's one of Richard's hidden talents. If he puts his mind to it, he does a perfectly flawless Frank Sinatra.'

'Really?' Kate's interest was piqued. 'I'd never have imagined.'

Richard shrugged self-deprecatingly. 'Emergencies only,' he said. 'Self-preservation.'

'We might need to lean on you in any case,' warned Colin. 'I can't imagine getting through the banquet without some fun and games overflowing into the dining salon.'

230

'What is it, Richard?' asked Robin, for he was looking decidedly preoccupied.

'I don't know, darling. It just seems so strange to be sitting here planning dinner and entertainment for the evening.'

'But why?'

'I don't know. I really don't. Maybe it's the weather. Maybe it's just our situation here. Maybe it's everything that's happened so far. But somehow I just can't see it happening as planned at all.'

And just as Richard delivered himself of this dark sentiment a waiter appeared bearing a tray. A waiter whom they had never seen before; certainly not the one they had given their order to or the one who had brought the food they had just consumed. 'One cold chicken salad and one poached salmon?' said the waiter. And then stood, open-mouthed, as they all started to laugh.

'This is very serious, if you and Dai are sure,' said Jolene. 'If Killigan is a prime suspect, then it all turns around. Billy's first set of records put Killigan at the centre of it all. The later ones move him out of the limelight altogether.'

'What do you want to do, Jolene?' asked T-Shirt. 'We could sniff around, try to get more proof.'

'Go and lean on Billy?' suggested Dai. 'He doesn't look all that tough to me.'

'Go confront Killigan himself?' suggested Jilly.

'No, said Jolene decisively. 'We leave well alone. I don't have any real legal jurisdiction and you guys certainly have none. This is American soil – sort of. We can continue trying to build a case, quietly, but we should do nothing that would prejudice the outcome of any eventual proceedings. And we call for back-up.'

'Agent Smith,' said T-Shirt dismissively.

'Agent Jones,' said Jolene with a tiny twinkle. T-Shirt was jealous. How delightful!

'Not even Agent 007 could get over here in this weather,' said Dai.

'It's too early for even the FBI to go confronting him, I'd say,' said Jolene. 'No, we just suggest to Jones that he take a close look at Killigan's stuff at Armstrong. At his movements and any records by or about him left over there.'

'Well,' said T-Shirt, mellowing. 'You've got copies of Killigan's log as well as Billy's, haven't you? Want to go share a hot keyboard?'

'Yes,' said Jolene, 'I do believe I do. But we'd better go talk to Agent Jones first.'

231

'Better hurry, then,' said T-Shirt. 'Wasn't there going to be a big queue to use the radio round at about two pm? It's almost that now.'

'Almost two?' wailed Jilly. 'No wonder my tummy thinks my throat's been cut! Come on Dai, bach. We've almost missed lunch!'

The little group split up, with the hungry heading for the mayhem in the dining salon and the hunters running on up the companionways to the welcoming bridge and the spacious radio room.

It was fortunate that the radio room was spacious, for quite a crowd was building up in it, spilling out onto the bridge itself. They were a cheery bunch, their ill-controlled festive excitement at odds with the grim demeanour of the captain and her senior navigating officers. And that grimness was only the merest reflection of the massive darkness still building relentlessly to port where the storm, whose wings were gathering high over them, flapping occasionally with the storm squalls and ice showers, was slowly, majestically rearing its hurricane-dragon head. Only the gathering, dangerous gloom and the captain's strict ban of anything alcoholic from the bridge kept the excited party in the radio room under any sort of control. Jolene and T-Shirt found themselves on the fringes of an animated, chattering group whose favoured language was Russian but who occasionally lapsed into English. They were, they found, too late to slip in to the radio officer's schedule. And even an appeal to the captain fell on deaf ears. Unless it was a matter of life and death, she ruled, they would have to wait to contact Armstrong. There were people here who had booked their calls weeks ago. And first in the queue was Billy Hoyle.

As two o'clock neared, the tension began to mount, for there was no sign of Billy. Everyone else was bursting to get their message home the moment midnight crossed the Urals. Even the radio officer himself would be sending a message to his mother in his native Yorsk. But Billy was slated to go first. And everyone else would have to take their turn.

As a distraction, the radio officer cleared the little screen of the computer beside his radio facilities so that the computer's clock counted up on the VDU. The computer's central programme was set to his own home time, and so the clock was counting, in big white figures on a bright blue screen, through the final seconds between 11:58:01 and 11:59:59, when Hoyle arrived, with Sergeant Killigan in tow and, of all people, Vivien Agran. At the sight of the entertainment officer, some of the party spirit left the little band. The lately-boisterous group fell back to allow her past.

Hard on their heels, Richard and Robin arrived also, with Colin and Kate, not to use the radio but to gaze out at the black clouds. Catching Jolene's eye, however, Richard flashed her one of his contagious, boyish grins. 'Hi,' he said, striding across the bridge towards her. 'You were next on the list for a visit. To chew the fat. How's the . . .' He stopped speaking abruptly when he noticed the subjects of her investigation impatiently crowding up behind the radio operator. As though his sudden silence was the signal, the clock on the bright blue background of the computer went to 00:00:00

A little cheer went through the crowd, for it was midnight in their homes too, and the beginning of the new millennium for their families and friends far away in Russia. But it soon died, to be replaced by demands that the radio operator get on with his duties.

Everyone crowded forward, with Mrs Agran and her new American friends right at the very front, threatening to overwhelm the poor radio officer. Richard saw him take from Killigan a 3.5 in. floppy and push it into the port of the computer which still read 00:00:00 on its screen above. He put it in the port but did not click it home, his fingers busy on the keyboard. Clearing the clock, no doubt, opening the communications channels.

But the clock was still reading 00:00:00.

Richard realised then. It had to be at least ten seconds after midnight but the clock still read 00:00:00. He walked across to where Varnek was standing by his computer, looking out at the lowering blackness. A winding sheet of snow whipped across the face of it, torn away brutally by an ice-mailed fist of wind. 'Do me a favour, Mr Varnek,' he said quietly, just audible over the first pummelling blow of the wind on the ice-laden clearview. 'Call up communications.'

Varnek followed the gaze of those bright blue eyes down to the screen and his hand moved, obedient to something compelling in Richard's quiet tone.

Communications filled the whole screen. Varnek looked up.

'Open any communications file,' said Richard. 'Radio, satellite VHF, TV . . .'

Again, Varnek's hand moved in obedience, opening the control and monitor file on the Internet function the radio operator was calling up as they spoke. It was as though the snow in the wind outside had found a way of leaking into the ether. Thin whiteness skidded wildly downwards and across the screen. A quick eye might distinguish some letters there. But it was mostly boxes, asterisks, circumflexes, exclamation marks and question marks: computer garbage.

Horrorstruck, Varnek looked up at Richard and down again at the screen. Richard looked through into the radio room, at the immovable clock frozen on the computer screen, set, solid as a tombstone, at 00:00:00. 'It's dead,' whispered Varnek.

'It's dead,' called the radio operator in a horrified echo. 'It's all dead.'

'And it died on the stroke of midnight,' said Richard. 'Captain Ogre, I'm afraid your computers have the millennium bug.'

Chapter Twenty-Three

'That is impossible, said Irene Ogre in her day room five minutes later. 'These computers are the latest model. Look at them. Pentium Processors. Intel inside. Windows Ninety-eight. They are proof against the millennium bug. There is no doubt about it. The bug is a – what do you say? – a damp squid. There must be some other explanation.'

'The machines are only as reliable as your suppliers,' said Richard gently. 'Where did they come from?'

'They were installed as part of the total re-fit at the St Petersburg dockyard in nineteen ninety-seven. I have all the paperwork.'

Richard nodded. He was beginning to feel a little better. Perhaps he was wrong after all, over-reacting. Since the mid-nineties, the millennium bug had been presented to him as a potential disaster of such proportions that he had had all computers, each programme and every chip aboard every ship he was responsible for individually checked and made guaranteed 2000-proof. He had overseen the virtual re-equipping of Heritage House, headquarters of his two London-based companies, Crewfinders and Heritage Mariner Shipping. From the automatic security gates of the parking in the basement to the global communications system at the hearts of both Heritage Mariner and Crewfinders on the topmost floor, every check that could be made had been made. Even so, he planned to call Heritage Mariner at midnight London time, just to confirm that all had come through into the new millennium unscathed.

But what was he thinking? It seemed highly unlikely he would be calling anywhere at midnight, London time. Or at any other time, unless Radio Officer Kyril could revitalise his defunct equipment.

'Right,' he said gently. 'Say there were regular supplies of reliable computer equipment coming into St Petersburg as late as nineteen ninety-seven, before the crash of ninety-eight. Say this is a one-off incident. The next thing to do is to check that all the other systems are up and running properly. I have to say that I don't believe they are.'

'What do you mean?'

'The galley is a shambles. Why don't you check that programme

235

first?' He gestured towards the quadrant that said GALLEY.

Her nose went up, her bright eyes flashed. Her expression said, 'You are wrong, you foolish man.' But she clicked on the octant he was pointing at. The whole screen went blue as this section overrode the others. 'You see?' she said.

'Open a file,' he answered. 'Try that one: DINING SALON.'

She clicked on the little icon and the screen filled with a blizzard of falling computer garbage against a background of flickering black. The speakers hissed like an angry sea. Irene gasped with shock.

'Yes,' said Richard quietly, almost to himself. 'That's what I got for lunch.'

Irene switched off and tried again. But none of the galley files she tried would open. Numbly, she tried the other octants, and the two central panels. Not all the sections had died. Mrs Agran's RECORDS program was still running.

'The bug seems to be switching them off in sequence,' Richard said, 'as if each machine is reading midnight at a different time. Is that possible?'

'Yes. There are ten systems. Each system is governed by one responsible member of the crew. As a part of the re-fit, when the systems were put in in the first place, we were all asked what time we would like the central computer clocks set to. This was good management. It was well thought out, well done. *Kalinin* spends her time wandering the world. We change the clocks as regularly as we change underwear. So each man and woman was asked what time they would like their computer at. Most of them said they wanted them set to home time. Chef comes from Magadan. Galley computer is set to Magadan time. You see the pattern. The exception was Mrs Agran. They were good Russian workmen. They refused to set her computers to United States central time, so she settled for the time zone of her first husband's home.'

'And that is?'

'Irkutsk. But her computers were brought in by different people.'

'Her RECORDS program will give us the name of the home cities of the third officer and the chief steward, won't it?' said Richard. 'And the time zones they would have had their central computers set for.'

Irene nodded and called up the information.

'It looks bad,' said Richard. 'The systems that have crashed are all the responsibility of people in whose home towns midnight has already struck. There are three of them so far. I know Mrs Agran may be an exception, but what was it James Bond said? Once is happenstance, twice is coincidence.' He looked up at Irene Ogre and forced all the power of his character into the cold blue stare of his eyes, 'And the third time is enemy action.'

The next logical step was to convene a meeting of all senior officers to discuss the probability of Richard's fears being right and to plan a stratagem should the crisis worsen. This meeting had to take place on the bridge since the weather demanded that the ablest ship-handlers be there at all times. The internal phone system had gone down with the communications program, but at Richard's suggestion they tested their personal radios and found that they still worked well enough for the chief and his engineers to join in the discussions.

The bridge was cleared of all passengers and crew who had been hoping to call home. Only Kyril the radio officer and the engineer helping him to try to fix his equipment remained, working in grim silence. Vivien Agran also remained. She would have to update passengers and direct staff about the problems they could expect. Unbeknownst to anyone, she had used the confusion of clearing the bridge to slip Killigan's disk out of Kyril's machine and into her all too convenient cleavage. Richard was there and he asked that Robin, Colin and Kate join them too. Robin knew as much about the bug as he did and a good deal more about computers. Colin and Kate knew more about the conditions gathering around them outside than anyone else on board.

'It is possible,' said Irene, opening the discussions, 'that *Kalinin*'s computers have the millennium bug. This may be why the communications system is down, and the problems we are experiencing with the lading records, accommodation and the galley computer may arise from this. If this is so, as each central computer clock reads midnight tonight and tries to roll over to tomorrow, the old chips will read 00 for the year and either seize up or decide it must be the year 1900 and act accordingly. It should be possible to either re-set the clocks or re-programme them to accept 00 as 2000 without crashing. But we'll have to be quick. Once a system goes down we may have to check and re-set almost by hand every chip in every circuit before it all comes up again. The potential problem is enormous. The computer systems have kilometres of circuitry, much of it printed and microscopically small, with thousands and thousands of chips. But the question only arises if the equipment is less than it seems,' Irene concluded. Her steady gaze rested on Varnek. A short silence fell.

237

Varnek met his captain's eyes, clearly weighing his words before he spoke.

'Yes,' he said. 'The equipment is almost certainly less than it seems. It looks like the most up-to date and expensive American equipment, running state-of-the-art American programs. But it is not. It was bought on the black market and put in on the cheap. And who by? By the mafia of course. You all know that, you Russians. Even legitimate businesses nowadays have their kickbacks, their little payments. The mafia are everywhere. A way of life. And what do the mafia know or care about the bug? Nothing. The men who put these systems in got them from businesses that had collapsed in Moscow, got them second-hand and cheaply from whomever would accept their roubles or their barter goods. They tarted them up, charged high prices and programmed them with pirate programs. Russia is, after all, the pirate capital of the world. So yes, it is possible they all have the bug.'

White light flashed across the gloomy bridge, as though a magnesium flare had been ignited and instantly extinguished close off the port bow. A rumble of thunder followed close on its heels that made the very teeth in their heads begin to tremble and chatter.

'That weather's deteriorating fast,' said Richard. 'We need to get all the help we can.'

'We'll need anyone with any skill in programming,' said Robin, interweaving her thoughts with his.

'We need the people who control the programs to tell us what time their clocks are set for so that we can prioritise the work,' continued Richard.

'We need guidance from the engineers about where the systems are located and the best way to get at the master computer for each,' said Robin. 'What do they call it? The server?'

'Can you get into the control mechanisms of all of the systems from one central computer?' Richard asked Irene. 'That would speed things up.'

'No, each system has its own server.'

'In the meantime,' rumbled Colin, 'you'll have to look for a safe haven and run for it with all the speed you can manage. If you lose your navigation computers, your weather or your propulsion in this lot, you're dead.'

'We need to check with you, Chief,' said Richard, running with that thought, 'on how quickly you can get the manual overrides on the engines in case the propulsion programs go down. As long as we've got steerageway, we have a chance.' He looked out at the storm

238

and saw a great bolt of lightning pounce down from cloud top to wave crest as though the distance was a mirror cracking from top to bottom.

'Are we all agreed on the priorities, then?' asked Irene. 'Find out who understands enough about computers, passengers or crew, to be confident of re-programming the central clocks. Third Officer Borisov, please do that, then try and get your lading program up and running again. At the same time, we must find out the order in which we can expect the systems to go down if it is the bug.' Thunder came, and she paused until it passed before resuming, 'Mrs Agran, please consult your records and establish what time every computer is set to, starting with the next to read midnight. Chief, could you please detail some engineers to guide experts to the relevant servers while the rest see about overriding their own computer systems if need be. Mr Yazov, we will look for the nearest safe haven in case everything goes down in spite of our best efforts. Radio Officer Kyril, you will continue to try and fix the communications as a matter of the highest priority. The instant we can get a message out, alert me. Our first priority must be to alert head office as to our situation. Then we will try for any help we can summon from nearer at hand. Anything else? Very well, it is now fourteen twenty-three local time. I would like everyone back here by fourteen forty-five at the latest. Mrs Agran, earlier than that if possible. Captains Mariner and Drs Ross, will you remain on the bridge, please. Your local knowledge and wide experience might be to our benefit here.'

Richard and Colin both automatically crossed to the chart table. Robin went to look at the weather printouts and Kate went with her. The next bolt of lightning lit their way. 'The gale will be at its worst between twelve midnight and one a.m. by the look of things,' called Robin. 'Just before we get a bit of respite in the eye. If we make it that far. Then it will hit hard again from the opposite quarter at three or four a.m.'

'Safe haven by midnight then, Colin,' said Richard. 'What d'you think? Mr Yazov? Any bright ideas?' The three of them leaned over the chart, following the line of *Kalinin*'s laid-in course, looking for the nearest storm shelter and, finding none near at hand, looking further afield. No one spoke for a few moments; they would have been inaudible against the field-artillery rumble of the thunder in any case.

'We could try for the lee of the South Shetlands,' suggested the navigating officer, Mr Yazov, uncertainly after the last echo had died.

'Turn and run back into the Gerlache Strait, in behind Brabant

Island there?' suggested Colin. 'It's a good, big, solid island, there are mountains there tall enough to cut the westerlies—'

'But all the channels east of Brabant are foul,' countered Yazov impatiently. 'Look, we would have to run by Liege Island, then Davis, Abbot and Harry Islands. If our navigation or propulsion systems faltered then . . .' He made a throat-cutting gesture.

'Here's where we're going,' said Richard. 'Right here. It's chancy but it's the only hope we've got. If we put on all the speed we can from now, re-programme the ship-handler to lay in a course a little more to westward – a lot more to westward, given the wind and the weather – we should make it just before midnight. It's the one truly safe haven to windward of the whole Antarctic Peninsula. If we can get *Kalinin* in through the narrows here, we'll have sheer rock walls on every side except to the south-east, and that's where the quietest weather will be.' The broad end of his right index finger was resting on the flooded volcanic caldera of Deception Island.

Richard's identification of a safe haven galvanised them even more successfully than Irene's string of orders. Having a tangible hope to aim at allowed everything to fall more securely into place, gave the whole of their desperate endeavour a pattern and a clear, acceptable purpose beyond the terrifying, unfocused goal of fighting something as amorphous as a tiny flaw in a computer programme, even though their lives depended on it. Kate, the sci-fi buff, muttered that it was all too much like *2001* for her taste and Richard grunted, 'You're only a year and a couple of hours out,' which brought it home to all of them with disturbing vividness.

Vivien Agran was back by 14.40 with a printout and some handwritten notes. She reported to the captain but her clear voice carried to them all over the wind and the occasional thunderclap. 'Second Engineering Officer Sholokov comes from Samara. I have checked with him and his computer is set up the same as the others. If it has the bug, it will die in twenty minutes. Then at sixteen hundred hours our time, midnight will arrive in Arkhangelsk. Vasily, that's your home town. What do you think?'

'We'll have to check carefully. I got my computers from the same batch as Kyril, Chef and the rest. If the weather programmes go down while we're still eight hours from Deception, things could get very rough indeed.'

There were general nods of agreement on that one, and the first flash of lightning from starboard emphasised that the first of the

240

thunderheads in the van of the army massing westward had passed right over them to hurl its fiery wrath onto the mountains inland. 'And finally, we have most time to try and fix the most important. The chief is from Murmansk and, Yazov, you're from . . .'

'St Petersburg,' said Yazov. 'So, we have until seventeen hundred. But I'd say navigation has to take precedence. Chief can override the engine systems and give us propulsion by hand if need be. If my navigating aids go down, then the best I can offer is a compass I got from a Christmas cracker last week, my not very genuine Tag Huer navigator's chronograph wristwatch and the captain's sextant.'

This raised several eyebrows on the bridge for they knew well enough that the lugubrious young officer had a couple of Magellan 3000 hand-held GPS systems at the very least to call on in extremis. But Yazov's point was well made. If push came to shove, the chief could power the engines and pitch the propeller manually, and the bridge could communicate with him, as now, by the VHF. But coming up to Deception through the full force of this storm, with the wind, the waves and the current all trying to hurl them sideways at more than a 100 m.p.h. would render even the most powerful Magellan global positioning system little more use than Yazov's Christmas cracker compass.

Third Officer Borisov returned with a small group in tow. There was little enough time to discuss their computer qualifications, and no chance at all to test the fitness of the applicants. The best Irene could do was to order Kyril to leave his communications program for the moment and oversee their work on the environment server.

Richard joined this little group and followed them as they went down into the engineering sections. T-Shirt and Max had both spent time preparing computers for the millennium and were both confident that if the system was familiar, they would be able to do the job. Dai Gwyllim had never worked with computers professionally, but he was self-sufficient in this as in all else. He had de-bugged all his own stuff at home in Wales and was likewise quietly confident. With the engineers and Kyril the radio officer, this was the backbone of the team. If they sorted out environment, they would split into teams and work on keeping the remaining three main programmes alive while Kyril, like Dr Frankenstein, went back to his rather more complex re-animation.

The environment system's central server was in the engineering section but well away from the engine room and the engine control rooms themselves. It was in a hot, bright, quiet little room, white-

241

walled and tall, with the equipment laid out on a steel shelf like a body in a morgue, and wires snaking everywhere. The VDU screen was dead so the first thing Kyril did was to snap it on. The screen flickered, went black. Tiny numbers whirled in the top left corner as the memory was checked. Richard looked at his watch. They had five minutes. Was that enough? He had no way of even guessing, for he had no idea what the delicate task involved.

The others gathered around the screen, talking impenetrably in the language only understood by computer buffs. No sooner was Windows up than it was gone as they went underneath it into the machine's basic program, clicking purposefully on little sections at the corners of screens that Richard had never noticed before, let alone thought of using. Uneasily aware that Robin or either of the twins would probably have made a more educated witness, he watched Kyril and T-Shirt settle into work.

'We have three ways to go,' said T-Shirt. 'And our selection of the best route is likely to be dictated by time at this stage. If we had all the time we needed we could get the clock up and re-program it to understand that 00 is the next logical step after 99 and everything is still AOK. I don't know about you, Kyril, but I don't think four minutes is going to be enough time to do that. On the other hand, we could just call up the clock and switch it off. Hope that the rest of the system ticks over OK until some other outside agency asks for time and date recognition.'

'That would be quickest,' said Kyril.

'But riskiest. Some chips will only continue working if they can keep checking with the central clock. If there are enough of those then the system'll crash in any case. Third and simplest is just to call up the clock, tell it the date is January nineteen ninety-nine and hope it'll run for another year.'

'Not possible. We can work within the day, if we're lucky,' said Kyril. 'But there are too many chips in here which know it is December the thirty-first, nineteen ninety-nine. If they come into conflict with the central clock, they'll close down.'

'But these clocks are accurate down to thousandths of a second,' said Richard.

'Yeah,' said T-Shirt. 'So it's a bit of a gamble, but it's all we've got. So here we are. Central clock. With no checks or back-ups, we hope. Current date is 12:31:1999. New date 12:31:1999. Current time is 23.58 and counting. New time? Whaddya think, Kyril? 01.58 and ENTER. That buys us twenty-three hours. If it works we can keep

242

doing it over and over until we think of a better plan – or until the ship is safe in dock.'

They sat silently, watching the figures spin. 'Seems to have bought that OK,' said T-Shirt. 'What do you think, Kyril?'

'I don't know. It was very close. We will have to wait and see, I think.'

'Well, we haven't time to just wait here and see,' said Richard. 'We've a hell of a lot more to do.'

'Yeah,' said T-Shirt. 'You're right. I'll set this up the way it was. Just take a minute.'

In a few moments the screen was back to blue. Automatically, he reached over to switch the VDU off, but Kyril stopped him superstitiously. 'Leave it on screensaver,' he said. 'It might just help.'

'Can't do any harm,' said T-Shirt accommodatingly, and so they left it. Richard, last out, turned back to close the door – just in time to see the screen click over to a picture of a dancing baby. He smiled automatically as though the baby was real and closed the door softly.

So that he did not see, the instant after the lock clicked shut, the baby freeze in mid-pirouette and slowly begin to fade.

The bridge was a purposeful bustle when Richard got back to it. The weather seemed to have eased a little, certainly the first thunderstorm had spun away towards the Weddell Sea, like the first wing of a blitzkrieg. Yazov had laid the new co-ordinates into the Differential Shiphandler and the requisite headings were already clicking into the computer guidance system. *Kalinin* was turning a little westward already and seemed to be riding slightly easier. Irene had called for full ahead and the ship's ice-strengthened hull throbbed to a new urgency.

Kyril was back in his den working on his dead equipment but the other programmers were nowhere to be seen. Robin was deep in conversation with Irene, two experienced captains debating the balance between speed and stability; retracting the stabilisers would give everyone a rougher ride but would add several knots to the ship's dash for safety. Varnek had pulled out another couple of charts and was preparing to slide them under the Perspex of the chart table. They were detailed charts of Deception Island, and he and Yazov were deep in conversation with Colin and Kate Ross about approaches and cross currents, and how to get safely in through the reef-fanged narrows of Neptune's Bellow.

Richard strolled over to Varnek's table and looked at the latest weather printout. The vicious storm was swinging in behind them.

That's why it had eased, a very temporary relief, as it gathered itself to strike again. The last six hours of their approach would have that and God knew what else running up behind them. The full force of the storm would come after them at hurricane force and worse, gusting off the Beaufort scale altogether by the look of this weather map. Winds of that force would tear great chunks of brash and bergy bits off the blue-white masses south of them and hurl them northward like torpedoes. Richard remembered that iron-hard lump of deadly blue ice which had come so near to crippling *Erebus* and he shivered. It would be a close-run thing. And they'd be lucky to pull it off.

'All laid in and running smoothly at fifteen fifteen hours exactly,' said Yazov to Varnek who held the watch. 'Coming up to full ahead at the captain's order. Destination, Deception Island.'

Varnek repeated the information to the captain for the log.

Richard unconsciously clasped his hands behind his back, narrowed his eyes and squared his chin a little, bouncing on the balls of his feet, feeling *Kalinin* beginning her wild dash for safety.

Robin, looking across the bridge and catching his unconscious gesture, smiled. Even in civilian clothes he looked so much in command here. But then she gave an uneasy little shiver. Thank heaven he wasn't responsible for this ship, these people, in this situation, in this much danger, she thought to herself. Thank God they seemed to have got the computer thing sorted out at least. She shivered once again.

And Kate Ross said, quietly, 'is it me, or is it getting cold in here?'

Chapter Twenty-Four

Kalinin's epic run to Deception took nine hours. For each and all of those hours, the forces of law and order aboard, other than Jolene, were held by duty and circumstance on the bridge as everything took second place to the survival of the ship and those aboard her. As the hours ticked by, safety and disaster came ever closer.

During that time *Kalinin* covered nearly 150 miles of heaving, storm-swept ocean, speckled with berg and bergy bits, crusted with growler and floe. The strange black water itself was made heavy and hard by temperatures and wind chills which should have frozen it solid in moments but for the power of the tempest agitation which simply refused to let the briny molecules fuse fast enough.

Had *Kalinin*'s hull not been ice-strengthened and her bows those of an ice-destroyer, she might well have shattered as though she was made of glass, the metal of her battered sides rendered fragile by the strange, sub-zero water, as *Titanic*'s were said to be. Had her propeller, unlike *Erebus*'s, not been guarded in a heated, ice-proof cage, she would have been crippled before the run got under way, for the storm did not hesitate for long but threw its terrible frozen armoury in behind them from the instant that the captain gave the order to go north.

The hurricane, gusting well off the Beaufort scale, swung in hard from the south and west as Richard had predicted, howling after them at velocities more than ten times their own speed. The wind, like the water, was armed with ice. Hailstones the size of tennis balls hurled forward and down relentlessly at one hundred and fifty miles an hour, shattering on impact, half melting under the awful physical laws of compression, and freezing on the instant. The tops of the black waves were twice as thick as whale oil and half as cold as liquid nitrogen. They tore off in chunks, already setting solid in the wind, and spattered like jelly onto the superstructure, clinging and transforming into deadly carapaces of ice. Ice can make a tree trunk from even the thinnest line, multiply the thickness of even the stoutest wall, make ice hills out of flat decks, up-end whalers and turn trawlers turtle within the hour. But *Kalinin* had been fashioned in Gdansk to run north at the world's far end, to override the waters between Murmansk, Zemlya and the Pole. She had a draught and a depth, a solidity in the ocean which shrugged off such danger. Her rigging lines were few and well-protected. The areas most at risk from icing could be heated from the engine room, for as long as the engines ran. And, like the pumps and the engines themselves, the system had a manual override to its computer controls.

And the ship was brilliantly commanded and conned. The details of her course and speed were largely in the control of the automatic guidance system which communicated with GPS satellites, weather sats and ice-warning sats. It was able instant by instant to take readings of wind and sea, drift, current, dangers ahead and behind, so it guided *Kalinin* with superhuman authority and accuracy at full possible speed north towards distant Deception. But the humans knew, as the machine did not, that the information, the accuracy, the guidance keeping them alive might well be a temporary thing, as prone as Major Schwartz's suit and *Erebus*'s ancient electrical system to total powerdown. The commander and her officers stood tirelessly at their posts, with one eye on the relentless sweep of the minute hand on the ship's old-fashioned analogue chronometer. They checked the information feeding into the ship-handler system, ready and able at a moment's notice to re-interpret information, override the system and get *Kalinin* out of trouble for themselves.

The strife outside was reflected aboard. Computer garbage whirled across the dying screens like a blizzard as the computers went down one by one and information, systems – and, latterly, people – began to freeze at the arctic touch of the bug. T-Shirt and Max worked with Borisov while Dai worked with Kyril and the engineers who could be spared, fighting like doctors in an epidemic to re-awaken the dead systems and keep the last few survivors up and running. The failure of the environment system at three, in spite of their best efforts, hit them all hard. The next hour passed in a whirl of activity as the weather system was checked and they passed on down to the navigation and propulsion systems.

The TVs had gone down with the communications, the heating had gone down with the environmental control system and the galley was beginning to grind to a halt. People were milling about with nothing to do, depressed, cold, hungry, bored and looking for mischief.

Vivien Agran did not have to look far for mischief, and had Varnek not been locked on the bridge like a monk in a monastery, she would

246

have called on him to do some lethal mischief long ago herself. She was in possession not only of the priceless Power Strip but the disk on which its specifications were stored, the one at the bottom of Ernie Marshall's bag, the other still tucked against her left breast. And, like Killigan and Hoyle, she had an Internet address where contacts would be willing to pay prices beyond immediate reckoning, if she could only get the information out. Her negotiation with Killigan had established some common ground, some shared ambitions and some apparent agreements, but no trust. When she failed to return either the Power Strip or the disk after communications failed, lack of trust became confirmed suspicion. Without Varnek and his cosh, Vivien knew she was exposed. While Killigan and Hoyle plotted and planned how best to reach and deal with her, the bored and the restless passengers began to beat a path to her door, looking for the recreational devices only she could supply. And it was her job to furnish that supply, no matter what the risk. Literally as well as figuratively, her door was always open, and since communications crashed, she could no longer rely on her computer to give her a clear picture of who was standing outside it.

Jolene was keeping her head down as well. The ship's computer network had crashed with the general communications system, but she had managed to find a couple of start-up disks, a systems disk and a word processor she could use on the library machine if she set it up as a stand-alone. It was frustratingly slow work, made infinitely more difficult by the fact that the ship was pitching and rolling with increasing ferocity, so that time after time she hit the mouse key or some part of the keyboard by accident, and scrambled the programs she was trying to use. It was a nauseating motion, too, this brutal up at the stern, down at the bow, sudden wrenching corkscrew to starboard that *Kalinin* was performing. It made Jolene's stomach rebel with increasingly acid disgruntlement, bringing the green sweat of seasickness to her tingling skin. And her sweat-dampened clothing let the increasing chill in with distracting intimacy. Even so, she did not really register the change in temperature until she noticed that her breath was clouding on the computer screen. God's teeth! If only T-Shirt could have been with her. The word processor fitted badly with the records she was trying to unlock. Simply finding Killigan's logs was frustratingly difficult. Finding the back-ups without access to the network's big file-management system was next to impossible. And when she did finally find something she wished to open, the pages of

247

computer babble made the files almost too impenetrable to read.

But Jolene was on target now. The pattern of what had been done in the past and what was planned for the future was beginning to emerge in her mind, with all the suspects in their proper places, and their guilt unanswerable. But as things stood, she was unlikely to get the chance to pass on her discoveries to any higher authority – other than the one whose name she kept taking in vain. And that brought her round full circle and made her, unknowingly, Vivien Agran's fellow in misfortune. For computers and disks were her Achilles heel independently of the bug; the man she relied upon to help her with this was involved in trying to save the system, the men whom she was fighting knew what she was up to and were increasingly careless of what they might have to do to stop her, and the man she was counting on for protection if the going got rough was trapped on the bridge and likely to stay there until *Kalinin* reached safe haven in the volcanic heart of Deception.

Richard stood on the port bridge wing looking back over *Kalinin*'s stern. Occasionally he would pull his binoculars away from his eyes and glance down at the battered face of his Rolex. It was coming up to four o'clock. Unless the computer boys had found a way to overcome the bug, they would lose the weather systems soon. Then the navigation and propulsion at five, unless the chief had put the overrides in place.

Vasily Varnek stood beside Richard, also straining his eyes to see through the combination of roiling murk, whirling ice storm and freezing spindrift. The rear of the bridge wing was brightened by a long window; thick-glassed, steely-hard and shatterproof. It was rapidly becoming disturbingly opaque as the ice built up on it but, mused Richard grimly, looking ruthlessly on the bright side, that at least meant that the forward-facing clearview section was getting an easier ride. A bolt of lightning, as well defined as an inverted tree of magnesium light, slammed down to the yeasty wave tops immediately behind them. Richard was surprised how rarely *Kalinin* herself had been struck so far. He had been waiting for the simple electrical power of the tempest to do what the bug had failed to do so far and rob them of their eyes as well as their ears. All the equipment aloft was in strong protective golfballs, wind-resistant and ice-proof, but the sheer power of the lightning strikes stalking their heaving wake was easily sufficient to burn out every circuit keeping their machines in contact with the weather satellites above.

Richard lowered his binoculars and walked slowly, carefully, to Colin's side, the twisting heave of the pitching deck playing havoc with his pin-supported knees. 'Colin,' he kept his voice low, 'if the radar went, could we send someone down to the forecastle head to act as lookout?'

The wild white walls of the ice storm actually seemed to close in front of the square bulk of the bridgehouse, as solid, overpowering, and deadly as the walls of the cleft in the moraine. They met in a howling distance where the forecastle head reached out over the wilderness ahead. Even as Richard spoke, the hull up-ended as a big sea, fanged with a solid ram of ice, came in under her transom. She dived forward and down to starboard, digging her bows in like a cruiser running at flank speed. A blue-black mountain of green water whirled into a whelter of blue-white foam and ran away, leaving thick, glittering tracks as though great slugs had gathered there.

'If you could get a man down there, which I doubt, he wouldn't last more than a minute or two,' said Colin.

'So we have to assume we can only keep watch from up here. And if navigation goes down, we'll need to keep our eyes clear with a vengeance.'

'Aye,' said Colin grimly. 'But ye'd better tell that to the god of storms out there. It's his ice that's blinding us. His thunderheads that have buried the sun. His hurricane that is pushing this ice storm. And his waves as high as houses that are coming after us at more than a hundred miles an hour.'

'Still,' said Robin, joining the little group, with Varnek's latest weather-sat print-out in her hand, 'the clearview's working well enough!' She held up the picture Varnek had just handed her. It was stamped with the fax arrival time: 15.55.

'Only for as long as we have power to heat the glass and move the wipers,' said Richard. 'We have to plan for worst-case here. If we lose navigation and the rest of our electrical power, how will we see to steer?'

'That shouldn't happen, even in worst-case,' said Robin. 'The alternators have manual override as well as the engines. Even if the system shuts down and shuts them down, the chief should be able to fire them up again and give us electricity!'

'Well, in that case,' said Kate, joining in as well, 'it's a great pity they didn't back up the environmental heating system with more old-fashioned electric fires.' She shivered. 'It is getting really cold!'

'Yes,' said Robin. 'I think I'd better go down and check on the twins. I'm sure Gretchen will have thought to wrap them up well, but . . .'

'You want me to come?' asked Richard. His eyes wandered back up to the clock: four minutes to four and counting.

'No, darling,' she answered, her still, level grey eyes fixed on him. 'You and Colin keep planning for your worst-case scenario. Even though you're not in command, you'll be worth your weight in gold braid if things get really tough.' She glanced across to Irene and Vasily Varnek. 'I, for one, would feel a lot safer simply knowing you're still up here, I really would.'

'I'll come, then,' said Kate at once. 'I could do with a few more layers. What about you two? Or does the worst-case scenario not include pneumonia?' She looked up at the ship's chronometer. 'And should we try to be back by four to learn the worst about the weather system?'

'No need to worry,' said Colin. 'But I could do with my big Arran right about now.'

'Me too, please,' said Richard, feeling slightly uneasy to be discussing such mundanities in the midst of such turmoil. During the next four minutes the tension on the bridge became all but unbearable. No one talked or moved. Varnek kept checking his weather monitoring system with almost frenetic insistence. And it was only when the minute hand was almost at the five past position that he said, 'Clock reading four minutes past midnight, January the first, two thousand, Captain. Your programmers have pulled us through on this one at least. Weather system still running.'

There were no cheers, but a great sigh of relief seemed to go round the bridge at the news. Then the lugubrious Yazov came across to the smiling Varnek with a print-out from the weather monitor's sister system.

'Ice-watch is down,' he said. 'It's been working well beyond its parameters for a while but now it's official. It can see the clouds but it can no longer see through the clouds.' He handed over the flimsy and Varnek, his mood darkening again at once, handed it on to Richard.

He looked down at the print-out. It was grainy and grey, with no detail, no co-ordinates, nothing. Except that, oddly, the flecks of meaningless white against the dull gunmetal background looked like the snowfall whirl of computer garbage on a screen monitoring a dying computer system.

Richard, like Varnek, dashed from the crest of relief to the trough of frustration, suddenly began to learn what it must have been like to be Nelson, running one-eyed through the blast. 'Take the port wing,' he said quietly to Colin. 'I'll take the starboard. We're on ice-watch now until the clouds thin or Deception comes in sight.'

Behind them, Varnek gestured and Yazov leaned over the green-tinged bowl of the collision alarm radar like an old-fashioned witch hoping to foretell the future from the entrails of some sacrificial lamb. He knew as well as the first officer and the captain that the machine was designed to warn them if they were about to hit metallic objects such as the hulls of ships. It was no more likely than Richard or Colin's mere human eyes to see icebergs made of ancient water and air bubbles, hard as iron and sharp as steel.

'Whaddya think, Borisov?' said T-Shirt, sounding almost drunk with fatigue. 'Think that'll hold it now?'

Borisov pulled himself erect and leaned on the second engineering officer for a moment, stretching his cramped shoulders, much in the way T-Shirt was unknotting his body against Max like a cat on a scratching pole. 'I can think of nothing else we can do,' he said in answer, easing himself up off the young engineer. 'If that does not overcome the bug then this system will crash within the next hour or so also.' He glanced at his watch. 'Hey,' he said. 'Look at the time. We must have fixed the weather system or we'd have heard by now. It would have crashed over half an hour ago. So maybe this one will be all right now too.'

'Well, whaddya know, Max! We're as good as we said we were.' T-Shirt straightened to clap his smiling friend on the shoulder. 'Still, the guys on the bridge have done fine without communications and all that other stuff so far. Unless Dai and Kyril have resurrected that now too. What do they want navigation for in any case?'

Borisov, lading officer and trainee navigator, gave a sour bark of laughter. 'You feel the way she's pitching?' he asked as the four of them began to file out of the cramped, chilly room which housed the navigation computer server. 'With or without the weather systems up and running, she has never moved like this in the ten years I have been aboard. This is bad weather, my friends, and we need all the help we can get. To run to Deception in this, blind as well as deaf and dumb, would kill us even before we reach Neptune's Bellows.'

'That's one hell of a corny name,' said T-Shirt. 'What is Neptune's Bellows?'

'It's the narrows you have to go through to reach the safety of Port Forster in the middle of Deception,' said Borisov. 'Even with everything aboard working one hundred per cent, on a still day in a dead calm, it is one of the most dangerous narrows in the world.'

As Borisov delivered himself of this little speech, so lugubrious as to be worthy of Yazov himself, the little band stepped into the lift which would take them up to the command bridge where they planned to report and get their next assignment. Like the rest of the electrical and mechanical equipment aboard – electrical equipment in the engineering sections and in the bridgehouse, deck gear, pumping, lading and cargo-handling equipment – it was safely under the purview of the still-functioning engine room system, which they had also fixed, like the weather and navigation systems, but which the chief was still preparing to override, just in case. They entered with unthinking confidence therefore, but as the door closed, T-Shirt suddenly slammed his hand onto the rubber protector. 'Tell you what,' he said. 'You guys go up and get the next series of what-to-dos. I got to pay a call.'

Then, typically, he was gone. Max shrugged at the other two. 'It's love,' he said, pulling the saddest face. They were all still laughing when the lift stopped dead in its effortless journey upwards halfway between Main Deck and Bellingshausen-Peary. The light went out.

The lights went out on the command bridge as well, as did every instrument and aid there, and for an instant they stared destruction in the face. Dai and Kyril called out from the radio room where they were crouching deep beneath the main shelf. Richard automatically looked at his watch but it was nowhere near five o'clock yet. This had to be something other than the bug then. Irene gasped, but the sound was subsumed beneath the terrible bellow of the storm. The helmsman, little more than a machine minder, looked upwards suddenly, his face a weird mixture of ice whiteness and shadow. Richard and Colin swung round towards the captain and Varnek swore. Then the power surged back. The VHF buzzed and Varnek spat a few words into the mouthpiece and got several, equally terse, in return.

'The chief apologises, Captain,' said Varnek when the little machine quietened. 'His preparations for manual override just hit a temporary problem.'

The lights and the equipment flickered back on. The lift doors sighed silently open and three very worried men spilled out onto the bridge. Behind them, echoing weirdly up the lift shaft, came a cacophony of sound which might have been cheering or screaming from below.

'You three,' said the captain, with creditable self-control, 'please go and check all systems to see whether that failure of power has caused us any further problems.'

252

As she spoke, a great lightning bolt hit *Kalinin*.

For an instant the ship was the centre of a tremulous cloud of electrical discharge which raced eerily beneath the ice shroud, leaping from molecule to molecule of metal, seeming to give off freezing sparks buried beneath the blue carapace. From the topmost reach of ice-thickened aerial to the lowest of sea-swept hull, the whole ship lit up as though she was made of fragile neon. Then the strange St Elmo's fire died, seemingly snatched away northward by the next black buffet of the wind. And as it did so, the lights and power flickered once again.

It had taken Jolene the better part of two hours to get to Killigan's logs. But she had them now: the top copy, last entered; another, twenty minutes older, and another, twenty minutes older than that one – its contents much the same. But then there was a final one, like Billy Hoyle's, the better part of four hours older still, buried away in the bowels of the record system. A very different story indeed. Without thinking, the minute Jolene cleared the screen of all the junk of incompatible systems, she strained forward to read what it said without printing it out. It was only when she was halfway down the first page – first of fifteen according to the screen – that she even thought to save her work. But when she pressed SAVE, she simply got a DISK FULL message. Full of the confidence engendered by experience and with watching T-Shirt handle the system, she reached across for another disk, waiting for the green light denoting communication between the current disk and the drive to go out.

Instead, everything died. The light, the screen, the ceiling light in the room and in the library outside. Everything. The ship gave another lurch up and forward as though she had been kicked in the rear by a giant. Down went *Kalinin*'s head. She corkscrewed so wildly that the monitor skidded across the top of the computer box. Jolene reached out through the gloom automatically, guided by the residual static glow of the screen. As her chilled fingers grabbed the icy plastic sides, the screen, the ceiling light and everything else flickered on again. The screen was blank, however. All her work was gone. The realisation of what was happening hit her then so forcefully that when the message PLEASE SUPPLY AN OPERATING SYSTEM jumped onto the screen, she cried aloud with shock.

And the door burst open behind her.

'Now,' drawled a deep, coldly disapproving voice, 'what's going down here?'

Still fighting to come to terms with what the accursed computer had done to her, Jolene swung round. Sergeant Killigan stood in the doorway, with Billy Hoyle looming behind him. She had never seen them look so threatening. Her mouth dried and her whole body ached for the safety of her powerful little Glock pistol with its red-dot sight. Then she remembered the last time she had seen the red dot and she really did experience cold sweat.

Killigan strode across the room. 'What have you got there?' he demanded quietly, his voice awash with venomous threat. He clicked the disk out of the A drive and threw it down with the others. 'Give the machine what it's asking for, Inspector,' he ordered. 'Give it an operating system and a processor. Let's see what you've got on these little disks of yours, shall we?'

'Get lost, Killigan,' she grated. 'This is a Federal investigation. The disks and what is on them are the property of NASA and the courts. They are no concern of yours.'

'I don't believe you, lady,' said Killigan. 'And neither does Billy boy here. He's told me all about secret back-up files and a shitload of other stuff. You're living dangerously. You know that? You got till I count to three to slip in the operating disk and call up what you were working on just now, or a series of very nasty accidents will happen to you and I'll call it all up myself.'

'Here,' said Billy, suddenly. 'Let me.' He shoved Jolene roughly aside and snatched up the SYSTEMS disk, jamming it into drive A while the word processor went into drive B. The screen lit up at once. LOADING PROGRAMME it said. The green light glittered as the system talked to the disk.

Defeated for the moment, Jolene tore herself erect, but Killigan stepped up to her, pushing his body between her and the door. Close as he was, he was still weirdly illuminated when the ghastly glow swept in through the library window next door. Like some strange white airborne miasma, the brightness spread, whitening what it touched like frost, making the plastic glow, making the manmade fibres of his cheap shirt gleam and crackle, bringing a strange odour to the air, an incongruous mixture of ozone and burning, like a distant, chemical beach barbecue. The sergeant's thin crewcut stood erect and flashed with sparks.

Then the light died again.

As though blaming her, as though preparing to carry out his threat, he stepped forward. She tensed herself for pain and retaliation. The thought flashed into her mind that now was the time to get hers in first.

254

And the light flickered on again. The dead screen cleared. PLEASE SUPPLY . . . Jolene's gaze flashed down to the little green light at the A drive. It was flickering hopefully, then it went red and died.

'Well, that's that,' said Billy Hoyle. 'The systems disk is screwed. Processor's wiped. Whole machine looks fucked to me. Unless the inspector here can read BASIC straight off the disks – if there's anything actually left on them after that little lot – she's finished with our logs anyway.' He threw the disks at her and she caught them.

'I don't need the disks, you son of a bitch,' said Jolene, enraged, waving them at him as though they were a fist closed in threat. 'I don't need the logs or anything more. I've got the whole picture now and I'm coming after you, you murderous bastards.'

Killigan glanced at Hoyle. 'Close the door, Billy boy,' he said, almost regretfully. 'The lady and I have to have a little heart to heart here . . .'

But before Hoyle had even tensed his muscles to obey Killigan, the outer door opened and T-Shirt slammed into the room.

'Jesus,' he said. 'Was that some light-show? You hear them screaming out there? What a rush, huh, Jolene?'

And, as though he was the love of her life, a soldier back from the war, she tore past Killigan and hurled herself into his arms.

T-Shirt swept her out into the corridor. With a single syllable of obscenity, Killigan moved to follow them, reaching into the conveniently baggy pocket of his army-issue parka for the butt of the Glock. Billy Hoyle reached out to restrain him, seeing all too clearly what was in his mind and knowing that pulping some nosy little broad in the privacy of a storm-silenced library was one thing but blazing away at a couple in a public corridor was something else entirely.

Killigan shrugged off his hand with a fierce look and Billy suddenly felt a little ice entering his own belly. The sergeant's reason was gone; his sanity rapidly slipping after it.

'Killigan,' he spat.

Killigan ignored him and tore the door wide. But there at the far end of the corridor were Borisov, Max and the second engineer gathered around T-Shirt, passing on the captain's orders and not even Killigan was mad enough to shoot at all of them.

He swung back to Billy, his face still thunderous. 'I'll settle with that little bitch later,' he snarled. 'Now let's go pay a visit to the other one. I'm fed up with taking all this crap from a couple of fucking broads.'

The next two women the disgruntled sergeant saw, however, were

Robin and Kate who brushed past them as they hurried down to the Mariners' cabin. Billy's eyes followed the women after the briefest of grudging nods. 'If I was going to off anyone, Killigan, I think I'd probably off those two and their nosy fucking kids.'

'Shut the fuck up, Hoyle,' snarled Killigan. 'If anyone's going to get offed, then I say who, if and when. Remember, the last thing we want to do is close all our options when we're stuck aboard this tub surrounded by the Russian mafia. I got the Glock, but I ain't got enough bullets to handle a whole fucking army of these guys if they get really pissed at us.'

It was this thought which preserved Vivien Agran for the time being.

Killigan and Billy did not go smashing into her cabin at once. They watched from the far end of the corridor until enough people had come and gone to convince them that she must be accessible and alone in there. Then they moved. Killigan hit the door hard, turning the handle, half expecting it to be locked. But it wasn't. He and Billy erupted into the little office area and she looked up from behind her desk, her face set like stone. 'I've been expecting you,' she said, her fingers busy on her keyboard.

But Billy had learned a fair amount from his last visit here and he snatched the whole thing away from her at once, before she could even try to send a message on it. The ship's network was still down – as dead as the door monitors and the corridor cameras – so she was effectively cut off in any case.

Apparently unmoved by Billy's action, she rose. 'Of course you want your property back,' she said coolly, opening the door of the secure cupboard behind her desk. At once Billy was there beside her, leaving the keyboard to dangle. He caught her arms and twisted them behind her back with clumsy but effective force, gripping fiercely through the padded arms of the hooded parka which she wore, unzipped, over her formal suit and blouse.

Killigan came across and looked into the cupboard then. His eyes flicked down to her supplies and up to her eyes. 'Now,' he said quietly. 'I bet you see yourself like this, Mrs Agran don't you?' He held up a magazine whose cover showed a powerful-looking woman dressed in black leather standing on the prone figure of a man. 'I just bet this is you, deep down inside, all dominant, in charge, ahead of the game.'

With sudden, brutal force, he hurled the magazine away, its thick, garish pages almost slapping her in the face. With a return stroke swift as a snake's he reached into the cupboard again and pulled out a box for a computer game. DEATH PUNCH it said in red at the top.

Beneath the title was a computer-generated graphic image of a warrior woman, her slightly angular bosom bursting open in a fierce cloud of blood as her massive, brutish opponent reached in to tear her heart out.

'I believe I could probably do that for real,' he whispered, tossing the box back in the cupboard and focusing his dead iron gaze on the strain of her blouse buttons. 'You want I should try?' He reared his arm back, half closing his fist into a taloned claw.

'No,' she said, a flutter in her level voice showing how fiercely she was fighting for control. 'Of course I don't. Take what you came for and go. Please.'

'Maybe I came for more than just the Power Strip and the disk,' he said. 'Maybe I came to make sure you can't come after us.'

Vivien screamed as Billy twisted her arms more fiercely, supporting Killigan's threat. The buttons over her bosom burst and Killigan tensed, as though the sudden shadowed gape was tempting him past the realm of reason and control into the strange world of the video game, where he could really tear out a woman's heart and walk away unscathed.

But just at this moment, a firm knocking came at the door and Gretchen's voice called, 'Mrs Agran, may I come in?'

'Just a moment, Gretchen.'

As Killigan hesitated, his mind coming back within the bounds of sanity, the screen on the computer monitor cleared to show Varnek looking fiercely out at them. 'Vivien,' he called. 'We have partial communications restored. Kyril and Mr Gwyllim have fixed the TV satellite reception system and managed to call the network back up and are working on the radio now. It is past five and we still have propulsion and navigation. We have a chance to get to Deception after all. Vivien? Vivien!'

Vivien jerked herself free of Billy Hoyle and fastened the buttons of her blouse. 'Take your stuff and go, Sergeant,' she spat at Killigan. Then she swung round to Hoyle, working her shoulders to ease the strain. 'And you had better find a safer place to hide this time, little man. Because when we get to Deception Island I am personally going to send you to join your friend, the late Mr Marshall!'

'Hey,' said T-Shirt gently, 'you're still shaking.'

'It's the cold,' she said, quietly. 'I am not afraid. I am simply freezing.'

It was half an hour after Max and Borisov had come to tell him the captain wanted the systems checked after the chief's ill-fated testing of the manual override. It was just coming up to five and T-Shirt was disobeying orders and beyond caring whether the systems he had spent the afternoon working on were going to survive the hour. They were in Jolene's cabin, sitting together on her single bunk, and she was curled against him, shaking like a leaf. The storm was worsening as far as he could tell, and the chill coming in over the failed environmental maintenance system was becoming quite fearsome, far beyond anything the little electric heater in the corner could handle. But even so, bundled in his warm, dry clothing, he was quite snug and for the life of him he could not understand why she was not. He believed her when she said she was not scared, though she had told him all about her confrontation with Killigan and Hoyle.

Her slim body seemed as well-wrapped as his own, and yet . . .

'Look,' he said easily, 'I'm not getting fresh here – not unless you want me to, that is – but I just gotta check something out.'

Before she had even the faintest idea what he was talking about, he slid his hand in through the front of her clothes, snaking his fingers down layer after layer until they found the skin between the outer swell of her left breast and her armpit. His breath hissed, drowning out her half-hearted, "Hey . . .'

'Mrs DaCosta,' he said. 'You are as wet as a drowning kitten under there and as cold as a Slush-Puppy. We gotta get your body temperature up, lady. And I know whereof I speak, for the redoubtable Dr Glasov demonstrated on Max, Dai and myself only a couple of days back just how to approach this very problem. But do not ask,' he said severely, getting up and looking down at her, 'do not ever ask how she took our temperatures.'

He leaned over. She slid back. She gazed up at him, her eyes clear and calm, colourless as pools of dew.

'Trust me?' he asked quietly.

She nodded. 'Oh yes,' she said.

'Now,' he said gently. 'This is without doubt the stupidest time and place to be playing doctors and nurses.' As he spoke he glanced up at the clock above the door. The word 'time' caused a sort of Pavlovian reflex now.

It was ten to five when he began to remove her clothing. As he worked, he piled the duvet round her so that as the layers came off they were replaced by warm swan's down. As he slid her pale, chilled, shivering nakedness out of wet shirt, clammy jeans and soaking underwear and into warm, dry wrappings, he continued to talk quietly and easily. He asked her about her past, probing into her family

258

background in Austin. He skated delicately over the matter of Mr DaCosta but managed to establish that the relationship, like the man, was dead. Then he told her of his own life, experiences and simple philosophies, as if he felt he should bare a bit of his soul while he bared all of her body.

When she was naked and wrapped in the duvet, he took the wettest of her clothing and draped it over the electric heater to dry. The little radiator could not heat the room, but it should be able to perform that simple function well enough. Then, still bundled in the duvet, he carried her through to the shower. Sitting her against the heated towel rail cushioned by the fluffy, water-warmed towels, he swiftly removed his own clothing, slinging it outside onto the bed. 'If this is getting too much for you I'll keep my shorts on,' he said. 'It's medicinal in any case.'

She shook her head, white-faced, blue-lipped, wide-eyed and shaking. 'I need all the help I can get,' she said. 'Shock treatment is good.'

'Hokay . . . '

When he, too, was naked he turned and switched the water on. Only when he was satisfied with its temperature did he come back towards her. With fastidious care he dried his hands and arms on a towel, then he reached down for her, lifting her to her feet and deftly whirling the dry duvet off her body and out through the door onto the bed, safely under the cloud of steam that was beginning to gather – even though the shower was little more than tepid.

'Now, where was I in the story of my life?' he asked, pressing the icy length of her against himself and stepping into the warmth of the shower stall. 'Ah yes, Special Forces training . . .'

When Max thundered joyfully on the door soon after five o'clock to tell T-Shirt that the systems he had fixed were still alive, there was no reply. When he came back at six to say that Dai and Kyril had partially restored the ship's network and enough of the communications system to allow them to receive TV pictures again, though they could still not send out any messages, there was still no reply. When he came back at seven o'clock to say that the environment system looked as though it was going to stay as dead as the lading and galley systems, any reply which might have been forthcoming was smothered beneath the duvet.

Jolene and T-Shirt emerged from her cabin at seven thirty and went in search of Mrs Agran. Jolene was wearing her own clothes and was aglow with warmth, especially because she was also wearing T-Shirt's parka over the top of them. T-Shirt was less well dressed and nowhere near as warm, though he, too, was all aglow. They were in search of Vivien Agran because they really needed more clothing. With the environment system still down, the temperatures in the bridgehouse were beginning to reflect those outside, save only for the wind chill. T-Shirt was armed against the cold with all of his vests and three shirts. He also carried his spare parachute snugly on his back, and his duvet tied round his neck like a warm cloak. They could think of no one else who might be able to supply the extra clothing Jolene still needed. T-Shirt doubted whether even Mrs Agran would have anything spare now, for everyone he saw was bundled up in every stitch they could lay their hands on. But as things turned out they couldn't find her. Her cabin was locked and no amount of knocking or calling could elicit a reply. A quick check of her usual haunts revealed nothing. Questions to passing stewards drew a blank. They found Anoushka, dressed for skiing at Aspen, but even she had no idea where her boss was. She told them there were no more warm clothes available.

T-Shirt's eccentric costume turned quite a few heads when the pair of them arrived in the dining salon at five minutes to eight, local time, at exactly the same moment as Richard and Colin, Robin, Kate and the twins. The weather was showing no sign of moderating. No more dead computer systems had been revitalised since six. They were still deep in the grip of a very dangerous situation and four hours' hard sailing from Deception and the promise of safe haven. But the millennium was just arriving at the Greenwich meridian, halfway round the world from where it had started, halfway through the twenty-four hours it would take to complete full circle, and four hours still away from *Kalinin* herself. It was four minutes to midnight in London, and Big Ben filled the screen.

'Why are you dressed like that?' asked Mary, wide-eyed.

'In celebration,' T-Shirt answered cheerfully. 'It's my impression of my favourite English king. Richard the Third.' And as he leaped and capered, whirling his cloak over the hunch of his parachute, the most famous clock in the world began to chime midnight.

As it did so, Lieutenant Borisov rushed in, white with worry. 'T-Shirt,' he called. 'Captain Mariner. Can you come with me, please?'

He took them straight up to the bridge, darkly silent, refusing to answer their worried questions, clearly fighting to get his thoughts in order.

On the bridge he took them over to Captain Ogre. One look at them called Varnek over to stand beside his captain.

'What is it Borisov?' she demanded.

Borisov took a deep breath. 'As lading officer I should have thought of it before. But I have thought of it now and we may have time to plan for it if nothing else.' He paused. No one said anything.

'We have managed to deal with the bug so far by re-programming the central clocks in the servers,' he said slowly. 'That way the systems will work until the components on the next level down – the circuits and the chips themselves – are asked to check the time and the date. When that happens we will have an even more serious problem, because we still do not know which individual chips are two thousand-proof.'

'None of them except Mrs Agran's if the servers are a good guide,' said Richard.

'Why would they be asked to check the date and the time?' asked T-Shirt.

Richard answered. 'On my ships there is an automatic systems check once every month. All the systems perform an automatic status assessment and report back automatically. Not the people, the machines. Automatically.'

'Yes!' said Borisov, his face alive with relief to have found such a ready understanding. 'This is the same on *Kalinin*. The systems will be asked to check themselves automatically. And the instant they begin this they will begin to close down again because every single chip, down to levels we can never hope to reach, will have to check on what the date is. And there is nothing we can do. It is something only head office can stop. Only they have the codes and the passwords.'

'When?' demanded Richard. 'When is the systems check programmed to happen?'

'Every month, at the same—'

'When?' demanded Richard and T-Shirt both at once.

Borisov looked at them all, his eyes wide with worry. 'During the first five minutes of the first hour of the first day of the month, local time. We have until midnight. Then we lose it all.'

Chapter Twenty-Five

Dai Gwyllim stuck his head out of the radio room door. 'I think Kyril's done it, Captain,' he said. 'You should be able to call out now.'

They all crowded round the door into the radio room, all except the navigating officer and the helmsman. The radio equipment glowed as brightly as a Christmas tree as Kyril programmed in the wavelength and the call sign for their main office in St Petersburg. The machine's memory had been wiped when it crashed. 'It will slow us, doing everything by hand,' said Kyril. 'But at least we can call out now, eh? That is good.'

'You have done well,' said Irene. 'You will receive special mention in my logs.'

'It may not be all that permanent,' warned Dai Gwyllim.

'And it will die again at midnight,' said Borisov to Richard, sotto voce.

'Not if we can get the codes and close down the automatic status check,' he answered gently, his deep voice confident, assured.

The storm outside took the ship and hurled it sideways, as though trying to throw it bodily onto the black rocks of the shore of Graham Land to leeward. They all staggered a little. The lights flickered. The lift across the bridge hissed into action, the car speeding downwards. A weather picture started spooling out of the weather-watch machine.

'We're through!' exulted Kyril. He flipped open the receive channel.

A slow, clear Russian voice began to speak to them.

'Give me the mike,' ordered Irene. As she spoke she reached in and took it from Kyril's hand. She pressed the SEND button and spoke. 'Hello, St Petersburg. This is *Kalinin*. We have an urgent message, over.' She lifted her finger from the button.

The voice droned on. Even though it was speaking Russian, it was obvious to Richard that it was the voice of a machine, pre-recorded.

Irene pressed SEND again. 'St Petersburg, this is *Kalinin* . . .'

The lift doors hissed open. Max and Jolene erupted onto the bridge just as Irene released the button and the mechanical message claimed the air again.

'T-Shirt,' said Max, urgently. 'It just said on the TV that some sections of Moscow have closed down. They don't know if it's the bug or some hacker with a virus and a sad sense of humour but bits of the commercial system aren't responding, some of the city's municipal systems, traffic lights and the phone system have closed down and—'

'Not just in Moscow, then,' said Borisov.

'. . . cannot accept your call,' continued the mechanical Russian voice. 'Account remains unsettled since January first, nineteen hundred. This system is closed until full settlement is received. We are sorry, this system cannot accept your call . . .'

Irene swung round. 'Mr Varnek,' she ordered coolly. 'This part of the system is not working properly but other parts may be. Please try and establish contact by fax. Mr Borisov, e-mail. Now! Kyril, put that on automatic call-back and try to raise America.'

'Only Russia has the twenty-four-hour office and the codes,' warned Borisov as he crossed to the bridge computer and tried to get out onto the Internet.

'Yes, but if there's anyone in the American office, perhaps they can get through to Russia more easily than we can and call us back.'

'Also,' said Richard, slipping a thought from a different priority level into the conversation, 'while you've got a line out, you might try calling Deception. There's an Argentinean summer station there. They might be able to help and they'll certainly need to know we're coming.'

'Good thinking. Kyril, you heard.'

'Yes, Captain. Dai, can you take that book and look up their wavelength and call sign please? I'll try America now.'

Richard strode away from the bustle, his mind still busy. He stood looking out into the storm-darkened gloom under a midnight sun. It was almost too dark to see. Only the lights defined the ship's outline in the whirling whiteness. He was forcefully reminded of the last transmission from the failing ice-watch, all gunmetal grey, fading featurelessly to dark slate with a wild whirl of specks just large enough to have white faces and black-shadowed backs. He leaned forward, unconsciously riding the corkscrew heave. Foam surged back up the deck like a tsunami wave and attained the square front of the bridgehouse, exploding up in a vertical wall of instantly-freezing foam. It set onto the clearview and the wipers and froze solid for an instant before the heated glass broke the icy grip of the stuff, the wipers swept back into motion, and, like Saul at Damascus, Richard could see again.

264

'It's getting worse. Shifting westward slightly,' he called to Varnek. 'Did the weather sat give us a time and place for the eye?'

'On this heading. Two hours.'

Varnek's answer made Richard glance up at the chronometer. He saw with surprise that it was coming up to ten o'clock. 'That should see us into Deception,' he said quietly to himself, 'if nothing else does!'

'Still nothing on e-mail,' sang Borisov.

'Fax isn't answering either,' called Kyril. 'I can't raise America, and all I can get from Deception is an automatic message saying they're currently unmanned but the refuge and supply centre is open for emergencies. But there's a very strange thing here!'

'What's that?' asked Richard and Irene together.

'It's a general warning. It comes every now and then on all the bands I've tried. Even the emergency band, so it must be important.'

'Warning about what?'

'Interference, I suppose you'd call it.'

'What from?'

'Mir. The space station Mir.'

'What about it?' asked Richard, intrigued.

'The Russian Space Agency is bringing it down tonight. Sometime between midnight and two our time it's due to enter the atmosphere. Somewhere over Argentina on a path over the Falklands just to the north of us, they think. They're warning about interference, possibly black-outs as it breaks up in the atmosphere.'

'. . . which promises to be the biggest fireworks show in history,' the English commentator was saying. Even two hours after midnight there, London was still on the air. Midnight had got as far as Cape Farewell in Greenland, and would soon arrive in Rio which was gearing up as only Rio could. But in the meantime, lacking anything else to talk about, the increasingly desperate anchorman was discussing the forthcoming destruction of Mir. 'Perhaps only the Russians, especially under their current financial circumstances, could have come up with the idea of getting rid of a two-hundred-ton space station simply by crashing it into Earth's atmosphere. I have here a representative of Greenpeace who, as you will imagine, has a strong and not particularly festive opinion . . .'

In spite of the storm, the continuing festivities and the cold, the twins were asleep at last. As the Greenpeace man was joined by a woman representing Friends of the Earth to observe that the space

265

station was due to break into four pieces – three of forty tons and one of eighty tons containing a nuclear reactor – and that no one seemed to know exactly where or when these things would actually land, Robin and Kate picked up a slumbering infant each and eased themselves out of the dining salon.

It was difficult to carry the children because they were so heavy now and the ship was rolling badly, but the women picked their way carefully along the corridor to the lift. When the car came, the doors hissed open to reveal Killigan and Hoyle leaning back into the rear corners. After only the slightest hesitation, Robin said, 'Going up?' and strode in. Kate followed, and an uneasy silence ensued as the lift rose one more deck to their level.

'What do you think those two are up to?' asked Kate as they walked along the corridor to the Mariners' stateroom.

'I don't know,' said Robin thoughtfully. 'But I don't like the look of them. When I've put the twins down, I think I'll stay with them. Could you go and find Richard and Colin? Update Richard as to where we are and tell him about those two – not that he'll be able to do anything about them. He won't want to leave the bridge.'

Once the twins were tucked down, with Robin anxiously but comfortably on watch, Kate went off to deliver her friend's worried message. Her first thought was to take the lift up to the bridge, but the thought of being trapped in it with Killigan and Billy Hoyle made her think again. So when it did not immediately answer her summons, she turned and made her way along the pitching corridor and up the heaving companionway instead.

She reached the bridge and walked into what was obviously an explosive atmosphere. 'Look,' Richard was saying, obviously trying to keep things calm, 'We just have to plan for it. OK, so the radio's down again. The radio on the Sikorsky is still unreachable and wouldn't raise much except local traffic in any case. From the sound of things, we'd never have got any sense out of St Petersburg in time. America might have been able to help but Borisov here doubts it. Fine. At least we know the equipment on Deception is there and functioning one hundred per cent. That's what we'll have to go for. The camp is up on the clifftop at Mount Pond and it's a bit of a climb from the beach—'

'Eighteen hundred feet sheer,' supplied Colin knowledgeably. 'Half a mile on the path and it is very steep too.'

'But once we're in Port Foster bay, we can send Zodiac with a team prepared to run up there and call whoever you want. We might even be able to send the Sikorsky, but I can't remember whether they have a landing area up there.'

'But it will be too late for us!' said Borisov desperately. 'All our systems will have shut down.' He looked at his watch; double-checked with the chronometer above the helmsman's head. 'We have just over one hour then. Total powerdown. All systems. Dead.'

'Not the engines,' said Richard. 'And not the ancillaries the engine room controls. At five to midnight we get the chief to switch to manual override. We'll still have steerageway.'

'Steerageway to where? We'll be blind and deaf, in the middle of the worst storm I have seen. And nothing ahead of us but Neptune's Bellows, a passage less than a kilometre wide with rocks and shoals on either side and winds tearing in and out all over the place. It is madness. We'll be dead.'

'No we won't,' Richard insisted. 'Not if we're careful. Not if we plan. Not if we're prepared. Ships have been coming and going through Neptune's Bellows for centuries. Most of them without all of this equipment.'

'Not in storms like this!' cried Borisov, looking around as though expecting applause for this clincher to the argument.

'Mr Varnek,' snapped Richard. 'When will we reach the eye of the storm?'

'At midnight, Captain Mariner.'

'And what will we find there?'

'According to the weather sat, clear skies and calm winds for one hour, maybe two.'

'Mr Yazov, where will we be then?'

'Waiting to enter Neptune's Bellows, Captain Mariner.'

'You see, Mr Borisov? It is a question of timing. Of being ready and having every eventuality planned for. In one hour's time, this weather will clear for one hour, perhaps two, before it all closes down again. In one hour and five minutes, we will lose everything except power and propulsion. Therefore we will need to know to within millimetres where we are and how we are heading. We will have moments to post watches on bridge wings and, if we can, on the forecastle head. If we are lucky we may even be able to get the Sikorsky up. As soon as the weather clears we will head at full speed towards Neptune's Bellows. And the moment we are through we will need to send teams, either by Zodiac or Sikorsky, to the base there.'

On this note, a distant cheer erupted, as though the passengers had heard and approved Richard's decisive words. Kate swung round and gasped with shock. The lift car stood open, unnoticed, its door wedged wide by Killigan's boot on the one side and Hoyle's on the other. The instant Killigan saw Kate recognise him and open her mouth to warn the bridge party that they were being spied upon, he moved. They both stepped back. The door hissed shut. The lift car was gone. The cheering carried on, distant but unmistakable. It was midnight in Rio, fifteen degrees to the east of them. They had exactly one hour left.

For the team on the bridge it was an incredibly busy hour and it passed in a flash of frenetic activity. The same was true for the men in the engine room. But for those caught in between, time dragged, the slow tick of the minutes only partially lightened by the colourful excesses in Rio. And there were a good number of people caught in between, for the team on the bridge was stripped down now to navigators and ship-handlers. All the computer people were redundant; even if they could fix anything, the respite would be pointlessly brief. Kyril stayed at his post, but he remained there alone, his equipment dead, his hope of communication with anywhere, near or far, put on hold until he got into the Sikorsky or up onto the deserted base on Deception. All the watch officers remained, on watch or not, just as all the engineers assembled with the chief below, preparing to switch over from the automatic to the manual systems at the captain's order in fifty minutes' time. Richard and Colin remained; no one else.

Kate returned to the Mariners' stateroom and passed back to Robin Richard's love and the knowledge that her message had been received. The hunch-backed T-Shirt, with Max and Jolene, went down to the dining salon in search of food and a little more partying. But Jolene was restless, all too well aware that Killigan and Hoyle were on the prowl and that Vivien Agran was nowhere to be seen. In the innermost pocket of her jacket, beneath the warm bulk of T-Shirt's parka, she still held the little pile of computer disks, wrapped in the printouts of Billy Hoyle's logs like a little present. Getting to a radio was a high priority for her, too, and she required a much less powerful machine than any of the others, for she only needed to reach Agent Jones at Armstrong. He was so close at hand, she had even tried to raise him on her personal phone, but the signal had gone down with the satellite dish and had not come up again.

She had a clear view of her duty beyond making that call too. Whether she could tell Jones what she had found and what she planned or not, it was her duty, clear and unavoidable, irrespective of the cost, to get back the Power Strip if she could and prevent its design specifications getting from the floppy disk onto the Internet. All she could do at the moment was to keep herself generally aware of the whereabouts of Killigan and Hoyle. But she had no wish to go looking for them. The next time they managed to get her alone for a couple of minutes they would not hesitate to finish their unfinished business with her.

The obvious thing to do was to ask the otherwise unemployed T-Shirt for his help. And Jolene knew he would not hesitate to give it. But sometime during that ecstatic time in the shower and those wonderful hours immediately afterwards, T-Shirt had managed to become so precious to her that she would far rather put herself at risk than do anything that might endanger him.

And so she and T-Shirt and Max sat with the others in the dining salon, watching a midnight carnival snaking through Rio with stories and comments from Montevideo and Buenos Aires. It was not until a little item came in from Gander, Newfoundland, whose time zone was on the half-hour between Rio's and their own, that she realised how late it was getting. Shaking herself into some kind of wakefulness, Jolene looked around. The first person she saw, in the distance, was Vivien Agran. She had changed her clothes, Jolene noticed. She was wearing black jeans, a black shirt, a thick, heavy black parka. Jolene raised her hand, trying to catch her eye to ask her about a parka for herself so T-Shirt could have his back, but she was gone, leaving an impression almost as disturbing as Killigan and Hoyle. Jolene sat back, mind racing, and suddenly realised she was sitting opposite the one potential ally she had not tapped for any favours yet. She leaned forward. 'Hey, Corporal Washington,' she said. 'How are you feeling?'

So far, anyone wanting to use the Sikorsky or the Zodiacs had gone down the deck. The Sikorsky sat on a platform above the main deck behind the bridgehouse. The Zodiacs were lowered from the poop further back still, and were boarded down a set of retractable steps which started at a little mezzanine dock, hardly more than a balcony, and reached to a little step-off point at water level. This was not the only way to get back to the chopper and the inflatables, however. A long passageway reached back at second engineering deck level, piercing the storage areas and ending at the bottom of a well with a ladder up its side and a hatch at the top. The hatch was in the main deck just below the Sikorsky's overhanging tail, within easy reach of the davits to lower the Zodiacs and one companionway up from the little mezzanine balcony. At 11.45, local time, Third Officer Borisov led a little squad of men down this passageway. His orders were manifold. He was to wait for the sudden quiet calm which would announce that they had passed into the eye of the storm. He was to expect a signal of confirmation on his VHF. He was not to expect the lights or power to fail as the chief switched over to manual power – though in fact he did expect this. He was then to lead his men up onto the deck. There he would ascertain, as best he could, whether the chopper would fly and the inflatables would float, and ready them all as swiftly as he was able. The pilot was part of his little command, as were the two most expert Zodiac coxwains. Kyril was with him. The radio officer would go first to the Sikorsky and try to raise any local bases he could on the chopper's radio while the pilot was doing his pre-flight. Once the chopper was ready or the Zodiacs could be lowered, Kyril and Borisov would signal the bridge and be directed into the helicopter and/or the boats. By this time it was assumed that *Kalinin* would have passed, safe and sound, at best speed possible, through Neptune's Bellows and into the calm, safe haven of Port Foster.

As Borisov led his elite team down the long engineering deck corridor, he was wrapped in thought, his mind – a dangerously negative force on occasion – far ahead of his feet, wrestling with ghostly problems. He was unaware that Killigan and Hoyle were also intent on making use of the quickest way off the ship and across to the communications equipment at the unmanned station on Deception.

'Do you realise what you are asking?' demanded Irene Ogre, drawing herself up to her full height. Corporal Washington met her, look for look on the level. 'Yes, ma'am, Captain. But I am a legally constituted member of the United States Army, ma'am, and this is American soil. I know you have firearms locked away for use in emergencies. This is an emergency, ma'am. I realise you cannot leave the bridge at this moment, so I want you to turn over the key of the gun cabinet to me, please. The inspector here and I have to go and place two men under arrest until such time as Federal agents can come and question them.'

'Killigan and Hoyle,' said T-Shirt helpfully.

Irene looked across at Richard, but for once he was no help to her. His frowning concentration was wholly on the chronometer, the GPS readout on the ship-handler, and the latest weather-sat fax on which Varnek and Yazov had marked the positions of the ship and the still-invisible Deception. It was impossible to believe that in ten minutes time they would break out of this storm wall into a calm sea and clear sky and find an island, twenty miles in circumference, two thousand feet in height, immediately off their port quarter.

'You see Deception, Mr Yazov?' called Richard, his voice reflecting nothing of the tension he was feeling.

'Clear as clear,' called Yazov from the collision alarm radar. 'If I had the sound on this turned on, you would be going deaf right now. As far as I can make out the detail, the mouth of Neptune's Bellows is seven kilometres due west of us, right about . . . NOW!'

On his signal, Richard reached over and hit the emergency left turn button. The button instantly overrode the automatic ship-handling system, swinging the ship onto her new heading due west. The helmsman had been awaiting this and he braced himself to hold the wheel as the game ship swung beam on to wind and sea which until now had been following them. Over she rolled like a corvette, until it seemed that the starboard bridge wing was going to go under. Then she began to right herself. Vicious spindrift came whipping across her foredeck from left to right. A great sea punched her on the jaw, wrenching her head round with massive force.

'How's that eye coming, Mr Varnek?' called Richard.

'Any minute now,' responded the Russian.

'It'll arrive on the dot of midnight, then,' said Colin from the other side of the writhing, wrestling helmsman.

'Yes. Very well,' said Irene Ogre to Washington. 'Take the keys. But I want no gunfights aboard my ship, Corporal, Dr DaCosta. This is not the Wild West.' The three of them ran over to the lift and Irene moved to stand at Richard's shoulder. 'How long until the chief switches to manual?'

Richard's eyes flicked up to the chronometer. 'Four minutes,' he said. 'Nine to powerdown. Where is the eye, Mr Varnek?'

'It's just coming over Deception. On this line we will run into it at the stroke of midnight, a little less than five kilometres this side.'

'It had better be there,' said Colin quietly, standing by with Yazov, ready to go out and act as lookout.

'It'll be there. Are you ready?'

'Aye.'

'Mr Yazov?'

'Ready.'

'Right. Off you go down to the A-deck door. Good luck, the pair of you. And for God's sake wait for my signal!'

Colin gestured out at the lethal, howling madness smearing itself across the clearview. 'You don't have to tell me twice,' he said grimly. 'I'll not be going out in that without a direct order. Why, man, it's almost as bad as December in Aberdeen.'

The guns were sturdy, not very remarkable, reliable. A Remington rifle and a Smith and Wesson .38 police special, a pistol, not an automatic, with chambers and no fancy red-dot sight. But Jolene felt so much better as she pulled it out of the case that she would almost have traded T-Shirt for it. Almost. She saw him looking longingly at it and remembered the section of his life story he had told her in the shower. The Special Forces section. 'You can't have it,' she said firmly. 'It's my security blanket. Humour me. And anyway, you look like what you really need is a broadsword.'

'And a horse,' he said. 'In fact, now you come to mention it, I'd give my kingdom for a—'

Corporal Washington snapped the breach on the Remington open and closed like John Wayne with a Winchester. 'Let's move out,' he ordered quietly.

But T-Shirt held up his right hand. 'Wait a moment,' he said.

The guns were in the captain's quarters up on Palmer-Hall Deck. Because they didn't know where Killigan and Hoyle were, Washington and Jolene planned to move downwards, deck by deck. But T-Shirt's work on the computers had given him an insight into the way the various programs worked, so he called up the accommodation section and swiftly ran through the corridor monitoring programme. Five minutes later he found them, one deck down on Byrd-Ellsworth. 'There they are,' he said in triumph. 'Got you, you—'

The lights flickered.

'Shit!' he said. 'What's the time?'

Jolene looked at her watch. 'Jesus! It's ninety seconds to midnight.'

'You want to watch these bozos for a bit?' asked T-Shirt. 'See what they're up to?'

'No,' said Jolene decisively. 'I don't want to watch them. I want to stop them.'

'Fair enough,' said T-Shirt. He stood up and prepared to follow her. 'Hey!'

'What now?' snapped Washington, beginning to run out of patience.

'They disappeared. I've got Mrs Agran now, but Killigan and Hoyle've gone. Now where the hell . . .' He began to flick through the corridor monitors again, holding the others up for a few more vital seconds. Then, 'Gotcha,' he said again. 'They're on Palmer-Hall. Hey, that's this—'

Jolene's watch alarm went off, interrupting him. 'It's midnight,' she said, and distant cheering echoed up from below.

'Cool,' said T-Shirt. 'Welcome to the new millennium . . .'

And everything went off. Lights, monitors, engines, everything.

'Speak to me, Chief,' said Irene Ogre, her face like a mask of ice. The only light on the silent bridge was coming out of the whirling heart of the storm, dull as pewter. 'You promised me that this was not going to happen. Speak to me!'

Richard was at her side, his large hand on the helmsman's shoulder, steadying the solid seaman as he fought to hold the ship on course while she still had steerageway.

'It's midnight, Mr Varnek,' said Richard.

'A moment more,' said Varnek. 'The last weather map was so clear. It can only be a moment . . .'

Under the straining silence of his uncompleted sentence, the engines suddenly rumbled back to life. Richard felt the kick of steerage slam up from the wheel into the helmsman's shoulder. He raised his VHF to his lips. 'Colin?' he said. 'Mr Yazov. Any minute now. And remember, the seas will still be running high and there are no safety lines out there.'

As he spoke, a flaw in the wind snatched the whirling ice away and he shouted, as though kicked in the stomach with brutal force. Just for an instant, there was Deception. Just where Yazov said it was. Just as Varnek said it was. A black cliff nearly five kilometres long, six hundred metres high, less than four kilometres dead ahead, coming towards them at all of fifteen knots.

Then the mad swirl was back again and he couldn't see the forecastle head, let alone four kilometres. The lights flickered back on then as the alternators kicked in.

'Mr Varnek,' said Richard. 'What is your computer saying?'

'Rest in peace, perhaps. Nothing else. It is dead.'

'The whole thing? You can't even access Mrs Agran's systems?'

'I tell you, Captain, I'd see more if I was looking up a dodo's ass.'

'Very colourful, Mr Varnek,' spat Captain Ogre. But whatever sharp words were spilling onto her lips were snatched away with the storm wall as they plunged into the eye, just as he had predicted. And, as Richard had already seen, there was Deception, a black wall seemingly immediately ahead of them, grinding down upon them. What made it particularly terrifying, other than its solidity and shocking proximity, was the fact that Neptune's Bellows was invisible, indistinguishable

273

from the unremitting bulk of it. And such was their speed as they plunged towards it, that even if Richard hit the emergency turn button again, they would ram themselves with massive force onto some black, ice-bound part of it.

'OK, Colin,' said Richard into his VHF. 'You're on.'

Colin Ross was used to the cold. He did most of his work on the ice at the Poles. He had man-sledded across the Big White when Ranulph Fiennes was still a lad. He made no great song and dance about it, but his left hand was prosthetic, the real one lost to frostbite a quarter of a century since. But he had never felt cold like this. Out on *Kalinin*'s foredeck, everything was thick and slick with ice; ice that seemed ambitious of attaining absolute zero on its own. The wild physics of the storm were still being worked out here as molecules of pure and salt water intermingled at temperatures far below zero, still in the grip of the awful forces which had been whirling around them until a moment or two ago. There was a frost fog in the unnatural calm, something born of the wild wish of the ice to be closer still to interstellar temperatures, to attain the blue perfection of glacier hearts where even light begins to freeze.

Nothing on *Kalinin*'s foredeck was flat or sharp or thin. Everything was coated in the crackling weirdness of this living ice, in transition to something worse. Colin regretted they had no crampons. Just to walk on this stuff while the ship was still rolling over the great storm swell was almost impossible. Almost, but not quite. On his first sure step, Colin saw the black cliffs of Deception bearing down on them like an obsidian avalanche, and he knew where he and Yazov had to be, no matter how hard it was to get there.

It suddenly occurred to him that he had shared no last words with Kate and he had a moment of poignant regret. But then he thought to himself, 'No, that's good. Now I have to make sure I get back alive to share them with her.'

At no time did it occur to him that Kate might not be alive to hear them when he got there.

Killigan exploded through the door into the Mariners' stateroom just before the lights came back on. It wasn't hard to do; the door was not locked. The red dot of the Glock's laser sight flashed around the little room, picking out the startled faces of the two women there. Kate Ross stood up at once, frowning in outrage. Robin, however, had used a Glock with a red-dot sight. She knew at once what they were up against here – in terms of armaments if nothing else – and pulled her friend back down.

'Yeah,' said Killigan. 'Yeah, this is good. You two broads will do. You two and the kids.'

'What will we do for, Sergeant?' asked Robin gently, her voice calm, her heart ready to explode.

'We're off on a little jaunt ashore, as soon as we reach Deception. And you guys will do as insurance.'

Robin's mind filled with a whirl of questions, pleas, propositions. Her breath hissed in as she filled her lungs to bursting, trying to calm her mind. Mother-like, she answered automatically, reasonably, 'But the children are asleep . . .'

'Wake them up. Get them out, lady. Time's a-wasting here and we've a shitload to do.'

The lights flickered on again. Robin, ship's captain to her marrow, noticed a slight hesitation in the engines. Oddly, in the light, Killigan lowered the Glock as though it was something unsuitable to be shown to women or children. But he did not moderate the hard grate of his voice one bit. 'Come on, lady. You got till I count three then I shoot your friend here. One—'

'Killigan,' came Hoyle's voice from the door. 'Killigan, we got company. And we got trouble.'

'Captain Mariner, get over here,' said Killigan. And Robin obeyed. She knew that the next step would involve the twins, or a shot through some part of Kate. Killigan grabbed her by the arm and pulled her outside the door so that she was half in front of him and half in front of Hoyle.

Half dazzled by the brightness and the abruptness of the action, Robin at first saw only an empty corridor. Then, at the far end of it, she saw a couple of sinister black dots. Gun barrels. She simply could not believe this was happening, let alone happening to her. Everything froze. Then there came a familiar female voice.

'Killigan. I'm a police-trained shot with a handgun and you know how good Corporal Washington is with a rifle. We could take you now. Both of you.'

'Then why haven't you?' sneered Killigan. 'Worried about your authority? Scared of what the Feds will say?'

'Concerned about your hostage there, Sergeant. Why not let her go?'

'And then what? What then, eh?'

'Take me instead. Let the women and the kids alone, Killigan. I'd make a better hostage in all sorts of ways. You know it.'

'That's true, Killigan,' began Billy.

'Shut up, Billy boy, let me think. You instead of the limey broads? Is that the deal? One woman instead of two women and two kids? Not much of a swap, lady.'

'That's it, Killigan. It's the best I can do.'

'Well, it's not good enough.'

'Then we can do better,' came a new voice. Vivien Agran stepped out into the light, hardly more than a shadow herself.

'Take me too. Two broads for two broads. Now that is good insurance, Killigan. Hoyle. Because you know Captain Ogre is going to send Vasily Varnek after you when she finds out about this and he will be taking no prisoners tonight. Besides, I believe I have a better market for your merchandise. I could probably get you ten million dollars, maybe more. Remember our little heart to heart, Killigan.'

'I remember. But where will we be going?' asked Killigan, hesitating.

'Ashore,' answered Jolene, speaking for both. 'Up to the base on the mountain.'

'With your disk and access to the Internet,' added Vivien Agran. 'And I have that other e-mail address. The address in America where they have no trouble with the Internet and the bug. And ten million dollars, like I said.'

'You think NASA values an experimental space suit more than a human life?' demanded Jolene, seeing Killigan waver. 'Come on, Killigan. You've won. Lets walk away from this. Look,' she added, almost as a desperate afterthought. 'I've got all the record disks too. All the evidence left against you so far.'

'All right, Inspector, and you, Mrs Agran,' said Killigan. 'You've got a deal. Both of you come on out here with your hands up and we'll make the swap.'

'I'm coming,' said Jolene easily. 'But I'm giving the pistol to a Special Forces man and Washington's still got the rifle. You're as good as your word or you're dead. I kid you not.'

Killigan watched the women walk out into the middle of the corridor, then Jolene turned back suddenly. Killigan tensed, then relaxed slightly as he saw her in a clinch with T-Shirt. That guy had been like her shadow recently, he noted. Then she joined Vivien Agran and came on down towards him. Killigan's mind was coldly busy. He had a market for the information on the disk and he had taken back the Power Strip itself. But the word was that Moscow and St Petersburg were closed to e-mail tonight, so if Agran was telling the truth, her offer was tempting – and he was beginning to feel a little trapped here. If he took one woman maybe he could get a better price and the realistic chance of escape from the bind he was in. If he took the other as well he had the chance of ensuring that all the records which might contain anything incriminating against him were wiped. Then Agran's offer would really make sense. It looked like a good deal to him, especially as he had one more card up his sleeve – and now was a good time for a little demonstration.

When the women reached him, Killigan pushed Robin back in through the door of the stateroom and caught Jolene by the shoulder. Hoyle grabbed Vivien. Using the women as shields, Killigan and Hoyle backed down the corridor. When they got to the head of the companionway, Killigan made a sign and Billy threw something solid and silver up the passage. It skidded along the floor and came to rest outside Jolene's cabin door. It lay there for five seconds, then it exploded, blowing the door into the empty cabin, hollowing the walls and denting the floor. 'Timers,' bellowed Killigan over the blast, the noise, the smoke, and the rain of glass from the shattered ceiling light. 'Bet you didn't know I still had them either. Major Schwartz brought them over with the Glock. Good as grenades, I warn you.' He grinned. That would give them something to think about. Slow down any pursuit into the bargain.

'What was that?' demanded Captain Ogre. 'It sounded like an explosion. Varnek, go and check. Captain Mariner and I will watch things here.'

Varnek went at once and Irene joined Richard at the helmsman's side.

'Are you there, Colin?' Richard said into his VHF.

'Here.'

'Good. What can you and Yazov see?'

'We see the entrance to the Bellows dead ahead. Can you come north a little?'

'Starboard a point,' said Yazov.

Irene tapped the helmsman on the shoulder and he adjusted the wheel by eye.

'As I said,' said Richard quietly but forcefully, 'it's important we take the north channel through the Bellows. It's extremely narrow. At this speed we need to be accurate and certain.'

'Then we must reduce speed.'

'Indeed, but it is a fine balance. If we reduce too much, these big seas will make it impossible to hold any line at all. And we must bear in mind that there is likely to be a vicious cross-wind running south to north across the Bellows itself, with a potential headwind cutting across that from inside the crater, blowing straight into our faces at the worst possible moment. The more impetus we have at the critical time, the better – assuming we've taken the correct line and aren't about to run bodily onto the rocks. That's why Colin and Mr Yazov are out there. They can see the state of the sea pretty well and feel the wind – smell it, even – better than we can.'

'We can until our noses freeze,' observed Colin over the VHF.

'Don't worry, Colin, you won't be out there long,' promised Richard.

'I see what you mean,' said Colin. 'The Bellows is opening like those rocks that nearly ate Jason and the Argo in the legends.'

'Just as long as they don't close as quickly on us,' said Richard easily. 'We don't have a Medea to help us along. And the only kids aboard to sacrifice are mine.'

The bridge phone buzzed urgently. Irene crossed and answered it, her eyes, like Richard's, never leaving the bulk of Deception which seemed to rear over them ever more threateningly as *Kalinin* sped towards the still scarcely visible northern passage.

'Richard,' said Irene after an instant. 'It's Robin. For you.'

Richard answered with his eyes still fixed firmly ahead and his mind on calculations far too complex to allow his full attention to the phone.

'Richard,' said Robin tersely. 'Killigan and Hoyle were just here!'

'Really, darling?'

'They threatened us, tried to kidnap us and have taken away Jolene and Vivien Agran instead. They're armed and dangerous. They have grenades and a handgun. It's a Glock.'

He did not say, 'That's nice, dear,' but it was a close-run thing. Then the penny dropped. He looked away from the deadly loom of the cliff. 'What? What did you say?'

Robin went over the details again.

'But they've gone now?'

'With Jolene and Vivien Agran. Yes.'

'Are you and the twins all right?'

'Yes. So's Kate. But you've got a bad problem. T-Shirt and Washington have gone after them. It's like the OK Corral down here. Well, more like World War Three.'

278

Richard looked across at Irene. What had she said? No gunfights? Fat chance. And she had just sent Varnek down to check up on things.

Abruptly, Irene's VHF buzzed. 'Captain,' came Varnek's voice, and a babble of Russian ensued. Richard could guess well enough what was being said.

Such was his concentration on the new situation and its implications, that when his own VHF buzzed he scarcely paid it any attention. It buzzed again. 'Yes?'

'Richard! What's going on there? Have you lost the plot or what?'

'Colin! You have no idea. What?'

'You have to cut your speed. We'll be into the Bellows' mouth in less than five minutes and I can't see the line.'

Richard simply dropped the phone. Robin and the twins were OK. The next danger that might harm them was this one if he got it wrong now. 'I don't want to cut speed, Colin,' he said into the VHF. 'There'll be a vicious side wind any minute and like as not a catabatic headwind pushing straight into our faces. You remember this place. If I've got it right, the cross-wind will push us north onto line and the headwind will slow us just about perfectly. If I've got it wrong, wallowing around in trouble trying to get some headway up will just pull us over onto the rocks below Fildes Point all the more quickly.'

'But if we don't find the line, we'll end up on the Ravn—'

'There, Colin! There!' Richard shouted it, and he could hear Yazov yelling too. On the corrugated heave of the ocean ahead there came a line the colour of graphite, as though drawn by a pencil from side to side ahead of them and roughly charcoaled in behind.

'I see it. The cross-wind. God, Richard . . .' Colin hardly ever swore.

Richard breathed in. Breathed out. 'Steady as she goes,' he said.

At full fifteen knots *Kalinin* came into Neptune's Bellows, heading straight for the Ravn Rock. Richard, on some higher level of seamanship – of reality, even – watched the wide calm reaches of Whalers Bay and Port Foster open up behind. As he looked, the ship's movement separated the spire of Petes Pillar from the great black wall of Cathedral Crags northward, to starboard, almost as though he was watching some computer animation. The instant that this massive majesty imprinted itself on his mind, Colin shouted, 'Now!'

Richard felt the whole of *Kalinin* begin to shudder. 'Hold her steady,' he told the helmsman. 'Steady as she goes . . .'

The brute wind shoved *Kalinin* sideways, Fildes Point and Petes

279

Pillar pouncing down on them. Her hull juddered and shook. Richard sent a silent prayer of thanks to the shipwrights of Gdansk who had built her to take poundings such as this. Up she went, northward, one point, two; not turning, simply sliding up across the Bellows as though sailing sideways as well as forward. Then Richard saw a gleam of light. A flashing point of brightness from deep within the massive throat of the place. It was the beacon on Collins Point, six cables in. 'Steer for the light,' he said, his voice rough with tension. 'Steer straight for the light.'

'Incoming!' yelled Colin, as though announcing a shell or a bomb.

'Then hang on!' yelled Richard back, and not a moment too soon. The wind of icy air in the storm's eye – heavy, thick, cold down-thrusting and wanting to push out across the ocean, trapped in the broken cup of Deception's great caldera – burst out through the cleft of the Bellows, and all but stopped them dead in their tracks. Out of nowhere, they were in the grip of a gale that was hurling out at them with awesome force, trying to rip the bridgehouse off and blow *Kalinin* like a thistledown away to Graham Land.

'Colin!' bellowed Richard into the VHF, awed and shaken by the huge force of the catabatic gale. 'Colin, are you all right?'

The radio leaped into life. 'NOOOOoooooo!' it shouted as Colin's voice was snatched unmistakably into the distance. Then there was silence.

'Colin?' called Richard again. There was no answer. Outside, brushing the bridge wings, majestic cliffs swept by; so they had not quite stopped dead as it seemed. The wind intensified, shrieking around them with the steadiness which could only be the breath of a god blowing out against them.

'Colin!' he called again. He turned and looked at Irene, pale and shocked. To have saved the ship but lost his friend . . .

But she did not see his wild self-doubt. Her eyes were on the black rock jaws brushing the outmost reaches of her precious command, as though she expected to see sparks flying off the outer edges of the bridge wings as they dragged along the sheer black cliffs.

But there were none. *Kalinin* was clear of harm, perfectly conned. Suddenly the wind dropped and Whalers Bay gaped pale and calm on their starboard. She powered into Port Foster, into a dead calm, still as a mountain lake, flat as a mirror under the pallid perfection of the silver sky.

'Cut your engines,' said Richard. 'Anchor where you want.'

He felt deflated, flattened, defeated. What on earth was he going

280

to say to Kate? Even Colin would be dead by now, frozen solid in an instant in the terrible cold of that Antarctic Ocean. He felt like crying until Colin came racing through the bridge door with Yazov close behind.

'Well done!' bellowed the big Scot, overcome. 'That was fantastic! I've never seen the like! I owe you an apology, though, Captain Ogre. I seem to have dropped your little VHF over the side . . .'

Chapter Twenty-Six

It had seemed so simple to Jolene. Independently of getting Richard's wife and kids out of the frame, the idea of offering herself as a hostage solved the most important of her problems: how to keep tabs on Killigan and Hoyle and what they had stolen. The long-term objectives were to stop them sending NASA's priceless information out onto the Internet, to confiscate the Power Strip and the floppy disk, to have the men arrested and hand the case over to Agent Jones. Short-term, it seemed obvious that they were going to get off the ship somehow as soon as it was safe from the storm, and when they did, she wanted to be with them. Going as a hostage was so much easier than going as a hunter.

It was uncomfortable, however. Killigan kept twisting her arm up behind her back even more fiercely than her big brothers used to do at home in Austin. Every now and then he would cop a feel of her tits too, though he still had the decency to pretend it was by accident. He didn't have to pretend too hard. It felt as though the ship was going over the Big Dipper at Disney World. Hoyle, however, was feeling Vivien Agran's torso with a great deal more freedom, really getting off on the power, as they hurried down the heaving passageways and companionways. When they got a chance to compare notes, Jolene decided to ask what utter madness had motivated her fellow captive to offer herself as a hostage.

As they reached the bridgehouse end of the long tunnel reaching aft towards the Zodiacs and the Sikorsky, *Kalinin*'s motion suddenly went from that of Kentucky steeplechaser to that of a gliding swan. At the far end of the passageway, visible as though down a reversed telescope, the group of men there suddenly became extremely active, disappearing up through the ceiling like a Santa Claus convention going home.

'Move!' spat Killigan and the four of them rushed down the length of the corridor together. Under the vertical chimney they paused again, their path further aft blocked by a pull-down ladder like a white-painted fire escape. Looking upwards, Jolene found herself watching a square

283

of pastel duck-egg sky silhouetting foreshortened figures bustling upwards and outwards onto the deck. Above the last of them, strangely geometric after all the roundness of bodies and equipment, loomed the tail of the Sikorsky.

'Me first,' said Killigan. 'Then the women, Inspector first, then you, Billy boy. And remember, ladies, any trouble and I just shoot the pair of you. I can off you both and miss Billy here easily. Think about it. You really don't want me to blow your pretty little asses away this early in the day!'

Up he swung, then stopped, half in the chimney, gun pointing, until the women were on the ladder behind him. Jolene followed Killigan closely, her mind racing, and she could feel Vivien close behind her. When she got to the top, she hesitated. Killigan was on the ice-slick deck beside her. Behind him, the helicopter team were trying to get the Sikorsky ready but it was obvious that they had quite a job ahead of them. The Zodiac team were working more quickly. The davits had been swung out already and were hanging over the stern like thin, swan-necked Narcissuses, admiring their reflections in the mirror of the water.

Jolene's wide eyes began to take stock of where they were, but Killigan snarled 'Move!' and she obeyed. Once on the deck she had little leisure for admiring the epic grandeur of her surroundings. The deck was slippery with ice and she was very worried that if she slipped and sat down suddenly, the Smith and Wesson .38 calibre police special pistol she had jammed deeply down the front of her jeans really would blow her pretty little ass away. Vivien Agran came carefully out of the raised hatchway behind her and stood equally uneasily on the deck. Jolene wondered hysterically whether she was also worried about slipping over suddenly because she had somehow seduced the big Remington rifle out of Washington and secreted it somewhere about her person. Jolene bit down hard on the hilarity that began to bubble up inside her. Maybe she wasn't quite as calm and in control here as she thought she was.

Billy Hoyle pulled himself out onto the deck and Killigan tensed himself to move, when events overtook them. It was inevitable that such a stiff, suspicious group should be noticed. They were out of place, out of character, out of time.

'Hey,' called someone from beside the Sikorsky.

Killigan had obviously made his decision. It was taking too long to get the Sikorsky ready, so they would go for the Zodiacs. But the Sikorsky might be readied in time to interfere with his plans. He

284

reached into his pocket, pulled out a timer. His thumb was actually resting on it when someone called, 'Killigan?' Almost regretfully he put the bomb away. 'Killigan, what are you . . .'

Killigan turned. Even at twenty past midnight it was bright. The pilot was easily recognisable. He was up on the undercarriage, preparing to open the cockpit door. A blood-red dot shone briefly on his thigh, and then it exploded open, as though one of the timers had been detonated in his leg. He fell and skidded across the deck, out of Jolene's sight, shouting with shock and pain. The others around the chopper dived for cover.

The stillness amplified the echoes of the shot. Jolene looked up. Half a kilometre ahead stood a cliff almost the equal of the Razor. It was the better part of a kilometre wide. From here it looked more than half a kilometre high: black, absolute, and as unforgiving as a guillotine blade bedded down into the purity of the still, steaming, water at its foot. It called its weirdly amplified version of the Glock's flat voice again, and from across the bay it was answered. Jolene saw that up on top of that sheer black precipice stood a sturdy radio mast and the hint of a collection of huts. Deception Base.

'Move,' spat Killigan again, herding them over and downwards, across the deck to the outer companionways. Beneath them sat the mezzanine deck, the folded steps. Everything they needed to climb safely down into the Zodiac. How safe they would be after that was anybody's guess. Jolene hoped fervently that T-Shirt was close behind and Washington was with him. And that whatever Vivien Agran had up her sleeve was not going to get in anybody's way. And, indeed, that whatever Richard Mariner did when he realised what was going on fitted in with everything else as neatly as the way he had slipped *Kalinin* into safe haven here.

Vasily Varnek caught up with T-Shirt and Washington at the inboard end of the long passageway out of engineering which led to the chimney beneath the Sikorsky. Just as he did so, the flat sound of a shot came echoing back to the three of them. 'What are they doing?' demanded the Russian officer, still unaware of the full complexity of the situation facing him.

'I'd say Killigan has decided not to go for the chopper. He'd never get it off the deck without major problems. And blowing it up would lead to unbelievable carnage; maybe even sink the ship,' said T-Shirt. 'So he and Hoyle will be pushing Jolene and Mrs Agran down to the Zodiacs right about now. If anyone stands up to them there'll be more shooting, I expect. If they don't, there'll be no more unless he wastes his bullets on trying to disable the second Zodiac. But he won't want to waste shots, 'cause he'll know there's a chance we'll come after him like gangbusters anyway, even though he's got the women with him. But he will want to take out the Zodiac if he can.'

'Wait a minute,' said Varnek. 'What is this you say? They have Mrs Agran?'

'Mrs Agran, Dr DaCosta, a red-dot Glock and a bunch of timers as powerful as grenades. Also a computer disk with NASA's most treasured secret on it and a burning desire to get to an Internet terminal – no matter what the cost, I'd say.'

'We've got to get after them,' said Washington.

'I'd advise you to wait a little,' said T-Shirt. 'You won't stop them leaving the ship without a good deal of bloodshed. But then they won't be able to stop us following them. An army of us, if we want. Even if they do manage to disable the second Zodiac, there's likely to be the Sikorsky if we can fly it. Or failing that we have two launches and two more lifeboats. And once they get up to Deception Base, where are they going to go?'

'But the women,' said Varnek.

'Precisely,' said T-Shirt blithely, sounding a little more confident than he felt. 'The women. We have to give them just a little space to put their plans into action. Jolene has plans, I'm sure. We must at least give them time to make sure of their own safety. Mr Varnek, I presume Mrs Agran is almost as heavily armed as Jolene DaCosta?'

Vivien Agran allowed herself to be hustled down the slippery companionway towards the little mezzanine deck. She and Billy were just behind Killigan and Jolene, and ahead of them the red dot of the nasty little pistol's sight moved through the misted air like a tiny searchlight. The mezzanine deck was cramped and crowded, the sense of compression surprisingly forceful – the deck above their heads seemed very near indeed. Vivien looked up, surprised to find it bearded with thick ice. No sooner did the glittering carapace register than she also noticed it was raining freezing drops of meltwater down on them as well. One Zodiac hung from the davits, ready to be lowered to the millpond surface of Port Foster. The other was still in its securing cradle.

On the mezzanine a few crewmen – easily intimidated by the sight of Killigan's pistol – were crowding back and clearly wishing there was somewhere to hide from the sinister little dot. Even Borisov stood back, no doubt assured by his relentlessly negative intelligence that any move would be fatal. Vivien's lip twisted. What a coward he was; how unlike Vasily Varnek, whom she dearly wished was here beside her now.

As she was hurried ruthlessly across the ice-thick deck of the mezzanine, she slipped, staggered, and was glad enough to be pulled upright by Hoyle's brutal hand on her upper arm. Still, with all this bending, twisting and dancing about, she was extremely grateful for the foresight which had led her to wrap the blade of Chef's sharpest 30-centimetre Sabatier carving knife with a strong linen drying-up cloth before she slid it down the back of her trousers, snugly into the space between her buttocks, its outline hidden beneath the skirt of her parka.

'You!' spat Killigan, pointing at Borisov with the finger of the laser sight. 'Get the steps down.'

Borisov did not hesitate. He hurried over and pulled the lever. Crackling and popping like an old man's joints, the retracted steps burst out of their icy covering and reached downwards.

'And that,' ordered Killigan, moving the dot from Borisov's breast to the dangling Zodiac.

Again, Borisov sprang to obey, so that when the little step-off point reached the stillness of the water, the Zodiac was sitting in place beside it. Down went the women, with Hoyle immediately after them and Killigan's red dot covering them relentlessly.

'You too,' grated the American, flicking the light back to Borisov. 'Start her up and sail us in.'

Borisov started down, then turned, his mouth opening, as though to protest, refuse, argue. The red dot was exactly in his eye. He closed his mouth and turned back.

Before he followed him down, Killigan reached into his pocket and pulled out the timer he had considered using on the Sikorsky. He flicked the LED display switch and chucked it across the deck so that it slid under the cradled Zodiac. He had few shots but a good number of timers – and he urgently needed rid of the Zodiac. That would slow pursuit perfectly after his crippling of the chopper pilot. He turned and ran down the steps. The others on the mezzanine ran wildly up the steps on their side and for the tiniest of instants the little deck was empty and still. The first Zodiac pulled away across the water, drawing a wide arrowhead of wake behind it.

Then Varnek exploded out of the bottom of the portside companionway, sliding like an ice-hockey player across the deck to kick the timer out over the side and slam with bruising force into the uprights of the railings above it. Through a galaxy of stars he saw the way the timer curved out through the perfect stillness of the midnight and settled deep into the placid water before it exploded. And then he was on his feet and tearing at the bindings of the second Zodiac, yelling at Borisov's little team to get back down here and help him.

T-Shirt was up by the Sikorsky, side-tracked into helping the wounded pilot. The wound to his thigh was severe: he would not be flying for a good long time. But it was not fatal. T-Shirt's mind was racing. This must be Killigan's equivalent of winning friends here. The renegade sergeant was trying to make sure that they would hesitate to follow him in the face of his gun and his detonator grenades, but doing so in such a way as to make sure they did not get hyped up on blood lust and the need for revenge. It looked very much as though he planned to come back aboard to get passage out of here. There was probably no other way to get off Deception – not for weeks anyway. Holding Jolene and Vivien Agran was clearly more effective than taking the popular wives of Richard and Colin and the equally popular children. There would have been no lack of a posse to head out after Robin and the kids; but the NASA inspector and the ship's madam? T-Shirt looked up into the silvery-rose perfection of the midnight sky. Who was going to risk life and limb for them? As though in answer to his rhetorical question, he heard Varnek bellowing at the crewmen, and grinned tightly to himself. That's one, he thought. Washington and me makes three. Richard and probably Colin will be along in a minute, he would lay his life on it. A couple more and they'd have seven, magnificent or not.

The pilot's VHF lay on the icy deck. T-Shirt picked it up. 'Send the doc down with a stretcher for the pilot,' he said to whoever was listening on the bridge. 'And send down another pilot if you've got one. They've taken the women and Borisov in the first Zodiac. Varnek will be going after them in the second one any minute now but we need to get up to the top of the mountain if we're really going to head them off.'

Richard swung into the stateroom on Palmer-Hall. 'Robin,' he said, 'We need you.'

'What?' She looked up from the tousled heads of her sleeping children, caught between the urgency in his voice and her bone-deep need to stay and continue guarding William and Mary.

'Killigan and Hoyle have taken Jolene and Mrs Agran ashore. Shot the chopper pilot in cold blood. Varnek's going after them in the spare Zodiac but we need to get the Sikorsky over to Mount Pond if we're going to finish this.'

'But what do they think they're doing?' asked Robin, rising. 'What is the point of it all?'

'To send out the Power Strip's design specifications on the Internet and make a mint of money.'

'Of course. But then what? Where are they going to go after that? Where can they go, Richard? This place is beyond the end of nowhere and that storm's going to close down again in an hour or so. Are they expecting to sit up there forever?'

'They've probably not thought that far ahead. It's all been make do and mend since the major asked for his suit that one last time on Christmas Eve.'

'I'm not convinced. There must be a way out of this for them. They couldn't be so stupid as to run up a blind alley with all of us coming after them and nowhere else to go. They must be planning to come back aboard.'

'OK. You have a point. The worry is that they might not *all* be coming back aboard. Can we talk about it while we go? In Mrs Agran's absence, the captain herself has detailed Gretchen to babysit.'

'It's all right,' said Kate Ross quietly. 'I'll look after them. They'll be safe with me.'

'Right,' said Robin. 'Who's coming?'

'Colin. T-Shirt. Washington will go with whichever transport they can get most serviceable most quickly.'

Robin stopped dead in the doorway. 'There's something wrong with the chopper?' she asked, her voice slightly cooler than the storm wind they had just escaped.

'No. It's iced up, that's all. After the storm.'

'We go on my say-so,' she said decisively, moving once again.

'Fine, fine.'

'I'm not taking that chopper up unless it's one hundred per cent, no matter what the emergency. Is that clear, Richard?'

'Of course, darling . . .' Richard's calm assurance was undermined a little by the fact that the wounded pilot was carried past the pair of them just then.

Robin's concerns were well-founded, as Richard soon discovered. Her first external pilot's check revealed clogged intakes and blocked exhausts, compounded by iced-up control surfaces and frozen landing gear. When they climbed into the cockpit, joined by Colin, and she began to run some pre-flights, things got worse. She soon discovered frozen fuel lines and a range of problems with levers, pedals, pitches and props that went far beyond anything Richard could understand.

She had just announced herself grudgingly satisfied that the exterior of the fuselage was free of ice when T-Shirt swung back into the picture like Tarzan with a hump, announcing that Varnek had gone, taking, among others, Corporal Washington and, unexpectedly, one of the scientists, Mendel.

Richard recalled Robin's suspicions that there was something more than they suspected actually going on here and he frowned.

Jolene had brought her big Cat Colorado walking machines with her and she'd never been so glad of anything in the whole of her life. She had put them on after her shower with T-Shirt because they were lined and warm but, as she stumbled up the slippery, cindery path towards the distant Camp Deception, the state-of-the-art footwear seemed to be all that could possibly make this walk feasible. Every now and then she glanced back, wondering what on earth Vivien Agran had on her feet which allowed her to keep up. All she had ever seen her wearing during their admittedly brief acquaintance was executive slingbacks with a medium heel. But for this little jaunt, the entertainment officer seemed to have supplemented her black jeans and Parka with some hefty-looking Timberlanders. Now that, thought Jolene, really *was* thinking ahead.

No one had thought to bring a torch, however, so the going got tougher the higher they climbed. The pathway they were following up from the black beach, where they had left Borisov with a couple of hundred sleepy seals, was swinging in partway under an overhang – though it was still possible to see it, like a pale ribbon, slipping over the shoulder of the hillside further up. The light from the sky was as clear and rose-tinted as it had been half an hour ago, but the angle of the cliff seemed to put them in shadow all along this section. On their left was a steep slope where about ten thousand gentoo penguins had made their nests. Jolene gasped. Choked. The fumes from the gentoo rookery down below burned at her throat and brought tears to her eyes. She wavered; slowed. 'Move!' snarled Killigan. That was about all he had said since taking her, she thought bitterly. Still, it wouldn't be long now until they reached the camp. The radio mast towered up on her right. The cliff fell away threateningly at her feet – though the truly vertical drop did not begin until after the pathway snaked over the rise just ahead.

290

Once they were at the camp, Jolene planned to wait for Killigan to take out the disk. She hoped she would have the chance to see him starting up the computer and keying in the e-mail destination. She had a photographic memory. Once she saw where he was planning to send the information, the gun would come out and the transmission would be terminated. Agent Jones would have the murderers of Major Schwartz and Leading Seaman Thompson. NASA would retrieve the Power Strip and the disk containing its most important design specifications. She would have the address of the main players in the market willing to pay for such information regardless of how it came to them. Everything wrapped up, neat as a Christmas gift.

Except that, like Robin, and now Richard; Jolene had her doubts. The plot seemed too simple. There had to be something else going on here – Killigan's escape route at the very least. Without it he would simply be the richest occupant of some army stockade for the rest of his life.

The pathway led up into the light, over the shoulder of the mountain and onto a plateau just large enough to contain a collection of huts and a stack of communications equipment. Unlike Armstrong, the huts were real huts, not Jamesways; they had wooden sides and real glass windows. After the high-tech twenty-first century set-up of the NASA camp, this all looked a little old-fashioned, out of date, shabby.

The radio mast towered over all – but in the earliest moments of the twenty-first century, it could not simply be a radio mast. Up its skeletal length, secured and well-protected against the fiercest excesses of Antarctic weather, there were satellite dishes, bowls and aerials of all sorts. It was obvious which was the main communications hut, for it crouched at the base of the mast, almost between its feet. At a decent, secure, distance away stood the camp's power source, a solid-looking generator hut, identifiable by the pile of fuel cans outside it. Other than that there were labs and dormitory huts, similar to the basic layout of Armstrong. Except that there was no transport dispersal area. If you wanted to get anywhere on Deception, you walked down to the beach and you took a boat. But the Argentinean scientific team who normally lived here in the summer must have taken their boats away with them, for they had seen no boats below.

'Hoyle,' shouted Killigan. 'Can you get the generator started?'

'Yeah. I guess.'

'OK. Do it. I'll take both the women with me.' As he spoke, Killigan let the red dot rest on Vivien Agran. It followed her as she came over to join Jolene. Then, inevitably, Killigan said, 'Move.'

As Hoyle went over to the generator, the three of them went towards the communications hut. The women walked side by side, with Killigan a little behind them switching the red dot from one to the other, letting the ruby line of light bounce over their shoulders as they walked so that they would not forget he had a bead on them. The penguins screamed in the distance. That was all. Apart from the crunching of their footsteps on the cindery gravel, and the whisper of their breath, there was no sound. The wind was dead calm. There was no surf on the inner lagoon. In the far distance of the vast skyscape revealed by their elevation here, clouds gathered and toothpicks of lightning glittered, but there was no whisper of sound from them.

'What do you reckon?' said Jolene, her voice only slightly louder than the rhythmic crunching of her footsteps. 'You going to get the disk off him and send it your own people instead? Is there really ten million dollars up for grabs or was that just a con to buy some time?'

Vivien did not respond.

'You think Varnek's going to get up here in time to give you an edge? You well tooled up?'

If the entertainment officer had any reply, she could not make it. The door of the communications hut was suddenly in front of them.

'It's open,' said Killigan. 'Agran, lead the way.'

As Vivien opened the door, a distant coughing roar alerted them to the fact that they had power. She reached for the light switch and the communications hut lit up. Everything was covered, closed down, carefully secured. Killigan pushed past them, confident about what equipment he wanted to use and how to get at it. The only thing that slowed him was the necessity of holding the red dot on the women. Then Hoyle ran in and took over, working with the speed of a well-trained expert.

The computer looked old-fashioned but functional. When they checked that it was connected to the power and switched it on, it lit up quickly enough. Its flickering seemed to fill the room. Jolene looked around, surprised. The strange light seemed to be catching the corner of her eyes, flickering at the window as though the sky itself was fluttering like a butterfly wing. She stepped back to look out of the window at her shoulder. Nothing. Perhaps it was the tension, she thought. For it was coming up to the microsecond when she would have to make her move. The e-mail address would be up any instant – either Killigan's or Mrs Agran's. It would all depend on which way Killigan would jump, now, at the last possible moment. She tensed for action. The flickering of the screen died and the icons came up.

With a bark of delight, Hoyle sat down and grabbed the mouse. He rolled the cursor over the plain green screen to the symbol for Internet communications and clicked on it.

From outside there came a high scream. Something thumped on the roof. They all jumped so badly that Killigan nearly shot someone. The outer edges of Jolene's sight began to flicker again. Shock, she told herself. Get a grip, girl. Her mind was racing, trying to work out how to get her hand down the front of her jeans without anyone noticing. But in fact that was the easiest bit.

'Can't get the Internet server up,' said Hoyle. He clicked again. The scream and the thump on the roof came again. 'It's the dish,' said Hoyle. 'Trying to connect us with our service provider via the phone satellite!'

No sooner had he said this than the screen cleared. 'We're in,' he said. 'That's our provider's logo. We're on the Internet. Now I know exactly what number I gotta dial. Here we go . . .'

Jolene focused all of her concentration on the screen, beginning to worm her fingers down the waistband of her jeans.

'Just a moment,' said Vivien. 'I've got one more offer to make.'

Hoyle's hands wavered. He looked up at Killigan.

'I'm sure I can get my people to go up over ten million dollars.'

'That's not much of an improvement, lady,' said Killigan.

'And the ride out. That I can guarantee. Remember that. You come in with me, you get a ride on *Kalinin*, safe and secret. You know I can deliver that. You can drop off at Ushuaia in three days with a down payment. You can walk away and never look back, with the balance wired anywhere in the world you want. All of you. No loose ends.'

'Except one,' said Killigan, and the red dot flashed blindingly into Jolene's eyes as he spoke.

The door burst open. Varnek and Washington erupted into the hut, Mendel a little way behind them.

Stasis. Except for Jolene pulling her fingers back out into the light. Silence. Stillness. Except for the weirdest crackling; a strange, faint odour. And a distant rumble, as though the second part of the storm was coming much more quickly than anticipated.

Jolene, her body tense as a spring, looked at the two groups she was caught between. The flickering through the window behind her came again, more powerful now. And as it did, Killigan jerked his gun round in one swift, fluid motion and shot Washington through the head.

Jolene didn't stop to think. The game had suddenly jumped beyond anything she had calculated or could deal with now so she threw herself backwards with all her might. The back of her head hit the glass of the window and shattered it with stunning force. Her shoulders took the glass and cleared it out of the frame so that she could pivot on her hips and roll free through the small frame which was just big enough to allow her body to exit.

She hit the cindery ground in a foetal position, rolling sideways, able at last to push her hands down the front of her jeans unobserved.

As she came up, there was Hoyle with Washington's rifle, coming round the corner of the hut, bringing the big Remington to bear. Jolene rested on one knee, ripping the pistol up into two-handed firing position, arms straight, flicking the safety off as it came up. As soon as the barrel was in line with his thorax she squeezed off a pattern of three and rolled away. Whether she hit him or not she did not know, but when she came up again, he was gone. She broke for the nearest cover, the labs by the cliff edge. Only when she hit the ground behind their reassuring bulk did she begin to try and take stock.

She should have been trying to work out what was going on and how she was going to retrieve the situation now. Instead, as she let the shells fall out of her gun and slammed in another complete load, she was wondering what in hell's name was happening to the sky. She had heard of the aurora australis, the southern lights. She knew about most sorts of atmospheric interference from the petty to the memorably epic. She knew that the spectacular light shows that the solar wind, for example, could trigger at high latitudes were becoming more vivid because the ionosphere was rippling down nearer the earth. But apart from the Fourth of July, she had never seen anything like this.

The entire sky above her head was full of flashing lights. Up at the zenith, they were like sheet lightning, flickering across the whole dome of heaven in a range of colours from rose-pink to blood-red. Beneath this were individual lines and streamers, light and dark, like the trails of great exploding rocket displays. They had no form. There were no dandelion clocks of fire. No ruby fountains, golden waterfalls or silver showers like there had been on the last night of the state fairs of her youth. But the upper sky was all ablaze in a most amazing feast of ill-organised pyrotechnics, all the more impressive because, like the aurora, it was all but silent.

'Hey, Inspector,' came Killigan's voice. 'What've you done to the Internet?'

Jolene rolled onto her stomach in the gritty ash and peeped round the corner of the hut she was hiding behind. She made no sound.

'Dish looks all right,' he shouted gruffly. 'So you must have screwed with something else, huh?'

Could he not see? she asked herself silently, wild with pettish frustration. Could he not comprehend? Whatever was happening above their heads was screwing with more than wavelengths in the light spectrum. It was screwing with everything.

Mir! It was Mir coming down! Right over their heads. Two hundred tons of it and a nuclear generator. Jesus! The most expensive light show in the history of the world. She raised the Smith and Wesson, looking for a target.

'Don't blame me, you sorry fucker,' she yelled. 'Blame the Russians. It's their space station.'

Black grit kicked up in front of her face. She had seen no red dot, nothing. She rolled back into cover. Silence. Except, right in the furthest range of her hearing, a strange, gathering thunder. Then, by a fluke of *timbre*, by a chance of auditory wavelength, she heard a tiny *tinkle*. She was distracted by the breathtaking sky. It was such a tiny sound after all, like a dime thrown onto the ground. Only at the last instant did she jerk into action, tearing the muscles of her belly as she moved with galvanic force. And not a moment too soon. The hut she had been hiding behind erupted into flames which rose as though challenging the majestic light show in the sky and rained down on her crouching back in splinters – splinters and nothing larger, thank God. She was up and sprinting for the next hut at once. Black grit kicked up from beside her foot. She noticed this and thought it was probably a bullet from the rifle with its heavier load. Bad shooting from Hoyle, unless they were trying to wound her and hold her as a hostage still. At this stage that didn't seem very likely. They'd kill her with the next shot, then.

Jolene dived to her right, hoping to God there was a building there. There was: an outhouse used as a chemical john, like the one Billy boy had tried to watch her using. But it was much, much smaller; this was Argentina after all. It was about a metre square, two metres tall. Unless she was going to stand behind it like a sentry in a sentry box it was going to be no use at all. She pulled herself to her knees, looking around. About three metres beyond the outhouse the ground sloped away steeply towards the edge of the cliff. Then a sheer drop of more than six hundred metres to a shallow beach and a deep lagoon. If the water they had experienced so far was anything to go by, the lagoon would turn her into something fit for Captain Birdseye in about three minutes flat.

Jolene fought to her feet and turned, using the chemical toilet as a shield, reaching out with her right arm round the end, balancing the weight of the Smith and Wesson against her burning need to draw a bead on a target – preferably Killigan – and blow the sucker away.

Instead, she saw Killigan's shoulder as he pitched another detonator at her. He should have been a pitcher for a major league team. The shot was accurate, perfectly timed and unstoppable. The last thing she thought with any clarity was, 'Strike one.'

Then behind her the Sikorsky reared up over the edge of the cliff and swept into the upper air, the power of its passage sucking her backwards onto the dangerous, cliff-edge slope. As her feet slipped down onto the cinder path, the whole outhouse blew up. A massive gout of red and yellow flame instantly occupied the space where she had been. She took one more giddy step backward, and then the blast caught her. It caught her, held her, lifted her, pitched her over the edge of the cliff and then it dropped her.

'There they are,' shouted Robin as she brought the Sikorsky up towards the cliff edge. She could see figures against the spectacular pyrotechnics in the sky.

'Can you see Jolene?' T-Shirt yelled.

'No,' bellowed Robin.

'She's a top-flight professional,' said Richard. 'She can take care of herself.'

'Glad I gave her back the Smith and Wesson though,' commented T-Shirt.

'We need to get over the lip of the cliff,' called Richard. 'See if we can put down anywhere.'

'All right, darling,' shouted Robin.

Robin's words drowned out Colin's more sensible, 'Is that wise? We aren't armed . . .'

And so they came up over the edge of the cliff, straight into the heart of the fire-fight. No sooner had the black edge of the vertical drop heaved in under the Sikorsky's nose than Robin was yelling, 'There she . . .'

And the outhouse went up. Jolene's body jerked backwards as though a line had been tied to it and she had been pulled over the cliff edge by a falling weight. All of them were in the cockpit. The men were crowding their heads into the cockpit through the door from the cabin. They all saw the lone figure, pale, intrepid. They all saw the explosion. They all saw her flying out and down beneath the rearing nose of the helicopter.

Then the blast which had chucked Jolene so casually over the edge of the cliff caught the Sikorsky and flung it upwards. Debris rattled against the nose, and Robin, for one thanked God that it had not been a brick outhouse. Flames licked at the undercarriage. The Sikorsky was riding the top of the blast bubble, seemingly pressed hard against the glittering sky.

'She's gone over the edge,' yelled Richard.

Automatically, without thinking, Robin reached for the radio. Opened a channel to *Kalinin*, sucked in breath to warn the ship. At the very least they should drop a lifeboat and look for Jolene's corpse. Shattered or frozen, it made little difference, as long as the death was quick. The instant Robin opened the channel to *Kalinin*, the whole of Killigan's armoury went up, triggered by the helicopter's radio signal. The communications shack erupted in a massive mushroom of fire large enough to topple the radio mast and ignite the generator hut. The Sikorsky, already surfing up on the wave of explosive power, swung upwards and backwards again, hurling back across Port Foster towards the southernmost curve of cliffs. Only Robin's natural genius as a pilot held them safely in the air. They were back across the harbour, skimming over Telefon Bay on the far side before Robin brought the Sikorsky under control. And it was only then, really, that they noticed T-Shirt had gone, vanished out of the helicopter altogether, leaving behind him on the cabin floor a duvet like the cloak of an ancient king.

The human body falls, give or take, thirty metres a second. So when she went over the edge of the cliff, Jolene had a little over twenty seconds to live. If she had sat in solemn silence, counting each second off on her watch, they could hardly have been longer than the seconds she experienced. At first she fell backwards, speed gathering, looking lazily upwards at the rocket show in the wild sky above her. She had the feeling of her arms and legs waving, swimming and kicking in the air. A roaring of air past her ears gathered, intensified. She saw the belly of the Sikorsky, outlined against the glory among the stars, soaring away from her – and that was all, really, that gave her a sensation of falling. But then an extra twist of movement flipped her over. At once the wind bit at her eyes at near hurricane force, for she was falling at more than one hundred kilometres an hour by now. And now that she was face down, the wind blasted past her ears with deafening force, so that she did not hear the destruction of Deception Base when Killigan's detonators all went off. She knew nothing else of the Sikorsky, blown like thistledown more than two kilometres across the bay, riding the blast wave backwards. All she knew was that her heavy head was pulling her down into her last high dive. The edge of the bay came into focus even to her streaming eyes, and it was chopping up towards her faster than a guillotine blade. Now, and only now, did she realise that she was going to die here, any second, and her heart felt as though it was going to break before her head exploded on the shore or her body froze in the bay.

But at the very moment when she gave up hope, T-Shirt slammed into her back. 'Hang on,' he screamed into her ear. Arms and legs flapped wildly, and even before she could realise how useless his sacrifice was, he had thrown away his hand-chute and was wrapped around her, holding her tight as tight could be while his big, wing-shaped parachute brought them safely and gently down into the instant death of the freezing ocean immediately below.

'There they are,' yelled Richard. 'I can see the parachute. How soon can we get to them?'

'I'll be as quick as I can,' called Robin and, in spite of all she had said about safety, she cut through the outer edge of the blast to drive the battered helicopter down across the bay. By the time they were over the parachute, two minutes had passed, however, and short of going swimming in the icy water themselves there was nothing they could do other than head flat out for the Zodiacs.

There was no room on the beach, so Robin hovered as low as she possibly could while Richard and Colin dropped out of the cabin and onto the black cinder shore. Here they found Borisov still sitting in his Zodiac, unsure of what to do. They focused his mind in no uncertain fashion. Piling into the big black inflatable they yelled a range of orders at him which it is unlikely he understood in any detail. The basic objective was clear enough, however. The Russian officer gave the Zodiac full throttle and it sped in a wide curve across the mirror-smooth perfection of the bay. The last of Mir fell away to the north of them, its flashing brightness beginning to intermingle with the gathering front behind the great storm's eye.

'How long?' yelled Colin.

'Ten minutes,' answered Richard.

'Then they're dead. It was the bravest thing I've ever seen, but we couldn't get the back-up quick enough.'

298

'Even so,' bellowed Richard, 'we have to find them, take them back with us.'

'We do,' called Colin. 'Though it's a bit like coming full circle.'

'What do you mean?' called Richard.

'We started with one member of NASA, frozen, and now we're ending with another one, frozen.'

'That's pretty grim, Colin. But I'm very much afraid you're right.'

The Zodiac skimmed over the placid misty water to the bright mark of T-Shirt's parachute. Unerringly, without deviating from the wide parabola of his approach, Borisov brought in the Zodiac. And as he did so, Richard and Colin reached out over the bow, hoping against hope to find hands reaching up for them.

It was Richard who saw them, side by side, their heads just above the water. As the Zodiac skimmed in, his ice-blue eyes, blue as the hearts of icebergs, fastened on them. Two soused black blobs of heads half sunk in the steaming water. He reached automatically, not really expecting any answer. They had been in the water for fifteen minutes after all . . .

But as he reached for them, they both reached back for him, and the droplets of the water which fell upon the skin of his reaching arms were warm. As warm as a decent bath. And he remembered. Deception was a volcano. Sometimes the sea boiled in here. At least it was always warm.

'Come on in,' said T-Shirt cheerfully. 'The water's fine.'

Chapter Twenty-Seven

All the major players left alive gathered in the main bar of the Hotel del Glacier in Ushuaia on the evening of Monday, 3 January 2000. It could not really be said that they did so on purpose or by prior arrangement, but most of them happened to be in the same place at the same time and there was just too much left unresolved for them all to drift apart so soon after the event. Like the survivors of any great experience, they came together to reassure each other that what they had shared was under control now; safely in the past, over at last – except, perhaps, for the occasional nightmare.

Kalinin had docked with the afternoon tide, less than twelve hours behind her schedule, after riding out the second half of the storm in the calm heart of Deception Island then running hard and fast due north across the Drake Passage. Those of her guests moving on as part of their schedule, like Dai, Jilly, Max and T-Shirt, had rooms booked here in any case. Richard and Robin, Colin and Kate, and of course Jolene, also had accommodation on the upper floors with their spectacular views of ice, sea, and the distant fires of Tierra Del Fuego. The Ice Pirates had flown Special Agent Jones north, leaving Gene Jaeger still holding his battered command against the Big White like Travis holding the Alamo against General Santa Anna. They had set down briefly at the British Antarctic Survey base Faraday to pick up Andrew Pitcairn and his chief engineer who had come shopping for a new propeller, then brought them all north to the southernmost city in the world. There were rooms in the hotel for these visitors as well. All the rooms were booked just for the night. The Rosses, Andrew and the chief would be heading south again with the accommodating American chopper pilots in eighteen hours' time, when all the rest would be heading even further north. The people from the FBI, NASA, Heritage Mariner and *Kalinin*'s passengers would fly up to Buenos Aires together, then away to all points of the northern hemisphere. They were returning, as T-Shirt put it, to all points from Carmarthen to Chattanooga. The cruise ship's depleted officer complement would return aboard their battered vessel and await developments from one

301

St Petersburg or the other. To none of them did tomorrow seem all that promising a day, except, apparently, to Richard, who was striving to lighten everyone's mood.

As though pulled together by some psychic bond, they began to assemble in a quiet corner of the main bar soon after 6 p.m. local time that evening. Richard and Robin had handed the twins over to the hotel's excellent nanny service, and William and Mary were enjoying the novelty of watching *Tom and Jerry* in Spanish. Richard called Colin and Kate down for a farewell drink, and Robin discovered T-Shirt and Jolene side by side in the bar sadly considering the prospect of imminent separation after three days when they had not spent one second beyond arm's reach of each other.

Then Special Agent Jones appeared, to separate the young lovers and confer with Jolene apart. She had much to report. T-Shirt drifted over to Robin's side, pleased to see a familiar face. But hardly had he sat down than Dai, Jilly and Max arrived, looking for him. Immediately, Irene Ogre came in looking for Richard, having thought of just one more thing she wished to get clear for the formal report she had spent the last hundred hours or so writing. No sooner had Irene got down to business than Andrew walked in as well. He hesitated when he saw Irene, but Kate caught his eye and called him over.

As the crowd grew, tables were pulled together until everyone sat in one big circle like the Knights of the Round Table come unexpectedly out of the past. There they sat, with a variety of glasses in front of them and an awful lot to say to each other. But after Irene had cleared up with Richard their exact heading into Neptune's Bellows at midnight on the New Year's Day, they all sat silent and a little listless.

At the far side of the bar a floor show was getting under way and Richard unconsciously hummed along with the little dance band which was playing a selection of popular tunes from the 1940s, looking around his dull companions with glittering ice-blue eyes. The only one there who would meet his bright stare was Robin, and she frowned ever so slightly, in wifely warning against doing anything too outrageous or inappropriate in pursuit of his all too clear ambition to snap these people out of their gloomy preoccupation. So he contained himself for the time being, beating a gentle rhythm against the table edge with his fingers.

'Buy you folks a drink? Bureau'll pick up the tab.'

Richard recognised the drawl he had heard when Jolene was talking to Armstrong base on radio and VHF, and he turned. Special Agent

Jones was tall, slim, angular, beautifully turned out in an Armani suit. And he was young. Jolene was standing beside him, frowning slightly, her water-coloured eyes sweeping round the glum group.

T-Shirt stood up at once, his lean face breaking into its most insouciant grin. 'Well, that's just plain neighbourly of you,' he said, just on the edge of over-acting. 'Make mine a bourbon and branch water.' He held out his hand, and Jones was able to take it easily, for they were quite close together, and much the same height. 'Madrell, Thomas S.'

'Yeah, I know, T-Shirt. Dr DaCosta told me. Jack Daniels or Wild Turkey?'

'I'm easy. Jolene probably told you that, too.'

'No, sir. She said you were a lot of things. Easy wasn't one of them. Now, about you other ladies and gentlemen . . .'

Special Agent Jones went calculatedly against stereotype in more ways than one. After buying a round of drinks, he sat at the head of the table and joined in the discussions that began to flow with the alcohol. He was happy to add what he knew to the pool of their knowledge. It was all a closed file now in any case, he said. Everybody who had done anything criminal in federal jurisdiction at any stage was dead, except for Fagan and he had given enough information to tie up any loose ends and establish himself as Killigan and Hoyle's dupe. Jones had just finished interviewing him in his secure accommodation aboard *Kalinin* and would be taking him home in custody tomorrow.

The pattern of evidence which would never now fill the closed file was simple enough. The story it told was unremarkable; the sort of half inevitable series of unfortunate coincidences which make up any part of life, said Special Agent Jones.

Sergeant Killigan, in his youth, long before secondment to NASA, had been stationed in Europe. As with so many other servicemen at that time, an approach had been made by a down-market stringer ultimately working for the KGB. A proposition had been made. A contact number had been given. Nothing had come of it, of course. What could a Marine sergeant on a short tour offer to the KGB? But then, in time, Killigan had come south to the Big White and the game had changed radically. He now had access to something worth selling, and just as his retirement was coming up. He had access to the Power Strip.

The KGB was no longer functioning, but his contact apparently was – and he knew a man who worked for the Soviet Space Agency who might be interested in a little industrial espionage. And so Hoyle the fixer, Mendel the scientist and Fagan the dupe were enlisted. Killigan promised them at least one million dollars each. No one's life was ever supposed to be put at risk.

The Power Strip would be removed from Major Schwartz's suit. Mendel would study it in his seasonally quiet laboratory, put the design details on disk and Hoyle would send the details to an e-mail address in Moscow under the cover of the millennium celebrations before returning the Strip for the suit's next outing, with no one the wiser.

But Major Schwartz's desire to do his job as well as he could threw it all into disarray. He called for the suit halfway through Mendel's illicit work on the Power Strip. The conspirators could find no way to stop him going out. So out he went and, despite their best efforts, disappeared and died. Aware of nothing untoward except a missing man and, immediately, a missing search team, Colonel Jaeger had called in help and complicated things even further.

Fearful now of discovery leading to serious charges and seeking to hide their tracks while he himself was trapped in the guise of Old King Pole at the colonel's reception, Killigan had deputed Hoyle to get rid of anything incriminating which might be discovered at the place Major Schwartz had been found. Either Killigan or Hoyle had stolen explosives and detonators from the stores. But neither man was an expert with detonators. What they had supposed were simple explosive timers actually had a radio-signal override. The section of the detonator in the back of Leading Seaman Thompson's head established that the detonation frequency, pre-set by the original supplier, was the same as *Kalinin*'s hailing frequency, which was unusually high, even for a Russian vessel. It seemed that Lieutenant Knowles had unknowingly set off the fatal explosion himself when he had tried to warn *Kalinin* that someone had been tampering with the Skiddoos.

Then Jolene had arrived, which had really scared the conspirators. Killigan slipped almost completely out of control, coming after the inspector personally while doing his best to destroy all of the evidence, no matter how much of his base went with it. But Killigan himself all too nearly went with it, and Hoyle took over, with Ernie Mashall joining the action for his own reasons.

'Poor Major Schwartz's coffin was used to smuggle a range of things from Armstrong to *Erebus* and then across to *Kalinin*,' Jolene supplied. 'Firm lesson in security procedures for all of us there, I think.'

'For all of us working as undertakers, that is,' said T-Shirt quietly.

Suddenly Richard threw up his hands with a sound of frustrated revelation. Everyone looked at him. 'Fool that I am,' he said. 'That night. The night Marshall disappeared, when we were searching the major's coffin. I smelt something out of place. And it was gun oil. It must have been from the Glock. I smelt it but I never realised what it was until now.'

'So,' continued Jolene quietly, 'Killigan was strong enough to smuggle his gun and timers onto *Erebus* but too weak or too nervous to use them there.'

'Or too restricted,' suggested Robin. 'Washington was in the bed beside him all the time.'

'Yeah. And Washington was the one man there who wasn't in on it,' agreed Jolene.

'Seemed like a straight guy,' said T-Shirt. 'He certainly trusted Killigan. Backed him all the way.'

'Until the evidence got too strong,' said Jolene.

'*Kalinin*'s people seem to have presented the last complication,' said Special Agent Jones. 'Hoyle continued trying to keep Dr DaCosta here away from the truth of what they were up to while he waited for Killigan to get out of the sickbay. But,' he shot a look at the morose Irene Ogre, 'your Mrs Agran seems to have added all sorts of new curves.'

'Like you said, Irene,' said Richard gently. 'The cat among the penguins.'

'Shouldn't that be cat among the pigeons?' asked Agent Jones, diverted.

'I prefer the captain's version. It fitted so well with the situation.'

'Right,' said Agent Jones vaguely. 'Anyway, Mrs Agran sidetracked Hoyle and damn near threw the whole plan off the rails. I guess we'll never know the exact ins and outs of it all, but she managed to get Ernie Marshall and Billy Hoyle's entire stock off them, including the Power Strip. Hoyle had to re-activate Killigan. Dai Gwyllim told us that. And when Killigan went to see her, she upped the ante.'

'As far as I can work out she simply doubled the sum Killigan was talking about,' said Jolene. 'Whether she could have delivered is another matter, I guess. But suddenly they were looking at more than two million dollars each – Killigan more than four million. It gave them second thoughts. All they had to do was send the information off the disk to an alternative e-mail address.'

'Which is what they were trying to do when the communications system all went down on *Kalinin*, at St Petersburg and Moscow,' said Richard. 'I remember the look on their faces, though I was pretty preoccupied myself at the time.'

'But then,' said Jolene quietly, 'things must have started slipping badly out of control as the storm gathered and we started the run up to Deception. I'm certain Mrs Agran had the disk and Killigan and Hoyle began to realise that they might have lost the lot. All she had to do was send it out herself and they would be left with their backs to the wall, no way out and nothing to show for it. That's when they started trying really hard to cover their tracks. Really putting the fear of God into me, trying to wipe my disks which I had informed them contained incriminating information which they thought they had erased from the network files. But still they hesitated to start any real mayhem because there was simply no way of escaping any unpleasant consequences, trapped on a ship in the middle of a storm so far from civilisation. Which brought them back to Mrs Agran in the end. Because only she had the power to guarantee safe passage out of the situation. I'm sorry, Captain Ogre . . .'

'No, Dr DaCosta, you are right. What you say is true,' Irene admitted bitterly. 'If Vivien had ordered me to take the men somewhere safe, not too far off our scheduled route, and dropped them secretly, I would have done so. I hold my command – held it – on her say-so. And that of Vasily Varnek. This you all know, I think.'

'But even then they could not trust each other,' continued Jolene softly. 'They all had to be side by side to be sure that the deal was done correctly. It is such an easy thing to send an e-mail, especially off a disk. If they had wanted, Hoyle could have even sent two copies, one to their original buyers and one to Mrs Agran's. Two identical files marked dotEXE waiting in two in-trays to be downloaded at the recipients' convenience. Two fortunes automatically wired in return anywhere in the world. The same as you do, T-Shirt – keeping all your banking in Lordsburg, able to get at it anywhere, anytime.'

'Lordsburg,' said Agent Jones. 'Isn't that where John Wayne was heading for in the movie *Stagecoach*?'

'I'm sentimental,' said T-Shirt.

'Surprised you don't keep your funds in Tombstone, Arizona, then.'

'Did once. Bank got robbed.'

'So the final stage of the plan probably shaped like this,' Jolene went on. 'With Mendel there to see his end OK and help with any problems with the disk and its information, they probably reckoned on taking Mrs Agran's deal, even though they only had her say-so for the money. Then they could get a ride back on *Kalinin* and disappear. Rich men. Footloose and fancy-free. No one any the wiser.'

'No one except for you,' said Agent Jones.

Jolene nodded. 'Once they had taken Mrs Agran's deal and saw a way out for themselves then I wasn't coming back. I see that now far more clearly than I saw it at the time. The disks from Armstrong and I were just going to vanish into the Southern Ocean like Ernie Marshall. Clean shot through the left breast and immolation in the generator house before they all came back, repentant, under Mrs Agran's and First Officer Varnek's jurisdiction seems the most likely scenario. And your two crew members, Irene, would have been witnesses to my unfortunate, accidental, death. Unless they had yet another double-cross up their sleeve.'

'Which we will never know now,' said Agent Jones. 'All we do know is that the Russian Space Agency stopped anyone receiving any details from the disk by crashing Mir into the South Atlantic just at the crucial moment, and that Killigan had primed enough of the detonators to blow up all the rest at once when the radio channel to *Kalinin* was opened. An explosive error, you might say.' He paused for an instant. 'Another round? J. Edgar Hoover's still in the chair . . .'

'Well,' drawled T-Shirt. 'Seems to me as though old J. Edgar's the only one who'll likely get the full story now, so I reckon the rest of us should just score it up to experience and get on with our lives. You got to admit,' he continued, leaning forward with his widest grin, 'it was one hell of a trip.'

From eight until midnight on Monday nights the occupants of the Hotel del Glacier bar provided much of their own entertainment, for Monday was karaoke night. The compere was well-practised in selecting victims and was expert in allowing just enough negotiation to get the best performance possible from each – even from those who had never sung with a dance band before. Tonight she had her eye on the big, boisterous group of foreigners who had arrived in the hotel at much the same time as *Kalinin* down in the harbour. Rumours of their adventures were rife around the port already and beginning to spread through the city even as far as the Hotel del Glacier. She watched the group go from dull quiet through increasing hilarity to their current cheerful state; thirteen extremely lucky people clearly coming to terms with the fact that they had come very close to death and lived to tell the tale. Soon, by the look of things, they would begin to split up into pairs and groups, drifting away from the party.

307

She was keen to get among them before that happened, however.

'We'll have to go up soon,' said Robin regretfully. 'The nanny service will be bringing the children back to our suite any time now. Nine thirty is their bedtime and I want them to have a quick bath before they tuck down.'

'We'll have to go soon too,' said Kate. 'Back to the Big White tomorrow. Tell me, Andrew, how were things in Faraday?'

But Andrew Pitcairn did not hear her, he was gazing at Irene, unable to stop himself mentally undressing her. Two double tots of Appleton over-proof rum hadn't helped his self-control in that respect either.

'Andrew!' Kate's voice interrupted some very intimate speculation indeed. He looked away from the object of his lust.

'Sorry?' he said.

'Faraday. How were things there?'

On the other side of the table Dai Gwyllim was saying softly to Jilly, 'Fancy a bit of a dance, darling? This karaoke stuff is dreadful to listen to, but all of the songs they've crucified so far have been great to dance to. Good little band, that is. What they really need is a good vocalist. Tenor maybe . . .'

'Don't you dare,' she said. 'You promise not to sing and I'll dance with you till dawn, you lovely man, you.'

Max, left alone when they began to move, looked speculatively around, but Jolene was deep in conversation with the smooth Special Agent and T-Shirt was watching them like a hawk. Colin Ross and the Mariners were exchanging what looked like a few final words. The epic Irene was looking at Andrew Pitcairn but he was telling Kate Ross about something. It was time, Max decided, to make the acquaintance of that little waitress from LA who had been making eyes at him since the incident at the Razor. He tensed himself to move when, with perfect timing, the compere arrived, all raven curls, burning eyes, flashing smile and skin-tight red frock.

Special Agent Jones offered to try Bruce Springsteen and T-Shirt boasted a pretty good Willie Nelson. The black eyes rested on Colin Ross who met them on the level. 'I suppose you've heard of the great Kenneth McKellar?' he said. 'Andy Stewart? Do the band know "Campbeltown Bay I Wish You Were Whisky"?'

'It is forties night. Fifties,' said the compere, her smile nailed into place. 'Big band. I have here the words to many famous American songs. Bing Crosby. Fred Astaire. Dean Martin. Tony Bennett . . .'

'Go on, Richard,' said Robin. 'Go for it, darling. Give everybody a break.'

And off Richard went with the much relieved compere to talk to the band before he did his bit.

'He'll sing until I stop him,' said Robin. 'Any of you who want to have a dance, do it now.'

With the exception of Colin and Kate they simply stared at her, trying to weigh the seriousness of her tone. The precise meaning of her words. But then the music struck up, swinging easily into another familiar standard. Richard began to sing and as soon as his voice crooned surely out of the loudspeakers, the little dance band itself seemed to be transformed. They might have been under the baton of Nelson Riddle or Billy May. They gave the music that extra style and swing which the performance deserved.

Richard opened with 'Come Fly With Me'.

With one accord the group at the table swung round, half of them certain an old record had been put on a turntable somewhere and this really was Sinatra's voice. But there was Richard, eyes half closed in concentration, singing with practised ease.

Dai and Jilly, already on the floor, swung easily into an intimate dance of their own. The magic of Richard's perfect, unfussy impersonation was pulling other couples onto the floor with astonishing speed. The compere beside the little ensemble simply glowed, her millennium made already.

A hand fell on Andrew Pitcairn's shoulder and he stopped mid-sentence to look up. Irene was staring down at him, her eyes fathomless.

'Dance with me,' she said.

He stood, entranced, and she swept him into her arms. He was happy to let her lead.

Her head came down towards his shoulder. 'I have dreamed of you,' she said. 'With your icy reserve and your iron control. You are men of steel, you English. I'll bet you have never looked at a woman and seen skin instead of clothing!'

'Well actually,' whispered Andrew, his blood like drums in his ears, 'now that you mention it, Irene . . .'

The tempo eased a little. Richard stepped into 'London by Night' as though it were a pair of shoes.

'What do you say, Dr DaCosta?' purred Special Agent Jones. 'How can any red-blooded American sit this one out? The Brits might think we were rolling over.'

She smiled civilly enough but he knew he didn't stand a chance. Even in his Armani suit he was outclassed. She didn't even have to answer. Her clear-water gaze, as limpid as the drops he had added to her bourbon, turned towards T-Shirt, and T-Shirt, of course, had been watching Jolene all along. They were moving sensuously across the floor even before the band swung into the instrumental heart of the song.

When Richard started spreading his velvet singing tones over 'You'd be so Nice to Come Home to', even Colin and Kate were up. Intensely sensitive to the personal relevance of Richard's choice of song, Robin leaned back in her chair, avoiding Max's eye until, abruptly, the stunning muchacha of a compere was there, asking Max not to sing but to dance. Then Robin was alone. The only one without a partner because, as always, her partner was centre stage, under the limelight, in charge of the action. Still, she thought, closing her eyes and leaning back to listen, he was an exceedingly good singer when, as now, the mood took him. And the message was still coming in loud and clear.

'Excuse me, ma'am.'

Robin looked up. And there was the young, eager, Armani-clad figure of Special Agent Jones. She smiled.

'You look like a lady who could use a dance partner,' he said. In the romantic gloom his eyes seemed almost luminous, as green as emeralds.

Richard finished the song. Then, really enjoying himself, the band well behind him and the atmosphere right, he started his final one, 'It's very nice to go trav'lin'. As he sang, he opened his eyes, confident of the rhythm, the words, the band and the delivery. His bright gaze swept across the room to the empty table, then quartered the faces of the dancers as though he was on a forecastle head, on the lookout for ice. He knew half of the people dancing there, but they were all wrapped up in themselves and their partners and not one of them was looking at him.

Except there.

There on the heart of the floor. Over the shoulder of an Armani jacket. One pair of level grey eyes which watched him all the time. As Robin danced with Special Agent Jones, Richard fixed that bright stare with his own and he sang to her alone. And she hummed along, falling into indulgent agreement with his choice of lyrics, their meaning and their particular relevance. No matter where they went travelling, on ice or ocean or foam, it was oh so nice to go home.

Acknowledgements

Going back over my notes I am struck by the way the subject matter of Powerdown has coloured the research materials. I read far fewer books than usual. They could not supply me with the information I required at the speed I needed it. Almost all of the research for the final third of the story came in the form of newspaper articles (more than thirty on the millennium bug from the London *Daily Telegraph* alone) from television, from the radio and from other media information sources such as phone-ordered pamphlets, and from the Net itself. There are websites on the bug, on NASA, on Deception Island, on Base jumping, to name but a few.

The book as it stands began not with the bug but with the Key Stage 3 English paper of a couple of years ago, which featured a travel brochure for Antarctic tourism. Its shape grew with the article T-Shirt refers to, in Volume 193, No. 2 of the *National Geographic Magazine*, published February 1998, about climbing hitherto unconquered peaks in Queen Maud Land, Antarctica. I had been looking for a backdrop against which to set a contained story dealing with the predicted effects of the bug, and here it was.

Horton Griffiths travel agents, Sevenoaks office, Noble Caledonian Limited and Marco Polo World Cruises all supplied details of actual cruises, though the ships described of course bear no resemblance to any of the ships actually booking now for cruises in the South Atlantic and Antarctic Oceans during the millennium summer. Kelvin Hughes, as always, then supplied charts and Admiralty Pilots of the area. The next step after Kelvin Hughes was onto the Net.

But I did read books without which this story could not have taken its current form. Sara Wheeler's *Terra Incognita* (Jonathan Cape 1996) gave a woman's view of the 'Big White' and influenced, I am sure, both incident and character. Captain Nick Barker's *Beyond Endurance* (Leo Cooper 1997) gave me the ship upon which *Erebus* was based so loosely – and no characters at all. The intrepid Captain Barker and his men would never, I am certain, behave in any way as disgracefully as Andrew Pitcairn's command. Nor, it must be emphasised, would the men of the British Antarctic Survey – or NASA, come to that – behave in the way some of the characters in this book behave.

Richard Adams and Ronald Lockley's *Voyage Through the Antarctic* (Allen Lane 1982) touched on many of the landfalls mentioned in the book, including the penguin rookery and Deception Island itself. The history of the BAS can largely be discovered in Sir Vivian Fuch's *Of Ice and Men* (Antony Nelson 1982). I researched southern ocean storms particularly this time, and much of the best work seemed to me to be in Sebastian Junger's *The Perfect Storm* (Fourth Estate 1997), although it is set in the North Atlantic, and Lyall Watson's *Heaven's Breath* (Hodder & Stoughton 1984).

The only published work I found immediate enough to mention with regard to the computer technology (apart from that published on the Net of course) is Patrick Douglas Crispen's *Atlas For the Information Superhighway* (South Western Educational, Cincinnati 1997).

Apart from these, and a range of others on Antarctica too numerous and long-used to mention again, including Scott, Shackleton and Fiennes, naturally, it was the papers, the videos, the phone and the Net. And people, of course. Almost exclusively on this one, I must thank people from The Wildernesse School. I must thank John Wright and Paul Clarke from the geography department for their help with a range of matters from southern hemisphere weather systems to modern Russian time zones. I must thank at least three of my old boys for information supplied – one as an engineering cadet on board a computer-controlled vessel, one as a computer engineer employed on making systems bug-proof (Y2K compliant, they call it) and one working now as a ship's entertainment officer. For obvious reasons they are happy to remain anonymous. Finally I must thank Roger Hood for sharing with me all his research into the likely effects of the bug on our own school and any other computers, systems and networks he could find out about; for guiding me around the Net where necessary and for acting as a down-to-earth sounding board for some of my more outrageous flights of fancy.

Peter Tonkin
Sevenoaks and Port Erin, 1998.

312